DUGAN UNDER GROUND

A Novel

TOM DE HAVEN

METROPOLITAN BOOKS

Henry Holt and Company | New York

Metropolitan Books
Henry Holt and Company, LLC
Publishers since 1866
115 West 18th Street
New York, New York 10011

Metropolitan Books™ is an imprint of
Henry Holt and Company, LLC.

Copyright © 2001 by Tom De Haven
All rights reserved.
Distributed in Canada by H. B. Fenn and Company Ltd.

Library of Congress Cataloging-in-Publication Data
De Haven, Tom.
Dugan under ground / Tom De Haven.—1st ed.
    p.   cm.
ISBN 0-8050-5741-2 (hc.)
1. Comic books, strips, etc.—Authorship—Fiction. 2. San Francisco (Calif.)—
Fiction. 3. Cartoonists—Fiction. 4. Hippies—Fiction. I. Title.
PS3554.E1116 D84 2001   2001030319
813'.54—dc21

Henry Holt books are available for special promotions and
premiums. For details contact: Director, Special Markets.

First Edition 2001

Designed by Kelly S. Too

Printed in the United States of America

1   3   5   7   9   10   8   6   4   2

This one, Kate, is for you, with love

"Hey! You want strange? I'll give you strange."

—Waldo the Cat

DUGAN UNDER GROUND

BIGGS
THE CARTOONIST

THIS IS AMERICA, AIN'T IT? AIN'T THIS AMERICA? You bet it is, Mr. Editor—and it's the WORLD'S GREATEST COUNTRY, too—LAND OF THE FREE, HOME OF THE BRAVE . . . where a brash, tough, cheerful-minded orphan packing a magic yellow wallet can make the hearts of young and old pound with UNPARALLELED EXCITEMENT. The THRILLING EXPLOITS of this hard-traveling little fellow and his talking dog are followed by millions daily. Are your readers among them? If not, today is the perfect time to add DERBY DUGAN to your ROSTER OF FUNNIES!

—King Features Syndicate promotion, circa 1954

The Sunday Page

[1]

In late September 1960, during another one of those wear-a-tie cock-tail parties that somebody, some couple, in our little circle liked to host four to sevenish on Sunday afternoons, a cartoonist friend offered me this piece of advice: "Kill the kid," he said, "keep the dog." His name was Dick Macdonald, and what he proposed struck me as so kooky, as so fucking *nuts,* that I burst out laughing. Dick looked slapped. He saw nothing funny. Well, he'd never had a sense of humor, the poor slob. He'd had a professional one, of course, just not a personal one. But you could say the same thing about most of us Fairfield County comic-strip men. If you'd met us—if you'd had car trouble, let's say, and walked into that house party asking to use the phone to call a wrecker—you'd have taken one gander at our collective stoop and the good cut of our sport coats, then registered the bland murmur of golf anecdotes and figured us all for a bunch of loan officers. Or druggists. "I'm serious," said Dick. "Bury the brat. It'll make you change your way of doing things. A death always does, am I correct?" Of course he was. He was drunk, but he was correct. He was drunk, but I was drunker.

Although our small tribe routinely spent the weekends drinking, I usually ended up more clobbered than anyone else. Still, I never fell down, I never passed out—and I never "accidentally" copped a feel off somebody's missus, so far as I know. At get-togethers, I usually just wandered from terrace to kitchen to living room, replenishing the ice and the mixed nuts without being asked, smiling at everyone's stories or clucking whenever that seemed called for. As long as I didn't start in again talking about poor Buddy Lydecker, retelling *that* old tale of woe, people liked me well enough, I think. But they felt bad for me, too, and not because I drank so much. They weren't hypocrites. No, they felt for me because—well, for a couple of reasons. May as well start with Ginnie.

We still lived together, but over the summer she'd taken up with young Bill Skeeter, a third-rate illustrator, and was there anyone, anyone at all, who hadn't seen my wife go zooming around Westport in that scumbag's white Triumph? With others, and there'd been plenty of others in the past, she'd always been discreet. Not this time. And good Christ, was I ever pitied. Poor Candy. Poor, pathetic Candy Biggs. How can he stand it? Why does he put up with her?

It was my career, though, not Ginnie's latest affair, that accounted for the constant barrage of advice from my peers. "Make the kid older, Candy." "Make him younger." "Give him a girlfriend." "Let him go blind." I scribbled down everything, every idiotic thing they said, right on the spot—at the post office, the stationer's, the art supply shop. The liquor store. I wrote it all down in a five-cent notepad. *Older? Younger? Girlfriend? Blind?* "Thanks!" I'd say. "Let me think about that."

Since we all knew one another's business and work habits, it was common knowledge among cartoonists in our part of the world that I never clocked in fewer than sixty hours a week at the drawing board, and still—still, goddamnit!—"Derby Dugan" kept losing papers and I kept losing income. Either I put the kibosh on that trend pretty soon, or my home-owning days in suburban Connecticut were numbered. So the advice, the tips, the "helpful" suggestions kept coming. My colleagues, God bless and fuck them, were trying to save my bacon. Even so—and I don't mean this too cynically—there was more to their concern than professional brotherhood. If my strip got canceled, which seemed a real possibility that fall, it would be yet another signal that newspaper comics, our common bread and butter, were in serious trouble.

Everybody used to follow the funnies, it was a national glue, like politics and baseball and polio scares. But over the past decade—since the end of the war, really, and the Second Coming of nylons and gaso-line—readership had slumped. And when it came to story strips like mine, it had taken a *plummet*. We blamed television, of course, we hated television, but it wasn't only the competition we got from *Wagon Train* or Gorgeous George, it wasn't only that, it was some-thing else, and we knew it. We just didn't like to admit it. City papers that had been around since the Gilded Age were shutting down, and the ones still left were edited now by a new breed of journalism school pricks with nothing but contempt for the "lowbrow" funnies. At every opportunity, they'd hack away some more at the comics, shrinking the sections or else jamming them full of ads for Brylcreem and Toni Crème Shampoo.

Times had changed. The whole country seemed, I don't know, dif-ferent. At least to us guys it did. We still had Sinatra, thank Christ, and John O'Hara novels, but on the other hand, big bands were kaput and so were men's hats. Now it was all compact cars, chlorophyll, and Calypso music on long-playing records. Bridey Murphy, Davy Crock-ett . . . the oral contraceptive! Negroes sat in. Lucy dumped Desi. And last July we'd all flocked to see the latest Hitchcock picture, expecting another *North by Northwest* but finding instead Janet Leigh in a daz-zling white brassiere! Twenty minutes later she was dead. So maybe, we'd started thinking, it was our turn now. Our day in the shower.

"Give him eyeballs, Candy." "Put some hair on his head." "Make him a cowboy." "A Cub Scout." "A ballplayer."

"Kill the kid," said Dick Macdonald, "keep the dog."

[2]

In April of '54, I took over "Derby Dugan and His Dog That Talks" from poor Buddy Lydecker. He'd been drawing it, six dailies and a twelve-panel Sunday page, ever since Walter Geebus, Derby's famous creator,

passed away suddenly in the mid-1930s. I became heir to a "classic"—
to the longest-running comic strip in America. King Features had made
boatloads of dough syndicating and licensing that "property," and
while I wasn't naive enough to imagine the company was sentimental
about "Derby Dugan," for sure they'd never pull the plug without first
thinking long and hard. But if Derby's client list kept dwindling, they
wouldn't have a choice, finally. If they had to, they'd sack it. That's
what they kept telling me in terse letters accompanied by smaller and
smaller checks.

Truth is, "Derby Dugan" was in decline long before the strip passed
into my hands. Poor Buddy's tenure had been less than brilliant. His
stories plodded, they hardly made sense, and till his final day on the
job he never drew a woman with a bosom, or a telephone not the can-
dlestick kind. He was sixty-something years old and tired, worn out,
but I was thirty-four at the time, still full of bounce and beans. I honestly believed I could turn things around. When I took over—and what
a mess, what a nightmare that was!—the daily was running in fewer
than a hundred papers, the Sunday in scarcely fifty. I promised King
Features I'd goose up the numbers. So what happened? During my first
year, I actually *lost* ten more carriers, including big ones like the *Detroit
Free Press* and the *Los Angeles Times*.

I tried everything I could think of to refresh the strip and save it
from the cartoon boneyard. A lot of my ideas misfired, badly. Blasting
Derby Dugan—a twelve-year-old!—into outer space just earned me
the scorn of longtime readers who didn't like their orphan boy finagled
with. Ditto for sending him back in time, to the Wild West, the Civil
War. The Age of Dinosaurs. And when I let him use that magic yellow
wallet of his—which multiplied ten-dollar bills like loaves and fishes—
to make himself a billionaire, I was accused of turning Derby Dugan
into a piggish miser. Readers hated it when suddenly the kid went out
and bought himself an airplane factory, a fleet of limos, and a Shetland
pony. So to correct that boner, I destroyed the factory and the limou-
sines in a series of Communist-directed firebombings, then simply pretended the stupid pony had never existed. Pony, what pony! You see
a pony? I don't see a pony.

Shortly after that, when Derby Dugan and his smart-ass talking dog
scrambled back onto the open road, my client papers were bombarded

with letters and telegrams from parents and teachers, church groups, welfare agencies, the cops, the FBI, the Teamsters Union, even Art *Link-letter*, everybody accusing me now of using the strip to encourage, get this, juvenile delinquency! According to my new critics, I was glamorizing truants, runaways, hitchhikers, and hobos! Talk about the country changing! When had *that* happened? Overnight, I guess. For six decades, Derby Dugan slept in alleys, froze in barns, trudged along in punishing weather ("Freedom's great, Fuzz, but sometimes it stinks. Sometimes it rains.") and nobody had ever complained. Now that stuff was child abuse, it was cruelty. It was un-American. I ought to be ashamed. I ought to be horsewhipped. Actually, I ought to be investigated—I might be, I probably *was*, an agent of the Soviet government! Glory day! When the complaints, and the cancellations, didn't let up or show any sign of *ever* letting up, I got this directive, finally, from Mr. Dan Sharkey at King Features: "Bring him home."

Home? Derby Dugan didn't *have* a home, at least he'd never had one for more than a month at a time, and always it was borrowed. That was the point! That was the premise! You couldn't—

"Bring him home, Candy. Put him in school."

And so, because I didn't own the strip, the syndicate did, Derby Dugan was legally adopted on Christmas Day 1959 by a couple of hardworking grocers (also named Dugan, conveniently) and went to live in a picture-postcard American town. I was so pissed I called the place Jerkwater. But they changed it on me, to Plainville. And there he'd wallowed, him and his dog, ever since. No matter how many drinks I had, the stories I kept dreaming up were puny ones, lighter than air, semihumorous weeklong "situations." Gone were the bloody six-month cliffhangers about spies and big-city gangsters, kidnapped movie stars, the Abominable Snowman, searches for lost Mayan gold, murder on an Indian reservation. I'd loved that junk, but now it was forbidden. And in its place? School-yard bullies, bicycle thieves, and (the pits, my friends, the absolute stinking pits) Fuzzy Trains to Become a Sheep Dog. This couldn't go on! The strip was even boring the crap out of *me*!

Earlier that summer, around the time Ginnie decided Bill Skeeter was the latest club she could bash me with, I'd tried to sneak a little of the old spirit back into "Derby Dugan" by using a series of lame sleep-walking gags as the lead-in to a noncomic sequence in which my boy sleepwalks right out of Plainville, tramping through a cornfield teeming with snakes and then into the woods, arriving finally down at a lake, where he steps into a rowboat with a treasure map carved into the transom, and—

Nice try, but no cigar. Dan Sharkey, my editor, returned the last six dailies that I'd sent him with a note clipped to the top one that read: "I'm not laughing."

After that I briefly quit telling stories altogether and turned "Derby Dugan" into a joke-a-day thing, like "Peanuts" and "Beetle Bailey." Those one-off strips were doing well, picking up papers, so maybe . . .

Only that didn't pan out, either, since I ended up losing both the *Rochester Democrat-Chronicle* and the *Providence Journal* in late July. God, was I desperate. So desperate I'd recently put the kid on a Little League team—the Little League, for crying out loud! He's a loner but he *joins,* a runt but he struggles, he *tries*—he can't hit the ball for shit but still he keeps stepping back up to the plate, he won't ever cave in! He's on the fucking Little League, he says "Yes, sir" to the coach and "Come on, fellers" to his teammates, and goddamnit, four more papers dropped us before Labor Day. What else was there left for me to try?

[3]

"Kill the kid," said Dick Macdonald, "keep the dog. Retitle the strip, call it 'Fuzzy.' He's noble, he's cute—he pals around with other animals."

"She."

"No fooling. She? All right, she. Pals around with funny animals. Make a note, Candy."

"I'll remember. But thanks."

"You've been drinking. You'll forget. Write it down."

So I did. I wrote it down on a cocktail napkin. That satisfied Dick and he clapped me on the shoulder. Then he zigzagged a path through the living room mob, avoiding cigarettes and staggering drunks, carrying his glass to the bar for repairs. I stayed put. Kill the kid? I thought. Kill the *kid*?

Suppose the syndicate let me. Suppose—suppose they decided it might be worth the gamble, that it might even get my face, or Derby's, plastered on the cover of *Time*. Just suppose. And like that, bing, I'd framed twenty different—but all "poignant"—ways to do it, from heroic sacrifice to lingering leukemia. I was a bad drunk and a mediocre boardman and I couldn't write a punch line to save my life, but until I'd been stranded in Plainville, I'd always been a good story man. Even when my plots got me in trouble, they were solid. What happens next? Not a problem. I'd think of something. I always did—I had the knack. Derby, I thought, could perish in a forest fire. Saving bear cubs. Saving *fawns*. Or he could—he could lunge between the president of the United States and a brainwashed Cuban. I knew exactly how I'd draw the boy wasted by cancer, which brush I'd choose.

I stood in a corner blocking out the party babble and thought about it: you can see just how desperate I'd become. Desperate, yeah, but not deranged. Because, let's face it, there was no way in hell I'd ever bump off that kid, a sixty-five-year-old kid as recognizable as Mr. Peanut or the Monopoly board. A kid who was in the damn newspaper being rousted by a cop the same day the headline read "Teddy Storms San Juan Hill." And who was there in the funnies being kicked by a mule the day it was "Wright Brothers Fly." Who was struck deaf, dumb, and blind when it was "Stocks Collapse" and who was shot in the head when it was "Japs Bomb Pearl Harbor." A kid who was thrown off a truck, thrown off a roof, thrown off a cliff, thrown off the fucking Chrysler Building when it was "Allies Hit Normandy," "Dodgers Do It," "Rosenbergs Are Executed," and "Court Kills Segregation." For six and a half decades Derby Dugan was there, day in and day out. He belonged. He meant something. And even if nobody much cared for him anymore, *I* did. I loved him. And I especially loved his optimism, so misguided, so fierce—how in the good old days, in the days before his exile to Plainville, I could run him over with a bread truck, splinter both his legs, and he wouldn't gripe, he'd never grumble, he'd just look ahead to the clean white sheets and regulated temperature of a hospital ward. Wasn't that better than a blanket in the woods? And if it wasn't? If it turned out, which it almost always did, that the hospital was a pit? At least it was dry. And if the doctors were quacks, itching to amputate? He could always steal a crutch in the night and get moving again. Find, *maybe* find, something better, safer, even, by God, delectable and fun—a nine-foot magician, a golden ape, a plate of scrambled eggs—right through that door, down those stairs, around the next corner. This is America, ain't it? Ain't this America? That's what he'd say, what I'd *make* him say. But Derby Dugan was the guy who truly believed it, that anything was possible. Oh, I loved that little bald kid. He was my boy! And no matter how black things looked, and despite Dick fucking Macdonald's crackpot suggestion, I'd rather have cut off my drawing hand than be the rotten son of a bitch who put Dugan under ground.

[4]

Less than a month after Richard Rodgers optioned "Derby Dugan" with the aim of turning it into a Broadway musical, Ginnie and I bought our house. What was I thinking? It wasn't as if *I'd* got much of the Rodgers dough. But Ginnie figured that a hit show—and how could it not be a hit, a record breaker, it was Richard Rodgers!—would result in a hundred or more, in *two* hundred or more, newspapers signing me up. That was in June of 1956, and she'd been so excited by the prospect, so whipped up by the absolute certainty it would happen, that we drove to Connecticut (we were living in New York at the time, on East Fifty-third Street) and mortgaged ourselves silly. When Rodgers bailed and Broadway got "Li'l Abner" instead of "Derby Dugan," we found ourselves owning a house we couldn't afford.

Originally I'd wanted to buy a modest split-level a foot or two outside of Wilton, but Ginnie said couldn't we go look at just one more—please? And I said all right, but just one. So we drove over to Green Farms, where she fell madly in love with an eighteenth-century Dutch Colonial. Low rooms, chair rails, leaded windows. A fireplace and hearth. So cozy! But more than that, and more than its coursed stone walls and gambrel roof, more than its lilac hedge and spring-fed swimming pool, more than anything else, I'm still convinced, it was the address that sold her: 1776 Founding Fathers Lane.

My wife, you should know, was a real sucker for Americana—pious or cornball, it didn't matter which. Three cheers for the red, white, and blue! Sure, hadn't she grown up in historic Freehold, New Jersey, where you couldn't turn around without bumping into some bronze tablet that began, "On this site, the Continental Army . . ." She plowed through doorstop volumes by Daniel Boorstin, displayed the flag on national holidays, and bought jigsaw puzzles depicting the battle of Gettysburg, the surrender at Jamestown, the midnight ride of Paul Revere—Lord, she even hung a facsimile of the Declaration of Independence over our bed. But the funny thing? The go-figure part? *Ginnie was from Hungary.* I mean, she was born there and lived there till she was almost ten, and she talked like Eva Gabor. You know what they say about immigrants being the staunchest patriots? There you go.

And now I bet you're saying, his wife was born in Hungary and her name was Ginnie? Virginia? Well, no. She named herself that, in high school. She'd nearly chosen Molly, after Molly Pitcher, the heroine of the battle of Monmouth, which was fought—Ginnie liked to point out—right there in Freehold. But she'd settled on Virginia after reading about Virginia Dare.

Years after she'd rechristened herself, I happened along and she nicknamed me. Come on, what boy growing up in Frank Hague's Jersey City would *ever* have been called Candy? And survived? My real name is Edward. Ed. Eddie. I was Eddie Biggs, or Big Ed Biggs, till Ginnie and I started keeping steady company and a certain Dinah Shore ditty was always playing on the jukebox. *Candy, I call my sugar Candy.* That's what she did, all right. And damned if it didn't stick. With very few exceptions (my brother, my father, and poor Buddy Lydecker), everybody has called me that ever since.

Ginnie Kis (her bona fide surname!) held a civilian job, file clerk, at Fort Monmouth, in Oceanport, New Jersey, while I was stationed there in the publication agency of the Army Signal Corps. My M.O.S. was "draftsman," and I spent World War II decorating the PX and the officers' club when not designing nose art and cartoon mascots for B-29s. How we met, it was like something cute you might see in the movies— we literally crashed into each other bolting for cover in a summer cloudburst. I retrieved her umbrella, she picked up my cap. We exchanged those things under a barracks overhang. From the first minute, the first glimpse, Ginnie had me rattled. She was a medium-size brunette, built slender, a little bit skinny-legged, but stacked better than Jane Russell. Could she fill a day dress!

A few nights later, I saw her again at a cocktail lounge in Red Bank. We talked for hours. My father, my brother. Her mother, her father. Her married sister with the scoliosis. Ginnie's parents still lived in Freehold and spoke poor English when they bothered to speak English at all. They owned a small restaurant, the kind we used to call a "paprika joint," in Manalapan. Or, rather, they had owned such a place. Her father played cards and kept losing. Till he finally bet and lost the family business. But then a month later he sneaked back to the restaurant with a can of gasoline and burned it down. "Jeez," I said, "really? So then what happened?"

"Nothing."

And I said, But . . . but—? He burned down his restaurant! *Something* had to happen next. And Ginnie said, well, nothing did—except that afterward "Papa" just loafed around all day smoking Turkish cigarettes while "Mama" took in sewing and twice a week cleaned mansions in Elberon and Deal. They were such greenhorns, said Ginnie, the pair of them. They'd never be Americans, she said, no matter how long they lived here, not real Americans, not like you and me, Candy—they dressed too funny and smelled of garlic. Plus, you could say to them "Amos 'n' Andy" and they'd give you a blank stare. Ginnie rarely saw them anymore. Honestly? She hadn't seen them in a year. Did that make her a bad person? A bum? No! I said, no, of course it didn't. And meanwhile I thought, *Nothing* else happened? It drove me nuts, what can I tell you? Guy burns down his own restaurant, something's got to happen next, something that relates. It's got to!

And so while Ginnie told me about her sister—how they got along, how they never got along, whatever—I was thinking . . . all right, clearly it's a torch job, there's the *evidence,* the gas can . . . so the cops come knocking, and they cart off Papa in handcuffs. Or . . . the cops finally come, but Papa escapes down the fire escape. Or—you know what's even better? He douses the place, strikes a match, starts the fire, but then he gets nabbed, immediately—because his car (What is it? A shitty DeSoto? It's a shitty old DeSoto) won't turn over. He's pumping the gas pedal, he's cursing the engine, *in Hungarian,* and suddenly it's

Get Out Of That Car With Your Hands Up! And maybe they'd call him a name. They're cops. They'd insult him. Call him a lousy bohunk. Or jeez, what about this? He gets away, makes a clean getaway, and the cops are baffled, they're stumped, they might even think it was an accident, faulty wiring, but the big scary guy who won the joint? In that poker game? *He* knows. And comes gunning for Papa, for Papa the Pyro, and—

Ginnie kissed me suddenly on the mouth. Full on the lips. So—fuck Papa and fuck the big scary guy—I said to her, "You feel like going for a walk?"

And later, strolling with me along the Navesink River, Ginnie said, "What, like 'Terry and the Pirates'? Like that?"

I said, "Yeah, like that. Like 'Terry and the Pirates.' And 'Popeye.' In this country," I said, "if a guy is smart and can draw a little and tell a good story? He could make bags of moola doing a comic strip in the paper. And when I'm ready, toots, I'm going to sit down and create a strip that'll knock everybody's socks off, believe you me."

Ginnie said, "Oh, I believe you, sugar," then we found a bench and sat near the river and we're holding hands, and she puts her lips to my ear and tells me her despised and abandoned Hungarian name. I know I'm being anointed, privileged, that it means she trusts me with her secret.

"But you can't tell anybody. Raise your right hand, I solemnly swear."

I swore, I raised my hand and swore an oath, and pretty soon she was calling her sugar Candy. I must have loved her like crazy ever to let her start with that. Oh, I did—no question! Just thinking of her home address, her *telephone number* put a sappy grin on my face. I said to her once, "I'm sorry if you wanted to stay and have another drink, but—but honey, I *hate* it when other men look at you." She said, "You do, do you?" And I said, "Yes, I do. It kills me. I love you, baby. I love you like crazy." And I still loved her like crazy fourteen, fifteen years later. Only she didn't still love me.

Hell, I couldn't blame her.

[5]

When I arrived home, far from sober, after Dick Macdonald's party in Westport, it was going on eight o'clock. Eight o'clock, Sunday night, the twenty-fifth of September 1960. I turned on every lamp downstairs, and there had to be a dozen. I'd read in *TV Guide* that Red Skelton, the comedian, was deathly afraid of the dark; well, me too. Me and Red Skelton, both. But as long as they sell lightbulbs, so what? And let me say this: I've always hated the dark for the same reason Derby Dugan has always loved scrambled eggs. Just because. Nobody ever locked me in a closet when I was a kid.

As a matter of fact, I had a very normal lower-middle-class childhood. It wasn't *entirely* normal, I suppose, since my brother, Gus, and I grew up without a mom. She was killed when Gus was three and I was still an infant. Trolley car, puddle of slush. Although my dad lived another twenty-four years after that, he never remarried. He had his bowling nights at the K of C and a couple of sons who played canasta with him, stayed out of jail, and went to Mass on Sunday. He was content. You get what you get. If you're going to be grouchy, go climb a tree. Feeling blue? Take it to the attic. That's the kind of a guy he was. On weekends he painted miracle scenes from the Bible on gessoed plywood.

Dad owned his own signage business ("For a Quality Sign That's Right. On Time. It's Tom Biggs!"), and beginning when I was ten or eleven, he put me in charge of paper signs. Every Tuesday morning, before school, I'd knock out dozens for his grocer clients: Hot Dogs 19¢, Tomatoes 29¢ LB, Stew Meat 49¢ LB. Gus was a whiz at numbers—he kept Dad's books—but hopeless with a brush and a mahlstick. For me, handling those tools felt as natural as handling a knife and a fork.

Dad said, "It's a good living, Ed. People need signs."

I said, "I know it, Dad, but I want to draw funny sheets. Like 'Terry and the Pirates.' And 'Popeye.' Here, will you take a look at what I've done?"

He said, "Can't you see I'm busy?"

Whatever I learned about wrinkles, gesture, posture, and sweat beads I'd picked up from a bunch of how-to-cartoon books that I found at the Jersey City Public Library and from diligently copying my favorite newspaper strips, but long before I could draw worth a damn, I was a real pro at the sign-writer's trade, thanks to my dad. By the time I was done with high school, I was slick and I was fast. And that competence was invaluable later when I tried breaking into the comics field.

Following my discharge from the army in late March of '46—Ginnie and I were married already—I found regular freelance work in New York City lettering talk balloons for Quality, Fiction House, Timely, Top-Drawer, and for most of the Archie titles. This wasn't what I wanted, of course—funny books, to my mind, were reading matter for cretins—but it paid the bills, or usually did. There was the occasional dry spell: a month when for no apparent reason I'd find myself with half the usual number of assignments, or a week, or two, spent waiting anxiously for a puny check. Those times could be tense. Ginnie would say, with just the slightest edge to her voice, "How is that comic strip of yours coming along?" and I'd tell her, "Good." Then I'd wrack my brains even harder than I'd wracked them yesterday, pushing, prodding, *praying* for an idea. How about—? What about—? A detective? A doctor? A judge? Done. Air force pilot? Also done. Caveman? Spaceman? Hillbilly? Done before. Gunslinger? Game warden? Done already. Done to death! All the really good ideas, the million-dollar ones, seemed taken. Why hadn't I noticed before? Every night I doodled, I sketched, I thought, What about—? How about—? I sharpened pencils, put them in a cup, moved the cup from one place to another for easier reach. I cut bristol board into proper strip lengths, and ruled panels . . . that stayed empty. I fixed a drink to loosen up. Then fixed a second. But stopped there. Then didn't. In the can-do era, in the can-do country, I couldn't do shit. "It's coming good," I'd tell Ginnie, and take her to Grant's Tomb, and Tammany Hall, and the birthplace of Theodore Roosevelt . . .

That Sunday evening, after I'd gone around the house turning on lamps, I cracked open a beer in the kitchen and sat down at the table. Leaning against the toaster was a rectangle of gray cardboard, the back from a Things-to-Do pad. I'd discovered it there Saturday morning. Ginnie had left it, a scribbled list of meals (lemonade fried chicken, tuna noodle casserole, fish cakes) that she'd prepared and refrigerated, in Tupperware, so I wouldn't eat just hot dogs and cold cuts or English muffin pizza all weekend long while she was off gallivanting. What can I tell you? She was loony, and most days knocked-out loaded on Miltown or Equanil.

I got up and pulled out the drawer below the cutlery drawer. Two cartons' worth of Chesterfield Kings, Ginnie's current brand. A week ago it was Tareytons. She changed brands half a dozen times a year. Even in her nicotine habit the woman was promiscuous. But so long as she wasn't on a mentholated kick, I'd help myself to a pack now and again. I'd never been much of a smoker myself. People told me I should be, though. *It'll help you think straight, Candy. Make the kid older. Give him a girlfriend.*

I was wondering if what I needed with that cigarette was a real drink or a second beer when the telephone rang out in the living room.

"Candy? We have a problem." It was Bill Skeeter! "Candy?" There was a long pause. So long that I had time to look over one of Ginnie's jigsaw puzzles on the coffee table—a Frederic Remington Rough Rider, the scene unfinished, scarcely begun. Most of the knobbed pieces, a mix of the bright and the drab, were still jumbled in the box. Other, similarly incomplete puzzles—"Buffalo Hunt on the Great Plains," "Independence Hall," "Mount Rushmore," that kind of thing—lay on flat surfaces all over the house. She'd begin one, grow bored or get stuck, and move on to another. "Biggs? Answer me! You there?"

"Oh, I'm here," I said. Then I said, "'We,' meaning you and I or you and Ginnie, or do you mean all three of us have a problem?"

"Listen. Could you get in your car and drive over here? Now."

"Well, gosh, I appreciate the invitation, but I was just getting ready to sit down and watch Ed Sullivan."

"Don't get cute, all right? I'm in no mood."

"No mood at all?"

"Just get over here! Come get your crazy wife, man, or else I'm gonna *throw* her out." He hung up before I could squeeze in another word.

Jesus. I hadn't expected things to crash quite *that* suddenly. In the past, even the silliest, even the very slightest of Ginnie's "love affairs" (with the traffic cop from Bridgeport, for instance) ran to half a year, at least. And considering how publicly, how brazenly she'd conducted this one, I'd steeled myself for a long, dragged-out humiliation. Instead, it was over, apparently, in just under three months.

I fixed a weak highball and carried it up to the studio. Just the guest room. Nothing special. Drawing table, swivel chair, taboret, filing cabinet, and a five-and-dime-store showcase that I'd picked up in Danbury at a flea market. Displayed inside it was my Derby Dugan collection. My Derby Dugan *museum*. Cereal premiums and gasoline station giveaways or cheap stuff that was sold in Kresge's and Woolworth's. Most of it dated from the thirties and forties, and almost all of it I'd got from poor Buddy Lydecker. He was glad to see me cart it away. Help yourself, sonny boy. So I did. I helped myself. To hats, lots of different yellow derby hats, and pot-metal toys, strap-on watches. Big Little books, rings, punch-outs, buttons, decoder badges, alarm clocks, Christmas-tree lights, pajamas, and wallets. Yellow wallets galore. There were, all told, a couple dozen different magic yellow wallets, and naturally all of them were "official." Some were actually made of cow leather, but most were cheap plastic. Some with a make-believe ten-dollar bill stuck inside and some not. Some with Derby Dugan's name stitched on the front, some without. But all of them bore Derby's picture somewhere on the cover. Winking Derby. Laughing Derby. Loafing Derby. Running Derby. Hitchhiking Derby.

Ginnie had been steadily pilfering a doodad here, a doodad there, and giving them to her lovers. Can you imagine? To her lovers! After a looting, she'd carefully, she'd fractionally adjust the space in between everything else that remained on a shelf, she'd close up the gap—so I wouldn't "notice." (She knew I would, and I did, but I never said boo.) I used to wonder what her boyfriends might say, what their mouths and their eyes would do, when they'd tear open yet another handsomely gift-wrapped box only to discover inside a twenty-year-old Derby Dugan mechanical rowboat with chipped enamel or a scratched-up Derby Dugan pennywhistle or a 1937 Derby Dugan Hobo Jungle board game. Smile, you're on *Candid Camera*!

I sat at the drawing board, sipping my drink and sorting through a small pile of swipes I'd dumped there last night. Stuff I'd torn from *Look* and *Life*. Ads for appliances, furniture, and automobiles mostly, but now that I was drawing a small-town, stay-put version of "Derby Dugan" I'd also started cutting out pictures of barns, silos, ramshackle filling stations, that kind of thing—boxy Protestant churches with tall steeples. When Derby was *Derby,* though, when that kid of mine was footloose and fancy-free, I'd sit down in the evening with a pair of scissors and a stack of magazines, everything from *Confidential* to *National Geographic,* and just go crazy, clipping the Alamo, the rocky coast of Maine, the Santa Fe Express, the Sunset Strip . . .

After I'd cleared my table and finished my drink, I still wasn't ready to go out and retrieve my straying wife, so I doodled with a fiber-tip pen: squares, spirals, tic-tac-toes, and the occasional derby hat. The occasional Derby head. Oval, circle, circle, circle. Then I grabbed a pad of vellum and roughed out some ideas for the dailies I'd be starting work on the next day, a batch that wouldn't be published till early November. Derby's at bat. Bases are loaded. There's a rain cloud. And *then?* Then for some reason I was thinking about poor Buddy Lydecker. I patted fingers around my chest till I found that scar, the place where he'd stabbed me, and that's when the phone rang again. "Patience, Billy, patience!" I'd picked up the studio extension. "A little patience, my friend."

But that time it wasn't Bill Skeeter calling.

[6]

Originally from Boston, or maybe the outskirts—the boonies!—Ginnie's latest Romeo had arrived in Westport the previous winter to take an instructor's job at the Famous Artists School. You must've seen the magazine ads for that home-study mill—all suggesting that illustrator wannabes who passed the Free Talent Test would then have their pricey lessons vetted by such pipe-smoking notables as Ben Stahl, Albert Dorne, and Norman Rockwell. But the reality was they got low-paid nobodies like Bill Skeeter. This is America, ain't it?

Before he landed that job, Bill had done line work for men's adventure rags like *Male* and *Saga* and painted covers for trashy paperbacks. I don't remember him ever telling me how old he was, but I'm guessing his late twenties. No question he was good-looking, with his curly brown hair and jazzman's goatee (hiding what I suspected was a weak chin), but God, but Jesus, the way he'd act! So full of himself and always trying too hard to impress. I think he thought he was Rembrandt. And that we all should think so, too. The little drip.

By the time Ginnie and I met him, at a pool party in late June, he'd already quit Famous Artists. The heck with *that* place, he couldn't breathe cooped up inside a goddamn cubicle all day, correcting bad perspective with a Conté crayon. He was bragging to anyone who would listen that he'd recently been hired to illustrate a novella by Geoffrey Household for the *Saturday Evening Post.* He only shut up to go take a jackknife off the springboard.

Ginnie said, "I bet he lifts weights!"

I said, "Lifts weights? He's skinny, for crying out loud!" He was, too, he was a real shrimp. And I thought his tiny licorice nipples looked sinister.

Next time we saw him—at Ginnie's insistence we had him over to the house, along with a dozen others, for a cookout on the Fourth of July—there was no more talk about his drawings for the *Post* (which, by the way, never materialized). Now, he just boasted that Art Paul, the A.D. at *Playboy,* had phoned to ask if he'd "consider" doing a double-spread painting in acrylics to accompany a new Ray Bradbury short story. What a crock! But Ginnie thought he was "simply adorable," a real go-getter, and she just *loved* his Boston accent. He sounded, she decided, "exactly like Jack Kennedy!" Oh God. Another one, I thought. And wasn't mistaken.

One evening a week or so later, I was cutting some patches of shading film when she came into the studio and casually mentioned, "I'm seeing Bill Skeeter." She could tell me that while I had an X-Acto knife in my hand and know she didn't have to worry. "I'm seeing Bill Skeeter." With not much inflection, and certainly no apology.

That was how she'd always tell me about a new man—and yes, she always told me. It was part of the package. It *was* the package. "I'm seeing Joe Hayser." "I'm seeing Paul Vessey." "I'm seeing Don Haldeman." "I'm seeing Hank Cahill." "I'm seeing Bill Haley." *Bill* Haley? No, that was the rock-and-roll singer. It was *Jack* Hayser, *Joe* Haley. "I'm seeing Jack Hayser." "I'm seeing Joe Haley." That's how she'd tell me, that's how she'd do it. And I never said anything back. What could I say? Don't? I couldn't say that. Because you get what you get.

Sometimes a plate of scrambled eggs, sometimes a big old bread truck speeding out of control.

[7]

Bill Skeeter rented a furnished apartment over the Thom McAn store opposite a restaurant called Amici's, where a lot of our local boardmen met on alternate Wednesdays for a spaghetti lunch. I used to be a regular, but that summer I'd dropped out. Did I really want to be sitting there with friends some afternoon and watch my crazy wife go bouncing through that crumb bum's street door? No, thank you. I preferred to suffer in private.

After thumbing the buzzer, I looked at dress shoes in the store window. Up and down the street nothing was open, and the sidewalks were deserted. It had started to rain a little. I rang twice more before trying the knob. It turned and I walked inside.

"What took you so long?" Bill stood at the head of the stairs, on the landing outside his apartment. He had on a white dress shirt with the tails out sloppily, uncuffed dark slacks, and no shoes. Backlit, his beatnik hair resembled a bomb flash. "It's ten o'clock."

"Don't exaggerate." I looked at my watch. "It's only a quarter of."

"Well, come up if you're coming." He didn't wait there but left his door open. Even though I took my time climbing the stairs, I was out of breath—I was gasping!—when I reached the top. That fall, I weighed 240, 250. A far cry from my weight today—175 last time I stepped on a scale—but in those days I was a great big guy. A strapping fellow. Big Ed Biggs.

The front room, the room facing the street, had three double-hung windows, so that's where Bill had set up his drafting table and French easel. There were a couple of standing lamps, a large upholstered wing chair, a wooden chair at a small boxy writing desk, a console TV, and a dozen coffee cans, Savarin cans, parked haphazardly all over the place. On the rug, the windowsills, the radiator. Each was crammed with brushes. Who needed so many? Nobody who knew what the hell he was doing! How much do you want to make a bet he stole those brushes from the Famous Artists School!

The walls, as I knew they'd be, were covered with tacked-up ink drawings and unframed acrylic paintings: Bill specialized in slutty American schoolgirls, drew mostly jailbait in white kneesocks and saddle shoes, but there was the occasional tentacled Martian, too, and quite a few private dicks arching an eyebrow at a tall stacked blonde with her blouse unbuttoned. Or a .45 automatic in her fist. Or both. I recognized the model for most of those babes. He hadn't used her face, thank God, just—all the rest of it, adjusted for age and the effects of gravity. I even recognized, vaguely recalled, the underwear.

"She's in there."

"Pardon me?"

"In the back." He pointed through an archway, pointed with his thumb, and I had a moment's impulse to walk over there, booting Savarin cans left and right, and smash that stupid face of his hard against the wall. But I didn't—because as quickly as the impulse came, it vanished.

With a little nod to Bill, I walked halfway down the hall and then stopped outside the kitchen. One of the chromium chairs was tipped over. Somebody, and I bet I knew who, had jumped up too quickly. Dinner plates and cutlery were still on the table. Bowls of food. Mashed potatoes, green beans, creamed corn. Glass of milk, glass of beer. Hers and his. (Ginnie didn't drink much alcohol. Hardly touched it.) A platter of stringy-looking, dry-looking, cold-looking pot roast. And on a tiny shelf with the clock radio stood a crude (but charming) Fuzzy the Talking Dog ceramic cookie jar, painted sun-yellow. Mine, of course. "From the collection of." I lifted it down, removed the lid, and Christ if that son of a bitch wasn't using it for cookies!

At the end of the hall, the bedroom door was open.

Ginnie had her glasses and her clothes on. Red sweater, white pleated slacks. Royal blue neckerchief. She sat in a chair reading a book. Staring at one. *The Making of the New Deal,* by Arthur Schlesinger, Jr. I said, "Need a lift?"

She never looked up. "Can't you see I'm busy? Can't you?" No, but I could see the future as clearly as I could see Ginnie wasn't wearing a bra. Next she'd say, "Go home, Candy. I'll see you tomorrow." And ten minutes from now, guaranteed, she'd be lying across that unmade bed, sobbing. My arrival always set things, and always the same things, in motion. "Go home, Candy," she said. "I'll see you tomorrow."

"Yeah?"

"Cross my heart." Which she did, she thumbed it. I looked at her sagging bust, as erotic to me then as—I don't know what, as that lamp, that ashtray, that *Argosy* on the night table. Five minutes, I thought, and she'll be pacing the floor. And if I stayed much longer, I'd hear that first deep misery groan. So I left her, and on my way back up the hall I stopped in the kitchen and reclaimed my cookie jar.

"Let's give her a few minutes, Bill, shall we? Can't we do that? And in the meantime—where's the rest of it?"

"What rest, what?"

I tapped the cookie jar. "The rest. Come on, brother, give."

Bill rolled his eyes, then, staying well out of my reach, he propelled himself across the room and yanked open the shallow center drawer in his writing desk. So peeved, so put upon! He reached in and took out an "official" Derby Dugan yellow plastic wallet. It was one of the ones—I think originally it was a mail-away premium offered by Ritz Crackers—that had a hard-plastic medallion of Hitchhiking Derby glued on the cover. When Bill tossed the wallet, I caught it, then checked to see if the fake ten spot was still tucked in the moneyfold. Good, it was.

"So *now* can you get her out of here?"

"Little while longer. This," I told him, "takes finesse. You don't want her screaming, do you?"

"Jesus, no." He was only a few feet away now, that's all. I could've grabbed him. "Listen, Candy. You think I should leave for an hour? I'd trust you with the place."

"No fooling, you'd do that?"

"Oh, shove it!"

Bill switched on the TV and I went back to check on Ginnie.

She was at the pacing stage already—boy, that was quick!—and turning mean. "I told you to go home. I'm busy!" I really had to be careful now. If I botched it—well, I didn't want to do that again. This one time when she was shacking up weekends with a Cuban immi-

gration lawyer on West Eighty-fifth Street in New York, I drove down
to get her, but she went kablam, smashing the guy's plates, the guy's
saxophone, and somebody in the building called the cops. I was terrified we'd all be arrested. "Derby" Cartoonist in Straying Wife Fracas. So
yeah, I wanted to be careful. She paced, sprinkling cigarette ash. "Go
home, Candy. And don't give me that look!"

"What's she doing now?" Bill said when I came back.

"Feeling mad at herself. Next she'll get sleepy. It won't be long."

"I don't want her falling asleep in there."

"Don't worry, I won't let her sleep all night."

"This is crazy! What's going on? She just—blew up."

"And you weren't even arguing, I bet. Just talking."

"Exactly. We were having something to eat. I don't even know what
we were talking about. Probably that stupid cannonball. She dragged
me all the way to Ridgefield to look at some two-hundred-year-old cannonball stuck in some crummy goddamn building. Last weekend it's the
cemetery in Bridgeport. Like I really care where P. T. Barnum is buried."

"Things a guy has to do to get laid."

"Shut up!"

"I'm just saying."

"Yeah? Well, don't." He lit a cigarette finally. He'd been dying to.
"We're having dinner, everything's nice, we're maybe talking about that
stupid cannonball, and then all of a sudden? She puts a hand to her
face, like this."

"Crying?"

"Not yet. I asked her was she feeling sick, but she won't talk. Then
boom! Jumps up screaming."

"But it's like you weren't even there, right?"

"Right! Like I wasn't even there. I said I'd drive her home, whatever
she wants. But she won't say anything! She hasn't talked to me in three
hours."

I nodded like a cop, then I laughed and sat down in front of the TV.
Steve Allen, Bennett Cerf, Arlene Francis, and Dorothy Kilgallen were
all wearing blindfolds, and Carl Sandburg, the poet, was saying no, his
occupation was entirely unrelated to athletics.

"I was on this show. Ginnie tell you? I was a contestant on *What's
My Line?*"

"Get out of here. You?"

"Four, five years ago. King Features arranged it to promote my strip. Not that it picked up a single paper afterwards, but I did stump the whole panel. Are you self-employed? Do you work at home? Is there a product involved? Yes, I am, yes I do, yes there is! But they never guessed, they never even came close, and I walked away with fifty bucks! And a carton of Winstons. And a case of Geritol. It was fun. Arlene Francis is a genuinely nice woman, Bill, in case you've wondered—just lovely. Refined. Hardly your type, though. And much smaller than you'd think. Very slight. Cerf's okay, but a little full of himself. Thinks he's funnier than he really is. Same goes for Steve Allen. But Dorothy Kilgallen? What a bitch! When the game was over and John Daly told them I was the guy who wrote and drew 'Derby Dugan,' do you know what Kilgallen said? 'I didn't realize it still ran.' The fucking gall! She works for Hearst, you know. Her stupid gossip column is *syndicated* by King Features, and that snooty crepe-necked old bitch says on *national television* that she didn't know 'Derby Dugan' was still in the paper? I could've killed her. But what the heck, right? Who cares? Who gives a hoot? You got anything to drink?"

"There's beer."

"If that's all you have."

He returned from the kitchen with Pabst in a can and put it down on the writing desk along with a church key. I got up and went over there, and damn if there wasn't one of my wife's jigsaw puzzles on the green blotter. It was only partly done, of course, with a messy hill of pieces set off to one side. "Washington Crossing the Delaware." She'd filled in a lot of the river, some ice chunks, some boat, and the general's hat. I opened the can of beer and chugged it. But when I pegged the empty past Bill's head—I was aiming for a wastebasket, which is where it ended—he turned pale. I must've laughed because he asked me what I thought was so damn funny.

I said, "Just now? You looked like I must've looked the morning that I—say! Did I ever tell you about poor Buddy Lydecker?"

His face turned even paler. "Yeah—yeah, you told me."

"When?"

"It must've been, I don't know—at your house. Fourth of July."

"You sure?"

"I heard the story, Candy."

Well, maybe so, but not from *me*.

I said: "It was a nuisance taking the train out to Long Island every morning, but if I hadn't accepted that job—"

"I know," said Bill, "your whole life would've been different. Candy, I heard the story. Can't you just take her home now?" He sat down in the upholstered chair and leaned forward with his head in his hands. But then he jumped up again, making a beeline for the hall. He passed so close to me I couldn't resist. I grabbed him by his arm and squeezed, hard enough that he winced. He didn't struggle. I was scaring him. Well, *good*. I dropped him back into the wing chair and pulled up the hassock for myself. He rubbed his muscle. I said, "Cut it out, Joe. I didn't hurt you."

"My name is Bill, for Christ's sake."

"What?"

"You said *Joe*."

I guess I had, and that was pretty amusing, but no big deal. Joe, Bill. What difference did it make? Bill, Joe, Don, Hank. Bob, Pete. Honestly, what fucking difference did it all make?

"Poor Buddy," I said, "was an old man of sixty or more when I went to work for him. This was in 1953 . . ."

[8]

"May of 1953. I can't remember exactly how I heard about the opening—somebody telling somebody telling somebody else, I guess, and I just got wind of it. You know how that all goes. The grapevine. But I can tell you this much: it wasn't something I wanted. Not at first.

"Hey, look, here I was a married man, I'm married seven years and still I'm lettering for comic books! Five bucks a page. It was embarrassing. You can't tell your neighbors what you do, they'd think you're a moron. This was right around the time people were burning comic books in the public square. Because Batman fucked Robin and Wonder Woman was a dyke—remember that?—and if you worked for comic books, if that was your business, your bread and butter, you were a pervert, and I was tired of it. I wanted to be a comic-strip man—but what can I tell you, Bill? All the truly great ideas? The million-dollar kind? Seemed used up already, so I—

"So when I heard about this job, this five-day-a-week job, I thought, Why not? Poor Buddy Lydecker wasn't paying much, God knows, but it was steady. It was a newspaper strip, you could hold your head up. And I'd always liked 'Derby Dugan.' Well, I'd always liked it as a kid, when old Walter Geebus still drew it. I knew all of the characters. Ma Billions. Sam Sandwich. Pitiful Jane. The Duke of Delaware. Abe Ongo. I loved all of them. Tim Topp. Zen Cohan. Uncle Wondrous. It used to be a great strip. Now, okay, it was a lame thing and sort of a joke among cartoonists, but still, still it was 'Derby Dugan,' it was in the paper every day, and I thought, Take it. It would only be temporary. Something different to do while I waited for that one last great original idea to come to me in a blinding flash. Take the job. So I did.

"I'd ride the train out to Hempstead every morning, then catch a bus from the station and arrive by ten. We'd sit right down to work, but every twenty minutes poor Buddy would jump up and go check on his mother.

"My first day, he'd introduced me to her. She was a little shrunken thing who sat propped up in bed, giving her full attention to Julius LaRosa singing 'Anywhere I Wander' on *Arthur Godfrey*. That's what I remember. Julius LaRosa and this itty-bitty mummy in a blue quilted robe.

"She'd been failing for quite a while, and poor Buddy was growing frantic. After I was there only a couple of months, he started spending less time in the studio, and my job gradually got larger. At first, I was the letterer and the cleanup man, period. He'd pencil all the figures, ink everything. But as Mrs. Lydecker grew sicker and needier he let me do some inks, then some more, until finally I was inking everything except character heads. He wouldn't let me touch those!

"The strip hadn't looked better since Walter Geebus died, if I do say so myself! I used a sable-haired brush, not a crow quill, eliminating poor Buddy's old-fashioned crosshatching. The clothing and props were still hopelessly out of date, but now at least they had zip and a clean finish. The strip looked good. And I wasn't the only one who thought so, either.

"I was in the studio the day Dan Sharkey telephoned. He was comics editor at King Features. I could figure out the gist of their conversation, even though poor Buddy tried to hide it. He had to keep saying 'thank you' and every time he did, every time he *murmured,* 'Thank you, Mr. Sharkey,' he'd make a fist. He never mentioned my name. I wondered if Dan Sharkey even knew that poor Buddy Lydecker had finally hired some help. I bet he didn't, and it turned out I was right.

"Anyway, the old lady was sinking fast, but in the meantime 'Derby Dugan' was showing signs of life. I tinkered next with poor Buddy's dialogue. First thing I did was substitute a 'Yikes!' for one of his 'Ye Gods!' He was so preoccupied that he never noticed: he came back, inked a few heads, signed a few strips, and never noticed what I'd done. So I began changing a few more things, and the more things I changed, the more excited I got. This wasn't just poor Buddy's strip any longer, it was mine too. Little by little, I added a touch here, a touch there. Do this, try that. The ideas just *came,* you know?

"Eventually, I went ahead and rewrote an entire daily. After I erased his wooden pencil work, I roughed out a fresh strip, lettered it, then drew and inked it. But I panicked. For sure he'd catch *that*! So I never showed him. When he came back later, he took a brush to a daily that I *hadn't* changed (hadn't changed much) and then signed it. I considered forging his name to the strip I hadn't let him see, but it's funny, I just couldn't. So it went out to the syndicate without a signature.

"On the trips back and forth to Hempstead I found myself daydreaming. Derby's on a train. Out West. *And?* Maybe . . . maybe there's . . . a blizzard. *And?* There's a maniac on the loose . . .

"The morning of the day Mrs. Lydecker died, poor Buddy looked like hell. I think he'd been up with her all night, and by the time I arrived, the guy was shaky. We'd never gotten close—sometimes the two of us wouldn't speak twenty words all day—but I felt for him that morning. It was a Monday, and Monday was when poor Buddy always wrote the week's continuity in a stenographer's pad. Usually it took him a couple of hours, and while he did that I'd cut Strathmore to size and rule up the panels. But that day he just stared at the pad. He'd jot a few words, strike them out, jump up and go check on his mother. He'd come back and say her breathing was funny. He'd sit down, he'd jump up, he'd leave. By eleven o'clock there was still nothing on his pad. I listened to the radio and drank coffee. Around noon, he ran upstairs but didn't return.

"After forty-five minutes or so I began to worry. I walked out into the hall and listened. Called his name. Got no response. Finally, I went upstairs and there he was, sitting at his mother's bedside, quietly weeping, the poor bastard. The old lady's mouth was open, but her eyes, thank Christ, were shut. I made a few calls—poor Buddy was a wreck, it was the least I could do. As soon as the doctor arrived, followed almost immediately by three guys from the funeral parlor, I caught an early train home.

"We had a tiny apartment on West Twenty-sixth Street that year, a fifth-floor walkup. Ginnie was still at work when I got in. She was a switchboard operator at Metropolitan Life and none too happy about it. Tell you the truth, she wasn't happy about much. After she'd had her third miscarriage in two years, we'd gone to a specialist, and he said, Hmmm, it could be an allergy, or it could be a tilted womb, or it could be scars, or do you know what? It could be just anxiety. You folks worried about something? Hell, yes! Money. We were always worried about that. We never had enough. So you can see how my going to work for poor Buddy Lydecker had seemed like a step in the right direction. It meant a little more money and a little less anxiety.

"But then Ginnie went to another specialist and that one didn't give her any more of that could-be-this, could-be-that. He told her what it *was*. Then he put her in the hospital and took everything out.

"Anyhow, I was just saying how come she wasn't home that afternoon, the day Mrs. Lydecker died. She was still at work.

"I decided to do some drawing, strictly for myself. Who knows? Something I doodled might be the seed of a terrific idea. An *original* idea. It was possible. But as soon as I put pencil to paper, all I could draw was Derby Dugan, Derby Dugan and Fuzzy the dog. It was automatic! The most natural thing in the world. And that's when it started. That's when the fever gripped. I didn't even hear Ginnie come in. She had to shake me hard, I was that far gone.

"She said, 'What's all this?'

"I said, 'Derby's on a train, see? There's a blizzard. And that's the maniac.'

"Later, after we'd had supper and watched some television, I started to feel, I don't know how to describe it exactly—depressed? But antsy at the same time. Ginnie said it was probably a delayed reaction to Mrs. Lydecker dying, to that whole sad business, and I agreed. Still, I couldn't quit bouncing off the walls! I had a rye highball, but that didn't help. Finally, Ginnie put on a pretty blue nightgown and took me to bed. After she fell asleep, though, I just lay there staring at the ceiling. Since we always kept a light on, I could see every little crack, and that brownish water spot—damned if it didn't look like Derby Dugan's head . . .

"I saw poor Buddy again at his mother's funeral, then he called me later at home. We had to get back to work. See you tomorrow. I still had a job, at least! Next day I showed up at the house, but instead of going straight to the studio, like we'd always done, poor Buddy—who was still wearing his flannel pajamas—invited me to sit down in the kitchen for a cup of coffee. He offered me sugar and milk and I thought, Jeez, eight months and still the man doesn't know I drink it black. He filled our two cups and then picked up a copy of that morning's *Daily Mirror*, folding it open to the comics page. He plopped it down in front of me. My eyes jumped from 'Li'l Abner' to 'Joe Palooka' to 'Miss Peach' to 'Derby Dugan.' To that unsigned 'Derby Dugan' strip. The one I'd written and drawn eight weeks earlier.

"I thought about acting innocent, playing dumb, imagining for a second that he might—but no, that was stupid. He *knew*. And he finally said, 'Let me tell you something, sonny boy. I've been drawing this goddamn comic strip for more years than I care to remember. I dream about it, I see that little bastard in my sleep! I go to write a check, I almost draw his stupid face! I scratch my head and suddenly I'm sketching Fuzzy with my finger. You understand what I'm saying?'

"I said, 'Yes,' and he laughed at me.

"'No, you don't,' he said, 'you don't understand what I'm telling you *at all*. I hate him,' he says, 'and I hate his mangy dog! But I'm stuck with them! And they're stuck with me. We're family!' He sounded angry but looked scared to death. '*We're* the family . . . and you're just a handyman in our house. You're the plumber, the guy that cleans the gutters. That takes down the screens and puts up the storm windows. *You got it?*'

" 'Yeah, I got it.'

" 'Then let's go,' he said. 'I have a lot of catching up to do.' *He* had a lot of catching up to do. Him. Not us. Just him. Well, la-de-da. I took my coffee and followed him to the studio, and we settled back into the old routine. I sharpened pencils. Went to the post office. Took down the screens, put up the storm windows. And 'Derby Dugan' sank back into mediocrity.

"I'd go home at night, sit around in a funk. My drinking picked up. Ginnie, of course, wasn't thrilled. 'Make up your own comic strip. Like you always said you would. Forget Derby Dugan.' But she didn't understand! 'The boy should be mine,' I said. 'He belongs with *me,* we belong together. We're family!' Ginnie looked disgusted. And she got furious whenever I'd sit down and start drawing Derby Dugan strips. It was a waste of time—who'd see them? Who'd read them? We'd argue, she'd dump out a new jigsaw puzzle, I'd get back to work. She'd go to bed, I'd stay up late. The blizzard raged, the train derailed. The maniac struck.

"Poor Buddy. After his mother's death, he stayed in his maroon pajamas all day and played the radio loud. He still left the studio every twenty minutes, either to use the bathroom or to take a slug from a bottle he kept stashed behind cereal boxes in the kitchen cabinet. The more he drank, the slower he worked. It got harder and harder for him to write scripts. He'd stare at his pad, snap pencils in half, sharpen new ones so pointy they'd break at the first pressure.

"One week he was so blocked that he dummied a complete Sunday page: twelve panels of Derby Dugan standing in the Lincoln Memorial reading off the fucking Gettysburg Address! And it wasn't even Lincoln's birthday! I couldn't hold my tongue.

"I said, 'Hey, Buddy? What about this? Derby's out West. On a train. In a blizzard. There's a maniac.'

"*He* said, 'Mind your own business.'

"Well, that did it! Mind my own business? That comic strip *was* my own business. And it was time I did something about it. You could say I was disloyal, you might see it that way, but I didn't. I was half crazy worrying about Derby Dugan all the time. The kid was being mistreated every day of the week, every day of his *life,* by that goddamn

Buddy Lydecker! If he didn't know how to treat the boy, if he couldn't treat that boy right, I knew somebody who could! You bet I did. Ginnie finally saw it my way, too. When I told her what I'd planned, she encouraged me.

"She said, 'All right, Candy, all right.' We were in total agreement. She *agreed* I should go see Dan Sharkey. She was one hundred percent behind me. 'All right, Candy,' she said, 'all right!'

"But it was damn hard just getting an appointment with Mr. Daniel Sharkey. He didn't know who I was, he'd never heard of me. I had to park myself outside his office, I had to sit there for hours, but finally—well, I got in. He was very sharply dressed. We had a nice conversation, a serious conversation. He was surprised I knew exactly when poor Buddy's contract came up for renewal. But I think he was impressed, too. I'd done my homework. And he seemed grateful when I told him just how bad poor Buddy's drinking had become. We both sympathized, of course. His mother's illness, her death, poor Buddy's age, but still—turning out a comic strip on deadline required a man's full and complete attention. It took a firm hand. A parental hand, when you came right down to it. We talked for quite a while, Dan Sharkey and I. But naturally it wasn't *all* talk: I had my samples to show, those strips I'd done at night.

"Of course, I didn't get any promise from Sharkey—I hadn't expected one. I'd gone there only to introduce myself, to present an option, to let him know I was available if circumstances should ever happen to change.

"After that, I felt better. I'd done what I could. It was like—as I told Ginnie, it was like when you know something awful is going on in the apartment next door, some terrible crime, you hear it through the walls, some maniac is torturing a poor innocent child, you see evidence, black eyes, broken arms, and finally, well, finally you go ahead and you call the cops. You have to. It's your duty. You feel good about it, you've done what you can. It was like that, I said. And Ginnie agreed. 'All right, Candy,' she said, 'all right.'

"Going out to Hempstead was easier after I'd talked with Dan Sharkey. I just put in my eight hours. Whenever I felt like jumping in and making a helpful suggestion, I bit my tongue. I'd bite and swallow.

There were times, though, when I simply couldn't keep quiet, much as I probably should have. Because poor old Buddy had turned a little bit, shall we say, absentminded. I'd have to point out, for example, that Ma Billions was wearing pearls this week, when he'd forget to draw them, or that Sam Sandwich had three buttons, not four, on his counterman smock. Or I'd gently remind him that in last Tuesday's strip the dishwasher at the mining camp was a Negro, so it might be a good idea if he was *still* a Negro in today's.

"But were my efforts appreciated? Not at all! I was glowered at.

"Months passed and I never heard back from Dan Sharkey. Ginnie began to think my 'brilliant idea,' as she called it, was all a big bust. We didn't quarrel, but there were strains in our marriage. A few cracks. Like in the ceiling! She kept urging me to work on my own stuff. But I had no interest any longer in creating a strip. New characters? Never! For me, it was the boy. The boy and his dog. Me and the boy and the talking dog. We were meant to be. I had to hold on, just a little longer.

"So finally it's the beginning of April 1954. I've been with poor Buddy Lydecker now for eleven months. Day in and day out, and his version of 'Derby Dugan' is drifting further and further into hell. Straight down into the raging fires of hell. But that's all right. Because I've decided his version isn't the real version—mine is, the version I'm drawing every night at home. The real Derby Dugan is living in my filing cabinet. He's okay! He's out West. There's a blizzard, there's a maniac. And I had to keep myself from laughing out loud all day long in that studio in Hempstead. I'd look at poor Buddy's version, his *abortion,* and want to crack up. I had to stop myself from giggling.

"So now it's April 2, 1954. That's a Friday. Train, bus, and there I am at the house again. I ring the bell like always, but there's no answer. So I let myself in and discovered poor old Buddy Lydecker in his pj's and his slippers standing at the studio pencil sharpener, grinding away. It looked like he'd been sharpening pencils for an hour—there were dozens of them on the table, fresh green HP drawing pencils all over the place, every one with a sharp new point. Was he drunk? Had he lost his mind? He just stood there, slumped over, cranking that pencil sharpener.

"I cleared my throat. Said good morning. But he didn't stop. So I walked back to the kitchen and filled the percolator, measured coffee, plugged it in. And still I could hear him grinding away. While I waited for the coffee to brew, I sat at the table. That's when I saw the Western Union envelope.

"All right, I probably shouldn't have looked inside, that was snooping, that was wrong, but I had this feeling. I hadn't considered how Dan Sharkey might give poor Buddy the bad news when it came time for that—but a telegram? That seemed pretty shabby, after eighteen years.

"I told him that, too, a month later. I said, 'Mr. Sharkey, I don't mean to criticize, but a telegram?' We were having dinner in a restaurant, Dan Sharkey, Ginnie, and me. It was his treat, I was his guest, but still I had to say something. 'A telegram?' I said. 'I think a man deserves a phone call at the very least.' And he agreed. Dan Sharkey took it well. He should've phoned, he said. 'Ten lousy words!' I said, and Ginnie glared at me across the table.

"A lousy ten-word telegram! I felt bad for poor Buddy Lydecker, it must've been a shock. Well, of course—listen to that pencil sharpener. A fucking telegram. I was folding it back up when poor Buddy came in. No use to pretend I hadn't read it, he could see the darn thing in my hand. What could I say? I said it was terrible, a shame. Then I got hot, I even climbed on my high horse and said it was a disgrace to fire him like that. Not even a phone call! But he just stood there. It was unnerving. I said, 'They should've called you, Bud. At the very least.'

" 'That's all right,' he says, 'I called them.'

" 'Good for you,' I told him, and I meant it. 'I hope you gave them hell. Eighteen years!'

"He moved closer, he *advanced,* and I guess I got some inkling of the trouble I was in, because right away I stood up. His eyes didn't look right. And his breathing was funny. He says to me, 'I asked Danny Sharkey what his intentions are. I was afraid—I was afraid he was going to retire the strip. But that's not the plan,' he says.

"Now, that same evening I told Dan Sharkey how I felt about the telegram, I also mentioned to him that maybe—that just *possibly*—it had been unwise not to warn me ahead of time. He agreed. He'd been wrong, he said, not to call before I'd gone out to Hempstead. And yes, he shouldn't have told poor Buddy Lydecker what his plans were for 'Derby Dugan.' He hadn't considered the ramifications. But for all the trouble he'd caused me, Dan Sharkey heartily apologized. 'And I appreciate the apology,' I said, 'but you put me in a horrible situation.' I might've said more, but right there Ginnie leaned forward with a fresh Raleigh in her mouth and Mr. Fancy-Pants Dan Sharkey clinked open his beautiful gold lighter and thumbed the striker wheel. And if I'm not mistaken, he looked right down her dress! 'A horrible situation,' I said.

"And it *was* a horrible situation! When I realized poor Buddy had found out not only that he was losing the strip but that I was *taking* it, I didn't see much point in my sticking around. Especially once he started calling me names. It was so pathetic! This old man in his pajamas calling me filthy names. Since I had no intention of being dragged into a shouting match, I went back to the studio for my jacket and newspaper.

"He followed me. But now he was bawling his eyes out. It broke my heart, just about, and I thought, Well, Candy, you have to say *something*.

"So I told him, 'Look, Bud, think about it like this: you'll never have to see that little bastard again!' He always referred to Derby Dugan as 'that little bastard.' Poor Buddy hated Derby Dugan. He'd told me as much! I hate him, he'd say, and I hate his mangy dog. Now he could relax, I told him, he'd never have to see those two again. That shut him up, at least, and turned off the tears.

"What happened next—this is the part of the story everybody knows, every cartoonist in the business. The part I must've told a thousand times. Poor Buddy is watching me grab my jacket, the newspaper, some personal items, then he takes a deep breath, lets it out—and wants to know if he can be *my* assistant!

"I don't think I've ever been more shocked. Could he be *my* assistant? He'd work for nothing, he says, he'd come into the city every day or as many days a week as I wanted him. Please! He's begging me, and I can see that he's struggling not to get all weepy again. But it's no use. Please, Ed, please! That little bastard, that mangy dog! They're his family! *Please?*

"He never should have asked me such a thing. Where was the man's pride? It was embarrassing. I mean, did Harry Truman plead with Ike to let him stick around the White House, did he ask could he be *vice* president? Of course not! Things change. Life goes on. Nothing lasts forever. All that stuff. So I *had* to say no. But I shouldn't have said it the way I did. I admit that. I made a mistake, but I was embarrassed—for him. I should've just said no, I'm sorry, and let it go at that. Instead I told him, 'Over my dead body,' and that was wrong. Or maybe I said, 'Go climb a tree.' It was a crazy minute. But whatever I said, it was cruel. It was wrong. It was a big mistake.

"Still, it doesn't excuse what poor Buddy—well, that's when poor Buddy Lydecker grabbed one of those pencils he'd sharpened and rammed it into my chest! Two inches lower and a bit more to the left and I wouldn't be here talking to you right now. He stabbed me and then he just collapsed in his chair and began to sob. Meanwhile, there's a fucking pencil sticking out of me, it's sticking out and there's not much blood, but it's deep. It's *in* there.

"I put on my jacket but couldn't button it! Then I took my newspaper and—I'm guessing I was in shock—I walked to the goddamn train station! There was a woman out sweeping her steps, I remember, and that woman just froze when I passed. And there were these two guys hanging on the back of a garbage truck. They hollered to me, but I waved them off.

"It was about a two-mile walk, then I had to wait for a train. People stared at me. On the platform and in the smoker. A conductor came and said something. I looked out the window. My body remained calm. My mind was a blank. I walked home from Penn Station and poured a drink. By then my shirt was bright red, it was just—soaked! The phone rang. That would've been Dan Sharkey, calling with the good news. But I didn't have the strength to get up from my chair to answer. So I let it ring and ring till finally it stopped ringing.

"Ginnie found me, hours later. I don't remember who pulled out the pencil, if it was her or the doctor. But apparently I wouldn't say how it had ended up stuck in my chest. I wouldn't tell her, not then, I just kept saying—according to her, all I kept saying was, 'Derby's on a train. There's a blizzard. There's a maniac.'"

[9]

After I finished telling my story, *that* part of it, the first words out of Bill Skeeter's mouth were these: "So—did you keep the pencil?" I kid you not! That's what he said.

I leaned forward and he flinched. That look moved on his face again, the same jumpy look I bet moved over mine when poor Buddy Lydecker found me in the kitchen with his telegram. I said, "Bill, what do you think? Sure, I kept it. And I wish I still had it to show you, but— well, as soon as people heard what happened, they just started show- ing up at my door in droves, they wanted to see it, touch it. It became a legendary pencil, a *historic* pencil, and before too long the green paint started chipping off. So here's what I did. I gave it to the Smith- sonian. You could take a train down there tomorrow, Bill. You could ask at the desk and they'll be glad to show you that famous pencil. A guard'll take you. It's kept in a special climate-controlled room." I winked and leaned back. "See for yourself."

"You're full of bull," he said, and I laughed. I laughed right in his face!

Although I wasn't quite done talking, here was a good place for a short break. So I excused myself and went to look in on Ginnie again. She was sleeping, of course. Ginnie's on a bed. There's a blizzard. There's a maniac.

When I returned, Skeeter looked both hopeful and anxious. "You leaving now?"

"Soon, Bill. But don't you want to hear the rest of the story?"

"What, there's more?"

You *see*? I had him hooked. "A little," I said. "Sit down and I'll tell you."

"I'd rather you left."

"So Ginnie called the doctor. Tetanus shot, maybe a sedative. But I don't remember that. The next thing I do remember, I woke up in the dark. Now, you might laugh, Bill, and I don't care, but I've never gone to sleep without a light on. At *least* one. That's just my way. Mine and Red Skelton's. We're not afraid of the dark, we just—I don't like it *being* dark. But Ginnie put me to bed and she'd turned off the lights.

"Now I was awake in the dark and it rattled me. I threw off the covers and got up. But then I nearly fell, I was so groggy. Around the door I could see a strip of light. The tiniest yellow crack of light. I called Ginnie, but when she didn't come, I shuffled across the floor. And kept staggering, first to one side, then the other—it was like the room was moving. Swinging on a curve. It was all I could do to keep my feet. Then I opened the sliding metal door and walked into an old-timey railroad coach with faded red upholstery.

"I recognized all of the passengers. Sheriff Pinch sat alongside of Tim Topp, whose crutches stuck way out into the aisle. Fat Ma Billions, wearing a shiny black dress and a string of pearls, played cards with the handsome Duke of Delaware and Lou Larynx, the crooner, while Pitiful Jane—sucking, as usual, on the end of her long red braid— peered sadly at them over the back of her seat. Oh God, just about everybody was there. Abe Ongo, alone, scowling as he read his newspaper. Yin Yi, the mysterious Chinaman, puffing on a cigarette stuck in the corner of his mouth. Zen Cohan, the hardware-store mystic, contemplating a handful of key blanks. Uncle Wondrous with his fluffy white Santa Claus beard. Everybody! Even Swami Tommy in his bedraggled turban. But each and every one of them ignored me whenever I stopped to pay my respects. It was like I didn't exist. Like I wasn't even there. But I was, Bill, I was *right there,* and it was amazing to see them all in the flesh. What a privilege!

"Then I spotted Derby Dugan himself at the far end of the coach. Him and his bright-yellow dog, on facing seats. I sat down next to the kid. He didn't look at me. But Fuzzy did: she growled. She could *talk,* but instead she growled. Finally, Derby turned, half turned, and the first thing I noticed? *His teeth were bad*—they were crooked and pitted, and ribboned with cavities. And I thought, God damn that Buddy Lydecker! This was neglect! Inexcusable neglect! No wonder Derby Dugan looks so miserable tonight. So I said to him, 'Hey now, son, where's that famous optimism?' I went to pat him on his shoulder, but he drew away—'Take your mitts off me, you,' he says. 'I ain't your son!'—and gazed out the window. I felt like swatting him. Can you imagine! Not my son! The crust! The fucking crust of that kid, after all I'd—

"Suddenly he let go with a deep-in-his-throat whimper, then ran a small dirty fist in circles over the glass. Outside, the snow was coming down hard, whipping around. I heard a bell—ding ding ding ding— and the train slowed to a glide. Derby pressed closer to the window, straining to see. The dog stood up, and looked out too. 'What's so interesting?' I said. 'It's just snow.'

"They ignored me. By then I was pretty damn annoyed. But I kept it in check and kind of insinuated myself between them, to find out for myself what they were looking at. We crept past a railroad crossing, the bell kept on dinging, red lights flashed. Stopped behind the crossarm was a black car—an antique sedan with running boards. In its head-lights, you could see how wild the storm truly was. And as the train inched slowly ahead, moving past that black sedan, the snow drifted practically up to its old-fashioned grille and fenders, the driver's door opened and poor Buddy Lydecker—who'd never operated a car in his life, so far as I knew—stepped out wearing only maroon pajamas. He stood there in snow to his knees and watched the train go past. A few seconds later he was gone, he was *back there,* we'd left him behind. The kid slumped into the corner of his seat, the dog curled up with her muzzle on her paws, and the pair of them looked at me with such loathing that I felt stabbed all over again. And then—"

"This is a dream, right?" said Bill Skeeter. "I hate it when people tell me those. I never listen."

"You listened to mine."

"Yeah, well, I wasn't sure."

"I had a fever," I said. "It was a fever dream."

"Yeah? So? What happened to the story?"

"This is part of it."

"No, it's not. Don't hand me that. If you're going to tell the story, tell it, just don't hand me any of that dream guff."

"So the kid and the dog looked at me like they both hated my guts—"

"And when you're done, maybe you could let me know *why* you're telling me this dumb fucking story in the first place."

"—then Fuzzy gets up and stretches, she does a great big stretch, and pins me with her glassy eyes and finally speaks. Finally! 'That was Dan Sharkey on the phone,' she says. 'Candy? That was Dan. Buddy Lydecker is dead,' says Fuzzy and I never would've expected this all-

American dog to have a Hungarian accent, but she does! Then the coach goes dark, and when the lights come back, I'm home in bed and Ginnie is leaning over me with a glass of water and a couple of tablets. 'Candy? That was Dan,' she says. 'Buddy Lydecker is dead.'"

[10]

"So we're out of the dream now?"

"There you go, William! Correct."

"And from here on it's all real?"

"It's all *been* real."

"Yeah, sure." Bill looked at his watch. "You want to finish? That'd be good."

"It was late the next morning when I woke up with Ginnie there. It was raining out—like it is now, a hard, noisy rain. I was surprised. I'd expected snow. But it was April, it was a rainy day in April, and poor Buddy Lydecker was dead. Booze and pills. Phenobarbital, Dan Sharkey told me when I called him back. But how did *he* know? I didn't ask. And who found poor Buddy? How did anybody even know to look? I didn't ask, and Dan Sharkey didn't say. But he did say they'd probably label it an accidental death, since there wasn't any note. 'And that's good news for us,' he said. Otherwise there'd always be a 'blot' on the 'Dugan property.'

"After he hung up, Ginnie sat down beside me. Could she ask me something? Would I care to explain how I'd happened to get a pencil stuck in my chest? So I told her, and she pressed her forehead with her fingertips and closed her eyes.

"That morning, Ginnie didn't go to her job. She brought me soup and dry toast on a tray, 7UP and tea with honey. I dozed and woke, dozed and woke. I'd wake with a groan and find her sitting there doing a jigsaw puzzle. Pushing pieces around. We didn't have much to say.

"Next morning I started drawing 'Derby Dugan.' Thank God I'm right-handed since I couldn't lift my left arm without a twinge. I cleared my table, turned it to face a wall instead of the window, laid out pen points and brushes, and put on the radio. And worked all morning. But there was no pleasure in it.

"At noon when the mail came, there was an envelope addressed to me by hand with a hundred-dollar bill inside. Also enclosed was a note from poor Buddy. It said he was sorry, sorrier than I'd ever know, and he hoped the money would cover any medical expenses. He hoped I could forgive him. Good luck. Signed John (Bud) Lydecker. P.S. DD carries the wallet in his *right* back pocket. P.P.S. Sheriff Pinch wears his star pinned to his *left* shirt pocket.

"I'd had no idea poor Buddy's real name was John.

"I drew till Ginnie came home. We had supper. Vegetable soup. Or ravioli from a can. Fish sticks? Something. I told her I thought I'd put in another hour at the board, two at the most, and she watched TV. Or maybe she worked on a new jigsaw puzzle. I kept on drawing and was still at it when Ginnie left for work in the morning. My fingers started to cramp around the pencil, the brush, and I put out a bottle of aspirin next to the bottle of ink. Bottle of aspirin, bottle of ink, bottle of Dewar's. I kept seeing poor Buddy weep. Poor Buddy—who'd taken such good care of his sick mother! The man was a saint. That man was a saint on earth and ought to be canonized! I was smashed by two in the afternoon. This continued. I was smashed almost every day by two in the afternoon. I lived with a crick in my neck.

"Dan Sharkey told me, 'We've lost the *Free Press* in Detroit, and the *L.A. Times* says they won't renew.'

"I said, 'I'm still feeling my way. Don't sweat it.'

"He said, 'This maniac story is dragging on. Wrap it up.'

"April, May, June. We found another apartment, on East Fifty-third Street, a nice two-bedroom. I claimed one of them for my studio. By then Ginnie had quit her job and planned to spend the summer months decorating. She had free rein. She could paint the place, buy drapes, a dishwasher, a garbage disposal—she could hang the fucking Gettysburg Address over our bed for all I cared.

"More cancellations came in. I killed the maniac, invented a time machine. I sent the kid, the dog, and Sheriff Pinch back to the age of dinosaurs. There wasn't another soul around, not for a million years. I practically lived at my board. Ate there and drank there. Drank there

and drank there. I worked all day and never missed a deadline. Ginnie
went to the movies, to musicals, to Schrafft's. She came home from
the five-and-dime with more jigsaw puzzles. 'The Alamo.' 'The Liberty
Bell.' 'Tornado in the American Wilderness.' We had less and less to
say. And she kept her distance. What, so now it was *my* fault? Now it
was my fault what happened? I gained weight, she lost it. July, August,
September, October. November. November 1954.

"Dan Sharkey said, '*Sacramento Bee, Newark Evening News, Des
Moines Register*—enough already with the dinosaurs.' Then he said,
'Ginnie, you are one superb cook, thank you so much. Yes, please, I'd
love a cup of coffee.'

"'No coffee for me,' I said. 'No pie. Nothing, thank you.' And then I
said, 'If you keep staring at my wife like that, Dan, you'll get a crick in
your neck.'

"After Dan Sharkey left, Ginnie was furious. Ever been cursed at in
Hungarian, Bill? Every word is a brick. Every syllable. It's a *club*. She
went in the bedroom and slammed the door. And I went back to work.
My kid was in trouble. That goddamn tar pit. It was sucking him under.
I'd been worried about him all through dinner. How could I concen-
trate on bullshit? *Des Moines Register!* Screw the *Des Moines Register*.
My kid was going under—unless. Wait a second. That branch! Directly
overhead. If only . . .

"But then Ginnie was standing there—no, it's worse than that, she's
lurking. Hovering there when I'm trying to work, trying to save that
poor kid's bacon, doing the best job I can, and she's blah-blah-blah,
she's blah-blah-blah! I'm making her nuts, this is too crazy, what's the
matter with me, the fuck is the matter with me, you should hear the
mouth on her, Bill, calling me names, but I have no intention of getting into a shouting match, I just—can't the woman see that I'm busy?

"Ginnie said, 'Come to bed—please! Please, Candy, please!'

"But Derby's in the pit. Up to his waist in tar. Reaching for that
branch . . . one more inch, one fraction of an inch—when suddenly
Ginnie grabbed my arm. There was a pencil in my hand and she
wouldn't let go! Goddamnit, let go!"

"I don't want to hear any more," said Bill Skeeter.

"Don't worry—I didn't stab her. Jesus. You thought I *stabbed* her? I never would've. There may've been a second there . . . but God, Bill, she grabbed me like some maniac, and my arm may've just. It swung around. But I never!"

"You all right? You don't look so good. Want me to get you a glass of water?"

"Another beer?"

"You don't need one."

Bill was right, too. I hate to admit it, but he was. Everything had turned blurry, and when I tried to swallow, I coughed. So I went to the kitchen, ran the cold water, and filled a jelly glass. God, was I thirsty! Telling stories is hard work, it's heavy lifting, it takes it out of you. Derby's on a train, he's in a rocket ship, he's walking down that old dirt road. He's lost in the desert. There's a cactus, there's a cow skull . . .

"What happened next, Candy?"

I said, "She's nuts, you know. And a pill popper, which I'm sure you've noticed."

"What *happened*?"

"She may've *thought* I was going to stab her—"

"What happened next?"

"She left me. But then she came back. Well, she didn't come back, I went and brought her back."

"I don't get it."

"Just what Dan Sharkey said! You two boys have a lot in common. He called me up a week later and told me where to find her, which hotel, and I thanked him and he said, 'You son of a bitch, I don't know why she'd ever go back to a lousy drunk like you, but that's what she wants, so get your ass over there right now.'

"He said over *there* but he should've said over *here*—know what I mean, Bill? He thought he was so smart!

"I said, 'Dan, you didn't have to call, you could've sent a telegram,' and he hung up. The son of a bitch hung up on me and I—I know that I shaved. And took a bath. I needed to be clean. After all, I hadn't seen her in a week and I just walked to that goddamn hotel. There was a woman out sweeping her steps."

"Candy, whyn't you sit down?"

"Don't wet your pants, kid." I put the glass on the dish drainer. "I'm fine." And I was, too. Fine as could be and ready to go.

With her small hands clasped together between her cheek and the pillow, Ginnie was sleeping like a little baby girl. I said to Bill, "What happened *next*? I walked to some crummy hotel in midtown Manhattan and took the elevator and—Ginnie," I said, "sweetheart? Time to go."

She pushed herself up a little.

I smiled at Bill. "What happened *next*? This," I said. "This is what happened next." I took her by an elbow, gently. She wasn't fully conscious yet. That would take a while. It always did.

As I led her slowly up the hall and across the front room, Ginnie never so much as glanced at pale Bill Skeeter, at poor Bill Skeeter, who went and stood near a window and pushed his fingers through his hair. I left her at the door while I went to the desk and for whatever reason took back her jigsaw puzzle, making sure that I scraped every piece into the box. Then, just on principle, I collected the Dugan wallet and that ceramic Fuzzy, and I thought, Bill's at the window. There's a cloudburst. There's lightning. And then I thought, Say something. You should say something to poor Bill. Some last thing. Some parting word. Something he can tell people whenever he tells the famous Candy Biggs story. But for the life of me, I couldn't think what. But then—and this was completely spontaneous, but it was perfect, it was just the thing—I set the cookie jar back down on Bill's drawing table. "Little souvenir," I said to that moron, that scumbag, that no-talent *hack,* who nevertheless would become, in just a couple of years, one of *Time* magazine's most-used cover artists. Can you believe it? Can you believe they'd let that little creep draw LBJ and Nikita Khrushchev, Helen Gurley Brown and—and the pope, for crying out loud. Makes you sick, doesn't it? Makes you want to—

"Just a little souvenir," I told him. "Keep it, Bill. Keep the dog."

By the time Ginnie and I got to my car, a hard rain had soaked us through.

[11]

So what happened next?

I ran my stupid Buick into a tree, that's what. I took it up to eighty, then steered it off Clapboard Drive, two, three miles past our house in Green Farms, where there was a sharp dip in the road. And hit an oak. Or an elm—I hit a big wet elm. Or an ash. Like I know from trees. What am I, a forester? Whichever kind of tree it was, I deliberately rammed the fucker.

It filled the windshield.

[12]

Yes, but wait a minute! Hold on! Why rush a good story? Let me finish it properly. Because it's so true what they say: it's all in the details. Just lay 'em on! So let me just—

Leaving Westport in the rain, I drove in silence while Ginnie hunted through her purse. She dug out a Chesterfield package but found it empty. Irritably, she crushed it, then slumped against the passenger door. I checked to make sure the lock button was down.

We sped past a movie theater showing *Exodus,* the same place where I'd seen the latest Hitchcock in July. With Ginnie. Who closed her eyes through much of it. Who put her lips to my ear after Martin Balsam was killed, and said, "I can't take much more of this."

Now she asked me to stop at that drugstore on the next corner, if it was open.

I said, "What do you need? Cigarettes?"

She said, "I'll get them."

"It's pouring out."

"I'll get them."

Apparently, the place *wasn't* open, but the pharmacist unlocked the door and let her in. Of course he did. Staggering and stoned-looking, she was still a beautiful woman. And her sweater was damp. It *clung,* and I remembered suddenly, but don't ask me why—I remembered what she'd looked like pregnant. Five, six months pregnant. And I remembered taking her to see Frank Sinatra at the old Paramount on Broadway (he sang "That Old Black Magic," he sang "Night and Day") but we left early because she was tired, she was uncomfortable, she was expecting, and on the way home we talked about names. If it was a girl. If it was a boy. And it was a boy. Almost. An unfinished boy. Like the last time. And the next time . . .

The pharmacist—who seemed young and good-looking, at least he did from where I sat in the car; good-looking but short, definitely short, a fucking *runt*—the pharmacist had gone around behind the counter, and now Ginnie was pointing. They both laughed. Or she did, *she* laughed, then *he* did, and I saw the way he looked at her. How could I miss it? I never missed it. And wasn't supposed to. They laughed again, laughed together, and that should've killed me, but it didn't. Things had changed.

I turned on the radio but turned it right back off. I picked up Ginnie's jigsaw puzzle and idly shook the box. It was perverse, I know, but I took off the lid, picked out exactly one knobby little puzzle piece, cracked open the vent window and dropped it through. The point being? I have no idea. I just did it. Then I tossed the box on the backseat and took out the yellow wallet I'd rescued from Bill Skeeter. I was rubbing a thumb across the plastic Derby Dugan medallion glued to the cover when Ginnie came back.

While she untwirled the red strip of cellophane from around a package of Benson & Hedges, I said I had something to tell her, something important, then told her I'd had a phone call from Dan Sharkey.

No, I'm getting this wrong. I'm rushing things again. While she untwirled the red strip of cellophane from around a package of Benson & Hedges, I said if she didn't mind I'd take one of those for myself. Let's just sit here, I told Ginnie, and enjoy our last cigarettes together, shall we? And then I'll start the car, turn on the wipers, the headlights, and drive us away. And then? Oh, then I'll just run this stupid Buick into a tree—how does that sound to you, baby? Like something you'd be up for?

Did I really say that? Of course not. I'm not sure I even thought it.

But we did sit parked at the curb while we both smoked. I do remember that. And that I said, "Bill told me you two drove into Ridgefield today."

"There was a tavern I wanted to visit. From the Revolutionary War."

"And something about—an old cannonball?"

She nodded, she smiled, she loved this stuff. "It's stuck right in one of the walls."

"Embedded there."

"Yes. A British cannonball."

"Did you touch it?"

"Don't be stupid. But I was just amazed that such a thing, a thing like that, could *last* for so long. Could stay in one place for so long. An insignificant piece of—ore."

"Well, it was embedded."

"But nobody pried it out, did they? At first they were just too busy, I guess. And then it was just . . . part of the wall. Why pry it out after it's been there so long?"

"Exactly. Take it out now and who knows what'll happen? The whole fucking tavern might collapse." I opened the vent window again and pitched out my cigarette. "I gathered from poor Bill that *he* wasn't all that impressed by your cannonball."

"Bill?" she said. "Bill who?" She tamped her cigarette in the ashtray. "Can we go now, please?"

And then?

I took that Buick Roadmaster up to seventy-five, pushed it toward eighty, and *rammed* it—

No. No, Ginnie said, "Can we go now, please?" and I drove out of Westport heading for home, and *then*? I finally told her about the call I'd had from Dan Sharkey.

"Remember him? Reddish hair, big ugly freckles, kind of thick around the middle?"

"When?"

"Did he call? Just before I left to come get you. He says to me, 'I thought I owed you a phone call, at the very least.' And I just knew he'd been saving up *that* line. You could hear it in his voice, the sheer *delight*."

"Look where you're driving!"

"And do you know what else he told me? That I'd done in the kid myself! That it was *my* fault! I said, 'Oh really? Who put him in Plainville, Dan? Who took him off the road?' But he wouldn't answer that one! Just said it's a *courtesy* call—so I wouldn't start work tomorrow on anything new."

"He canceled your strip?" Ginnie's lips moved, but it wasn't a smile. It resembled a smile, it was a good likeness, but I knew that woman, everything about her—Christ, I even knew her secret *name*—and I can tell you it wasn't a smile. She said, "He canceled your strip?"

"A courtesy call," I said. "How considerate! He says, 'We'll run all the dailies you gave us, but that's it. "Derby Dugan" ends in November.' But I told him, I said, 'It's the middle of a story—don't you even read it? The Plainville Patriots are on a winning streak, Dan. Derby's at bat. It's top of the ninth. It's the big game! Let me finish the story, for Christ's sake!'"

"Candy, you're driving too fast!"

"'Just let me finish the story, Dan!'"

"Goddamnit, Candy, look at the road—you want us to have an accident!"

"I told him, I said you can't—you can *not* leave him standing at home plate forever, you just can't. Let him knock that fucking baseball over the fence! Out of the park! And let him run! We owe him that. That's what I said. 'For all that he's suffered we owe him that much.'"

"Candy—!"

"But Sharkey hung up!"

"Candy, oh God, please slow down!"

"The son of a bitch hung up on me!" I said. And then . . . *then* I twisted the wheel and just launched that ten-ton Buick off Clapboard Drive, where there was a sharp dip in the road, and—

No . . . *then* I eased off the gas, just a little, and kept driving.

I drove all the way home.

Ginnie said, "Put the car away and come inside. We have to talk about this."

She said, "What are you doing? Where are you going?"

She said, "Candy!"

She called her sugar Candy, and I threw that big-ass Buick into reverse and backed it down our driveway, fishtailing at speed, and I left her standing on the steps, below the coach light, at the front door, in the rain. Then I shot around the next corner, left off Founding Fathers Lane into Clapboard Drive, and . . . *then?*

Then I crashed into an oak or an elm or an ash or whatever the hell it was, on purpose. On purpose, I'm ashamed to say. And that should've . . . done it. Should've *finished* things, but no. Instead of rocketing through the windshield, as physics would have it, I flew out the driver's door window! Sideways! And was thrown clear. Not that it was any picnic, mind you, it ended me up with a ruptured spleen, a chipped spine, and a fractured hip, four busted ribs, three French hens, two turtledoves, and—Jesus bleeding Christ, I look back on all of that now and I get the shakes, I fucking shiver. I was out of control. But now it's different, *I'm* different. I can sit here with a plate in my skull and every goddamn bone and joint screaming Don't move! Don't move! and with my hands like this, you can see how they are, they're ruined, they're wrecked, and still . . . still I can say, I can tell you kids with absolute candor that I'm happy. And content. I couldn't be more content. Or optimistic. I can't see how. But that Sunday . . . really, that entire stinking period in my life, but that Sunday, especially, I was—

Oval, *then* circle. First an oval, *then* a circle. Goddamnit, Roy. What're we gonna do about this guy? You don't keep an eye on him every second, what's he do, he does it backward. For all of his chops, he'll do it wrong. He'll do it "his way." Am I right, Nicky? But *whose* way? My way, if you please, Mr. Looby. As long as you're here, you'll do it my way. And don't hold your pencil like you're squeezing a pimple, for Christ's sake. What'd I tell you? Lightly. Gently. Caress it. It's your tool, sonny boy. So love it. You loving it, Roy? Then what are you waiting for? Draw him again . . .

And now I lost my train of thought.

But I guess I was just saying I was nuts. That's all. I went crazy. And when I look back, I still get the shakes. Both my legs were shattered, here, here, and here, and here, and up here, and a fractured collar bone, and that fancy exit tore off my left goddamn ear! But when they sewed it back on? At Norwalk Hospital? Well, you can see for yourself, they sewed it on too high! Look here. See here? Makes me look like Mr. Potato Head! So—

I went through the driver's door window, through the glass, and landed facedown thirty feet off the road in some field but it might as well be a fucking bog it's been raining so hard, and—

Goddamnit, first an oval, then a circle. What'd I tell you, Roy? How'd I show you? And—

And I'm lying in that field, I could've drowned, there was so much water, and what do I see? My own left ear! Now, there's a sight I'll never forget—

Like poor Buddy Lydecker in his maroon pajamas, crying.

Or Ginnie sitting on a bench by the Navesink River telling me her secret name, or—

Derby Dugan waiting for a pitch that won't ever come, or—

Holy mother of Christ, my *ear* just floated off . . . and then I heard a siren, please be the ambulance, please, but I wasn't afraid, not a bit, there'd be clean white sheets and scrambled eggs, and then . . . then suddenly these sodden pieces of jigsaw puzzle streamed past my face. Some were caught in the grass, but others were swept away, and then—

There it was. The yellow wallet. That yellow wallet. There it was, and it bobbed and dipped like a raft in a gush of black muddy water, and then it spun around in a countercurrent, and the next thing I knew, the *last* thing I knew, it was gone.

They found my ear, Roy, but they never found that.

BOOK TWO

THE BROTHERS LOOBY

Keep your cast small and tidy. Nothing extraneous. Your protagonist. A handful of supporting characters. Possibly a sidekick. An antagonist or two. Or three. And you'll need a base setting. An orphanage, an office, the Pentagon, the moon. Put things in motion quickly. Start with a bang, whenever possible. Explain later. Fill in as you go along. And, of course, it's always a good idea to make your hero suffer like Job.

—from "Creating the Adventure Strip," Lesson 21,
The Bigfoot Professional Cartooning Home-Study Course

The Dailies

MONDAY, APRIL 17, 2000

They tell me here, they go, "Talk to your brother, it doesn't matter what you say, just *talk*." So I'm talking. I've *been* talking. But I don't feel like it anymore—that okay? All right with you if I shut up for a while and just sit here? Or maybe I'll go down the gift shop and buy a pad of paper—some paper and a pencil, do some drawing. That could be interesting, although me and drawing, we got a pretty limited relationship these days. We're friendly, but we're not friends. Like, whenever I'm on the phone? I have to have a pencil in my hand and a scratch pad nearby, so that doing business or shooting the shit I can doodle heads. Say I get a call and there's no pad and pencil within easy reach, I'll say, "Wait a sec, could you?" Then go look. I'll come back, say, "Thanks for holding," and start right in doodling my tiny little heads— heads only, in profile, with thick brows, googly eyes, blobby noses, mouths wide open, tongues hanging out, spittle flying. I do left-facing profiles, right-facing profiles, I'll scribble hair on my heads, wild hair, or scratch in a little fringe above the ears. Sometimes I'll indicate a neck. But that's as far as I go, bodywise. I do heads only these days. Only heads. Beyond that, Roy, I lack all confidence.

So maybe I'll draw. But no—because you know what? I think I'll watch TV. Go right on dreaming, Roy, or whatever the hell it is you're doing, and I'll see if there's anything on worth watching. Be good if some good movie was on AMC. *The Searchers* or something.

Which reminds me: I saw a pretty good one last night. They got free Cinemax where I'm staying, so I might as well take advantage of it. Nothing else to do. What, I should walk around Richmond checking out the Civil War monuments? It's *raining*. Or sit at some bar? Well, I don't drink, not anymore. Don't drink, don't smoke. Ever since my "sudden massive coronary." Don't drink, don't smoke, don't give a rat's ass about Robert E. Lee.

But I was starting to say about this movie. It was just coming on when I got back to the hotel from seeing you. These guys have to break *into* Alcatraz. What was it called? I'm so bad with titles. It's, like, four, five years old. Sean Connery, Nicolas Cage, and that other guy, what's his name, with the scary eyes? Ed Harris. Ed Harris, Sean Connery, Nicolas Cage. *The Rock*! I watch dumb action movies, what can I tell you? But the *point* being, Roy, this picture was, like, filmed in San Francisco. A place I've been. Almost thirty years ago, but still: it's a "place I've been."

Funny, whenever it comes up, like say when Jerry Garcia died— whenever I mention that I spent a little time in Hashbury during the so-called hippie era, people are so *interested*. Did I ever see *Janis,* go to the Fillmore, and blah blah blah. All that peace, all that love. Must've been wild, it must've been great. Well, jeez, I hate to sound geezery, but I always have to say it wasn't anything like that, at least not when I was there. The streets were crowded, that's for sure, and nobody seemed older than twenty-five, and twenty-five was *old,* and the kids wore bells and paisley and headbands and shit, but it all seemed pretty ratty by then. More junkies than anything else, and skanky runaways offering to blow you for two, three bucks, and panhandlers galore. Like I have to tell *you.*

But I was just saying. About San Francisco. "A place I've been." There's no reason to ever go back, but at least I got there once, thanks to you, and um—goddamn, Roy, besides drop acid, smoke dope, and draw your last comics, just about the only thing I saw you do that summer was change your shirt, and you did that ten times a day. At least. Man, you'd just peel off one soggy T-shirt and pull on a dry one—

always a duplicate dead-white Hanes with our famous imp's grinning face on the front—then you'd start drawing again. Half an hour later, guaranteed, that fresh shirt was soaked. It was *sopping.* You sweated like James fucking Brown, man, and the days weren't even hot! It scared me. Worse than that, and this scared me the most—you know what it was? Those nosebleeds. All that blood! It was like somebody punched you. Crazy Roy. My crazy brother. Sweating and bleeding and tripping and bleeding and sweating and tripping, and drawing every day, morning till night, sometimes straight through the night, and meanwhile—meanwhile I'm parked at that table across the room, inking your stuff, giving it weight and bulk and a logical source of light. *Rendering* it. Finishing what you'd started, big brother, same as I'd done for you practically all of my life.

"How you doin', Clyde?" Remember that? You'd go, "How you doin', Clyde?" whenever you'd, like, *notice* I was still there. Still breathing. "How you doin', Clyde?" You always called me Clyde. I can't remember when *that* started, I guess back in our Stone Age. Since I can remember, it was Clyde, nothing else, and you never called me Nick. "How you doin', Clyde, you doin' okay?" "Good, Roy. Doin' just *great.*"

This summer coming up? It'll be thirty years. You believe it? Right after the "incursion" into Cambodia and the Kent State "massacre," as if you ever paid attention to stuff like that. You were Mr. Nothin' Doin', the famous nutball cartoonist, so everybody naturally assumed you were gonzo antiwar, but they got it wrong. They called your stuff "political," "satirical," "rebellious," but they misread. You weren't draft meat, you had no fucking *spleen,* you didn't give a shit. Well, me neither. Even back then I had the eyesight of a mole, and there was that unexpected bonus. When they said "heart murmur" at my physical I'd never felt happier! Like Candy Biggs always said, "You can't pay attention to everything, boys. Eliminate. Subtract. Pick your focus and forget the rest." You didn't give a crap about Vietnam, and neither did I.

But, God, was it ever a big, serious bone of contention between me and Noreen. She'd get bent way out of shape hearing the latest body counts, watching skirmish video on the Cronkite news, and I'd tell her, "So watch something else if it bothers you. Change the channel, Noreen." She'd get "offended," and there'd be another long, loud, shitty night. That definitely was a thing that brought me and her to our "parting of the ways." A "contributing factor." The fucking war.

Another thing was how much time I spent every night inking pages for DC Comics. She liked the income, *that* she enjoyed, but she kept saying to work faster, work faster—Christ, it was only the stupid Elongated Man, it was just Space Ranger, and did I really have to spend so much time making those ridiculous superheroes look sleek and solid? I'd say yes. Yes, I did. If I was doing a job, I was going to do it right, and that miffed our Noreen. I slaved at a miserable little print shop every day, inked comic-book pages at night, and all I got from that girl were complaints—I never hung out with her and the kid, we never *did* anything. Well, guilty, Your Honor. But I had work to do. I was busy.

So that was definitely another big—

Plus, she was so tightfisted!

Noreen, secretary of the treasury. Bank guard Noreen. It drove me nuts! I had to walk around the Shop-Rite carrying a white envelope full of coupons. Ten cents off. Buy One, Get One Free. I shopped with newspaper coupons! Did you? No way. She'd never been that cheap when it was you and her. When it was *Roy* and Noreen. But *Nick* and Noreen? "Did you use the coupon? Why didn't you? I told you to." Fuck it. We always seemed to be arguing. About the stupidest, stupidest things. She'd turn on *The Flying Nun,* I'd groan (even though I kind of had the hots for Sally Field), and she'd call me a real dick. "You're a real dick, you know that?" My turn to fix supper? I'd whip up some banana pancakes, she'd make herself a green salad—for spite! Me and Walt, we're enjoying our pancakes, she's chewing her lettuce. People eat greens, she'd go, human beings eat salad greens. Yeah, well, people eat pancakes, too. Human beings eat pancakes. And like, I preferred Bufferin, so what's she bring home? *Anacin.* Or so, like, given my choice, I'd choose to brush with Colgate. But oh no, she has to have Crest. Noreen's teeth demand Crest. She even went ballistic every time I took off my glasses and cleaned them on my shirt. I was "obsessive," I was "wearing out the lenses." *Wearing out the lenses.* Plus she even criticized the frames. Why'd I have to wear those ridiculous black ones? Couldn't I get something less clunky? A little more stylish? I looked like a damn loan officer or like what's-his-name—Barry Goldwater. Yeah, right, Noreen. I don't *think* so. God, could we argue about the stupidest things, or what?

Sure, there were *good* days, good *weeks,* don't get me wrong. And holy God, she *looked* great, didn't she? Didn't she, Roy? And she felt even better. And—we both liked *The Prisoner,* that was something we shared. Both liked Dylan (but she liked Donovan equally!). We both liked Vonnegut. *Rosemary's Baby.* The book *and* the movie. And James Bond. Aretha. Onion soup. Cheese fondue. Oral sex. (I said "oral sex," Roy. No reaction?)

Me and Noreen. Nick and Noreen. It wasn't all bad, there was *some* good stuff—let's hope so, right? We lived together almost three years, so let's hope there was. But mostly we had our problems. Really, though, you know what? All those problems? That aggravation? That aggression? Were on account of you. And the reason I finally split? Same thing. You, baby. Nobody but you.

I never told you this because—well, because you never *asked,* but what finally happened? She "caught" me inking over one of your published stories. I think it was "Eugene Takes It Like a Woman"—or maybe it was "The Imp Strikes Out." What's the one where he's chased on to a bus, turns out it's a minor league baseball team, they're all a bunch of Nazi homos, they boink him in the ass? Was that "The Imp Strikes Out"? Anyhow, it was one of those funny, filthy six-pagers you did in '69 for *Motor City Comics.* At work I'd made stats of it, and every night, just as soon as Noreen brushed with Crest and went to bed, I'd slap down another page on the light box. Use an overlay. And a brush. I used a *brush,* Roy. You and your fucking Rapidograph. It broke my heart. And your lettering! I couldn't read half the words. And your spelling! You needed me, Roy. That was so obvious.

It was crazy, I know, inking those stats. It was redundant, it was pathetic, but what the hell. It felt good sweeping a loaded brush across Eugene again, making our nasty little runt look right. Making your kindergarten printing legible, unjumbling it, bouncing every word that needed some bounce, putting *i* before *e* except after *c.*

Till one night Commando Noreen "caught" me. And hit the roof. She felt "betrayed." I'd "betrayed" her! I was supposed to hate you,

Roy, and everything about you, including your comics—especially
them—and look what I was doing! I *had* to hate you, it was my duty.
I had to hate you because *she* did.

Except, come on, that was the biggest crock of all time. Noreen
didn't hate you—she couldn't. You'd always been her magic boy and
always would be, no matter what. But if *she* didn't hate you and if *I*
didn't hate you, then what the hell were we doing together?

That was a question we dodged—again. And just yelled our heads
off. Till poor Walt started crying, and Noreen told me to leave. "Go live
with him," she says, "go on! That's what you want, isn't it? Go on, get
out of here!"

So I did. I got out of there.

And that was so unlike me. Nick Looby wasn't a flatleaver, he was
the good brother, the responsible one, the "nice guy." You knew me
best of anyone, Roy—was that not completely out of character? Leaving? But I did. I left. Got my old mint-green Bonneville tuned up,
bought four new tires, left Mom a note in her mailbox, said good-bye
to Candy Biggs, and set off driving across the fabled continent of North
America, Jersey City to San Francisco. All by myself. Was that not completely unlike me? You were the guy, Roy, who could just leave—who
could get up and go to the bathroom and next thing we hear you're in
Milwaukee. You could do that, but not me. You could leave, our dad
could leave—but Nick? Nick Looby would never leave. Except I did! I
left home that summer—me, the Looby with no sense of direction—
and went looking for you.

Candy said I was making a big mistake, I'd be sorry. And damned if
he wasn't right. He was right about that, coma boy.

MONDAY, JULY 6, 1970

Although Nick hasn't seen or talked to his brother in over three years—not since the end of May 1967—he has kept track. No problem. Ranked somewhere between Tiny Tim and Abbie Hoffman on the celebrity continuum, Roy Looby has become an American notable, a name printed in boldface. *Roy,* for Christ's sake! Partying with Grace Slick and Peter Fonda, acclaimed by Allen Ginsberg, banished from the Playboy mansion—after pestering some bunny for a hand job during a Shel Silverstein concert. And was it the Kinks that asked him to illustrate their next album jacket? Or the Byrds? One of those bands. But he turned them down. *"'I don't listen to that stuff,' deadpanned* **Roy Looby***, the scruffy underground cartoonist, then joked that his own musical taste runs the gamut from Gene Autry to Fred Waring and the Pennsylvanians."* Except that Roy wasn't joking, it *did*. Gene Autry, Fred Waring, Ethel Merman, Bing Crosby, Patti Page . . .

In April, Canadian customs busted Roy's comic book (*Lazy Galoot* #2) for obscenity, the same week Spiro Agnew called Roy "Roy *Loopy*" in one of his rants against youth culture. Bootlegged Imp Eugene bumper stickers keep turning up on mud flaps and microbuses, not to mention on Tommy Smothers's acoustic guitar, and the character's signature crack—the nihilistic "Nothin' doin'!"—has been pirated by ad men to sell everything from margarine to lawn mowers. Roy, however, refuses to sue for copyright infringement. *"Why should I?' said* **Roy Looby**, *22, the bald, cranky, and increasingly reclusive hippie cartoonist."* He lived for a while in Milwaukee, then Chicago, then Austin. Detroit. Ann Arbor. Philadelphia. Boston. Denver—but with a question mark: maybe, maybe not. Conflicting reports. Definitely Long Beach, though, and definitely L.A. Now he's in San Francisco.

Last month there was a long article about Roy in *Rolling Stone,* the issue with Captain Beefheart on the cover: ROY LOOBY HUNKERS DOWN. According to the story by Ben Fong-Torres, Roy's been staying in the Haight, on Waller Street, occupying the top floor of a ramshackle Victorian mansion with blue scalloped shingles and gingerbread. There was a photograph: tribally painted hippies mustered on the wraparound porch, a small black arrow pointing to Roy's turret window, his "attic domain," which is "strictly off-limits."

It sounds to Nick like Roy has carved out his own Fortress of Solitude, like Superman.

"Do you *hear* yourself?" says Candy Biggs. "Your brother is *not* Superman, kiddo." He leans forward to jab a finger, but cringes. Too much action too quickly taken. "If he's super anything, he's super son of a bitch."

"I know." Was this a good idea? Coming over here to say good-bye? Probably not. "I *know*," says Nick.

On the console TV, an afternoon game show returns after a blitz of commercials. Today's categories: Western Movies, The Mighty Mississippi, Famous Volcanoes, Kings of England. Let's have Famous Volcanoes for five hundred, Richard. In August 1883—

"Krakatoa," says Candy Biggs, answering before the contestant, some "homemaker" from Salt Lake City, can even wrinkle her brow. Then he plucks an undershirt from the basket of clean laundry on a hassock beside his chair. He smoothes it flat on his lapboard and neatly folds it before adding it to the jockey shorts, dungarees, and pajamas piled in a second basket, on the opposite side of his chair. "And don't make me laugh, Nicky. Drive cross-country? You? You get lost going to Paramus."

"I do not!"

"This is a dumb idea. No offense."

"You don't think I can drive by myself to California? I can too. And I'm doing it."

"Then you're just crazy."

"Like you should talk."

Abruptly, Biggs stops pressing wrinkles from a dark-blue polo shirt. "Have a nice trip, Clyde."

"Oh, come on. I didn't mean anything."

"Listen to me, would you? I read the same article you did—and *who's* crazy? 'Fortress of Solitude.' Sounds to me like Roy's living in his own personal loony bin."

Well, maybe. There *were* a few things in that *Rolling Stone* profile that *did* strike Nick as a little bit . . . strange. But it's possible that those were all, and only, a big goof, that Roy was pulling another mindfuck (same as he'd pulled last year on that gullible writer from the *East Village Other* when he claimed he'd run away from an orphanage at fourteen to work on an Indian reservation). Even so, Nick still has to admit (to himself, not to Biggs) that some of the stuff in that article and some of the quotes *were* flat-out strange. Fuck strange—flat-out *spooky*. Stuff like: "With the Cab Calloway Orchestra blasting from KLH speakers, Looby draws righty, smokes lefty—and because he doesn't quit his drawing board for twelve, fifteen, sometimes eighteen hours at a stretch, he keeps a Skippy jar nearby to piss in." Stuff like: "His diet consists exclusively of vitamin pills, popcorn, and Hawaiian Punch." And quotes like: "'When I'm done what I'm doing,' he says, 'you could cut off my hand, I wouldn't give a crap. Till then, cocksucker—you do that? I'd grow another one and just keep drawing.'"

And what exactly was Roy drawing, all "hunkered down" in his "attic domain"? What was he *doing,* for twelve, fifteen, eighteen hours at a stretch, that you could cut off his hand, he wouldn't give a crap, he'd just grow another? He wouldn't say, or show the guy from *Rolling Stone* a single page. Not even a panel.

"Go home, Nick," says Biggs. "Call up Noreen and tell her you're sorry."

"I don't think so."

"All right, then forget Noreen. You're going to walk out on your *kid*?"

"I'm not walking out on *any*body!" Nick almost said, *My* kid? "I'm just taking a trip."

"Then go." Biggs sits up straight before turning his full attention, but not really, back to the game show. "John Ford," he says.

"I want to see Roy, that's all."

"John Ford, you fucking idiot!"

"I miss him, Candy. I can't help it."

"What do you *want* from me, Nick? What do you want me to *say*?"

"I don't know—have a safe trip?"

"Have a safe trip, how's that? You leaving now?"

"Yeah."

"So leave."

"I'm leaving." And he is. Nick wants to, and he will, he's *leaving*, but in a minute. Just give him another minute to—to clean his glasses. They're smudged, for Christ's sake, he can barely *see*, he can't drive a car with his glasses all smudged up. He takes them off, breathes fog on each lens, polishes them both with the tail of his shirt—and watches Candy Biggs pair his clean socks (all identical, all black). Christ, thinks Nick, *Christ*. He looks bad, even worse than usual. That stone-gray stringy hair, too long for a guy his age—when was the last time he washed it? And those bags under his eyes. They look like fucking walnut shells. And that cheesy acetate shirt printed with nautical flags, God, and those Army Navy store dungarees. How long's he been wearing those, a month? And those crummy-looking brown bedroom slippers. It's been *years* since the man wore a pair of shoes.

Doing it casually—so as not to appear to be cataloging, or indulging in nostalgia, although he's doing both—Nick looks around the living room: at the half-eaten grilled cheese sandwich and coffee thermos on a snack table; at the shitty old Sylvania TV; at the junky air conditioner with bath towels—a blue, a black, and a yellow—wadded below it. At the aluminum walker in the corner. The heavy, rubber-tipped cane lying on the floor behind Biggs's feet. At the laundry baskets, one of them blue plastic, the other rattan. At the lapboard—the same wooden board that Candy Biggs once upon a time used for drawing comic strips—covered now with balled socks. Was the place *always* this dreary back when he and Roy used to hang out here day after day? When they'd come straight here from school and draw for an hour, for two hours, then show what they'd drawn to Biggs, who'd roll his eyes and say, "No, do it over." Say, "Too wordy. Simplify." Say, "If you can't draw hands, Roy, draw hands till you *can* draw them. Avoidance is the clearest mark of the amateur."

He'd say, "Draw it before, then draw it after. Skip the central action once in a while, let the *reader* provide it."

He'd say, "Pick a place, pick a situation, pick a danger. Setting. Premise. Plot. For example, Derby's on a train. There's a blizzard. There's a maniac."

He'd say, "Oval, circle, circle, circle." And he'd say it again. "Oval, Roy, *then* circle . . ."

"Well, I guess I'm going now," says Nick. "See you when I get back? Candy? I'll see you when I get back, all right?"

And Candy Biggs says, "Edward the *eighth,* you ninny! Edward the goddamn eighth!"

Nick lets himself out.

TUESDAY, APRIL 18, 2000

Hey, Roy? That nurse who was just in here checking on you? Skinny Carol? Skinny freckled nurse Carol with the great little ass? Carol Collins? Was saying to me this morning how incredible it is, your face doesn't have a line in it. And I got the impression she was doubly amazed since, well—you're living in a men's shelter, so it's not like you couldn't have a care in the world. She's right, too. Not a line. Not a *wrinkle*. In fact, even with the cool head bandage, the scabs, all the cuts on your face, you don't look much older than you did the last time you were in the hospital. Last time *I* know about, anyhow. Sixty-four to seventy-four to eighty-four to ninety-four, ninety-five, six, seven, eight, nine—thirty-six years ago. You were, what? Sixteen. So I was fifteen. Good grief, huh? Fifteen and sixteen, that time you were in St. Francis for, you know, your spleen. When you had that surgery. And I came to see you every day. Brought you comic books, brought your schoolwork, did your homework, and I—didn't I read you a novel? *A Tale of Two Cities*? No, what it was? It was *Great Expectations*. The old lady in the wedding dress, remember? And Pip? The guy's name was Pip. The hero? Actually I don't remember too much of it myself, I don't remember the *plot*, but I—

Man, I was so fucking scared you'd say something, tell Mom, or Uncle Neil, or *some*body, say how you'd *really* got that wicked bruise on your stomach. But you never did. How come? How come, Roy? How come you never did? Shit, you never even mentioned it to *me*!

That counted for a lot. Not that you didn't deserve what happened, but you never said anything, never told, never squealed, and that counted. For a whole lot.

You know something, guy? It still does.

TUESDAY, JULY 28, 1970

It takes Nick three solid weeks. Twenty-one days on the road, and on the twenty-second day he rolls into San Francisco. What took him so long? Where'd he go? Where *didn't* he go! Whatever the best, the most direct route is to California, he missed it.

He tried driving straight west, due west, but somehow he'd always veer off and end up heading *south*west or *north*west. That does tend to happen when you're left-handed, have no inborn sense of direction, and cross the country without a map. You end up passing through states you haven't thought about since eighth-grade geography. There really *is* a Minnesota! And a Wisconsin! And Nick actually drove through Texarkana. Abilene, Kansas, birthplace of Dwight D. Eisenhower . . .

He knew he shouldn't have meandered like that. It wasted gas, it wasted money, and gave him too much time to think. He considered picking up hitchhikers—plenty of hippies out thumbing rides this summer. But Nick didn't know for sure if he wanted the company. Besides, he was afraid they'd knock him out and steal his car. Or kill him.

Every night he slept in a safe family-style motel and lay in bed reading old comic books he'd brought along on the trip. He meant to stop

at the Grand Canyon, but then somehow missed it, and it just seemed
too much trouble to go back.

He turned twenty-one in Nebraska.

The first week, week and a half on the road, Nick called Noreen three
times, and each time she hung up on him. He could distinctly remember when Roy called, after *he'd* left. Noreen pleaded with him to come
back. Nick heard her—well, he was over at the house, he was keeping
her company, he was holding her hand. Trying to help her out in any
way that he could. He was there. The responsible Looby. The good
Looby, the nice—

Yeah, so what happens when *he* leaves? When *he* calls? She hangs
up in his fucking ear. And never once asks him to come back. Never
even suggests it.

To Nick, driving a standard-transmission Pontiac in San Francisco
seems only slightly less nuts than climbing Mount Everest with bakery
string. Those hills! Jesus, Mary, and Joseph! But even so, he finds
Waller Street and the blue Victorian house that was pictured in *Rolling
Stone*. More amazing still, he finds a two-car-length parking space right
in front. That should be his tip-off, the warning signal: you luck into a
honey of a spot directly outside the place you've driven thousands of
miles to reach, and for sure it's too good to be true. And so it is: Roy
is gone, he's moved out. Of fucking course! If that *Rolling Stone* article
made it easy for *Nick* to track Roy down, it made it easy for his
brother's pesty fans to do the same thing.

And if there's one thing Roy Looby can't stand it's other people.

On the porch, Nick speaks with two long-haired barefoot guys in
disintegrating T-shirts and faded blue jeans. No, man, they tell him,
sorry. Roy left. He's *gone*. A month ago? Five weeks? Something like
that. He's *gone*.

Nick wishes now that he dressed cooler. That he'd ditched his
khakis, his polo shirt, his Thom McAn Romas and bought a pair of
boots, some bells, a white crepe "blouse" from India, the kind with little mirrors sewn on. And those horn-rimmed glasses! He should've got
himself a pair of wire-rims. Tinted. If he didn't look like some Young

American for Freedom, some conservative *Republican,* he might have an easier time cadging information.

The other housemates whom he talks to, standing in the downstairs hallway, are guys wearing tie-dyed shirts, and they just keep shaking their heads. We're not gonna tell you nothing, man. They don't actually *say* that, they're trying to be good hippies and act guileless, but underneath all their laid-back horseshit is a definite Go Get Fucked. Nick even shows them his New Jersey driver's license—See? Last name Looby, I'm his brother, his younger brother—but they don't believe him. Or else they believe him, but it's just that being Roy Looby's brother doesn't cut it with them. They seem like people not likely to put much stock in families, as a rule.

In the front parlor stands a full-size Indian teepee. A naked chubby girl of twenty or so is stretched out on her stomach in front of it reading a mimeographed booklet of poems. She has a pimply ass. God, though. This is only the second in-person naked girl Nick has ever seen. Roy lived *here?* Where girls sprawl around naked? Jesus. Don't stare. Or else look past her, at the Gandhi poster.

After spending forty minutes in the house and on the front porch learning nothing about Roy's current whereabouts, Nick gets back in his car. Then driving again, just driving, stalling out half a dozen times on those stupid, stupid hills and narrowly avoiding a broadside collision every two minutes, he ends up, at dusk, in downtown San Francisco. Leaving the Bonneville at a pay lot, he checks into the Hotel Calamax on Sutter Street, and ten minutes later, for the first time since leaving Jersey City, he freaks. And bangs his head against the Formica table in his boxy room, giving himself a red lump at his hairline. (At least he *has* a hairline, at least he has *hair.* More than you can say for Roy.) What he needs right now? Is to go walking. Stretch his legs. Take in the sights. Have a good long stare at Alcatraz. Otherwise he might call up Noreen again.

But Nick doesn't make it any farther than the lobby. There, he stops dead and looks out through the revolving door, glimpses legs and torsos moving, registers the full dark. Turning around, he almost runs back to his room. Eats Pringles, drinks a Coke, removes his glasses, and cleans the lenses with his undershirt. Crawls into bed. He sleeps for twenty minutes, then wakes suddenly, dry-mouthed, and tries to reconstruct a dream he just had.

Already it's vague, it's unraveling. Something about—he was back in Candy Biggs's parlor, on the couch . . . waiting for Roy to show up. Biggs looked anxious, *guilty,* and kept pulling on that ruined ear of his that sits too high on the left side of his head. What else? Nick fidgeted, cracked his knuckles, tapped a foot, tapped the other foot, then reached for a bottle of India ink but knocked it over. A black puddle spread across the coffee table. Surreally slow. As Nick apologized to Biggs and Biggs called him clumsy, the spillage divided like an amoeba, then divided again, then again, and again, till there were twenty or more small puddles, then *not* puddles—pieces, instead, from a jigsaw puzzle. Then Nick was climbing a flight of stairs, arriving at the top, stepping over and around paintbrushes and rollers and roller trays, and water-damaged books, and stacks of old newspapers, and loose phonograph records. Suddenly Uncle Neil appeared wearing his brown uniform. He said something, but Nick can't remember what, and maybe the big old goof tried to *give* him something. It seems to Nick that he might've, but then Uncle Neil was gone and Nick had arrived in front of a door. When he pushed against it with his shoulder, it gave an inch, but only that: it was fastened on the other side with a hook and eye. He needed something to slip the hook, so he reached for his wallet and took out a Diners Club card he doesn't have in real life. But as he was returning the wallet to his back pocket, it suddenly dawned on him: this wasn't *his* wallet, it was Roy's.

Roy's magic yellow wallet.

What was he doing with *that*? Nick felt an urge to flick through it—he knew he'd steal any cash or condoms that he found, but what excited him was the possibility of discovering something secret of Roy's. A letter. A photograph. A dirty drawing. A *clue.* Quickly, he put away the wallet, or perhaps he threw it away, before he could give in to temptation. That's when he woke up.

Nick gets out of bed now and snaps on every light. Clicks on the television, finds an old black-and-white Japanese monster movie. Grabbing an ashtray, his cigarettes, and matches, he flops back down. How come in his dream he had Roy's wallet? What was *that* all about? What was that supposed to mean? It had to mean something.

Didn't it?

When Roy and Nick Looby were in parochial school, Uncle Neil Cannon (not a real uncle) read the gas and electric for a living. Once a month he would clatter down into your cellar, this smiley uniformed guy with a big metal flashlight and a meter man's book, and unless you followed behind and watched him closely, ninety seconds later he would spring back upstairs and zip out your front door with a locking pliers or a plumber's friend, even a cut-glass creamer that your grandmother got at her bridal shower. And you never noticed. He would always take something, but you never noticed. That was because Uncle Neil could figure just where to stick things so they wouldn't jut out or suddenly drop. Christmas balls, staple guns, napkin rings, baseball cards, café curtains, curtain rods, Sax Rohmer novels, little cans of semigloss enamel with brittle drips on the paper labels. Back issues of *Argosy, Real Male,* and *National Geographic.* Gene Autry records, Ethel Mermans, Fred Warings, big old shellacked 78s. Which you never missed. "People don't know their cellars," he'd tell Mrs. Looby. "And they don't know their attics, either. They don't know their asses, they don't know their elbows."

What was it with Uncle Neil, a compulsion? It must have been a compulsion, liberating useful things and items of crap wherever he found them—a little dab o' danger to glamorize a job he found even duller, he said, then he found the eleven o'clock mass, which he attended, and dutifully ushered at, on Sunday mornings. Most of the stuff that he took he dumped right away, in a vacant lot or a nearby sewer, but some of it, the glassware and tools, the records and curtains and touch-up paint, he gave to Cathy Looby. Reading matter he gave to her boys.

Mrs. Looby wished to Christ that Uncle Neil would stop bringing over so much junk. It was illegal, taking that stuff, it was stealing, it was a venial sin. Plus, it only ended up stashed down in *her* basement. But since he also gave her cash money, twenty dollars a week, always two tens, to eat at her table, she had to be careful. And watch what she said. In those days, Mrs. Looby feared that if she asked Uncle Neil to cut it out with the crazy generosity, he might take offense—he was easily offended; well, he was Irish American—and find someplace else to have his daily meal and Sunday dinner. And since there was no husband, no father—the rotten bastard had split for parts unknown in 1950, when Roy and Nick were still babies, two and one—she could not afford to lose the extra income. But she also kept her mouth shut because she felt sorry for the guy, him with that silly butch cut and that god-awful eczema at his hairline, and no family of his own, no prospects, a homely neighborhood bachelor in his middle forties. The poor thing. He means well, she told her sons.

So the cellar swag kept coming, till one late afternoon in the fall of 1960 when Nick was eleven and Roy was twelve and up and down Lembeck Avenue every Catholic family (which was practically every family on the block) had a KENNEDY FOR PRESIDENT sign displayed in the front window or staked in the lawn, Uncle Neil arrived at the Looby household with something he'd stolen that changed the boys' lives forever.

Years later, Nick can still recall the look on Roy's face when Uncle Neil removed it from the lining of his uniform cap. Roy's eyes grew wide and his mouth dropped open. Instantly, Nick could see it was the one thing in the world his brother most wanted to own. Needed to have. Roy hadn't known that a minute ago, but now he did.

It was a wallet, a bright-yellow wallet, sized for a child. Roy held that chintzy thing like it was precious beyond price, something holy, a holy relic, and turned it over in his hands. "Who's that?" he asked, pointing at the hard plastic cartoon character—a kid in a high-crowned derby with his thumb out in the universal gesture of a hitchhiker—that was pasted on the cover. "Who's *that*?"

"Why, that's Derby Dugan," said Cathy Looby, and Nick thought she said it exactly the way people—sheriffs and schoolteachers and ranch hands and "old-timers"—said, "That's the Lone Ranger," at the end of every TV episode.

That's Derby Dugan.

From then on, Roy carried the wallet. Used it for his cash and ID. Except that it was never just a wallet, of course. Nick supposes that a shrink or anthropologist would call it a talisman. Call it Roy Looby's talisman, or his totem. But primarily it was Roy's *inspiration*. And secondhand, it was, it would become, Nick's inspiration, as well.

. . .

Even though he still considers that dinky wallet the cheesiest-looking thing he's ever seen, too corny for words, a piece of crap, it has galled Nick (just a little, though, not a lot, and only occasionally, not often, not *very* often)—it has galled Nick Looby how his brother just grabbed it on that long-ago afternoon, just assumed possession. Not that Nick ever really wanted it, not then, not ever. Stupid wallet.

But so why the stupid dream?

WEDNESDAY, APRIL 19, 2000

Noreen used to talk about being a nurse, didn't she? Me and you, we'd
be yapping away about the "cartoonist's life," the "business," the "profession," quoting all the stats and jargon we'd picked up from Candy
Biggs, and poor Noreen, like maybe there'd be a pause, like maybe
we'd shut up for a second, and she'd go, "I might like to be a nurse."
A nurse, or maybe a teacher. Well, yeah. "In those days," et cetera.
"Young women," et cetera. And it's true, in those days the young
women *we* knew either got married straight out of high school and had
a bunch of kids or, like, you were a nurse for a couple of years or a
teacher, *then* you got married and had your kids. Started your family.
You put on weight, you went to the PTA, you turned a little goofy, or
a lot, and then you died. Oh, fuck me, listen to me, what a cynic. What
a jerk. Like I know anything about anything or have any right to make
sweeping pronouncements. Like anything was ever that simple. Even
in Jersey City. But it's our "curse," Roy. Our "professional curse." We
simplify, we subtract, we exaggerate—and make sweeping fucking
pronouncements. Hey, we're cartoonists. Or we used to be.

"In those days, young women . . ."

"In those days, asshole boys . . ."

· · ·

I only bring up that shit about Noreen and nursing because—I don't mean it was a date or anything, but last night I spent some time with Carol Collins. Nurse Carol. But it wasn't a date or anything—hell, I'm fifty, she's twenty-five. I'm fifty and don't make movies, don't own Microsoft, and she's twenty-five. So all it was, I drove her home. I was leaving, she was leaving: hey. Her car was still in the shop, it was pouring rain, she'd called a cab, it hadn't come: hey. No big deal. But here's the great thing, or maybe it's not so great: when I asked could I give her a lift? She didn't "demur." Apparently my vibes are harmless. Nothing about me said to her, Ted Bundy II. She accepted my offer instantly, with a smile.

But the minute we got to my car, I felt stupid. I felt mortified. She looked at the door and then she looked at me—and I gave her back a little shrug, that meek kind where your head sinks down like a dog's.

What a cool car I drive! A '91 Ford Topaz with SIGNS BY CLYDE, FOR ALL YOUR SIGNAGE NEEDS painted on the passenger door in that swooping Nick Looby style, undeniably "professional," unquestionably corny. SIGNS BY CLYDE. Oh, good Christ.

People still ask all the time, "Who's Clyde?" Customers call up, they ask for Clyde. Either I tell them, "I'm Clyde—it's an old joke," or I tell them, "Clyde's dead—I took over his business." Depending on what mood I'm in.

Carol Collins didn't ask me who's Clyde. But I volunteered the information anyway. "Clyde's dead," I told her. "I took over his business."

"You're a sign painter," she said, totally flat, no judgment—but I know by now that no judgment in somebody's voice always implies one. And it's this: God, how boring.

So I got past the "company car" ordeal, but then I was feeling this weird anxiety. You know what it was? I was afraid there might be clues in the car she could read, that would give her some negative impression of me. Some "unfavorable opinion." Can you believe that? Why should I care what she thinks? It was so stupid. For example: there were tapes in a caddy, just a bunch I grabbed before leaving home, not a conscious *selection,* just a random bunch, but it made me sick to my stomach that all of them were "classic rock." She'd think I was stuck back in the damn sixties. Why *Blonde on Blonde,* why The Band, why the Doors, why Linda Ronstadt, and why, for Christ's sake, had I taken the Beatles? And not just the Beatles, the *early* Beatles! What I wouldn't have given right then for, I don't know, a Pearl Jam tape! Or Beck. Something by him, *anything* by him. And I don't even know what the hell Beck sounds like, I just read about him in *Entertainment Weekly.*

But then—"Wow," she goes, "*Beatles '65.* Would you mind if we listened to this one?"

If it hadn't been raining, I would've rolled down the window and slung out my elbow, I was all of a sudden feeling that good!

And now I'm trying to remember why I even started telling you all this in the first place. I know I had a reason, but I can't—oh! Here we go, I remember now. We're driving along—naturally, she's giving me directions, head straight up Broad Street, hang a right, take a left, and then, bless her little heart, Carol says, "I told my mom and dad about your brother, and they both heard of him."

Her "mom and dad." Not *Carol,* her mom and dad. Carol's "mom and dad" heard of you!

But here's the funny part. Mom and Dad? Said, Roy Looby? Oh sure, he's the guy who created Mr. Natural and Fritz the Cat.

Jesus, Roy, not even a flush? Not even the flicker of an eyelid?

Of course, I had to correct the mistake, and I said, "No, that's Robert Crumb. My brother created the Imp Eugene."

That's what I said, Roy: I said my brother created the Imp Eugene. Gave you all the credit. What the hell, right? It's bad enough you're a tramp on the street, you're a guy in a coma—I should give her the full-fledged soap opera? We were having such a nice conversation, I was driving her home—so I just told her you created the Imp Eugene and let it go at that. I gave you full credit.

Big surprise, though. She'd never *heard* of Eugene. I said, Oh, he was this little runt with a bowler hat and a sneer on his face—the unhappy hippie. And if she wanted, I said, I could show her some of your stuff. So I might. I might just call up Joel Clark and have him ship me down a bunch of those reprint books he did. But I'll start her off with the early strips, the clean stuff. Take her slowly through the collected works, and if she doesn't wig out (I don't *think* she's a prude), I might even let her read the masterpiece.

Which I haven't looked at myself in thirty years, not since the day you finished it. I haven't looked at it once—but not because "they say it's cursed." I don't believe in any of that horseshit. No, it's just—well, you know. Those "negative associations." Like I see a package of chocolate macaroons in the supermarket? I get totally bummed, I smell church candles, day lilies. I avoid the cookie aisle for just that reason. Because, like, I was stuffing my face with chocolate macaroons when Uncle Neil called to say that Mom was dead.

Mom is dead, by the way.

And that song "Every Breath You Take"? Same thing. I can't listen, it freaks me out. It's the soundtrack to my heart attack. I hear that song and it's the fifth of March 1993 all over again, I'm stenciling a big *J* on a Dodge van, that song's playing on the radio, and suddenly it's like I got hit in the chest with a cannonball. Negative associations. Like, I think about "The Last Eugene," automatically, I think about—

Cora. And Clarky, before he got pathetic. And Victor and Mickey. And Breitstein. Elmer Howdy. Your nosebleeds. All that *other* shit. Which I don't want to think about. So I won't.

But all I'm saying, I'm just saying I might show Carol some of the old stuff. The good old stuff. The good old stuff from the good old days. Who knows, man, you might chalk up another fan.

But if I hear that word *genius*? That word comes out of her pretty little mouth and I swear to God, Roy, she won't get another ride home from *me*.

WEDNESDAY, JULY 29, 1970

Although he never smokes the day's first Marlboro till after two or three cups of coffee and some kind of breakfast, usually a Pop-Tart, this morning Nick lights one up on an empty stomach. Though he feels sick and headachy by the fourth drag, he smokes it down to the filter while reading take-out menus—Italian, Chinese, macrobiotic—that he finds propped against a fat-bottomed ceramic lamp. Devise some plan, he thinks, today's plan of attack. Instead, he turns on the TV, looking for cartoons. But the pickings are slim: it's a weekday. Aquaman, Archie, the Banana Splits. How come every single idiotic kids' show has to teach some dopey *lesson*? Like "responsibility," like "tolerance," like "teamwork." Like "respect for the environment." They're all so fucking preachy. Jeez, who writes these things? Billy Graham? Whyn't they just shut up already and light the Acme dynamite? Crank up the Cab Calloway and send in the mice!

This year, Nick had started keeping Walt company every Saturday morning. He'd let Noreen sleep in, get up by seven, and toast the little guy a waffle, drench it with syrup, watch him eat. After Walt finished, they'd head straight for the cellar, to Nick's drawing "nook," in what used to be a coal bin. Once Nick switched on the TV and the swivel lamp, their weeky ritual would segue into its second, its major, phase. Walt on the "carpet remnant," elbows planted in a pillow, Nick on a stool behind him, setting out brushes and pen staffs, shaking nibs from an envelope. Nick working, freelancing, inking someone else's pencils, some hack cartoonist he'd never met, somebody living in upstate New York or down the Jersey shore, in Florida, Delaware, Michigan, even the Philippines; inking whatever pages came that week in the mail, a "Blackhawk" story, or a "Tommy Tomorrow," occasionally a war story for "G.I. Combat," but usually just another superhero six-pager, and always a second-stringer like the Elongated Man. He never got to ink Batman or Superman or Green Lantern or Flash. Not that he was complaining. Twenty years old and he was inking for DC Comics. Pretty good, no? Well, Noreen didn't think it was such a big deal, and for sure Roy wouldn't, either, if he knew.

Using a Winsor & Newton #4, Nick soon would be lost in the pure sensual pleasure of flowing ink. Not so lost, however, that he didn't lift his head every minute and check out what the kid was watching. Usually some Hanna-Barbera crap. "Birdman and the Galaxy Trio." "Underdog." "Moby Dick and the Mighty Mightor." Pathetic. But Nick kept his opinions to himself. If Walt liked it, he liked it. Nick always felt hesitant about foisting himself, his personality, on the kid. He felt like . . . he felt like . . . he felt like he *shouldn't,* that it wasn't his place. Since it wasn't his kid.

Together they would stay there in the cellar for two, three hours. Nick took regular breaks to stare at Walt, at his profile, seeing what made him smile (complicated accidents) and what made him laugh (embarrassing situations). He'd get up and bring the kid a bowl of Cheerios, a glass of juice, a chewable vitamin. Around eleven, Walt would turn fidgety, flipping channels, watching nothing for longer than ten seconds, growing bored with cartoons. Good for him. Then suddenly he'd be standing at Nick's elbow, leaning forward on tiptoes, peeking at the wet bristol board, watching Nick's hand pivot on his wrist. Watching him dip the brush and twirl it to a point against the rim of the ink bottle. Nick loved it when that started, when the kid came over and seemed interested. His heart speeded up. But he'd pretend not to notice Walt. Well, he might smile, give the kid a wink, but that was all. He never was sure whether the kid enjoyed their Saturday mornings together or—even if he realized that Nick was *consciously* spending time with him. Hard to tell.

But Nick enjoyed them. Loved them. Same as twelve, fifteen years ago, he'd loved spending Saturday mornings with Roy. Nick and Roy. *Just* Nick and Roy. Playing hide-and-seek. Playing with badly painted toy soldiers. Coloring in coloring books. Swapping last night's dreams. (Roy's always were better, wilder than Nick's. Nick would dream he'd forgotten to do his homework and now there was no time, Roy that he'd been shot into space and was circling the world in a nose cone; Nick would dream he was floating a foot or two above the sidewalk, looking down at his shadow, Roy that he was part of a Western posse on horseback chasing outlaws; Nick would dream he was lost in the woods, Roy that he was back in 1,000,000 B.C., running from saber-tooth tigers, leaping over hot lava, trudging through a swamp that turned out to be a gigantic lake of tar.) Those Saturday mornings, those perfect Saturday mornings. Spent swapping dreams, coloring, playing games, but never watching cartoons, at least not before Uncle Neil brought home that wallet.

For one thing, the Loobys didn't own a television set until 1959. The last family on Lembeck Avenue, and probably in all of Jersey City, to buy one. Not that the boys ever suffered, they weren't deprived: they could always traipse across the street to Noreen Novick's house, watch programs there. Puppet shows, mostly. Kukla, Fran and Ollie. Howdy Doody. Claude Kirschner and Clownie. Then cowboy stuff. Hopalong Cassidy, Lash LaRue, Roy Rogers. Tons of cowboy stuff. Davy Crockett. But no cartoons, no animated cartoons. The brothers just weren't interested, not till after the wallet. Not till after Roy began drawing—obsessively copying—the wallet's plastic medallion. Derby Dugan, Derby Dugan, Derby Dugan. Roy at twelve, at thirteen, sitting crunched up at his end of the sectional, still in pajamas, the wallet in his lap, a pencil in his hand. Drawing on a pad of cheap white paper their mother had bought for him at Kresge's after he'd filled her good stationery tablet with Derby Dugans, Derby Dugans, Derby Dugans. Roy glancing from the wallet to his paper, paper to his wallet, then looking up for a second at Heckle and Jeckle or Mighty Mouse on their red-mahogany

Emerson with a picture screen the size of a porthole in steerage. Commercials for Bosco, for Maypo. Then cutting his eyes back to the wallet, the medallion, to his pad. And Nick at eleven, at twelve, watching Roy. Watching TV, watching Huckleberry Hound, Tom and Jerry, Daffy Duck, but watching his big brother, too. And watching Roy far more closely. Watching him draw.

Just watching.

Derby Dugan, Derby Dugan. Over and over again.

Derby Dugan.

It was weird, so unexplainable (and if the stimulus were not so dopey, almost mystical), Roy's instant passion for that character, for that *image*: a puny little boy with an oval head, circle eyes, a circle nose, and a ludicrous ten-gallon yellow derby hat. A patched black suit jacket and a striped gondolier's jersey, blue jeans, and combat boots. But who the heck was he, this Derby Dugan?

Cathy Looby had recognized him at once, the day Uncle Neil brought home the scavenged wallet. "He used to be in the funny papers," she said. "And when I was a girl, he was even on the radio. Derby Dugan and his dog that talks," she said with a fond, slightly abashed smile, reciting it like some drilled-in product slogan. Maxwell House, good to the last drop. 7Up, you like it, it likes you. Derby Dugan and his dog that talks.

Roy said, "A dog? What dog?"

And Uncle Neil, ever corny and eager to please, made a wild flourish with his arm and snapped his fingers. "Fuzzy! The dog's name," he said, "was Fuzzy."

The dog's name *was*? Nick would never forget the positively crestfallen expression on his brother's face. It was like Roy had suddenly discovered some marvelous treasure, pirate's gold, only to have it wink out, be an illusion, a stinking mirage. The dog's name *was* Fuzzy? Derby Dugan *used* to be in the funny papers? But was no longer? Did comic-strip characters, like countries after wars, like grandmothers after surgery, like fathers after the birth of two sons, disappear for good? Vanish into thin air? Roy's delight turned to confused dismay— Nick saw it happen, saw the change come into his eyes, the corners of his mouth, not five minutes after the wallet first materialized, like a magician's trick, from Uncle Neil's meter-man cap. Their mother didn't notice, and neither, of course, did Uncle Neil. But Nick did.

He noticed *everything* about Roy, or tried to. "I bet you Derby Dugan's still around," he said that day in early November 1960. "I bet you we can find him."

And the way Roy looked at him then, with an expression Nick recognized as a blend of relief, gratitude, and shared jeopardy—he's never forgotten it. Or the blast of sheer joy that blew through his chest, through his bones, when Roy smiled suddenly from ear to ear. "I bet you we can, too, Clyde. We'll find him."

That was the beginning. Not the wallet, that was just the catalyst. The real beginning, the actual moment when both their lives began to sketch out a single shape, was the moment when Nick and Roy Looby agreed to set off together on a quest to find Derby Dugan.

Everything started there.

When Nick sees himself now in the bathroom mirror, he almost plops. Jesus! *I have pimples again!* Three weeks of chili dogs, candy bars, pizza by the slice, and dime bags of potato chips have taken their toll. And his hair looks like barn straw, sticking out all over the place. Behold! a sleazebag. Not that Nick Looby (thick glasses, bad skin, and the physique of a custard doughnut) ever felt he was anything special to look at in the first place, although years ago, when his brother, seemingly overnight, had developed into a cartoonist with professional chops and Nick was left feeling so blackly jealous, Uncle Neil told him, "Don't sweat it, Nicky, at least you're better looking." Which wasn't saying much. Roy Looby has always been to handsome what down is to up. Those bulging eyes, that spongy-tipped nose. Plus—well, he's been shinily bald, a skinhead, since the age of nine.

One day his hair just started to fall out, and it kept right on falling out till there was nothing left. Alopecia areata, said the pediatrician, commonly called juvenile baldness. No rhyme or reason: just because. Roy didn't care. It didn't bother him. In fact, he liked it. He *liked* being different, liked it so much that when some hair started growing back— silky white, not black, as it had been—he begged his mother to shave it off. But it never came to that, since it all fell out again, in clumps, a few weeks later.

· · ·

At a busy coffee shop around the corner from the Hotel Calamax, Nick takes a window booth, then—after cleaning his eyeglasses with a napkin from the metal dispenser—pages through a copy of the *San Francisco Examiner* that someone left behind on the bench seat. He's not so much as glanced at a newspaper or magazine since he left New Jersey, and in the car he never played the radio, only his eight-track tapes (mainly *Abbey Road*). Nick has pretty much lost touch with the world. But it doesn't seem like he's missed a whole lot. Dockworkers striking in England, riots in Italy. Vietnam, Vietnam, Vietnam. The Nixons on vacation. And in New York City, a two-year-old baby died yesterday of an LSD overdose. Oh God, Nick can just imagine how Noreen would react to *that* little item: she'd cringe while her face turned blotchy. Then she'd burst out crying. Then she'd run, scoop Walt up, pecking him with kisses, kisses, frenzied kisses. Scaring the piss out of the poor little guy. But she's a good mom, Noreen. She is. A little tightly wound, but good. And Walt—

Enough. It's not smart to think about the kid. Nick should miss him like crazy, he *knows* that. But he doesn't. Not really. He's missed his brother every day for three years. But he doesn't miss Walt. So here comes the ten-ton guilt. Time for another cigarette, time to find the comics page.

That turns out to be nearly as depressing as thinking about Walt. Same old boring strips, same old boring gags. There are hardly any story strips, three or four sclerotic oldies, and each gag strip that he skims—they're all too slight to actually read or look at for longer than a moment—seems scripted by a committee of white suburban den mothers and tossed off with a felt-tip pen. Because Roy always did, Nick calls the stuff published in newspapers these days "watercooler comics," phony feel-good American clichés masquerading as humor. No pain. Frustration, yes, but no real pain. Tape 'em on the water-cooler, folks, and above the office coffee machine, or tack 'em on the cafeteria bulletin board. Guaranteed good for a chuckle. Cute kids, cute parents, cute dogs. Cute world. Say this for the old "Derby Dugan" strip: it was never cute. There wasn't a cute thing about it, including the orphan boy himself.

• • •

It was weird (that word again) how quickly, how *completely* Nick's brother fell in love with Derby Dugan in the fall of 1960. But he did, and when he'd looked so disappointed, so heartbroken when it seemed likely the character was past tense and long gone, Nick said, "I bet you we can find him," and then Roy said, "I bet you we can, too."

So began the quest.

The "Derby Dugan" comic strip didn't appear in either of the two Jersey City dailies, so the Loobys purchased copies of every other newspaper they could find in the neighborhood candy store—the *Newark News,* the *Star-Ledger,* the *Journal-American,* and *Daily News,* the *Post,* the *Telegram and Sun,* the *Mirror.* But it was in none of those, either. Where was it? Where was *he?*

It was Cathy Looby, of all people, who found him. She had a married sister living in South Jersey, near Philadelphia, and not long after the yellow wallet came into her boys' possession, she was talking to Aunt Cookie on the phone and happened to mention Derby Dugan— not surprising since Derby Dugan and the mystery of his current whereabouts was practically the only thing that Roy cared about anymore. That Roy and Nick both cared about. Roy and Nick *both.* Their mom said, "Do you remember it? I think it used to run in the *Bayonne Times* when we were kids," to which Aunt Cookie responded, "I don't have to *remember* it, Cathy, I *see* it in the *Philadelphia Inquirer.*" As soon as Roy heard that, he begged Mom to call Aunt Cookie right back and ask her if she'd cut out the strip every day and send it to him. "To us," said Nick. "Right," said Roy, "to *us.*"

When the boys got the first batch in the mail, Roy cleared the desk in their bedroom and carefully laid the strips out in tiers. Aunt Cookie had sent Wednesday's through Saturday's, four strips, and in each one Derby Dugan was at bat in a championship Little League baseball game. On Wednesday, he swung and missed, and Fuzzy the dog, watching from the home team's dugout, laid a paw across her eyes in deep distress. On Thursday, Derby Dugan hit a foul ball—and felt the first drop of rain, and said, "Go away, dark clouds, I'm busy." (Roy thought that was great. "Go away, dark clouds, I'm busy." Yeah, that was cool, he liked that—"Go away, dark clouds, I'm busy"—and briefly adopted it for his motto.) In Friday's strip, the sun came out but the other team's pitcher—Nick and Roy could tell he was a creep by the way he was drawn, with a piggish nose and beady little eyes—the pitcher threw an illegal spitball, which Derby swung at and missed. In the last panel, his teammates all cried, "Don't let us down—we need a hit, we need a homer!" On Saturday, Derby Dugan (radiating a halo of sweat beads) was still coiled in his batting stance . . . the mean pitcher pitched . . . the ball came closer, got larger in the last two panels, and a final caption read: "WHAT HAPPENS NEXT?"

The brothers Looby couldn't wait to find out, and when a full week passed without the arrival of another envelope from Aunt Cookie, Roy picked up the phone and called her himself. Nick stood next to him, heard Roy say, "What?" and watched him pale. "What do you *mean?*" said Roy and sat down. He said, "Why *not?*" and hung up.

"What's the matter? Roy? What's wrong?"

"He's gone," said Roy. "Aunt Cookie says he wasn't there on Monday—that where he used to be now it's 'Hi and Lois.'"

"But it's the middle of a story! He can't be gone! It can't stop there!"

But he was, and it did.

Strange day, the day that Derby Dugan vanished. Roy turned sullen, then testy, then cruel, telling Mrs. Looby at the supper table that her slumgullion looked like dog puke and tasted even worse, and when Uncle Neil said, "You apologize to your mother right this second," Roy looked at him with scorn and replied, "Oh, shut up, you're not my father, you're not *anything,* except twenty dollars a week." Then he shoved back his chair and left. When finally Nick was excused from the table and went looking for Roy, he couldn't find him. He was afraid, then almost certain, his brother had run away (it wouldn't have been the first time), but at last Nick thought to check in the attic. Surrounded by cartons of junk and summer clothes, Roy was kneeling on the floor using an old cedar chest for a table. He'd propped the yellow wallet against one of their grandmother's tall vases, and with a brown Venus Paradise pencil he was carefully copying, in Mrs. Looby's tablet of good writing paper, the medallion glued to the wallet's cover: Derby Dugan with his thumb stuck out. Hitchhiking Derby.

Nick just stood behind his brother and watched.

. . .

A waitress comes over and says, "Ready to order?"

"Absolutely," says Nick, folding the newspaper and tossing it on the bench next to him. "Orange juice," he says. "A large one." Load up on that vitamin C! "Cup of coffee," he says, "and, um, can I get two eggs scrambled?"

THURSDAY, APRIL 20, 2000

This might be the first piece of cake I've had in—I bet you it's over a year. And it could be longer. I just don't eat sweets like I used to. Before my heart attack? I was 240, 245, and that was nuts. It was fucking suicidal. So now I watch my diet, I'm pretty strict with myself. I guess I'm around 200 these days, and that's still heavier than I should be. Well, I've never been skinny—except during that delightful month I spent with you in California when I must've dropped down to something like 160, I was a goddamn *stick*. But compared to you that was *fat*. Cora used to say if you lost any more weight, you'd disappear. Which was pretty clairvoyant, no? Well, we hardly ate anything. All we did was work. And drink that god-awful red piss you liked so much, that Hawaiian Punch.

This is all by way of saying I hardly touch sweets, almost never, but today I made an exception. I couldn't resist. When it comes to good chocolate cake, a *bakery* cake, I'm still a sucker, and this one's got real whipped cream, not that sugary stuff. I'm tempted to go back out there and ask for seconds. But I'll be good.

One of the nurses, today's her last day, that's what the cake's all about. They're having a little going-away party, and I was invited. The nurses like me, I think. I'm the "older gentleman" who dropped every-thing to come and sit at his brother's bedside. Yeah, they admire me. They said, "Mr. Looby, have some cake with us." They asked me to take pictures for them. Of the "gang." They even insisted that *I* get in a picture. Somebody used Carol's Polaroid, and—look, see? Nick Looby and the nurses! Nick and his girls. That's Joyce, and that's Faye, and that little tiny thing is Angela—she's very religious—and that's Carol, that's my friend Carol Collins . . . and there's Clare and Debbie and Meghan, and I don't know that one's name—she's pretty though, isn't she? And that's Dr. Matheson, and that's Hank—he looks like a rapper but he's really sweet, he's an orderly—and that's Mrs. Mundy, whose husband just had a liver transplant and he's doing great. And that's me. That pasty-faced individual with the sheepish smile: that's me. God, I hate how I look in pictures, it's always a shock. And I definitely look my age. You wouldn't see me in that picture and think I was forty, would you? Or even forty-five. I *look* fifty. And could pass for older—well, you never completely recover from a heart attack, I don't care what they tell you.

And you know what I'm thinking about now? What I'm suddenly reminded of? *Noreen's* camera—that Polaroid she got one Christmas? Remember that smelly stuff, that gunk she had to rub on every picture with a little squeegee thing? God, she must've taken five hundred shots of just you. You at the drawing board. You on the front porch. The back porch. You with one foot planted on the cellar doors. You in your winter coat. You lying on your back reading comics. Lying on your stomach reading comics. You on the hood of your green '62 Beetle, you climbing *up* the stairs, you coming *down* the stairs, you—

Remember the day I helped you guys move into the house on Blofeld Street? That four-room box you rented? Noreen had just started wearing maternity tops, and since she couldn't help with any lifting, since she couldn't carry anything, she took pictures instead. "For pos-terity." She took Polaroids and supervised. "Bring that straight into the kitchen." "This stays in the living room." "Roy, do you think you want to put your drawing table in the bedroom? Do you think you might want it between the windows? Straight into the bedroom, Nicky. And just set it down between the windows."

We really could've used some help, but who were we going to get?

Candy Biggs? That's a laugh. Uncle Neil? Even though he was mad at
you for knocking up Noreen, he would've helped us except that whole
week he was in bed with gout. Gout! Kings get that, but *meter readers*? So Uncle Neil was no help and forget about anybody in Noreen's
family. They wouldn't even go to your wedding, such as it was—they
were all so humiliated, the whole damn lot of them.

So it was just you and me, humping everything into your new
house, your "first home," cartons and cartons of shit, your old phonograph records and your bagged comic books, and pots and pans that
Noreen bought at Bamberger's in Newark, and your crummy Westinghouse stereo and Noreen's Schwinn and her collection of stuffed animals, and her jigsaw puzzles and her board games—she never threw
anything out, she still had Candy Land!—and a secondhand air conditioner and that portable TV I got you guys for a wedding present. And
Noreen's going, "Watch the door frame" and taking another picture,
and she's going, "Careful, careful," and taking *another* picture, and
she's going, "You think you'd like the bed there? Put it down there."
God, that day sucked. I didn't want to think about what was really happening or that after I moved the both of you guys in I'd drive home
and—there I'd be. There I'd be. Me and Mom. Me and Mom and Uncle
Neil. That day just sucked, that's all. It just sucked.

Hey, though! Remember when we dragged in the mattress? And
heaved it down on the box spring? It looked so inviting that we
crawled on top of it and collapsed, and Noreen said, like, "Get up, you
two, get up, you're all sweaty," and you told her, "Make us," and you
weren't nice about it, either, but she laughed anyway. You could say
anything to that girl and she'd laugh, *you* could—she laughed and then
she went and got that fucking Polaroid again and took a picture of me
and you lying there side by side.

I wish I had that picture. I wish I had *any* of them. But I have to tell
you, she tossed them. I was surprised she did, but she did. One day
she just took all those shoe boxes where she kept them and—*pfffft!*
Out they went. I can't remember what prompted *that,* but it might've
been the same day we saw you and Victor Zits on *The Mike Douglas
Show* acting like a pair of matching assholes. God, you were so fucking stoned, so obnoxious, and you said No, no, Mike, it wasn't true that
you'd grown up in New Jersey, that was a dirty lie, you'd never even

been to New Jersey, thank God, and besides, ha ha ha, you'd never grown up. It might've been that day, I kind of have it in my head it was. And I'm sorry now I didn't go take those shoe boxes out of the trash can. That I didn't salvage them. But I was afraid Noreen'd find out and there'd be, you know, another fight. So I let the garbagemen cart them away.

After you split I don't think Noreen used that Polaroid more than half a dozen times. She bought a used reflex camera, and whenever she took baby pictures of Walt that's what she used. And that Polaroid just ended up—I got no idea where it ended up, it just disappeared. For all I know she tossed it on purpose. So I'd quit bugging her. Because—okay, I admit it: for a long time I tried getting her to pose. You know what I'm saying? Like she used to pose for you up in the attic, same thing but for the camera. I'd go, "Come on, Noreen, that's what people use these things for," and I'd go, "I'm not asking you to be, like, *gross* or anything, just how about some artistic shots?" And she'd go, "Yeah, right. Dream on, Looby." I could always tell when Noreen especially hated my guts—she'd call me Looby. But not only that, she'd really stretch out those *o*'s, stick in a whole bunch of them: Looooooby.

Dream on, Looooooby, dream on.

Anyhow, this cake is very damn delicious.

THURSDAY, JULY 30, 1970

Nick woke late this morning, having spent the last twenty-one hours in his hotel room, most of that time in bed. Sleeping, napping, or rereading back issues of *Walt Disney's Comics and Stories*. MICKEY MOUSE in "Milktime Melody." DONALD DUCK in "TV Trouble." GYRO GEARLOOSE in "Where's the Fire?" The good old stuff. From the good old days. Stories that he and Roy had loved, and pored over, when they were kids. CHIP 'N' DALE in "One Bad Apple." THE JUNIOR WOODCHUCKS in . . .

But enough! Nick came out to California for a purpose, on a *quest,* and so far all he's done is waste time. So today—today is the day. He's going to find his brother, somehow.

After he showers and gets dressed, Nick heads back to that generic coffee shop where he ate breakfast yesterday. But then, pulling open the door, he changes his mind and walks on. Two blocks farther up, he finds a lunchroom with faded café curtains and busts of Laurel and Hardy, Clark Gable, and Harpo Marx in the window seat. He walks inside and takes a padded stool at the empty counter. A cook is beating hamburger patties with a spatula. Every time they burst into flame, he hits them again.

The moment he sees Nick take out his Marlboros, the cook says, "I'm not gonna be one of those pains in the ass always telling the other guy to quit, but the fact is, smoke bothers me now." The waitress laughs—she's heard all this before. A surgical scar, bordered by tiny perforations, runs from her wrist to the elbow on her left forearm. She looks Mediterranean.

Nick puts away his cigarettes. The cook salutes him. In his shirt pocket is a pack of Lucky Strikes. "This?" he asks, as if Nick just said something about it or pointed. "I'm no hypocrite, look," he says, taking out the Luckies pack and shaking it. Up jump two sticks of chalk. "I carry it for the weight. After twenty-five years and suddenly no pack in your pocket, it's like no zipper on your pants. It's like no *pants*. Something's wrong, something's *off*." He turns and wallops another burger. Nick orders a cheese steak. He knows exactly what this guy is talking about. After twenty-one years and suddenly no *brother* in your life, it's like no zipper on your pants. It's like no *pants*. Something's wrong, something's *off*.

When Nick finally hits the pavement again, it's a little past one. Left seems a good direction, left is good, so Nick turns left, and a few minutes later—maybe five, maybe twenty—he finds himself on a busy corner staring at a tall granite Corinthian column and a bunch of palm trees. He crosses the street, sits on a bench in the park. Think. White-haired tourists stroll by and kids in trippy T-shirts. Leafleteers wearing Castro caps and field jackets with black armbands. You can hear dueling music from different radios, the Beatles, the Doors. Tommy James and the Shondells. Tommy James and the Shondells? In this hip capital, everything is not hip. Is that bell Nick keeps hearing a trolley car? How is he supposed to find Roy? *Think.*

Instead, his attention is snagged by a girl with large breasts—yow, they're even bigger than Noreen's! She has long, rippling, almost kinked red hair and green-tinted glasses. Her face is small, or seems small, surrounded by that gush of wild hair, and her chin comes to a point. Fringed blouse, blue jeans, and Dr. Scholl's exercise sandals. She pauses for a moment, ten feet away on the path that cuts diagonally through the park, adjusts her Navajo bag higher on a shoulder, then sets off walking again—almost loping.

Nick follows at a discreet distance, admiring the roll of her buttocks, the tight fit of her jeans, that amazing head of hair. Near the corner, she stops again, this time to use a pay phone. Nick stops too, idly scoping merchandise in the deep window of a little head shop. Carefully fanned out among the bongs and beads and I Chings are a dozen or so underground comic books. *Big Ass, Snatch, Despair, Jiz, Zap, Uneeda, Motor City Comics, Mr. Natural*—and both issues of *Lazy Galoot.* On the cover of number 1, the Imp sits crouched, hiding out, on a shelf in a dark closet empty except for dozens of wire hangers hooked on a clothes bar. On the cover of number 2, he's blasting down a two-lane blacktop, literally heading for the hills, bowler hat spinning off his bald head, in your basic never-was roofless coupe with doughnut tires. Goddamn, Nick *hates* Rapidographs, the line you get is never . . . it's always . . . no matter what, it's just—it's *uniform,* there's no personality. This stuff of Roy's demands a brush. Nick's brush. That is so . . . evident. It's just so fucking evident.

In the window, he can see the red-haired girl reflected: she's still talking on the phone, gesturing freely, frowning now. When she looks directly at him, Nick considers going into the head shop. Instead—and this is completely unlike him—he turns and looks back at her. Not smiling, not flirting, just neutrally looking. He can't see her eyes behind those shades, but her mouth is set in a combative expression. So now he smiles, what the hell, and points to the phone. Take your time, but I need that once you're finished.

Moments later, she hangs up. "All yours." At the corner, she stands with one foot in the gutter, one on the curb, waiting for a break in traffic—but she's also checking out Nick to see if he's really going to make a call. Well. He doesn't want to seem like a fool, so he picks up the receiver and digs in his pocket for change. Gets a long-distance operator, dials home. Dials Noreen's number. One-thirty in California means—twelve-thirty, eleven-thirty, ten-thirty—ten-thirty in Jersey City. She won't be there. She'll be at work. Perfect. No, wait, wait! It's three hours ahead. It's *four*-thirty in Jersey City. She'll be—

"Hello?"

The moment Walt's timid, small voice reaches Nick's ear, he almost hangs up. Three weeks ago, the boy never would have answered the telephone. Changes already. Time marches on. "Hey, it's Nick. It's

Nick. I miss you, honey," figuring it's all right to call a boy "honey," at least until he's—what?—eight, nine? "Miss me?"

"It rained on the floor."

"Did it?"

"Mommy used pots."

"Well, that's good. So nothing got wet?"

"The *pots.*"

"But that's all right, right?" Oh man, this is murder. "So where *is* Mommy? Is Mommy there?"

"Mommy's taking a nap."

God, thinks Nick, at four-thirty in the afternoon? She's letting the poor kid run around by himself? He could trip over those fucking pots! What's the matter with her?

"Can you make more spaghetti?"

"What?"

"In the *pot.* It got rained in. Can you make more spaghetti in there?" And would you just listen to how this little guy pronounces "spaghetti"! Three years old, not even three, and he can say it perfectly! None of that "sketty" or "getty" baby talk, not Walt! Smart kid! "Can you? Can you?"

"Oh yeah," says Nick, "oh sure you can. No problem."

Another long pause, during which an operator's voice tells Nick to deposit seventy-five cents more. He drops in the coins, they clang, and finally Walt speaks again: "What's that?"

"I'm putting money in the phone."

"Why?"

"Because it's a pay phone."

"Why?"

"It's a phone on the street, honey. So you have to pay."

"What street?"

Nick looks for a sign. "It's called, I think, wait—Geary Street. I'm on Geary Street, sweetheart. In a place called San Francisco. That's in California. Walt?" A loud clunk, followed by the sudden blat of animated-cartoon music. "Walt?" Followed by a click! Then a dial tone.

Well, *that* was great, *that* was satisfying. *That* sucked. Did Walt hang up because he's mad at Nick, or was it just time for Scooby-Doo?

What's Noreen been telling him? All of a sudden, Nick is so homesick that it's like some gigantic hand is pressing down on his skull so hard that his knees finally bend and he winds up squatting below the street phone, like Eugene in the closet. Exactly, thinks Nick, like the Imp Eugene on the cover of Roy's comic book!

And that's when he has a brainstorm.

Printed in minuscule type on the inside front cover of *Lazy Galoot* is a Market Street address for the Final Reckoning Press. So to Market Street is where Nick is headed now. He's actually sprung for a map, a little touristy thing with color bursts to indicate Places of Interest, and so far so good. This street coming up should be—*yes!* And if he turns left now, he should run straight into—*fuck!* No, wait, hold on: if he turns right. Turns *right*. Which he does, then walks four long blocks, keeping his eye on descending door numbers. And here we are, Daniel Boone!

The Final Reckoning Press occupies a freestanding brick building that used to be a neighborhood movie theater. Though dangerously tilted, the original bulb-ringed marquee is still attached. The ticket booth, pasted and overpasted with psychedelic dance posters, resembles a Parisian kiosk. Be open, thinks Nick, please be open. And so it is.

Inside, all the orchestra seats have been ripped out and replaced by a dozen or more gray metal desks, a couple of layout surfaces (caterer's tables in a former life), and a huge homemade light box. For a moment Nick feels completely at ease. Smell that ink! On the proscenium stage, a Multilith press, thumping and rocking like his mom's old Westinghouse washer, spits out a run. Nick could don a paper pressman's cap, get straight to work. Oh yeah. Feels like a temptation. Feels good.

After wandering around for a couple of minutes, though, Nick begins to feel less good and virtually invisible. No one pays him the slightest attention. There are fifteen, twenty people, young men and women, but mostly men, cutting stencils, marking up overlays, checking proofs, collating pages, and stapling four-color glossy covers (*Loud Groan Funnies* #4, with a Kim Deitch drawing) onto black-and-white comic books and doing it primitively—by hand, assembly-line style.

Nick watches a couple of hippie kids load stacks of those just-stapled comic books into supermarket shopping carts. The guy is long-haired with bad skin and the girl is blond with that dreamy Mama Michelle look. Both are barefoot and dressed in identical fringed blouses and red elephant bells. They roll their carts across the room and stop at a cluttered desk where an enormously fat guy sits in a *Front Page* swivel chair. There's a wood-and-metal nameplate, but the original engraved name has been masked by a strip of oak tag with hand lettering on it that reads: JOEL CLARK, PUBLISHER.

"I thought we were gonna get *Lazy Galoot* this week," Nick hears the girl say. "I thought a new issue was coming out."

"Maybe in August," says the fat man, Joel Clark. In his late twenties, early thirties, he's by far the oldest person in the place and a guy, thinks Nick, if you saw him on the street in that filthy tentlike yellow T-shirt, you'd feel contempt for. A guy if he sat down next to you on a bus, you'd close your eyes—to block out his scraggly beard and dirty fingernails.

"August?" says the girl. "You *said* June."

"It's not like I fucking *lied,* Judy. There's no book because we're still waiting for the material. Soon as I get the *material,* we go to press, okay? In the meantime, see what you and Allan can do with that," says Joel Clark, pointing at the comics in the shopping carts. "Some very good shit in there."

"We could sell a hundred copies of a new *Galoot,*" says Allan. "And we wouldn't have to do nothing but stand on the corner. But this stuff, you know?" He shrugs. "We're gonna have to, like, hawk it."

"So hawk it, Allan. Earn your keep."

After the two kids leave, disgruntled and pushing their carts ahead of them, the fat man spots Nick loitering nearby. "So what can I do for you? State your business, don't just stand there," he says, sounding like a Top 40 deejay or a ham actor, that kind of loud, declamatory voice. "Hey! You! Hey! This isn't the coma ward."

"My name," says Nick, "is Nick Looby?" Why the question mark? Like he's not sure? He thinks he's Nick Looby, but he could be wrong? God. Be a grown-up. Clear your throat and be a grown-up. "I'm Nick Looby." His voice falters and he takes a short breath. "I'm looking for my brother, Roy."

"Clyde!" says the fat man, this Joel Clark, rising from his chair almost in slow motion to offer Nick a small and pudgy hand. "Roy always said you'd show up eventually."

After shaking Nick's hand, Joel Clark ("But call me Clarky") makes several phone calls. Hi, Victor? Hey, Howdy? Hey, Mick? Hi, Breitstein! "Guess who I got standing right here at my desk? Clyde Looby! *Clyde's* in town!"

Even though Nick has never liked being called Clyde, he relishes the tingle now at being "announced." This is the first pleasant surprise.

The second is discovering that Roy hasn't moved to Taos or Timbuktu, just to Marin County, less than an hour away. "I could give you directions," says Clarky, "or if you don't mind waiting till Saturday, you can follow me up there."

"Yeah," says Nick, "let's do that." But why not just go see his brother today? Why hang around? Why put it off? He's surprised at himself and thinks about changing his mind, about saying to Clarky, Yeah, why don't you give me those directions after all. I'll shoot up there this afternoon. "No problem," he says, "I can wait till Saturday." Chicken.

"You got a place to stay?"

"I'm at the Hotel Calamax."

"Listen, you want to," says Clarky, "you could crash tonight and tomorrow at Roy's old place. He won't mind. And I got a key."

Nick doesn't even have to *think* about that one. Deal. And he gladly takes a lift back to the hotel in Clarky's hunkajunk yellow-and-white Town and Country station wagon. Clarky suggests that Nick grab his suitcase and shit and leave by the service entrance, fuck the bill, but Nick just laughs. After all, he's the good Looby, the responsible Looby, the—

After he's checked out and gotten his Bonneville from the pay lot, he follows Clarky back to Waller Street. Together they trudge up through the old mansion with its heavy savor of lavender, patchouli, and marijuana to Roy's vacated rooms.

Three of them, all poky. Wide-plank floors, walls grimy, cracked and crazed. Gas mantles everywhere but none that work, and neither do any of the fancy electroliers, but maybe those just need new flame bulbs. One of the rooms you can't walk into, it's so crammed with unopened cartons of *Lazy Galoot* numbers 1 and 2. There's a bedroom, and then there's the studio. The abandoned studio. A couple of tall bar stools, an ocean-blue beanbag chair, el cheapo stereo, an empty bookcase, but no drawings, no *scraps*. Nick paces around, looking for—what? Clues? "I'd like to call Roy, just to let him know I'm here."

"Wish I could help you out, Clyde, but there's no phone at the camp."

"The camp?"

"Somebody told your brother about a boys' summer camp that went out of business. You could rent it, so he did—he's got it through October."

"The whole *place*?"

"You'll see it soon enough."

"So how's he doing? He doing okay?"

Did Clarky flinch? Or was that just Nick's imagination? "I haven't seen him for a while. But he's all right, I guess. Working hard."

"Still 'hunkered down'?"

"Clyde—"

"It's Nick."

"I take a run up there, Nick, I deliver the groceries, then I turn around and drive straight home. He's working, is all I can tell you."

"On what? A new Eugene?"

"God, I hope so! None of my other books is selling worth a shit, so we really need to get out an issue of *Galoot* by the end of summer—we *really* do. So yeah, I'm praying it's a new Eugene and he's done with it soon." Clarky shrugs, then sticks out his hand like a happy car dealer. "I'll be back later with the guys. We'll have pizza or something. Good to meet you, Clyde."

"Nick."

After he watches Clarky trudge down the stairs, Nick shuts the attic door and locks himself in. Walks around. Checks the fridge. Nothing inside but a bottle of One a Day brand vitamins. He looks in the bedroom, gets down on his knees and looks under the bed, then checks the closet. The shelf is empty, wire hangers are clumped together in several places along the wooden clothes bar.

Returning to the studio, Nick flops down in the beanbag. Crunches pebbles, trying to get comfortable. Through the "turret window," he watches the sky turn purple. He feels giddy. Blood beats in his ears. Superstraight Nick Looby, Nick of the Buddy Holly glasses, the Barry *Goldwater* glasses, the wrinkle-free Banlon shirt, and the beltless khakis—crashing in his famous big brother's former "attic domain"?

Fuckin' A.

Almost home, he thinks. Almost home.

FRIDAY, APRIL 21, 2000

When they called me last weekend? I figured it was a prank. Then I thought it was some goofy mistake. But they kept saying, "Don't hang up, sir, we have a card, we found a card in the patient's wallet."

In case of emergency call Nicholas Looby.

No emergencies before this, Roy? Nothing? Lucky bastard. Then out of the clear blue sky, as Mom used to say. Out of the clear blue sky a stupid fucking bakery truck . . .

In case of emergency call Nicholas Looby, Jersey City. No address, just Nicholas Looby, Jersey City. Like Santa Claus, North Pole. Like who needs a street address, right? You *knew* I'd still be there, didn't you?

Yeah, I'm living in the old house. The old homestead. Why not? I *inherited* it. My neighbors are all Muslims now. From the Middle East. Two doors down, where the O'Neills used to live? I'm pretty sure they're keeping a goat.

In case of emergency call Nicholas Looby, Jersey City.

I'm the only one. The last Looby in Dirty City. The house looks good, though. I fixed it up. Got a new black leather sofa. Well, now it's only new*ish*. Cost three grand. And I got books. Do I got books! I belong to every book club in the known universe. What can I tell you,

I like to get mail. I don't read much, but I own a shitload of books. And a bunch of them have your name on them. The "collected works" of Roy Looby, "edited by Joel Clark." I even got the pirated stuff, those Hong Kong editions, the ones Noreen didn't get any royalties from. And I got that deluxe coffee-table thing, Clarky's magnum opus, *Nothin' Doin': The Imp Eugene and the Art of Roy Looby.* You ever read it? I think I own five, six copies. Well, I'm mentioned.

And I got a checking account, I got a savings account, I got a Powerbook. I'm doing all right. If I wasn't, do you think you'd be in a private room? Who do you think's footing the medical bills, oh brother of mine? Speaking of which, I couldn't *believe* what—but no, let's forget that, okay? I'm doing all right, and we'll leave it at that.

You know me, I'm a straight shooter, a regular Dagwood Bumstead, I play by the rules, I try to play *fair,* which is not to say I think life has played strictly fair by me! But I don't complain, Roy, truly I don't. Because I'm a grown-up. I grew up. Like poor Candy told us about a million times, you get what you get when you're a grown-up. So why complain? And being a grown-up has its perks, its . . . attractions. I've seen my share of women over the years. None of them great beauties and I wouldn't call what happened with any single one of them a "relationship," but there was sex and a certain level of commitment. For a while, at least. And. Well.

How about you? *You* ever grow up? Inquiring minds need to know. Did you? Noreen used to call you an infant. A baby. At best, a boy of twelve. You never paid any attention to bills and stuff, life insurance, health insurance, car payments—you couldn't balance a checkbook. And she loved that about you, thought it was adorable. And if you hadn't split on her? She would've *always* loved that about you. She probably would've—but I don't know if she'd admit it.

I do grown-up things like transfer balances from one credit card to another, to get a lower interest rate. Subscribe to both *Time* and *Newsweek.* And I get the *New Yorker,* but God, can they pile up. And three, four years ago I even bought *Mother Jones* for a while. I was scared of Newt Gingrich, thought I might even be turning "political." But I never read a single article. So I guess not. I guess I'm not *that* grown-up.

Shit, how'd I get off on all of that? When all I meant to tell you, Roy, was just this: yesterday the hospital called me up—at the motel where I'm staying. Asked could they send over your things. Send them on! I said. Absolutely. So what's waiting for me down in the lobby this morning but that filthy fucking duffel bag of yours. I don't know what I was expecting to find inside. Well, I wasn't expecting anything, really, but I know what I was *hoping* to find. A sketchbook. Or two. Or three. But you didn't even have a pencil! Not even a pencil, you prick.

Three Goodwill-type shirts, a pair of Farmer Gray dungarees, seven—seven, not six, not eight, but seven!—dirty black socks, a torn movie ticket from a theater in Sioux City, Iowa. Rolling papers and a pouch of tobacco. Tobacco. Band-Aids. A book of matches from a gas station in Harrisburg, PA. Yellow balloon that when I blew it up said Grand Opening but didn't say of what. Or where. Cheap little penknife with a picture of a cowboy riding a bucking bronco. "Rodeo Days, Reno, Nevada." That's what it says under the fucking cowboy. And a raggy white envelope, looks like it might've been a pay envelope, but there was nothing inside, no receipt, no check stub.

And that's it. That's all. No keys. No cash. No credit cards. Jesus Christ. No magazines. No books. I stood looking down at all that shit spread out on the bed and then it hit me: *where's the wallet?* I was ready to call up the hospital and start screaming theft. But then I thought to check the pants you'd had on, and sure enough, there it was.

And it looks exactly like you'd expect it to look after somebody's been carrying it around in his back pocket for almost forty years. I swear to God, though, I can't imagine how it didn't just disintegrate! A crappy piece of plastic like that! How?

Well, it's *magic*, huh, Roy? It's a *magic* yellow wallet.

FRIDAY, JULY 31, 1970

Nick cleans his glasses on his shirt placket, holds them up to the window, making sure he's got all the smudges, all the fingerprints, then he puts them back on, rebuttons his shirt, and resumes watching Cora Guirl—or Purple Cora, as she's known around here—do a jigsaw puzzle called "Claretcup Cactus." She has short-cropped, baby-fine black hair and dark-gray eyes, and purple everything else: lipstick, cowboy shirt, jeans, knee-high boots with three-inch heels. Even the scar that runs from the corner of her left eye raggedly down her cheek to her jawline is purple. Nick wants to know how she got that scar—come on, though, you just don't ask a question like that. But he'd bet money Roy knows.

Upstairs in the attic apartment last night, Cora mostly just lounged in the beanbag chair, blissed out on wine, cannabis, and Twinkies, while Nick, who was stretched alongside her on throw pillows, tried to glimpse a tit in between her shirt buttons. And while everyone else who'd showed up with Joel Clark talked about their favorite dead cartoonists, Cora maintained a glassy half smile and said nothing. But whenever Roy's name entered the conversation, which it did somehow every ten minutes, suddenly Cora was alert, she was *there,* leaning forward, paying attention.

Nick recognized the expression on her face.

Well, Christ, he'd seen it enough times on Noreen's.

"You live here in the house, Cora?"

She nods, foraging now through puzzle pieces scattered on the industrial spool slash coffee table. "But I'm moving soon. Too many people. Too zooey." Abandoning the puzzle, Cora flops back on the old junk-store sofa. "But when Roy was here? It was ten times worse. Bikers and dopers showed up day and night to hang out with the Imp Eugene. Like he was real! Like him and Roy were one and the same. It was nuts. Not to mention all the guys from Hollywood and *companies* and shit. Wanting Roy to sign on this dotted line and that dotted line— for animated cartoons or Imp Eugene rolling papers, or bedsheets, or yo-yos, or just all kinds of stupid stuff. Roy used to hide out in my room—he even hid in the closet a couple of times! When it got to be like Grand Central Station."

Nick sees an opportunity to change the subject. "You from New York?"

"No. Why?"

"Grand Central Station."

"It's just an *expression.*"

"Yeah, well, so where—"

"Milwaukee."

"How'd you end up out here?"

"How's anybody? I just, you know, came. I used to be a fifth-grade teacher." Cora's eyes close, then pop wide open. "But I changed my mind. Now you tell me something."

"What?"

"About Roy. Tell me something about Roy. What was he like?"

Oh God, not again. Last night it was the same thing. Hanging out in the attic with Clarky and Victor Zits and Elmer Howdy and Fritz Breitstein and Mick Ahearn, the charter members of the Lazy Galoots Comix Collective, it was the same damn thing, same deal. Tell us about Roy, tell us about Roy, Clyde—that kind of pestering shit. And it was funny, it was like—like they didn't know Roy *themselves.* Like they'd never *met* him, not really. These were his pals, his fellow cartoonists, but still. Still it was, Tell us something about Roy. Tell us something, Clyde. Elmer said, "He dug Basil Wolverton, right? I can see Wolverton in those long crazy faces Roy likes to draw, and the bug eyes, and those postapocalyptic landscapes. That stuff had to be Wolverton swipes, but I'd ask Roy and he wouldn't answer. Clyde, you ever see him reading Basil Wolverton's comics?" Victor Zits said, "Maybe Wolverton, and maybe Chester Gould, but definitely Walter Geebus. Who else, Clyde?" Ahearn: "What's the deal with those Gene Autry records, Clyde—all that old music? Is there some fucking rhythm he picks up?" Elmer: "I seen him once stoned and sitting there, right there, listening to Patti Page! He had to be goofing, man. He doesn't really like that shit, right, Clyde?" Zits: "Harold Gray, maybe—in Roy's figure work. That cool stiffness and the crosshatching, I think it comes from Gray." Clarky: "I don't think so, I don't think Roy ever looked at 'Orphan Annie.' Did he, Clyde?" And Fritz Breitstein said, "You ever notice Roy unties his shoelaces when he sits down to draw? I do it myself now. It makes a big difference, too, you're looser. When'd he start doing that, Clyde, untying his shoes?" Zits: "And John Stanley. Stanley's work on 'Little Lulu.' The simple layouts, mostly. Clyde, he studied that Stanley shit, didn't he?" Elmer: "I found this old Julie London record in a junk store, got it for a dime, I figured Roy'd think it was a hoot. But he said, 'Why would I want *that*?' He wouldn't take it! Like what's the fucking difference between Patti Page and Julie London? Clyde, how come he'll listen to fucking Patti Page and not Julie London—how come?" And then the more personal questions. Clarky said, "So tell us something we don't know about Roy, Clyde. Surprise us." And Zits said, "How about some history, Clyde? How about some *pre*-history? What was it like growing up with a guy like Roy?" Ahearn said, "Tell us, Clyde," and Elmer said, "Come on, man, spill."

"Okay," said Nick. "After Roy caught the bug, the cartoon bug? He never went a day without drawing. He could have the mumps, he could have the flu, he could have poison ivy so bad he looked like the Incredible Sun Demon, but it wouldn't stop Roy. He drew every single day. Well, I did, too. We both did," said Nick. "Yeah?" said Clarky, "but what did he draw?" "Well," said Nick, "at first he copied stuff, we *both* did. Then we drew our own stuff . . ."

And now this morning in the downstairs front parlor here's Cora Guirl wanting to hear more. What was he like? What *was* he like—like Roy was already past tense, finished. What was he *like?* Nick says okay, let him think, and thinks about this: when his brother, at fourteen, started writing to amateur cartoonists whose names and addresses he found listed in the back pages of *Cracked* and *Castle of Frankenstein* magazines. By return mail he got eight- and ten- and twelve-page mimeographed fanzines full of awkwardly drawn cartoons and badly typed ravings about favorite comic-strip characters, about EC horror comics, about *Mad* magazine. So there was *that* about Roy. Early on he got hooked, he hooked himself, into a loose network of like-minded comics fanatics. That's what he was like.

What else? Roy's all-time favorite movie was *Pinocchio.* Whenever they released it again in theaters or showed parts of it on *Walt Disney Presents,* he'd watch. Entranced. *Pinocchio* was *it. Really* it. Besides *Pinocchio* there wasn't a single movie Nick ever heard his brother admit to liking. Roy *kind* of liked *Thunder Road,* and *Hercules Unchained* and those clunky, nightmarish Ray Harryhausen monster movies: *The Seventh Voyage of Sinbad, The Three Worlds of Gulliver, Jason and the Argonauts.* But the only picture that Roy *loved* was *Pinocchio.* Oh, and he kind of liked *The Searchers,* too.

And? What else?

Well, there's this: Nick remembers discovering the word *misanthrope* in a seventh-grade vocabulary list and remembers that when he saw the definition he realized, holy cow, that's Roy. That's the definition of Roy: a "hater of mankind." His brother had never had a friend in his life (besides Nick, of course) and never wanted one, either. Mrs. Looby worried about him. "Oh, go outside and play, Roy, go on!" He'd make a face—and stay indoors. Other kids on the block called him names. Even before his hair fell out, they called him names. "Hermit." "Loner." "Weirdo." And he *was,* he was all of those things, and all of those things, Nick realized finally, added up to being a "hater of mankind." A misanthrope.

So one afternoon while Roy was trying to decide on a cool title for a fanzine of his own ("Hey, Clyde, how about 'Hermit,' how about 'Irate,' how about 'Jeer,' how about 'Knave,' how about 'Lynch'?"), Nick casually said, "How about 'Misanthrope'?"

Roy's head snapped around from the giant finger-tabbed Webster's. "Clyde, you're a genius!" It was one of the few compliments his brother ever gave him. Maybe the only one. "'Misanthrope' it is," said Roy. "Now let's get busy!" And what did getting busy mean? It meant that Nick stole ditto masters from the supply closet at school, so Roy could draw on the stencils with a ballpoint pen. Nick ran off a hundred copies at the stationer's, folded and stapled them, stuck on postage stamps, and mailed them out. (Well, he mailed out roughly twenty; the rest his brother kept in a carton.) "Subscribers" wrote back to Roy, praising his "stuff" (Victor Zitorsky, aged sixteen, of Philadelphia, was on their first mailing list, and so was Elmer Howdy, aged twelve, of Muscatine, Iowa), but Roy just sneered at the compliments. "I still suck," he said, "and if they like this junk, they suck, too!"

What was Roy like way back when? He was like that.

And? He could be a royal son of a bitch. One for instance? Okay, how about the time—it was in early May 1967—when both Loobys were sitting in a pizza parlor on Ocean Avenue drinking Cokes, smoking Marlboros, and Nick was saying yeah, sure it needed supporting characters, every strip did, supporting characters and possibly a sidekick, but. But. "I don't *like* these guys," said Nick, "all right?"

"*Like* them?" said Roy. "They fuck with Eugene's head, you're not *supposed* to like them. They're his *antagonists*. I'm just giving the little guy an antagonist or two. Or three."

"Well, they're stupid-looking."

"You don't like 'em just 'cause I made 'em up without *consulting* you, don't give me any of that shit about stupid-looking."

"Okay, all right—it would've been nice if you told me what you were gonna do."

"Get used to it," said Roy.

"And their fucking names," said Nick. "Woozy. And Floozy. And Claude! Claude, for God's sake! They're stupid names."

"You could've done better?"

"Damn straight I could've. I came up with Eugene's name, didn't I?"

"Like hell you did."

"What, so now you're saying I didn't?"

"Who cares, all right? Just lay off, okay?"

"I don't want to argue with you, Roy, I just—I don't *like* these new characters you're doing now. They're creepy. They're ugly. They're not funny!"

And Roy said, "If you don't wanna ink 'em, Clyde, don't ink 'em."

"Fuck you," said Nick.

Roy laughed, then hoisted up his green backpack from the floor, thunked it on the table, undid the snaps. "Can we talk about something else now? 'Cause I wanna show you this." He pawed through his sketchbooks and pulled out a letter, an invitation from Mickey Ahearn and Fritz Breitstein, two guys he used to swap zines with, saying, Hey, Roy, get your ass out here to Milwaukee, come jam with us on a comic book, we're gonna *publish,* no more of this *mimeographed* bullshit. No more dittos. Nick said, "Milwaukee? Pabst Blue Ribbon! Very cool. But we're never gonna get Noreen to go to Mil*wau*kee." Roy made a face, like don't be stupid, Clyde . . . and three and a half weeks later, he was gone. Got up one Tuesday night during *The Fugitive,* told Noreen he'd be right back, and then just . . . left. What was Roy like? He was like *that,* a guy who could make up new characters behind his partner's back, give them stupid names, and never apologize; who could head for the bathroom but end up in Wisconsin. Who could walk out on his wife when she was eight and a half months pregnant. And on his brother without even saying so long. Nick could tell Cora that Roy was like *that.* Or he could tell her that he was a misanthrope. Or that his favorite movie was *Pinocchio.*

Instead, he tells her, "All he did was draw. Roy drew all the time."

Cora looks at Nick for an uncomfortably long moment. As if she's going to say something, tell *him* something. Nick feels so positive she means to tell him something he really should know that he leans forward. "Well, he hasn't changed," says Cora, then she breaks up the unfinished puzzle. After she's thrown all the pieces back in the box, she gets up from the sofa and walks out of the room without another word.

As soon as she's gone, Nick goes to the front window, holds back an edge of the filthy white curtain. It's crunchy with grit. Mick Ahearn and Victor Zitorsky (do *they* live here too?) are smoking on the front porch, both of them astraddle milk crates painted orange. Nick would like a cigarette himself, but he left his pack upstairs. So why not just step outside and mooch one from Roy's cartoonist pals? Because he's had more than his fill of them. And not just because they grabbed his shoes last night and painted big tits and droopy cocks all over them. In acrylics. No, that didn't bother him, it was even kind of funny. No, it was the looks. That's why he's still so pissed. The snotty looks they kept giving him! Like, *this* is Roy's brother? This jerk? And all because Nick didn't know who Claes Oldenburg was, or Jasper Johns—because of that, they should treat him like a big joke?

He lets the curtain drop and wanders around the parlor, peeking inside the teepee, pulling the cushions off the crummy sofa. No loose cigarettes anywhere. On the mantle is a folded pair of wire sunglasses with almond-shaped tiny lenses. When Nick picks those up, he discovers a tightly rolled fat stick of grass. He pats down his pockets, finds a matchbook, and what the hell, what the fuck, lights the joint.

Last night, for the first couple of hours, Nick passed along the communal reefer without toking, without partaking, but he caved in finally to social etiquette. Besides, by then the Galoots were all winking at one another and smirking at Nick. Even their girlfriends were! (Even *Cora* was.) So at last he blew a little dope, and, as usual, he regretted it.

Whenever he smokes dope, Nick ends up trembling for hours, tormented by mortality fears and grotesque paranoia. He's always *sure* the narcs are coming. They'll smash open the door, drag him away, throw him in a cell with pissed-off Black Panthers. But worse, and far wiggier, is this: his body temperature plummets and then he expects, at any moment, that his heart will stop.

Last night it was the same old story: inhale, exhale, and remember, Nick, thou art dust and to dust thou shalt return. Great. Just fucking great. And meanwhile his brother's pals were painting boobs on his good Thom McAn Romas and yakking it up about Andy Warhol and that Oldenburg guy, and that other berg guy, *Rauschenberg,* and Man Ray and Marcel Duchamp, and talking about comics like *they* should be in museums too, for Christ's sake.

And now, this morning, after crawling into the teepee and taking another hit, holding smoke in his lungs for a silent count of ten, Nick thinks, Fuck those guys. Especially Victor Zits, who actually has a Palmolive complexion. An emaciated, beady-eyed gunslinger type (black T-shirt, vest, jeans, and boots). Zits the art school graduate. Yale, no less. Well, big deal. Zits acting so amused, so *be*mused, at Nick's igno-rance. (All right, no, he never went to an art museum in his life, but neither did Roy!) Zits talking Rauschenberg and Oldenburg, Warhol, and Looby. *Roy* Looby. All in the same breath, almost. Roy was an "artist," Roy was a "genius," and blah blah blah. Artist? Genius? Roy was a *cartoonist. And you can be my helper, Clyde.* Yeah? Gee, Roy, thanks! Oh God. Oh shit. Nick thinking, Oh fuck. I'm stoned, I'm stoned again right now, and sitting perfectly still (for some crucial rea-son) on the water-stained parquet floor inside this airless teepee . . .

I want to be a cartoonist, said Roy. *And you can be my helper, Clyde.*

Helper! What did that mean? Nick was clueless, but Roy was too, so they just improvised, Nick correcting his brother's lousy spelling in the talk balloons, erasing words if they were especially illegible, then relet-tering. Cleaning up Roy's graphite smudges. That early stuff, their first strips, done when they were thirteen and twelve, fourteen and thir-teen, Christ, it was crap—not too far removed from stick figures. "Fedora Flannagan and His Mutt That Mouths Off," which later became "Chapeau Sammy and His Wisecracking Cur," which later still became "Beret Baruch and His Palaverin' Pup." *Baruch?* Roy had seen the name in a newspaper headline, some rich guy. Together they did twelve-panel "Sundays," and three- and four-panel "dailies," and sixteen-page comic books ("Roy Looby's Comics and Stories") that Nick stapled together. That was another job for the helper. The helper stapled.

Crazy, but for a long time it never dawned on either of them that comic strips were inked. They just assumed they were drawn with a pencil, that you pressed down really hard with a soft pencil—a pencil or a grease crayon. That's what you did. That's how it was done.

One time, though, while the Loobys wandered around a stationery store, Roy suddenly pointed. Jammed into a wire rack full of artists' manuals (How to Draw Trees, Birds, Cats, Horses, Heads, Clowns, Landscapes) was an oversized paperback book titled simply *Cartoon-ing.* They didn't have three bucks, so they huddled behind a display of photo albums and flipped through it. The step-by-step instruction—sketchy ovals and circles that turned miraculously into fully modeled drawings at figure 2—seemed completely bogus. Any moron knew there had to be more to it than that. Even so, the book was valuable, was crucial.

"The one universal in all comic art," it said, "is India ink."

Of course! First you penciled, then you lettered, then you *inked.* Why hadn't they figured that out for themselves? Before leaving the store that afternoon, they bought (instead of a Mother's Day card) a pen staff for a dime, three nibs for a nickel, a cheap watercolor brush, and a bottle of indelible black ink, India ink, capped with a cool squeeze bulb.

"Clyde? You all right? Clyde?"

Roy had one hell of a time, though, using the brush. Ditto the pen. No matter how much he practiced, and he practiced every day, he couldn't get the hang of them. Using a pencil had come naturally, like breathing, like chewing, like *sleeping,* but give Roy a loaded brush or a crow-quill pen and he was a klutz. Even after they'd switched from typewriter bond to bristol board, he'd splatter, he'd smear, he'd leave dribbles of ink running down the page. He just couldn't do it.

Nick, on the other hand . . .

So Roy decided—one day in a pissy mood Roy *announced*—that helpers inked, sometimes. They lettered, they stapled, and sometimes, if the cartoonist was too busy, they also inked. "No big deal," said Roy. "Just follow my lines." And Nick said, "Sure, Roy, no problem."

Together, the boys sat in the attic, working on lapboards that Uncle Neil had had specially cut for them at a lumberyard. For hours every afternoon they sat in that raftered, stuffy attic, drawing comics. When their mom came home from work (she had an hourly wage job with the Hudson County Police, recording descriptions of the previous day's traffic accidents; the fewer the accidents, the less she worked and the less she made, but give her a solid week of rain or a good ice storm and there'd be steak on payday)—when Mom got home, she would bring them a pitcher of Kool-Aid and a sleeve of Hydrox, and then along around 5:00, 5:30, Uncle Neil would arrive at the house and check out what they'd done: "Whoa! This is terrific! I can't believe it! Cathy, did you see this?"

To Nick, those days were idyllic. He felt so good all the time, he always felt so—glad. To *be* there. To be Nick Looby. And especially to be Roy Looby's younger brother.

"Clyde? Your hands are ice-cold! What's the matter with you?"

It was great, it was idyllic, till Noreen Novick from across the street started coming over. Whenever she laughed at some dopey little gag strip they'd done, Roy would grunt, he'd shrug, he'd shake his bald head. He was never satisfied, not with his progress and not by the work. "Oh, but it's so good!" said Noreen, said Noreen, said Noreen. "Isn't it good, Nicky? Your brother is so talented!"

"CLYDE!"

"What?"

"What do you mean, what?" Cora is kneeling beside him now in the teepee. When did *she* get here? She tilts her head, amused, then smiles and gives him a playful shove. "Jesus, Clyde, your hands are freezing, you're shaking all over. What the hell've you been doing?"

Nick just stares.

"Your brother is so talented," said Noreen, and Nick kept wanting to say right back to her, I'm not? And I'm not? That's what he wanted to say but never did. He just agreed with her and went on being his brother's helper. Helpers inked.

In late 1962, when Roy was almost fifteen and a freshman at Snyder High, he found a coupon for the Bigfoot Professional Cartooning Home-Study School nearly buried on a page of ads for miniature monkeys, trick baseballs, and bike speedometers at the back of a *Sugar & Spike* comic book. Send Away, it said, For Our Free Talent Test. He did. Without telling Nick about it, he sent away. A week later, not even, the test arrived in Roy's self-addressed, stamped envelope, and here's what it said to do: Draw a desert island, a horse in a speeding gallop, the military budget; draw a man, now draw his wife and make her a scary monster.

Because there was no inking involved, Roy passed with an A-plus grade reported on a postcard that also listed the Bigfoot School's schedule of fees. The complete course, twenty-four lessons, cost more, said Mrs. Looby, than a hi-fi/television console. Roy just clasped both hands to his tragically bald head. "Please?" he said. *"Please?"* Uncle Neil would have liked to sponsor Roy, he could see the kid had real talent—why, hadn't he already sold a crayon portrait of the pope to a Catholic weekly?—but, well. Seeing as how Uncle Neil wasn't a *real* uncle, just a "friend of the family," it wouldn't have looked right if he went and footed the boy's tuition. People might wonder. They might talk. Of course, if he were to *become* a member of the family—and their mom said, "That's all right, Neil, I understand, but thank you." She reluctantly cashed in savings bonds that their late grandmother had bought for them both, for Roy and Nick *both,* when they were babies.

And how did Nick feel about that? Resentful? Not exactly. Not yet. He felt hurt. Jesus Christ, look at his hands! Didn't anybody notice Nick's *hands*? They were permanently speckled with India ink! And that goober-sized callus on his left middle finger! How had he gotten that? From scratching his ass? Damn. Wasn't Nick talented, too? Apparently not. Apparently all *he* did was go over his brother's pencil lines and make them look darker. When he realized everybody thought that's all he—

"Clyde? Hey! You're breathing funny, breathe normal. Clyde!"

Once the Official Student Supply Kit was delivered and the attic "studio" reorganized according to the Official School Diagram (A. Table; B. Chair; C. Lamp; D. Shaving Mirror), Roy announced one day that he was canceling *Misanthrope* and putting their jointly produced comic strips and comic books on "temporary hiatus." Nick was stunned. Sorry, said Roy, but from now on he'd be too busy with his *course work* to do anything else. Nick said, "Yeah, but what about me?" What was *he* supposed to do? Couldn't he still be his brother's helper? Absolutely, said Roy. And put Nick in charge of buying supplies, everything from masking tape and Pink Pearl erasers to rubber cement, tracing paper, push pins, and manila envelopes.

"Okay," said Nick, "but—"

"And," said Roy, who had by then already glanced over Lesson 1 and picked up some important new terminology, "from now on, Clyde, you're not my helper, you're my assistant, you're my studio assistant. And the studio assistant does whatever I tell him."

Although Nick studied the first several lessons, too, and practiced some of the drawing exercises, from then on he mostly just sat in the attic and watched Roy.

Except, of course, for the times when Roy told him to cut out magazine pictures for his new "reference morgue" and file away the clippings. And for the times when Roy needed some prop—get that ax from the cellar, go find Mom's bowling ball—or when he needed a live model. Left foot forward, Clyde, right arm back. Make believe you're running. Make believe you're a lumberjack. Pretend you're bowling. Pretend you're up at bat. Don't move. Do this. Do that. Studio assistants did this, they did that.

"Simon says, Do this," mutters Nick. "Simon says, Do that."

"*What?*" says Cora. Then she says, "Oh shit! Victor, get your ass in here! Clyde's gonna puke!"

By the summer of '63, Nick had had enough. "Studio assistant." Try "go-fer." Fuck that, Roy! And fuck you, too.

He started palling around with Larry Bozzo, a kid his age who lived on Stegman Parkway. Together they went to see *Hud, The Birds, It's a Mad, Mad, Mad, Mad World.* They listened to the "Good Guys" on WABC radio and haunted record stores, buying singles by the Ronettes, Skeeter Davis, the Chiffons, Little Stevie Wonder, Peter, Paul and Mary. The first and second Bob Dylan albums. They rode a bus to Bayonne and found the house where Sandra Dee grew up. Boz said the word *Laos,* he said the name *Sandy Koufax,* he read *Catcher in the Rye.* The world was full of stuff besides comics. Imagine that! Nick became an honor student, did chores for shut-ins, watched television. Jerked off. Read *Catcher in the Rye.* Read *Fahrenheit 451,* too. But still, something was missing. Something was *lacking.*

From time to time, he'd go up to the attic when Roy was out and look through his latest stuff. Jesus, he drew that? And *that?* Oh my God. He realized that he sounded like Uncle Neil. And Noreen. *Your brother is so talented, Nicky, so talented, so talented.* Yeah, yeah, but while Mr. So Talented was making phenomenal progress in composition and modeling, the crits of his work that came back from the Bigfoot School (and which Nick felt no compunction about reading) often complained about his "rendering." His inks were "cold," they were "hard." They were "fickle." Mr. So Talented had an Achilles heel!

"You *see?* He's not so great, Noreen!"

"What?" says Cora. "Clyde, look at me, okay? You know where you are? Clyde!"

"He didn't smoke the fucking jay that was—? Ohhh shit!"

"What?" says Cora. "Victor, what? What's the matter?" Then she says, "Use the wastebasket, Clyde, the *wastebasket*! What jay, Victor? *What jay?*"

The thing about Noreen? (Nick is vomiting.) She was always coming over to the house to see Roy: after school before she had to go to work, after work before she went home. Noreen's family owned a catering deli on West Side Avenue. She prepared salads, ran the slicer machine, designed buffet platters. She carefully batted cereal boxes from high shelves with a broomstick, then caught them. She smelled of kielbasy and vinegar. It was in her clothes, in her hair, and Nick always wondered if it was in her skin, too. In her *cleavage*. He would've bet money that Roy knew. The prick. How come *he* got everything? How come?

And they didn't fool Nick, those two. He knew what they were doing when the attic door was shut and latched with a hook and eye. Well, he didn't *know*, but he could imagine. He'd be lying on the living room couch watching TV or doing his homework, or—or he'd be outside cutting grass, raking leaves, and he could just imagine what they were doing up in the attic, he *did* imagine. And sometimes crept up there and peeked through the old-fashioned keyhole. But all he ever saw was the table, the chair, the lamp, and the shaving mirror.

Noreen would come down later looking flushed, looking guilty, with her parochial school blouse and blazer wrinkled and misbuttoned. And because she knew that Nick was on to her, on to *them,* she always treated him nicely, always "chatting" with him for a little while before she went home. Noreen. Whose breasts by the time she was in high school had grown so large and so heavy that guys in the neighborhood called her "The Shelf." And whenever Noreen—whenever The Shelf—talked to Nick on her way out of the house, he'd pick a spot on her forehead, even a pimple sometimes, and pretend it was an optometrist's examination light: he kept his eyes focused *right there,* because otherwise—

"Can you stand up, Clyde? Try to stand up," says Cora. "Victor, you are such an asshole!"

"Me? Me? *I'm* an asshole? *He's* the asshole—him!"

"Up, Clyde, up! Come on, you can do it! UP!"

. . .

Snooping in the attic one afternoon, Nick found a 12 x 18 Strathmore pad filled with hundreds—it seemed like hundreds but was probably just dozens—of pencil sketches that Roy had made of Noreen's locally famous rack. He'd indicated her neck, maybe her shoulders or some torso, but her naked boobs were all that Nick saw. And Jesus Christ, he nearly had a heart attack! He couldn't breathe, couldn't swallow, he got a freaking boner, and a cloud of gnats-that-weren't-really-there whirled up in front of his face. Then—then all he could do, and he did it without thinking, it was crazy, he *knew* it was crazy, but he sat down at his brother's table, grabbed a sable-hair brush, and began to ink those incredible knockers. He inked his way through the entire sketchbook, using a boldly cursive line and working with such gigantic concentration that he never noticed when Roy came in. At first Nick wasn't aware of Roy sitting beside him on a chair, and then he was, but neither of them spoke.

Nick just inked, and Roy just watched.

Finally, though, Roy said, "Any time you want to give this hopeless fuck a few pointers, I'm ready."

"Still having some trouble, are you?"

Roy didn't answer for about ten seconds. Then he said yeah—yeah he was still having some trouble. Yeah.

This was killing Roy, just killing him.

At that moment, and this was nothing new, Nick would've said, Take *me*! Take *me*! if the Red Chinese Army had burst in, demanding the blood of a Looby. Because he loved his brother then, and not just abstractly, fiercely. But Nick hated him, too. As much as he loved Roy, that was how much he also, and quite suddenly, hated him. And that would last. It would be the way that Nick felt, the ordinary way, the normal way, and it would not change.

He said, "You wanna start now?" and Roy said yeah, why not, and Nick told him—first thing he told him, he said Roy's whole problem with brushes? Was that he held them like a freaking *pencil*. "You don't hold them like that, man, it's completely different."

"Okay, okay."

"And you don't move your whole arm, just your wrist."

"All right, *just show me.*"

It was a mystery, it didn't make sense, how completely helpless Roy could be with a pen and a brush. It was—you know what it was like? Their mother with an automobile. Driving on the highway, Cathy Looby could light and crush out cigarettes, drink milk shakes, change the radio station, turn around and talk to her sons in the back, make not-*too*-unkind little jokes about poor Uncle Neil. She could steer while leaning across the bench seat to get her Blistex from the glove compartment, she could apply *lipstick,* she could do it all, completely at ease. Driving on the highway. But in the city? Driving in the city? She was like a statue, she was a nervous wreck, and there wasn't a curb she didn't bounce over making a right-hand turn, or a one-way street she didn't go down in the wrong direction. Roy was like that with a brush, with a pen, with India ink. With pencils he could do it all, and perfectly, but when it came to rendering, to finishing, he was sloppy, flustered, and tense.

With Nick's help, though, with his guidance, Roy improved. Nick (who had never needed any dopey mail-order school, who'd picked it all up by instinct) showed his brother how to hold a pen, a brush, and how to lay down beads of ink, get an easy flow, apply a wash. How to feather, how to crosshatch. Here, do this. Now, do this. Not bad. Now try this. Roy said, "Shit!" Roy said, "I *hate* this!" But Roy never once said thanks.

Several weeks passed, and Roy—practicing with a brush, with a pen, a brush, a pen—neglected his correspondence course. He said, "Maybe I should get back to my—"

"Not yet," said Nick, "first try this." Try this. Try that. Try it again.

More weeks passed, then one day Roy got a letter from the Bigfoot School, inquiring why he had fallen so far behind. He'd been rolling right along but now he was lagging. Roy freaked at the criticism. And Nick said, "Listen, Roy, if you want? I'll help you catch up. You want me to?"

For a moment, Roy looked confused. Then he said, "I guess. Yeah, all right."

"All right," said Nick. "You wanna start now?"

So they did, with Roy penciling layouts and guidelines, breakdowns and figures, and with Nick applying the inks. Lesson 8, "Building the

Body." Lesson 9, "Rendering Hair." Lesson 10, "Visual Hyperbole." Lesson 11, "Faces Young & Old," Lesson 12, "The Art of Stereotyping." Lesson 13, "People as Animals." Roy penciled, Nick inked. Roy penciled, Nick inked. God, it was like old times. Yeah, it was also cheating, but they never mentioned *that,* they never talked about it. In fact, they hardly talked at all. Roy penciled. And Nick inked.

His friend Boz called and said, "Hey, Nicky, wanna go see *How the West Was Won?*"

Nick said, "I can't, man, I'm really busy."

Life was good again. Changed, much changed, but good . . .

Nick is slumped in a straight-backed chair on the high front porch, drinking a glass of orange juice. "All of it," says Cora. "You're gonna be fine. Just fine. It's all stupid Victor's fault."

"*Who's* stupid?" says Victor Zits. "*Clyde's* stupid! Serves him right for smoking somebody else's shit. And screw you, Cora."

"Clyde? You're gonna be okay, I promise. That wasn't grass, honey, it was hash, and it wasn't *just* hash, sweetie, it was—"

Nick groans—and everyone on the porch jumps back. But nothing happens. "Drink your juice," says Cora, "you'll feel better," and Nick tries to, he tries to finish it all. Damn, he's *always* tried to do what's right, he's the *good* brother, the responsible Looby, the nice guy, but he suddenly coughs, spraying Tropicana across the porch railing, the steps, and, "Oh fuck," says Victor Zits, "my good boots!"

Boots? Not boots, Nick's *life,* his *life* was good again. Because Roy did all the pencils and he did all the inks. Lesson 14, "Linear Movement." Lesson 15, "Hands & Hand Gestures." Lesson 16, "Drapery & Clothing." And Nick was feeling—jeez, he felt so buzzy that day, buzzy and *scared,* but there was Roy, unfazed, calmly drawing, hard at work on his latest lesson. The portable TV set was on, and they both glanced up together, just in time to see Jack Ruby gun down Lee Harvey Oswald. Nick gaped stupidly at the screen and when he looked away, when he looked to Roy, his brother had just filled a sheet of newsprint with lightning-fast sketches of those Stetson hats worn by the Dallas police. While everybody else in the entire fucking world was busy being appalled by the jailhouse tumult, Roy Looby was figuring out how to render cowboy hats crisply in line.

"Cowboy hats!" says Nick to Purple Cora and Victor Zitorsky while they walk him into the attic, into the Fortress of Solitude, then drag him across the floor and throw him down on the beanbag chair. "Goddamn cowboy hats!" says Nick, and Cora says, "What?"

And Roy said, "One knee down, Clyde, the other one bent, make believe you're tying your shoelaces." Lesson 17, "Everyday Actions."

Roy said, "Make believe you're at the finish line, you just broke the tape—arms up, Clyde, way up in the air!" Lesson 18, "Strenuous Action." "Chest out, head back. Good!"

Roy said, "Make like Boris Karloff, like you're Frankenstein with your arms straight out." Lesson 19, "Characters & Caricature." "Now kind of curl your fingers," said Roy. "Make believe, make believe— hey, Clyde, just make believe you're gonna grab Noreen's tits."

Nick felt blasted, he felt *stunned*. Then something shifted inside, and he felt—enraged.

Roy saw his brother's face and laughed, then he grabbed Nick's hands and bent the fingers, just so. "*This* is how you cop a feel. In case you're curious. Which I know you are." He winked and Nick hit him on the side of his head. Then he hit Roy in the same place again. Then he hit him in the nose and blood sprayed. And then—and this was so completely unlike him, "I *never* do things like that," says Nick to Cora, and Cora says, "Things like what?" Like pick up the baseball bat that was lying there on the floor with Roy's other props—a bowling ball, a tennis racket, an iron, a toaster, galoshes, an ax. Nick reached down and picked up that Louisville Slugger with the Brooks Robinson signature and took a swing. But missed.

"Cut it out, Clyde, you crazy?"

Nick swung and missed again.

"Are you nuts? Cut it out, you maniac!"

The third time Nick took a swing—and he swung the bat just as hard as he could—it connected. Roy went down clutching his stomach.

"What's so funny?" says Victor Zits, and Cora says, "Clyde's not laughing, he's *crying*," and Victor says, "Fuck he is not, he's *laughing*," then Victor shakes his head scornfully and says, "Jesus H. Christ, *this* guy is Roy Looby's brother? This *jerk*?"

SATURDAY, APRIL 22, 2000

Holy God, Roy, you gave me a scare! You scared the shit out of me. I don't remember even driving back over here last night, that's how automatic it was. Bet you I made it in fifteen minutes, door to door. Carol said your heart stopped. So now we're even. Yours stopped last night, mine stopped seven years ago. *Officially* it stopped seven years ago. For like almost a minute. Yours too, they tell me. So we're even now. It's like we're—

Roy? I could be crazy, but that Dr. Matheson—your doctor? Keeps reminding me of Uncle Neil. That big moon face, and his stoop? And what's that flaky red stuff called? You know what I'm talking about—that runs along your forehead, right here. What's that called, that skin condition? I forget.

But speaking of him, I had a talk this morning with Dr. Matheson. And Dr. Stang. We had a "conference." In the "conference room." Coffee was served. And they were both saying how I should maybe think about "notifying" some people. Relatives, loved ones, et cetera. As a precaution. That's all. Like when Mom that time? Had that operation? Same thing. Nobody thought she wasn't gonna *make* it, stupid little gall bladder, but still—right? The priest, right? Where was the harm? Not that I'm calling any priest on *you,* Roy. Oh God, no. "Nothin' doin'!" But I'm just wondering now if it's not such a bad idea. Maybe I should at least think about calling up some people. And when nothing happens, which it won't, where's the damage? At least they'd know. They'd be "notified." I could say, "Nobody knows, for sure. He stepped out in front of a bread truck. There's a Wonder Bread bakery up the street from the homeless shelter, the men's shelter, and Roy just . . . he just." I could say, "Right now it's all wait and see." What do you think? Should I call some people? But who should I call? I mean, Spiro Agnew's dead, so is Allen Ginsberg, and how the hell do you even get in *touch* with Grace Slick?

So what about the Galoots? That blotter-doin', hash-smokin', fast-talkin' old gang of yours. What about them? Breitstein, I heard, got married—some Japanese woman from Japan and for all I know he's living over there. After the undergrounds went belly-up in the midseventies—no more head shops, no more cheap rent, no more war, get a job—I never saw any of his stuff again. Bet you there wasn't anything to see. Bet you he quit drawing. Mick Ahearn? Same thing. He's a "master" carpenter now, that's what Clarky tells me. In the Bronx or Brooklyn, someplace like that. Paris. Lake Hopatcong! Somewhere. Elmer Howdy? Well, this I love: Elmer's doing children's books, he's "illustrating" them. From *Lazy Galoot* and *Cunt Comix* to the Caldecott Medal. Is that a riot? So what do you think? Scratch Elmer? Oh, let's scratch him.

All right, then. Who else among the Galoots? Victor, of course. Mr. Zitorsky. Mr. Yale University Fine Arts Department. Mr. *Zits.* Actually, and this is pretty funny since I never liked that dickhead, but he's the only member of the old bunch I've actually talked to in the past thirty years. I even have his phone number, if it's still current, which it probably isn't. Or it could be, I guess, depending on whether or not his parents are alive. That's where he called me from, his parents' house. This was like in '84, '85, around then. Calls me up asking if I could put him "in touch" with somebody at DC Comics—he's hoping to find a little "freelance work." This is Victor Zi*tor*sky, Roy, same guy that laughed at me in San Francisco when I didn't know who the hell Claes Oldenburg was. Yeah, but when he called me? It was the Age of Reagan, not Aquarius, and he was back in Philly living with his mom and his dad, laying carpet for a living, and it's like, "Anything you could do for me, Nick, I'd sure appreciate it." "Nick," he says. First time he ever called me *that*. Nick, he says, not Clyde. Well, he's asking a favor. So now it's Nick. And he'd "sure appreciate it." I could've what? Told him to fuck off? Roy, I could've.

But I didn't. After a while, you put things in perspective. Well, some of us do, the ones that grow up and grow old. Besides, the poor bastard seemed desperate. Plus he sounded high as a kite. Clarky told me heroin, but who knows? Poor old Victor. I said to him, "I wish I could help you, Vic, but I haven't done any comic-book work in ten years," and that was the truth. I never went back to that stuff, not after Camp Galoot. Not ever again. I went to college, started my own signage business, and never inked another comic book. Or read one, either. "I'm sorry," I said. "I can't help you, Vic," and he said, "That's all right, Clyde, what the fuck." But could you imagine—Victor Zitorsky, creator of "Double Dingus McGee" and "Vagina Ballou," drawing *Batman*? Or how about Wonder Woman? He'd cut off her tits on page 4! The guy never had any drawing chops, never. Well, he didn't need 'em, right? He was an "artist." Always talking about "excellence." Like he knew from—

Eczema! *That's* the word I was looking for, Roy. What Uncle Neil had, that skin condition? That flaky red stuff? Eczema.

I don't know if I told you this, but Uncle Neil is dead. So I guess we can't call *him*! A bachelor to the end. Died a drunk and a Good Humor man, just about a year after Mom.

I *did* tell you Mom is dead, right?

God, though, was Uncle Neil crazy about her, or what? Always asking Mom to marry him, and Mom always saying, "I appreciate the offer, Neil, but I'm already married." And him saying, "Talk to the priest, get an annulment, you were *abandoned*, it's not fair." We used to laugh, didn't we? He was like a sad song. His unrequited love. Yeah, but. But he sure loved Mom, didn't he? Us, too. He wasn't family, but he loved us, too, all of us fucked-up Loobys. And jeez how we used to laugh at him. Even her, even Mom did. He was a meter reader, then a Good Humor man, a big dope. He had eczema.

Well, he's dead. And so's Mom.

So I can just forget about calling *them*.

And let's also forget about calling Victor Zits. Okay?

Yeah, because the more I think about it, Roy, the more I'm thinking not a good idea. If I told Victor about your accident, about your "critical condition"? He'd zoom down here in record time, you bet he would, but then he'd probably try to stick a pencil in your hand—draw, Roy, draw! Mr. Yale. Mr. Artist. Mr. Artist hyphen Rebel. Yeah, right. Mr. Coattails!

All of those guys talked a good game, but none of them had any chops. No chops at all. I mean, who reads any of their old strips anymore, who even *remembers* "Barky & Blacky," Mickey Ahearn's fornicatin' Dalmations? Or "Special Ed"? Anyone still remember Elmer Howdy's Special Ed—"His I.Q. Is Minus 2"? Or Breitstein's "Blessed Virgin Mavis." Shocking! Pornographic! Blasphemous! If you saw that shit today, you'd cringe. Any half-ass sitcom is edgier. *Disney* is edgier.

If it weren't for you—and they *knew* it—if it wasn't for you, Roy, even back then nobody would've paid those guys much attention. Compared with your stuff, their stuff was . . . but I don't want to be cruel. What the hell. And who cares? But why you ever consented to publish *Lazy Galoot* with *that* bunch, or let their pretentious hippie drivel share space with the Imp, it's always been a mystery. You could've published with anybody you wanted—you could've published with Crumb, or Shelton, or Kim Deitch, or Jay Lynch, Bill Griffith, with *any* of those guys. Art Spiegelman. Guys in your own league. Instead you published with Elmer and Victor and Mickey and Breitstein. What'd you get out of it? I mean, any fool could see what the *Galoots* got out of it.

I remember Victor that night in San Francisco saying that he'd never drawn better than after he watched you and that once you left, that once you took off for your hideout in the woods, it just wasn't the same. He said, "We never wanted him to stop. We'd sit and watch him draw for hours. 'Don't get up, Roy, don't stop. Don't, man. What do you need, Roy? Don't stop. You need anything? Don't stop. Can we get you anything? A Coke, a toke, a tab? Anything you need, Roy. Don't stop,'" says Victor. "Don't get up," says Victor, "just *don't*."

But you did. You finally got up and walked out, you walked out on those guys the same way you walked out on Candy and me and Noreen and—

Let's just forget about poor Victor, okay? I'm not calling him. And that's that. Or any of the *other* Galoots, either. So let's move on.

Cora Guirl? Jeez. The amazing Purple Cora. Well, I don't think we need to spend much time deciding whether or not to call *her*. Assuming I had the slightest idea where to find her, which I don't. Clarky says she changed her name half a dozen times that he knows about, changed her life like you change your shirt. Cora? Not Cora, no. Never.

Clarky? He knows already. I called him yesterday about—well, specifically to ask if he'd FedEx me down some of your reprint books. Since I promised Carol Collins. Remember I told you? And she's eager to get them, too! Especially *The Last Eugene*. She can't wait to see it. Mostly because I told her that I'd done it *with* you, that we did it together. She laughed, though, when I told her "they say it's cursed." Well, she's a nurse, she believes in *science,* right?

But anyhow. Clarky? He's already been "notified." I probably shouldn't have, but I did, I told him about you, and he was, like, "What? What? What?" Quack! Quack! Quack! He said I should call up the *New York Times,* and I said, "Yeah, right—and don't you, either." How much you want to bet he does, though? Fucking Clarky, he's a stand-up guy, but he's such a hustler, too. I don't think he's had a real job since Final Reckoning Press went out of business. All he does, best I can figure out, is write these long, long essays that he publishes in scholarly journals with circulations of like forty-three. "Cubism in 'Polly and Her Pals,'" "Gender Issues in 'Krazy Kat,'" "Religious Themes in 'Brenda Starr.'" Ai yi yi, but that's Clarky for you.

God bless him, he's still beating the drum, he still loves the stuff. And he sure loved *your* stuff, Roy—he's still your number one fan, although I get the impression he feels like an idiot sometimes. He put so much fucking work into that book he wrote about you and when it finally came out? It sank like a stone. No reviews, no sales, no nothing. It was like nobody cared or remembered—except him. But he's still your champion, Roy. So I bet you he does call the *Times*. Naturally he'll try to worm his sleazy way into the story.

You should have heard him. He says to me, "Nicky, this is so fantastic, they'll want to know—it's news." And then, no offense, Roy, but I said, look—look, I said, they got Kosovo, they got Elian Gonzalez and a bunch of pissed-off Cubans, they got the West Nile virus, you think they're gonna stop the presses for Roy Looby? It's not like Jimmy Hoffa turned up, it's only Roy. No offense. And Clarky says, he goes, "You crazy?" then just rattles on and on about you. You're mentioned in every book ever written about the sixties, you're in the freaking *Encyclopedia Britannica*. And I said, "Clarky, nobody *cares,* just send the goddamn books," and he says, "How do you want to pay for that, Visa or MasterCard?"

So Clarky knows. Who else should I call? Candy, sure, he's an obvious choice, but what's he gonna do, hop on a plane? He can't even get out of bed, most days. The poor gimp is over eighty now, and it's not like we keep in close touch, but I thought—well, since he always talks about you. Like if I drop by his house, he still brings up your name, every time. Yours and Buddy Lydecker's. And no, you still can't get out of Candy's house without listening to some version or another of the famous Buddy Lydecker story. Still can't. "And then he rammed a pencil into my chest!" Some things never change, Roy. Some do, some don't.

He's crazy as a coot and you can't figure out how he keeps going. Last time I saw him? He was saying how they want to put him back in the hospital, do another bone job, *more* surgery. He's not gonna do it, but. No more operations, he told me, and can you blame the guy? He'll just stick to his painkillers, thank you very much. Long as they keep writing him scrips, he's cool.

But speaking of operations. Hospitals? You know what Candy *always* mentions? The famous origin story. Yeah, but he'll insist it was scarlet fever you had and I'll say no way, Roy never had scarlet fever, it was a ruptured spleen. And I should know, right? Since *I* ruptured it, with a fucking baseball bat. But you can't argue with Candy Biggs. So you had scarlet fever. In 1964 you were in the hospital for scarlet fever. Okay, fine. But I'll tell you, pal, he's turned that little story into something so—

Put it this way. After Buddy Lydecker? You're the cheese. The main event. Even though you broke his heart, Roy, you're still the main event.

Summer of '64, there's Candy Biggs in St. Francis Hospital, recuperating from his nineteenth major surgery, his twenty-fifth, his whatever.

He's bluer than blue, he's down in the dumps, he's *below* the dumps, he's under *ground.* Then one day—they should make a movie, Roy, or, like, a religion—one fine day the poor mad fucker looks out through the open door of his semiprivate room, he looks across the hall, and—Jesus, Mary, and Joseph!—sees you! Except, of course, it's not *you,* not yet! He says to me, "Nicky? Your brother looked exactly like Derby Dugan!" Well, you did. The bald head, the yellow wallet. The blank eyes. Candy looks through his open door and there you are, but it's not *you,* not *yet,* it's just this bald-headed scrawny kid sitting up in bed holding a bright-yellow wallet in both hands like he's reading a comic book. "It was Derby Dugan—back from the dead." You were sixteen—right? Sixteen, almost seventeen, but you still looked twelve. "It was Derby Dugan back from the dead."

God, we always have a good laugh about that, me and Candy. And I can just imagine how he must've felt. Well, shit, I don't *have* to imagine, I *know.* Because I felt the same damn way, I'm sure, last weekend when they called me up and said you'd been hit by a truck. And to tell you the truth, I still feel that way. I'm sitting here watching you breathe, and it's just. It's like. I can't. Roy, I never thought I'd—

You know something? I'm gonna forget about calling up Candy Biggs, if that's all right with you. What's the point? Why add to his miseries? He's sure you're dead, he's buried you, so maybe it's best we just leave it like that. All right? All right, then. So who's next?

Well, there's Walt, there's always *Walter.* That's what he prefers to be called. Your son? He's Walter, not Walt, and he's been Walter since, oh jeez, long before he got out of high school.

He's married now, you know. Our boy is all grown up and married! Where *do* the years go? I never met his wife, but I hear she's a looker, she's French Canadian. Martine. You like that? Martine. He met her when they both worked on the same TV series up there in—I want to say Montreal, but it might've been Toronto. Some little half-hour cop show, they never showed it down here in the States. And I have it in my head she's a film cutter, but I could be wrong. They got married in Quebec, that I'm sure of. Two years ago? But I didn't attend. I wasn't invited.

And that hurt. I was hurt, Roy. I was. I understood. But even so. Did I ever forget his birthday? Or not send him a check? And when he graduated from NYU, I sent him one hell of a check! Sent him a card, too. With a note. "Go to Europe, kiddo, buy a Jeep, do whatever you want, I'll be looking for you at the Academy Awards—good luck!"

And when he wanted to make his first film? His "independent film"? Who coughed up five grand, and it wasn't a loan, either. I wasn't investing. I said, "Don't even think of paying me back. Just invite me to the premiere"—which he didn't. Not like there ever was a premiere-premiere, we're not talking *Pulp Fiction,* it was just some twenty-minute documentary about I don't even know what. Illegal immigrants? Something like that. Getting the shaft. Something like that.

I think he hates my guts, if you really want to know. Like, when he was in high school? Every summer I'd say, "You want to come work for me, you can be a sign painter, you can be the wall man, you can work outdoors, get a nice tan, I'll pay you top dollar." Every June I called him. And every June he'd say, "No thanks, I'm working at Chicken Delite." He'd rather work at Chicken Delite? For minimum wage? Yeah, that's right, he'd rather. Well, he's always been close to his mother. Although I don't think Noreen sees much of him herself anymore. What with him living way up in Toronto. Another place I've never been.

How about yourself, Roy? Old Ramblin' Roy? Ever been through Canada?

Ever think about Walt? Does he ever cross your mind? *Did* he ever?

Anyway. There's always him, there's Walter. I could always call him.

Then, of course, there's Noreen. Noreen Novick-Looby-Bozzo. Remember Larry Bozzo—that kid I used to be friends with for about half a year, way back? She married him. Our Noreen. But hey—you know what? Me and her? We're cool, we've made our peace. It took us long enough, but these days we're cool. We're fine. I could call her up and she'd be like, Oh hi! Perfectly civil. More than that. Friendly, almost. Not quite, but almost. And why the hell not? Thirty years and she's gonna hold a grudge still? Like I said, you get perspective.

She's had her problems, her "female problems," and I get the impression her marriage sucks, then her poor mother with the Alzheimer's and that wild girl she had with Boz. Laurie. Oh good Christ, I won't even go into *that,* but she was a handful, Laurie was. From what I hear.

Laurie Jane Bozzo. With her drug habit, her rehab, and those safety pins in her nose. The crazy boyfriends. Then she marries a fucking *Iranian,* and I'm talking a Muslim that *practices*—Laurie goes and marries a practicing Muslim who turns around and brings over his entire family. Can you imagine? Our Noreen, milk-and-cookies Noreen, having to put up with that? When all of a sudden you're faced with twenty-five Iranians at your door, what's Nick Looby, that fucked-up flatleaver, in the bigger scheme of things?

So when I was in the hospital that time? Following my "sudden massive coronary"? I don't know how she heard, but she did, and she came to visit. I hadn't seen Noreen in, oh my God—ages! And I didn't recognize her, not right away. You wouldn't believe how's she packed on the weight. The Shelf is now an entire bookcase! She's a *pantry.* But it's still Noreen. That same pretty face. You can miss it at first, but when you look hard, when you really look? She's still the girl next door.

She brought me some magazines. Magazines, couple of Sue Grafton novels. Not that I'm a mystery buff—I've never been—but it was the thought. She stayed about an hour and at one point even held my hand. We never talked about you, by the way. We talked about my "condition," my "prognosis," and we talked about Walt. About Walter.

And at one point—now, let me think, how did it go? She was being the proud mom, I guess, telling me all about this music video he'd just made, it's on MTV, and she goes, um, something like what a good eye Walter has. Every single frame, she goes, it's like a perfectly balanced picture. I had to bite my tongue. Bite and swallow. Because I wasn't *about* to speculate to our Noreen where the kid might've gotten *that* particular talent from. His "good eye."

On second thought, Roy, I don't know about calling Noreen. I mean, with all those Iranians around her house, does she need more grief? And would it *be* grief, or would it be just like a royal pain in the ass? "Just one more thing"? Besides, if I called Walt, don't you think *he'd* tell her? We could let *him* decide. I mean, who knows her better? Not Boz! Not fucking Larry Bozzo! What's he know? Guy who still drives around with a Bob Dole sticker on his stupid Windstar—what's *he* know?

So we could let Walt decide what's best. Maybe we should. Although it's entirely possible I won't be able to reach him. He could be away on a shoot. He could be—Christ, he could be following around garment workers with his movie camera! Or seals! What do I know? What do we—?

Funny, but I'm stuck now thinking about that time I was in the hospital and Noreen came to visit. When she was getting ready to go? She turned quiet all of a sudden. Very still. She looked at me and then I knew—man, I just knew!—I knew exactly what she was looking for. The old me. The old Nick. The Nick-that-was-Clyde. Her lost second Looby. I don't know whether or not she found him, but she did squeeze my hand, leaned over and squeezed my hand, and I couldn't help it, her top dress button wasn't closed and I had a peek. Her cleavage, Roy, looks half a mile deep.

And I was reminded that day, as I'm reminded again right now, of a day maybe two months after you'd split from Jersey. Walt was something like six weeks old. I came over to the house to ask Noreen if there was anything I could help her with. And while we're talking in the living room, the baby starts crying. "The baby." *Walter* starts crying. She went to get him and came back and sat down and started nursing him. Nudged her nipple right into his mouth. You really missed something there, Roy. You really did. They got dark brown. I forget now what we were talking about, me and Noreen, but even as I held up my part of the conversation, most of my attention was focused on this one drip of bluish milk running down the curve of her left breast, beading along the bottom, then dropping onto her jeans. It was like . . . it was like . . . I don't *know* what it was like. But it was amazing. She caught me staring and smiled. You missed something really special there, Roy.

So!

So.

So here's what I think. You want to know what I really think? Forget notification. Forget I tell anybody. And you know how come I'm not gonna? Because of that little card you had stuck in your wallet. That In Case of Emergency Call Nick Looby card. Because it said to call *me*. If you wanted somebody else called you would've put down somebody else, am I right? Somebody else's name. Seeing it that way, I'm just following your wishes. So it's just you and me again. Me and you, Roy, like old times. Just the two of us. A. Table. B. Chair. C. Lamp. D. Shaving Mirror. And us. Me and you. You and me. You wanted me called, they called me up, and here I am. Thanks to that little card you stuck in the wallet. Speaking of which, you had sixteen bucks in the billfold. A five and eleven singles. And it goes without saying you can have it all back, any time. Ask and you shall receive. Sixteen bucks.

The wallet, though? It's mine. From this day forward? That wallet, buddy boy, is mine.

SATURDAY, AUGUST 1, 1970

Two, three minutes ago, they drove through a quaint little town with fancy clothing shops and gourmet food "emporiums," BMWs parked at oblique angles to the high curbs, and a bookstore with a hundred copies of *Everything You Always Wanted to Know About Sex* but Were Afraid to Ask* displayed in the front window. Now they're traveling a secondary road, out in the country, Nick in the Bonneville following Joel Clark in his station wagon. Man, are they going to be there soon? Nick's head is pounding. Even though he slept almost eighteen hours, he woke up this morning with what his mom always referred to as a "splitting headache." Thanks to that fucking "opiated hash." Which is *another* damn thing. Earlier today when Nick was packing the car, everyone that he met on his way in or out of the Waller Street house winked at him, chuckling about Clyde's Major Freak-Out. Nick had, and still has, a hard time seeing the humor. First off, anybody could have made the same mistake. Hash you smoke in a pipe, correct? In a pipe. You don't roll it in a *joint,* who rolls hash in a joint, who? And second off—oh, forget it. The hell with everybody. He could've ended up in the hospital, in the *psycho* ward. Or dead, even! That's funny? No. Nick thinking in the car, No, I'm sorry, no, that's not funny. Plus, he made a total fool of himself, yammering like a retard and then puk-ing in public. Oh my God. He'll be pounding his pillow with a fist for weeks to come. Months. Years!

Great, isn't it? The day when he's finally going to see his brother again, he feels cranky and raw, so edgy that he just wants to . . . he just wants to . . . man, Nick just wants to *bark*!

Up ahead, he sees the station wagon's left directional signal start to blink, and half a minute later, both cars turn off the blacktop onto a dirt track. But then Clarky slows down, puts on his right directional, and pulls to a stop on the grassy berm. Nick parks behind him. What's going on? The fat man heaves himself from his Town and Country, and for a second Nick sees Orson Welles: the glossy dark hair, the choirboy face, the black tunic, the bulk. Clark trudges back to the Bonneville, leans down at the driver's window.

"I need to tell you something."

"What?" says Nick.

"I don't know how exactly to tell you this, and I don't want to worry you, but I know you haven't seen Roy in a while and I think you might be surprised that he's kind of . . . *withdrawn* from things."

"What's that supposed to mean?"

"It means, Clyde, that whatever it is that Roy's been doing the past couple of months, this secret project? Whatever that is, it's turned him . . . it's made him . . . he doesn't want anybody *near* him. The only reason *I* get to see the guy is because he needs a few things every couple of weeks, and I bring them."

"What, yesterday he's a fucking genius, today he's a nut?"

"No! No, he's just—well, you'll see. I just thought I should—"

"Warn me?"

"*Prepare* you."

Nick says, "If you're finished preparing me, can we go now?"

"Sure," says Clarky with a low-wattage smile. "Let's go see Roy." He turns and heads back to his station wagon.

On the rustic frontier-fort entrance gate, the name Camp Friendship has been painted over—in black enamel, it looks like—with a new name: Camp Galoot. "This is too weird," says Nick to himself as the Bonneville rolls slowly down between facing rows of red-roofed cabins, the porches sagging, the doors standing open. Bunks, mildewed bedding. All of the cabins have names plucked from *Roget's Thesaurus:* "Amity," "Rapport," "Peace," "Concord," "Fellowship."

At the far end of the midway stands an old gray farmhouse, and as Nick drives up to it, there's Roy, it's Roy, it's his *brother,* it's really him, seated in a rocker on the wraparound porch. He's not wearing a shirt, and his chest looks like something you'd see on a starving guy from Bangladesh. Sunglasses. Straw hat. Cut-off jeans. His bare feet are crossed at the ankles, propped on the railing. In his lap is a bright-blue mixing bowl.

Oh hey, don't get up, thinks Nick as he steps from the car and climbs five plank stairs to the porch. Don't get up or anything, Roy.

The blue bowl is filled to the brim with popcorn, and now the reunited brothers Looby both stare down into it, mutually fascinated by the red droplets that suddenly spatter the white puffy kernels.

"How you doin', Clyde," says Roy without looking up. "You doin' okay?"

Nick wants to say, Roy? Roy, your *nose* is bleeding!

Instead he just says, "Fine, Roy. I'm doin' great."

BOOK THREE

THE IMP EUGENE

"Imagine this. Imagine you're bored, it's a rainy day, there's nothing on TV, so you take down that stack of old jigsaw puzzles from the top shelf in the junk closet. And *then* imagine—perhaps you're more than just bored, perhaps you're feeling petulant, or possibly you're house-bound with a fever—imagine that some perverse impulse grabs you and that, gleefully, you open up every single one of those puzzle boxes and dump out their contents in a pile. Go ahead! Go on! And imagine next that you mix them all together with your hands, all those irregularly shaped pieces from that Kodaky picture of butter-cups, that portrait of Bert and Ernie, that majestic view of the Rockies, that penny gumball machine, the palace at Versailles in summer. All right? Finished? Now imagine *this:* that you try to *assemble* those hun-dreds and hundreds of tiny, incompatible cardboard bits, and that—impossibly, *magically*—you manage to unite them into a perfectly dovetailed picture of . . . the moon! And not *just* the moon, the moon on *fire*! This is how we should look at *The Last Eugene*."

—from *Nothin' Doin': The Imp Eugene and the Art of Roy Looby*

Comics and Stories

TRAVELIN' NICK

IN

"THE BROTHERS LOOBY AT SUMMER CAMP"

Our Story So Far: In July of 1970, Nick Looby journeys solo across the great American continent to see his long-estranged brother Roy, a notorious underground cartoonist. In our last installment, Nick finally arrived at Roy's "hideout," an old abandoned summer camp for boys in northern California. What surprises are in store for our hero? Let's see . . .

Tacked up around the cabin's knotty-pine walls were fifty-four, fifty-five . . . were fifty-six panel-ruled art boards, two-ply Strathmore cut 11 x 17 with 10 x 15 image areas, and as I watched, my brother Roy jumped antically from board to board—to this one, to that one, to that one there—all the while slashing at them with an HB pencil, drawing a primitive stick figure in one ruled panel, a tiny oval in another, a right triangle in still another. He kept dancing around the cabin floor, head moving, feet shuffling. Putting two short vertical lines inside that panel *there* and a half dozen parallel squiggles *there*. Then he pivoted, scrawling still more squiggles inside *that* panel. He couldn't keep still!

I said, "Hey! Whoa! What do you think you're doing? Hey!"

Roy twirled around to wink at me, then turned back to the wall, hesitating a moment, but only a moment, before crouching down to sketch three . . . ovals? circles? in an outside panel of the second tier of that page there. Roy's left foot tapped while his right leg jiggled; you'd think rockabilly was playing. He gave a wild falsetto hoot and wiped his forehead with an arm. Then he grabbed a low stool, set it down, and straddled it. Nose six inches from the wall. The back of his T-shirt was soaking wet, sticking—you could see his ribs. He leaned forward and roughed out an oval, then a circle, then another circle, then another. Working quickly, instinctually. And I could tell—because I'd seen this particular sequence of gestures, these *marks,* being made a thousand times before—I could tell that Roy was sketching the Imp Eugene. He leaned all the way forward, the bald, damp crown of his head touching the art board, then he shuddered once and didn't move again.

"Roy?" I pushed away from the sill and crossed the cabin floor. Feather-tapped him on the shoulder, expecting a sudden flinch. But nothing happened. Roy was sleeping. Passed out. Comatose? Man, this was all just too weird.

Our reunion had not gone particularly well.

Since my arrival, I'd had no idea what to make of Roy's behavior. Bleeding on the stupid popcorn, treating Clarky like homemade shit, jumping around like a fucking cricket—this frenzied *stick,* this maniac in Ray-Bans, could this really be the same guy I grew up with? My brother? My partner? What the *hell?* At first, I was embarrassed, then I got mad. Then I got embarrassed again. The way Roy talked to Joel Clark! "You know what you sound like when you fuckin' breathe, man? A fuckin' carburetor." When I heard that, I thought, Like Roy knows from carburetors. But thinking also, Jesus, why is he being such a *creep?* What did Clarky do, except bring him his Hawaiian Punch, his vitamin pills, his oranges, his stupid *toilet paper.* His Preparation H.

Man, if Clarky took offense, he could've flattened Roy, he only outweighed him by, like, two hundred pounds. But no, the big guy just stood on the porch and took it, even laughed a little. Roy passed him the bowl of popcorn. "Help yourself, fat man, you must be starving." Then he stood up from the rocking chair, wobbled, lurched, laughed again, smirked at me (I'd been watching from across the porch), and finally staggered into the house, screen door banging shut behind him.

Clarky stood there holding the blue bowl in his hands. All that blood-spattered popcorn. "Maybe Roy's pissed I brought you," he said.

"Maybe."

"I *tried* to prepare you."

"Yeah, yeah . . ."

Welcome to Camp Galoot.

Now here I was in Roy's studio, in Amity cabin, trying to light a cigarette, and just look at that burning match shake in my fingers. You'd think I had palsy. This was so—it was *nuts*. I sat down at a small table and looked around—at the pole fan humming in a corner, at Roy's inclined drawing board, at the pages tacked to the wall, at the high raftered ceiling, at my conked-out brother. And all of a sudden I couldn't breathe, I was so homesick.

Or was it heartsick?

Or was I just pissed off?

Except for how was I doing, Roy hadn't asked me a single question! Not: Are you hungry? Not: How long was the trip? Not: How come you're here? Not: How come you're here *now?* It was like he couldn't have cared less.

After I crushed out my cigarette on the floor, I walked over to Roy and took him by the upper right arm, giving him a shake. Nothing. "Roy. Yo, Roy. Hey—" then breaking off when my attention jerked suddenly to the art board tacked to the wall in front of me.

Although eight of its twelve panels contained various combinations of roughed-in stick figures, circles, triangles, rectangles, and squiggles, four panels were completely, even tightly penciled. From two feet back, though, you couldn't even *see* the drawings, Roy had used such an impossibly light hand, such a hard lead. But close up, there they were. There they fucking *were!* Eugene digging a tunnel. Riding on a bus (or maybe a train), staring out the window, his reflection staring back. Eugene sleeping under a banquet table. Pissing on a war monument. I moved down the wall, going left to right, peering closely, discovering similarly faint, *super*faint, line work—crisp, detailed, sporadic pencil drawings—on nearly every page. A panel here and there. Two in a row. A complete tier of them. Nearly four dozen cartoon drawings. But with all of the blank or quirkily notated panels in between the finished ones, it was impossible to get any sense of an unfolding story, a *narrative,* and while there were differently sized talk balloons indicated throughout, each contained only two words, the same two words, plus an exclamation point, dashed off in Roy's bastardized Palmer Method penmanship: NOTHIN' DOIN'!

"NOTHIN' DOIN'!" said the Imp Eugene while copping a feel off a chicken-headed girl in the Tunnel of Love. While blowing a doobie with a group of dog-men dressed in cowboy outfits—vests, chaps, spurs. While standing on the high board, jerking off—firing an arc of spunk—into a kidney-shaped swimming pool crowded with bare-breasted bunny-mermaids. While climbing through a window, climbing *out.* "NOTHIN' DOIN'!" "NOTHIN' DOIN'!" "NOTHIN' DOIN'!"

"Clyde? Roy?" It was Clarky, on the porch, his enormous volume silhouetted against the screen door. "I'm gonna be heading back to the city in a couple of minutes. Just thought I'd tell you guys so long. Everything all right?" When I stepped outside, Clarky looked behind me. "Where's Roy?"

"Snoozing." I reached back to pull the screen door closed, and it was such a custodial and clumsily possessive gesture that Clarky laughed, although he *looked* annoyed. Too bad, fat man, I thought, and sat down in one of the two Adirondack chairs on the porch.

"How long's he been working on this 'secret project'?"

"Since late spring. You get a look?"

"Kind of."

"And?"

I shrugged.

"Because it's not just me, the other guys are getting pretty antsy, too."

"What?"

"Zits and Elmer and Ahearn. Breitstein. The Galoots. They want to put out another issue as bad as I do. But we can't do it without something by Roy. What's the point? It's the Imp that everybody wants. So, come on, Clyde, don't be so damn mysterious. What's he doing?"

"I don't know, but whatever it is, it's over fifty pages long and still growing."

"You're shitting me."

"I shit you not."

"That's a fucking *novel*—Jesus! What's it about? Is it funny? What's it *called*?"

I turned my palms up.

"Don't be such a tease, Clyde. Are we talking brilliant shit here, is that what we're talking?"

"Oh, for Christ's sake." I stood up and jumped down three steps to the ground.

"Clyde! At least tell me what it's called?"

I flipped him the back of a hand and kept walking. At the house, I climbed to the little second-floor bedroom where I'd left my suitcase. I emptied my shaving kit and filled it with pens and brushes and templates, a French curve, a roll of white artist's tape, and a bottle of Higgins ink. Then I zipped it up and took it with me and tramped downstairs and out again into the bright afternoon, heading back to Amity cabin.

There were panels to be inked. And no matter what had gone down, or what was going down, was I not still my brother's inker?

TO BE CONTINUED

OUR NOREEN
IN
"SHELF LIFE"
(PART I)

It's the Monday after Easter in the year 2000, and driving her Volvo back from Gerald's Den of Beauty on this threatening-to-rain April morning, Noreen feels slightly sick to her stomach, her mood flip-flopping between high giddiness and the kind of dread she used to suffer, but no longer does, whenever a blowup with Boz seemed inevitable, when it was certain to happen tomorrow, or "as soon as he got home," or the next time he criticized her, called her fat, or even just opened his big mouth and uttered so much as a single word. It's strange. One moment she feels almost aroused (remember that?) and the next she's bracing herself for a quarrel. Stopped for a light at Twenty-first Street and the Boulevard in Bayonne, Noreen turns the rearview mirror toward her and primps. She did it. She really did it. Had it done.

Noreen is a redhead now.

"Oh, go wild, Mrs. Bozzo," Gerald had kept nagging her for months, but in that fun winking manner only young men of his, you know, *persuasion* could ever get away with. "You owe it to yourself." "But I've never *been* a redhead, Gerry," she said. "Let's stick with just a cut and a rinse. Don't I at least get *some* points for hiding the gray?" He would close one eye, make it squinty like a pirate (or like Popeye, she'd think), and tell her, "Not many!" They'd smile. But today? "Do it, Gerry," she said, "do it," and they'd both, quite suddenly, burst into hectic, coughing laughter. (Gerald had such a dirty mind, but she liked it.) "Now, you're sure now, Mrs. Bozzo?" "It's Noreen, for goodness sakes, Gerry, and yes, I'm sure. I'm positive. But not *brassy* red— please, I don't want to look like those old ladies you see coming out of the Jewish Community Center." "Hon, you are *so* not old." "I'm fifty today, Gerry, that's old." "Today! Well, happy *birth*day. Let's start the celebration then, shall we?" "Start *and* finish it, I'm afraid," said Noreen, "but yeah, let's. Let's just do it."

That time they hadn't laughed at how she phrased it, because that time it hadn't sounded at all smutty. It sounded weary and last-ditch, a capitulation. A shrug in language.

Never before in her life has Noreen colored her hair, and she's certain her husband will think she's completely lost her mind. What tiny bit is left. He'll gape and snort and flutter his lips. Even on her fiftieth birthday, he won't lay off the wisecracks. This evening Noreen has to pick him up at Newark Airport—she can't remember, if she even paid attention when he'd told her, where Boz flew off to last Wednesday. Cleveland first, then San Diego? Or San Diego, then St. Louis, *then* Cleveland? (He couldn't come home for Easter? Well, he wanted to— sure he did. What, Boz wasn't a family man? He resented the implication! But he had a golf tournament on Saturday afternoon, a client thing, and he couldn't make any good flight connections for Saturday night, so he figured, what the hell, might as well stay over, play a little more golf on Sunday, and then fly home Monday. Did Noreen have some problem with that?)

At the gate this evening—you just watch—first he'll make believe he doesn't recognize her, then he'll say something snotty, intentionally too loud, so that other deplaning "business travelers," his brothers-in-sales, will glance over at the big fat wife with the new head of wine-red hair and snicker as they straggle up the ramp. Unless, of course, he just stops dead in his tracks to press a hand to his forehead, pantomiming, for the millionth time, God-give-me-strength-what-did-I-ever-do-to-deserve-*this*.

Later—wait and see—he'll swear he was only kidding; he loves it, he'll say, she looks great. But only after she's frozen him out. Only after he decides he wants to park it tonight and figures he'd better be nice. Oh, what the hell, thinks Noreen. She's too old to worry about that shit anymore.

She thinks, April 24, 1950. Oh my God. Nineteen *fifty*. Harry Truman was president. When she was a young girl, she used to see Harry Truman, "the former president," on television, on that old mahogany Emerson, a floor model, that her family owned. By then he was a "crusty" old guy, crusty and "revered," and Noreen would think, He was president when I was born. And now he's way back in history with ghosts like Woodrow Wilson and Grover Cleveland. Laurie probably wouldn't even recognize the name. Say "Harry Truman" to Laurie and you'd get that blank stare. Heck, one day the name Ringo Starr came up, Noreen can't remember the context now, but Ringo's name came up in conversation, and Laurie said, "Wasn't he one of the Beach Boys?"

But enough. Noreen can see where this train of thought is taking her, and she doesn't want to be always tearing Laurie down. God knows, the girl has tried these past few years. She really has. Maybe she smokes too many cigarettes and drinks beer every single day (which is bizarre as well as unhealthy, since Heydar won't touch either alcohol or tobacco), but she's clean, no more drugs, thank God, and she's a good mom. A little high-strung, maybe, but a very good mom.

After all this time, though, it still brings Noreen close to tears (and yet equally close to stitches) whenever she realizes that her only grandchild, her beautiful three-year-old granddaughter, is named Zeeba! Zeeba Rahimiam. Life. What're you gonna do? But *Zeeba*?

Noreen's Tudor-style house is on Avenue A at West Thirty-fifth Street and sits on a raised corner lot adjacent to the county park. Her neighborhood used to be an exclusive doctors' enclave, but now it's mostly "effective" middle-aged salesmen like Boz who live in the big houses. Usually with their second wives, second families. Noreen and Boz have owned their house for going on thirteen years, but it was a compromise purchase. Boz wanted something brand-new, in a development community; Noreen did not. She would have been happy—as happy as her life would allow her to be—to stay put in Jersey City. No way! said Boz. He'd had enough of Dirty City. You had your break-ins, you had your crackheads, you had your *towel*heads moving in all over the place, turning beautiful old homes into mosques. And Islamic "schools." As if those taught anybody anything except how to build bombs. All right, said Noreen, all right. So they finally compromised on Bayonne, just due south, but with a much better element, a citizenry and not a pack of welfare wolves.

And what happened? Their house was robbed twice in five years, Boz kept finding crack vials in the rock garden, and Laurie Jane started dating an Iranian she'd met at the Bayonne municipal swimming pool. And whose fault was that? Noreen's. Noreen's, of course, because—as Boz never missed an opportunity to point out—she was too fucking scared to go someplace new and try something different. You're a typical Polack, he told her once, and she slapped him so hard she broke capillaries in his cheek. Then he said he was only kidding. He was only kidding, for Christ's sake.

After she parks in her driveway, Noreen thinks suddenly of her parents and grandparents, sees them hard at work in the old deli on West Side Avenue (the family sold it years ago, right after her mom was diagnosed with Alzheimer's, and now it's a Korean Pentecostal church). She can almost hear them all speaking Polish and, for just a moment, feels utterly calm. Noreen puts both hands on the wheel and remains in the car, idly staring at Heydar's banged-up old Fairlane, at the peeling paint and rust patches and the PRAISE ALLAH bumper sticker. She thinks, A granddaughter named Zeeba and a son-in-law named Heydar. (Cruelly, Boz has always called him Hey-dere, pronouncing it the way some Bronx bus driver would say hello to you.) Zeeba and Heydar, she thinks, and now it's her mother's voice that Noreen very definitely hears in her head, her mom speaking accented English to her, saying, "What kind of nationality is that, what kind of name is Looby?" Mom really s-t-r-e-t-c-h-ing out those *os*. Looooooby. What kind of name is Looooooby? Nine-, ten-year-old Noreen Norvick saying, "Polish, I guess," and her mom scoffing, saying, "Polish! It ain't Polish. You nuts?" And little Noreen saying, "Jeez, Mom, then I don't know, and what's the big deal anyhow?" and her mom scolding her then for saying "jeez," for taking the name of Our Blessed Savior in vain.

"Missus?"

Noreen jumps in her seat. Then laughs, embarrassed and relieved, and rolls down the window. "Heydar, you scared me. How are you, hon?"

Planting smooth brown elbows on the door, he leans in. "I'm well. Are you? I saw you come and then you didn't get out—are you feeling all right, missus?"

"I'm fine, Heydar, just ruminating." Ages ago, she gave up asking him not to call her "missus." Okay, if he couldn't bring himself to call her Mom or Mother, that was understandable, but couldn't he at least call her Noreen? At first, and for quite a while, it angered her, tremendously—she felt she was being mocked, somehow—but not anymore. The last time she ever said anything about it—and this was only a few weeks before Heydar's mother and four older sisters arrived from Iran by way of London—was the day she finally got fed up and said, "If you insist on calling me 'missus,' then you might as well put on a little white jacket and bring me a cold drink anytime I snap my fingers." Oh shit, that was so awful; how could she ever have said such a thing? Laurie was rightly furious; poor Heydar, on the other hand, thought it was very funny, he didn't hold it against Noreen at all.

Afterward, in fact, the two of them got along better than ever. They did gardening together, and the grocery shopping, they watched *Jeopardy!* in the evening, and sometimes he called her "Saint Missus" because she volunteered three times a week at Bayonne Hospital and because every so often she'd make a tray of lasagna or bake something, usually a fruit pie, and then deliver it to somebody named Candy Biggs in Jersey City, even though Heydar could tell that seeing the old man depressed Noreen. "Maybe next time you should let *me* take it to him," he once said. She said no, that was all right, but thanks. It was odd how her son-in-law picked up on the subtle things, that he took enough interest in her to try and figure out her moods. And gradually Noreen realized how much she liked him. She even began taking Heydar's side whenever he and Laurie had one of their periodic marital spats at the dinner table. He was actually a very sweet young man. And while she'd felt like wringing his Islamic neck when he imported his entire family from England, he soon proved to be a very responsible young man, too, quickly finding a place for them to live. The other Rahimiams were all now ensconced in a garden apartment down in

Freehold, about an hour away. Which was perfect. Not that Noreen disliked Heydar's people (Goli, Farrin, Darya, Mahbod, and Parto). No, they were very nice, and *industrious;* every single one of them now worked the night shift at a shopping-cart factory in Keansburg. Of *course* Noreen didn't dislike them, it was just that, well—who could blame her for wanting them out of her house?

Heydar pulls open the driver's door and offers Noreen his hand. Then, registering her dye job, an enormous smile breaks across his thin face. "Missus! You look like a movie star! You look like . . . like Susan Sarandon."

Noreen laughs and is a moment away from voicing some appropriately flattered yet self-deprecating reply when she looks up at him fully and sees that Heydar is holding to his face her thirty-something-year-old Polaroid camera, he's pointing it at her, and clicking, clicking, clicking the shutter release.

"Do you think they still make film for this? Do you think? Because I could take pictures of you looking so glamorous."

"Where the hell did you get that?"

Looking both confused and caught, Heydar lowers the camera, then points a finger to the sky. But no, he doesn't mean it came from Allah, he means it came from the attic, Noreen's attic. "I'm sorry," he says. "Should I not have taken it? But you said we could use whatever we found."

"I meant baby clothes, Heydar, for God's sake! I said you could help yourselves to Laurie's baby clothes. And I thought I told you both that *I'd* go looking. I don't want you two throwing stuff all over the place." She thrusts herself out of the car, and he steps away.

"We thought we would save you the trouble, missus. And since we had nothing else we had to do—"

"Well, maybe it's time you both did." Oh damn, she regrets that instantly. Noreen has told Laurie a hundred times that she *wants* her to be a full-time mom, that she's *happy* to have them live with her and Boz (especially since Boz is away more than he's home). She certainly doesn't expect her daughter to go out and take some minimum-wage job, and it's not like Heydar hasn't tried to find decent work. He has. He checks the want ads every day, makes phone calls. Since he was laid off at Maidenform, it's been tough for him, he has his pride (naturally—he's Middle Eastern), but the only work he's been able to get since February is a couple of shifts a week at McDonald's, which Heydar finds humiliating since almost everyone he works with there is either a high school dropout or mentally retarded, and the manager is a three-hundred-pound black man who calls him "ayatollah."

"I didn't mean that," Noreen says now. "Forgive me?" She touches his wrist, lightly, and poor Heydar obviously doesn't know what to say or, really, what he's done wrong. He tries handing her the camera, but Noreen shakes her head, refusing it—"I don't know if you can still get film. You'll have to ask them at the Rite Aid"—then steps around him, going into the house by the back door.

She can't believe that silly old camera turned up. She's even a worse pack rat than she thought. Noreen would've sworn she'd tossed that thing long ago. The way she'd one day tossed all the pictures she'd taken with it, two shoe boxes full of them. Pictures of Roy, mostly. Mostly? Almost entirely. Roy at his drawing table, on the couch in his living room, on his front porch, in his backyard. Pictures and pictures and pictures of unsmiling Roy Loooooooby. Roy's hands, even. Even Roy's silly wallet. She remembers once arranging—"composing"—a shot that ended up looking like a goddamn shrine: Roy's wallet, a bunch of Roy's pencils, the wrapper from a Mounds bar Roy had just eaten, Roy's house keys, Roy's high school ring, turned so you could read "Class of 1966." Jesus, there was something very, very sicko about all that—about her, about her *then*.

She was with Nick, Nick was still living with her, when she tossed the pictures, and she'd more than half expected him to sneak out later and retrieve them from the garbage can. Poor Nicky. He'd thought she got rid of those stupid photographs because she couldn't bear to look at them again, because she felt so hurt, pissed off, that whole "woman scorned" thing. She'd known that's what Nick believed, so then why hadn't she been kind, been smart, and told him the real reason? That she'd done it to put Roy out of her life for good, so that she could be— or at least try to be—genuinely with Nick. Give it a chance.

In those days Noreen was still trying, even if sometimes, God knows, she didn't act it.

Fucking camera. Fucking Heydar. Fucking *birthday*.

In the living room the big-screen TV is on, but nobody's watching, nobody's there, one of those things that bugs the shit out of Noreen. She turns it off and goes upstairs to find little Zeeba, in just underpants, fast asleep on the twin bed in her son's old room. The walls are still as Walter left them when he moved out twelve years ago, after college; nearly every inch is papered with movie posters—*Taxi Driver, Citizen Kane, The Godfather, Part II, Eraserhead, The Searchers*. And standing propped in one corner is his electric bass guitar—a relic from the time when he had aspirations of being a rock star, playing in Hudson County bars on weekends and rehearsing weeknights down in the cellar, he and his three bandmates. What was it? Liquid Light. The name of the group. Liquid Light. Finally, though, Walter had decided he wanted to make movies instead. Although Noreen was relieved to hear it, she can't imagine her son earning any less money as a rock-and-roll musician than he does now.

"Laurie?"

"In the attic, Mom."

When Noreen joins her daughter there, Laurie is tearing open the folded-in flaps of a large cardboard carton that an air conditioner originally came in; now it's packed full of winter coats. You can smell the mothballs. Other cartons have been pulled down from their stacks, opened, left open. Laurie has on tight jeans and a pale-blue work shirt; her dirty-blond hair is pulled back into a ponytail. For all of her alcohol and substance abuse, she still looks about sixteen, and she's twenty-five. "I wish you'd let *me* do this," says Noreen. "I know exactly where everything is." Well, not true, apparently: she hadn't realized she'd kept that old Polaroid. "I don't want everything left all—"

"Holy Christ! Mom!" Her daughter jumps up from a crouch, laughing in delight. "Let me see, let me see." She looks, looks closer, then walks all the way around Noreen, who for some reason has decided to close her mouth and stand perfectly still; it's like she has agreed to an official inspection. "I like it, Mom. Yeah. Oh yeah, it looks good. I *love* it."

Noreen wants to say, "You really do?" She wants to say, "Thank you, sweetie." But instead she says, "Well, I don't. It's just, it's not me. It's too youthful."

"Oh, come on. You look great." Laurie gives her a tight hug, says, "Really, really great," and this almost salvages Noreen's day. But some impulse she hates and wishes she could squelch beats through her till her face, from her hairline to her triple chin, is just one big scowl. "I'm gonna dye it back to its natural color. This was just an experiment that failed."

Laurie steps away, disappointed. "Whatever."

"Your father's gonna hate it."

"Whatever."

"I hate it when you say that. 'Whatever.' 'Whatever.'"

"Sorry." Laurie starts rummaging through the carton of winter things.

"You're not going to find any of your old baby clothes in there. I wish you'd waited." Knowing she's being sniffy and despising herself for it, Noreen steps around her daughter, darting from carton to carton. She points. "In there. That one." She reaches, but Laurie beats her to it, lifts the carton, swings it, brushing it against Noreen's left breast, and then sets it down on the attic floor. Flaps open, tissue paper torn away, and there they are, Laurie's little-girl dresses, washed and ironed and neatly folded. But looking faded. Mother and daughter stare for a moment, neither speaking. Then Laurie digs in, making selections.

"Where did Heydar find that old camera?"

"What?" Laurie glances up, but then immediately turns her attention back to a green-and-yellow sundress. "I don't know—he was snooping around over there," she says in her bothered tone. Makes you want to just slap her.

Noreen picks her way around wooden crates filled with tax stuff and Boz's paperwork from sales jobs he left years ago, boxes labeled Summer Clothes, labeled Halloween Stuff, a long box with the artificial Christmas tree inside, a reel-to-reel tape recorder, a manual typewriter that looks like it must weigh a hundred pounds, a box labeled N.S.A., meaning Noreen's Stuffed Animals, a stack of old jigsaw puzzles and board games (God, look, her old Candy Land!), and here's a large supermarket carton with the orange Tide logo printed on all four sides. Noreen recognizes it from several different moving days over the past twenty-seven years. But it had always been duct-taped closed. Now the tape hangs down in gray sticky twists and the top flaps are standing up.

Noreen pulls over an old dinette chair (several brown-edged holes in the seat plastic, from when Boz still smoked), sits down, leans over the carton, and digs in. And now here's a crumpled and badly torn poster of Donovan, "Mellow Yellow" Donovan lounging under a tree in a brown Edwardian suit, and here's an Indian blouse still blinding white with tiny mirrors sewn on the front and sleeves (she can't remember, or even imagine, wearing such a thing), and here's a paperback copy of *Hotel* by Arthur Hailey and a copy of *Valley of the Dolls* (hot stuff) and a copy of *The Harrad Experiment* (whoa, controversial) and a copy of *A Modern Priest Looks at His Outdated Church* (from when Noreen still cared about that kind of stuff) and *The Source* by James Michener and, oh wow, *Everything You Always Wanted to Know About Sex* but Were Afraid to Ask,* with that garish yellow cover you saw everywhere in those days, that famous asterisk. And here are some never-burned candles (the Tower of Pisa, a monkey in a fez, planet Earth, a Buddha) and a bong with a broken chimney. Good God, thinks Noreen, it's a fucking sixties time capsule. And smiles, thrilled. Hey, why not? Sentiment, sentimentality, whatever: it feels good.

"Laurie? Is that Zeeba crying?"

"It's the telephone, Mom. God. Can't you tell the difference?"

"Ex*cuse* me."

Neither of them moves to go answer it, and finally the phone stops ringing.

Noreen resumes her exploration, next finding in the carton a stack of carefully folded T-shirts. Howdy Doody face, James Joyce face, Bob Dylan face, "Imagine If They Gave a War and Nobody Came," some tie-dyeds, a continuous-line Picasso nude. And here's her blue-and-white McCarthy for President button, the one Nicky teased her for wearing, saying the guy was such a drip. Which he was. But at least she got involved—more than you could say for Nick. Or Roy, for that matter. More than you could ever say for the Loooooooby boys.

Down at the bottom of the carton is a bulging envelope; Noreen picks it up, bends up the clasps, opens the flap, peeks inside, and discovers that it's stuffed with movie-ticket stubs, diner napkins, her first driver's license (oh, look at that girl's face; no, *don't* look at that girl's face!), the program from a 1965 high school production of *Camelot* (if she opened it, she'd find her name—misspelled: Novak, Noreen *Novak*—among the list of "Knights and Ladies"), some holy cards she'd picked up at the wakes of her great-aunts and great-uncles, certificates for excellence in Latin and social studies, and a clump of postcards held together by a red rubber band. Oh Lord. All the postcards she'd mailed home from London, the time she was there with St. Dominac's high school band. After she'd come home, Noreen had asked everyone she'd sent one to, to give it back, if they wouldn't mind—she'd like to keep them all as souvenirs. (Only her grouchy Uncle Paul refused, probably rather than admit that he'd already tossed the damn thing!)

Noreen slides out one of the postcards: Piccadilly Circus, addressed on the back to her mom and dad, the message written in girlish purple ink, "I hate hate hate HATE flying, but we got here safe. The hotel is nice but no hot water tonight we're going to see a play, Love N." Noreen flicks through the batch and pulls out another, and her stomach clenches. The picture is of Buckingham Palace, the stamp bears a picture of the Queen, the postmark is dated 1-11-67, the addressee is Roy Looby, and the message reads: "Dear Roy, I was hoping this place would seem more foreign, but it doesn't, except they have 'Wimpy Burgers' instead of White Castles. Can't wait to see you again. I want to come home. I <u>need</u> to <u>talk</u> to <u>you</u>, All My LOVE, (your) Noreen. xxxooo"

And what she needed to talk to Roy about, had to tell him? Was that she was pregnant, three months already, and no, there wasn't any doubt.

Oh good God, that time in London was the longest ten days of her life and the single worst trip, even worse than the one to Aruba with Boz in '92, when he forbade her to wear a swimsuit because he'd be too embarrassed being seen with her. It was just awful. Wondering what Roy would say when she told him, what he'd *do*. What would happen to her. She looks at the postcard's color picture for another few seconds, then sticks it back into the rubber-banded deck.

"Mom?" says Laurie. "You okay?"

"Oh sure. Just thinking."

"What about?"

"Nothing really," says Noreen, because that's the simplest thing to say and because she couldn't share these particular thoughts with her daughter. What she's thinking about is this: for Noreen, the biggest mystery about Roy Looby has never been what happened to him after he disappeared from the face of the earth in 1970; actually, she's never been too intrigued by that. No, the thing Noreen has never been able to figure out is why Roy agreed to marry her in the first place. Why would he "do the right thing," and do it with guts, too? ("Shit," he said when she told him. "Damn," he said. "Crap," he said. "Fuck. So what now?" he said. "You wanna get married, or what?" and when she'd said yes—she did, of course she did—Roy said okay, and her family's subsequent scorn never fazed him.) Why did he marry her but then two weeks, *two weeks* before she gave birth to their son just walk out one night without even saying good-bye?

That's the mystery. And fuck everything else.

After returning the postcards to the envelope, Noreen leans over to wedge it back into the carton and notices a small, flat, laminated square sticking out from one of her old address books. It looks like a playing card . . . but, oh my God. Oh. My. God. It's that crazy thing she got from that weirdo guy, that black guy, that day, that day at that hotel! On one side is a repeating diamond pattern, and on the other is a drawing of a gigantic egg lying on its side in the bed of a child's slat-sided red wagon.

If Noreen will ever die of sadness, it will happen now . . .

TO BE CONCLUDED

SPECIAL BONUS!

"YOUNG BRIDE BLUES"

(AN UNTOLD TALE OF OUR NOREEN WHEN SHE WAS A GIRL)

Beginning in high school, Roy and Nick Looby regularly attended conventions for comic-book fans. They'd ride the PATH train from Jersey City into Manhattan on a Sunday morning, then wander fifty times around the "ballroom" of a sleazy downtown hotel, a firetrap if ever there was one. Finally, in late afternoon, they'd go home tired, carrying plastic shopping bags filled with secondhand comic books, old comic-character toys, animation cels, even sometimes a piece of "original comic art." Noreen had never gone with them, but following her marriage to Roy in the first week of March 1967, she decided she really ought to. It's what a wife did, a wife went. But after her first experience, she promised herself never again.

It was not Noreen's idea of a day well spent to mill and meander among a couple hundred boys—twelve-, fifteen-, twenty-five-, thirty-year-old little boys—who haggled over and paid outlandish prices for back issues of *Action Comics, Vault of Horror, Little Lulu,* and *Donald Duck*. The whole thing struck her as silly whenever it didn't strike her as downright creepy. There were trestle tables everywhere, manned by unsmiling dealers and arrayed with individually bagged comic books, as well as with "valuable" collectibles—Olive Oyl Pez dispensers, stuffed Pogo dolls, Little Orphan Annie wigs, Zorro caballero hats, and Spider-Man board games. Lord love a duck.

Noreen felt dispirited watching all of those ungainly, pencil-necked enthusiasts jam into an airless "exhibition room" to gape at amateur superhero and "funny animal" art (god-awful stuff!) or into the equally stuffy "pro room" to listen to career cartoonists hem and haw at cheap little microphones, answering questions like, "What kind of brush do you use?" "Do you work best in the morning or at night?" "How much does The Hulk weigh?" Most of those poor men, in Noreen's opinion, looked washed-up and sorrowful, even half in the bag. God! There was a room where you could watch old movie serials, chapter after goofy chapter of *Captain Marvel* or *Flash Gordon* or *Dick Tracy vs. the Phantom Empire,* and another room where you could bid wildly on, say, the boots that George Reeves wore as Superman on TV. This was a lot like Purgatory, but even so, she was a good sport about it, smiling whenever Roy looked around to see if she was still with him.

Roy, of course, loved it. He thought the fans were real dopes, and he had nothing but contempt for superhero comics (Noreen almost felt sorry for Nick whenever Roy needled him mercilessly for reading *The Flash* or *Fantastic Four*), but Roy loved to cram shopping bags full of what he and Nick called "the goods"—a fragile 1932 "Thimble Theatre" Sunday color page from the *Boston American,* for example, or a "Toonerville Folks" panel, vintage 1928, from the *St. Louis Post-Dispatch,* or a turn-of-the-century "Little Nemo" tearsheet from the *New York Herald,* or—this acquired on the day Noreen accompanied him—the artwork for a Depression-era "Derby Dugan" comic strip. The dealer wanted thirty bucks for it, but Roy offered him twenty and he took it. Noreen thought, Twenty dollars? For that old thing?

"A Geebus!" Roy had exclaimed. "A beautiful Walter Geebus original! Check it out, Reeni, check it out!" And she did—after Nick did, of course; he always grabbed anything of Roy's before she could put her hands on it. Nick always got first dibs. He was such a pain. Such a pest. Such a—

"Derby's in all four panels!" said Roy. And yes, Noreen could see that: a tied-up little boy being dipped into candle wax by increments throughout all four panels. Charming. People-in-the-past *enjoyed* this sort of thing? No wonder there was World War II! "Have you ever seen anything so beautiful, Reeni? Isn't it great?" Roy had asked her, and because she was married now and trying to be a good wife, and a good wife goes along to get along, she said, "Really great." But for crying out loud! The cardboard (or whatever) was creased and grimy and dog-eared, freckled with coffee stains, and the four pictures—she knew she wasn't supposed to call them "pictures," she was supposed to call them "panels"—the four *pictures* were all marked up with blue pencil. Why on earth would Roy want to own such a thing? Well, okay, because it was "Derby Dugan," and Roy was nuts about "Derby Dugan," and if that was what he wanted to spend their money on, okay. Not worth an argument. But twenty dollars?

It was tough watching Roy buy corny old cardboard with hardearned money (*you* try making salads and sandwiches eight hours a day, every day, in your family's delicatessen, especially when they're pissed off at you for getting pregnant, quitting school, and marrying a Loooooooby). It was so tough on Noreen that she decided for the sake of their new marriage that her first "con" would also be her last.

So on a warm Saturday in late April of 1967, she went to New York again with Roy (and Nick, of course), but this time she dropped them off at the hotel. They arranged to meet in the lobby at four o'clock. While Roy and Nick traipsed around the ballroom, she'd have her hair cut, do a little shopping, stroll through the Village, maybe see a movie. Good plan? Good plan. She was almost seven months pregnant.

At the hair salon on West Eighth Street, Noreen told the girl not too short, okay? and the girl said, "Okay, sure, but let's shape it a bit." Noreen watched in the mirror, and it seemed to her the girl was cutting off way too much. Maybe she should say something? But maybe not. After all, *she* wasn't the stylist; what did *she* know?

Noreen's friend Mary Pasco had started getting her hair cut here, she loved the job they did. Well, it was New York City, said Mary, who, unlike Noreen, was a little bit of a snob—"It's New York City, Nor, it's not *Jersey* City, you just get a much better cut"—and finally Noreen had decided to try the place. The cuts were expensive, and Roy never much liked the results—one time, he'd howled, said they'd made her look like the schoolteacher in the Our Gang comedies. Nick had said he liked the cut, he'd complimented her on it, but so what? Who cared what stupid Nick thought? After that experience, she considered going back to her regular haircutter at Journal Square, but there was a funny thing about Noreen. She made habits easily, too easily in her opinion. And she had a profound sense of loyalty, of allegiance. One haircut here, for instance, had made her a regular; it was her place now, and she knew she would keep coming back, whether she was pleased with the results or not. Besides, how could she ever return to her old haircutter's? They must hate her there!

She decided finally she couldn't watch the girl cut her hair, it was making her too nervous, it was making her crazy. She closed her eyes and paid attention to the radio, instead. It was tuned to one of those stations that Roy liked, the kind that played big-band music, which always left her cold. It was strange, being married to a young guy who liked old music. But Roy wasn't like everybody else, and that was good. Wasn't that good? It was good. She listened to a Frank Sinatra song and then something by "Count Basie" (How come those old-music guys all called themselves Count and Duke? What was *that* all about?), and then the news came on.

Noreen wished she could put her fingers in her ears, she hated the news, it was never good, never. Usually it was Vietnam, Vietnam, which made Noreen want to burst into tears, and always it was somebody mad about something, and—

The newsman, the announcer, was talking about catshit. Well, he didn't say that, he said "fecal matter." Same thing. He was saying that, according to a recent study, catshit causes birth defects, maybe, and that jogged to mind a dream Noreen had had—last night? last month?— and forgotten till now. She was bathing her new baby—suds on the water kept her from knowing its gender—when suddenly the baby changed into a cat. And not a real one, either. A clock cat, a kitchen clock, a black-and-white Felix the Cat with a pendulum tail. But here was the thing that made her dream so really grisly: *Roy liked the cat better*. He patted it dry, that awful thing, then hung it on the wall and set the hands at half past ten.

When the girl was done cutting her hair, Noreen said, "You don't think it's too short, do you?"

"Short looks good on you."

"You think? Yeah? Okay." Noreen tipped the cutter four dollars. It pained her, being so generous with tips, but this *was* New York City and she didn't want to be ridiculed behind her back as a cheapskate. When she left the salon, the warm April breeze touched her skull and she could feel it as if she were as bald as Roy. In that moment, Noreen knew for certain she had not gotten the perfect cut. And with her chunky, booby figure, now she'd probably be mistaken for a bull dyke! Oh my God. Wait a second, she was *pregnant,* and *showed.* How could she be mistaken for a dyke? Get a grip, Noreen, get a grip.

She hated it when she got flustered, and she was flustered now, so flustered that, unthinkingly, she bought a ticket at the first movie theater she spotted, a place that sold coffee in the lobby, but not popcorn, and sat through a picture that not only she had never heard of but that had subtitles! Oh no. And it had nudity, too. Full frontal nudity. Noreen sat in the dark wishing she had a figure like those women in the movie; French women had such reasonably sized breasts. By the time she left the theater, she felt like a circus freak, she felt lumpish, and was on the verge of tears. Plus, she felt stupid. Did other people understand what was going on in that movie? Did they? That couple. Were they supposed to be married, or what? Were they in love, or what? And that other guy, the swarthy one with the glasses? Why was he always following them around? Was he in love with the woman? Or was he in love with the *man?* That was possible, Noreen realized, since it was a foreign film. It was all very confusing.

She still had time to kill before meeting Roy and what's-his-face, so she wandered around the Village, looking at shoes, at cheap jewelry, at jewelry not so cheap, even, though just briefly, at bridal gowns in a shop on MacDougal Street. (She didn't want to be reminded of her own wedding at City Hall; nobody had been there except Noreen and Roy, and Nick and Mary Pasco, the witnesses. And there'd been no reception and no gifts—well, Nicky gave them a small Korean TV set. What a horrible day! Her parents had been so mad at her! What, they would've preferred she had an abortion?)

Wherever Noreen walked, she kept seeing antiwar flyers pasted on walls. Stop the War! Stop the Madness! Stop the Killing! Rally! Moratorium! She noticed, and guessed she did because she was a cartoonist's wife, that most of the caricatures of LBJ and Robert McNamara were pretty badly drawn; they were "unprofessional." Roy could draw those guys under the table! He could draw rings around them, her husband could.

She thought maybe she'd make a circuit of Washington Square Park, but then felt too fainthearted to do it alone. She was such a weeny Jersey girl! But already she'd gotten some comments from males passing by; a couple of black guys with space-helmet Afros and dripping chains had made kissy sounds at her, checking out her breasts. Winter, with its months of heavy coats, was much easier for Noreen, it really was. She was so clearly "expecting" and *still* they ogled her chest! Jeez, though, her boobs were almost ridiculously big these days, so big she suspected that Roy was more aghast than aroused by them. And he never asked her to model for him anymore, like he used to.

Noreen passed a tiny shop with record jackets and movie posters and comic books—old ones and new ones—displayed in the front window. The shop was below sidewalk level, four steps down. She returned to look more closely. If Roy had been with her, for sure *he* would've stopped, and she was so used to being with Roy that now she had to stop as well.

A lot of the comic books were clipped on a wire that stretched across the window, and glancing at the titles quickly, Noreen noticed several back issues of *Walt Disney's Comics and Stories,* one of Roy's favorites. She decided to go see what they were selling them for.

"I Am a Rock" was playing on the radio as she walked in. A heavy-set woman in a yellow caftan leaned on a display case and read the *Village Voice.* Her cigarette burned in a black plastic nightclub ashtray. Nearby, a baby-faced kid with a bristly Erik the Red beard flipped through used record albums. Noreen had to step around cartons of junk and squeeze down impromptu aisles, but she made it at last to the window display. Twisting around, she looked up at the Disney comic books. Two *Uncle Scrooges,* a *Chip 'n' Dale,* half a dozen *Comics and Stories.* She yanked one of those from its clip. On the cover Huey, Dewey, and Louie were sliding down a banister, moments away from plunging into a washtub, Uncle Donald standing by with a scrub brush. The comic was sealed in a clear plastic bag, and Noreen hoped there'd be a price sticker on it somewhere, but of course there wasn't. She hated having to ask salespeople for a price—she felt it committed her to buying.

"Any three for ten."

Noreen said, "What?"

"Any three books in that area for ten bucks."

"Even this one?"

"Any three, I said. Any means any."

God, Noreen just hated people who read the *Village Voice*.

She looked again at the Walt Disney comic and thought, He'd really like this. He'd smile and say, Thanks, great, wow, where'd you get it? She could make Roy happy—very goddamn happy—with a crummy little comic book that cost three bucks. Then—and this surprised Noreen, it took her by complete surprise—she felt angry all of a sudden, at *Roy*. She could make him happy with a comic book? A comic book and a goddamn plastic cat!

Until she got pregnant, Noreen had never had a single doubt that Roy was destined for success, for bigger and bigger contracts, an ever-growing stock portfolio, a home in Westport, Connecticut, where all of the big-name cartoonists lived and had Sunday afternoon cocktail parties. Roy's strange friend and teacher Mr. Biggs used to tell her about those parties, and Noreen had liked to imagine herself in that situation. She could see herself. Making dips. Cracking ice. Oh! I'm so glad you could make it—come in, come *in*!

But since she got married and dropped out of school, Noreen drove to work each morning with nothing but doubt in her mind. What if she hadn't married the next Charles Schulz, as she had believed. What if she'd married Joe Mediocre by mistake? Roy had turned so moody! Not that he'd ever been what you'd call happy-go-lucky, but lately—lately he was just a *bear*. He sulked and then he got snappish. "Get your hand off my dick, I'm trying to work here. Can't you see I'm busy?" *That* was new. He'd never complained before. Did she look like a cow? She looked like a cow, didn't she? She did. She looked like a cow.

Noreen left the creepy-lady shop and walked quickly to the hotel on Broadway, Broadway at Bond Street, and waited for Roy and Nick in a dim, shabby lounge just off the lobby. But after a few minutes, she decided she might as well go up and see if she could find the guys. She took the stairs. It was only the second floor, and besides, no way was she riding in that death-trap elevator.

The ballroom appeared more crowded than last time, and Noreen was almost certain she was the only female in the place. She drew a long breath, then waded through the conventioneers, all of them carrying identical yellow plastic shopping bags. Suddenly, she could sense dozens of sets of eyes—boy eyes, boy-man eyes—tracking her, stealthily checking out her bazooms, and she'd just about decided to hell with this, she was going back downstairs, when she looked between a group of beanpole teenagers and sighted Roy. How could you miss that Yul Brynner head? It almost always surprised Noreen when she'd see Roy from a distance and realize just how short he was. When they were both kids, she'd always assumed he'd grow. But he really never had. She'd married a short guy, and that was a little funny because Noreen was sort of tall, for a girl. She was five-eight. Roy was like five-five, or maybe not even.

He was seated at a card table, surrounded by several guys roughly his own age, all of them standing, all of them displaying bad posture, all of them watching Roy with funny little smiles. Each of them wore sneakers, jeans, a white T-shirt, and black horn-rimmed eyeglasses. They resembled a little gang. Of nudniks. They were watching Roy draw, she realized—he was drawing and they were watching, and those funny little smiles? Were smiles of admiration. She felt momentarily peevish, then exhausted. She wanted to sit down. She needed to.

"Hey, Nor."

"Oh. Hiya, Nicky. So how's it going? You guys having fun?"

"Yeah, sure. It's great." But he didn't look as though he were enjoying himself. Nick seemed mopey today, a little sad, and she noticed that the shopping bag looped over his wrist was empty. She caught him glancing toward Roy, and the two of them watched him scribble his signature on a sketch (Noreen could recognize that little gesture, that *flourish,* from a mile away) and then pass it to one of the nudniks.

"What's going on?" asked Noreen.

"Just a bunch of guys who used to subscribe to our fanzine—remember that? Remember *Misanthrope?*"

"Are they paying for those drawings?" Roy had finished another one and was grinning, saying something, and all six guys—no, there were *seven* of them—laughed and nodded. "Are they?" Till she'd said that, Noreen had no idea such a question was even in her mind. Now she regretted asking it. It made her sound. It made her sound. Noreen didn't *know* how it made her sound. Mercenary? Well, if it did, she didn't mean it to. And she was happy that other people recognized Roy's talent. Of course she was. She guessed she just wished it wasn't a bunch of nudniks. "So are they?"

Nick said, "Jeez, I don't think so. It's just, you know, they asked him if he would. Make sketches for them all."

"Is he going to be much longer?"

"You want me to go get him?" said Nick, eager, it seemed, for the excuse to do just that. "Is it four o'clock already?"

"Twenty till. No, that's okay," she said. "Let him be."

"Hey! Nor! Where are you going?"

"Back downstairs. You guys can meet me there when you're ready."

"I'm ready now."

"What's the matter, Nicky?" Turning back, Noreen touched him on the wrist. She didn't know why she did that, she usually never felt sympathy for Nick the pill, Nick the *pest*. But he looked so unhappy, and he *was* her brother-in-law now. "What's wrong?"

"Nothing's wrong, okay?"

"I was just asking. See you guys downstairs."

"Want me to come? I've had enough of this crap."

"No," said Noreen, "that's okay. You're in charge of bringing Roy down at four."

"All right. See you in twenty minutes." Then he called to her when she was walking away. "Hey. I like your haircut."

"Yeah, well, I don't," said Noreen.

Back in the lounge, she claimed a small marble-topped bistro table and ordered a Coke. An extremely tall black man sitting alone on a Victorian horsehair sofa nodded to her. She ignored him, but he got up and came over. All of a sudden, Noreen found it difficult to breathe. The man put down a pack of cards in front of her on the table. "We're both waiting for people, am I right?" he said. He had on tight black pants and a white turtleneck and wore a heavy gold chain that made Noreen think of Sammy Davis. And what teeth! Amazing teeth. Maybe he was an actor, or wanted to be. She tried to be polite and at the same time appear unwelcoming. When he sat down across from her, Noreen got up.

"Whoa," he said, "relax. I'm waiting for my mother, she's coming down in a couple of minutes with her new husband. So I thought we could just, you know. Wait together. I won't even offer to buy you a drink, if it'll make you feel better."

Noreen sat down again and wondered why she decided not to tell him who *she* was waiting for. So far, she hadn't noticed him checking out her boobs.

He tapped the cards. "Ever seen anything like these?" He picked one up. On it was a picture of a red metal wagon with slatted wooden sides and a gigantic egg-shaped white stone lying in the wagon bed. The stone had a perfunctory face daubed on it, just filled-in black circles, two eyes, and a nose. But wait a second, it wasn't egg-*shaped,* it *was* an egg, a humongous egg—because, look, there was a thready little crack oozing the slightest speck of yolk.

"Never have," said Noreen. "What's this, a tarot deck?" She wasn't sure that she pronounced that right. She said TAR-o, but maybe it was tar-O.

"No, ma'am. But same idea. Tell your fortune. See this *c* with the circle around it? Copyright Marcus Bailey. That's me." Smiling, he checked his wristwatch, a gold thing with a black face. "Want me to tell your fortune—the Marcus method?"

Noreen said, "Oh, I don't know," but when he looked disappointed, she changed her mind. "Sure, why not?"

He shuffled the deck and then spread out seven cards on the bistro table, facedown. "Pick any three," he said, "and then turn 'em over."

One of her picks was that crazy-egg-in-the-wagon, another one showed a mastodon sinking in a tar pit; pterodactyls flew overhead and there was an erupting volcano in the far distance. Her third had a picture on it of an old-fashioned car with a rain cloud hovering above the steering wheel and bolts of cartoon lightning zagging out of it. "That's a 1947 Chrysler Town and Country," said Marcus. "You dig antique cars?"

Noreen said, "Not really."

Marcus studied her cards, stroking his goateed chin as he peered.

His *hmmm* actually created a slight vibration that Noreen could feel at the top of her chest. "You're gonna have a daughter," he said.

Putting a hand to her stomach, Noreen said, "Really? Where's it say that?"

But he shook his head. "If you're interested in learning more, you can buy a deck for yourself later on this year. Okay? They should be on sale in time for Christmas at E. J. Korvettes and other fine department stores. All right, babe? For now, let me just *read,* okay?"

"Okay," said Noreen, "but I don't think I'm gonna have a girl. I just have this feeling it'll be a boy."

"I'm telling you what I'm telling you," he said. "Hmmm. You got something to do with a butcher shop? I see meat, you around meat a lot?"

Noreen laughed. "Yeah. Go on."

"You around meat a lot, for real? All right, Marcus! Butcher shop?"

"Delicatessen," said Noreen.

"Close enough." Marcus Bailey frowned, then began tapping the card with the '47 Chrysler on it. "This ain't your car, honey, it's your husband's. That's your husband's car."

She smiled. "We own a VW."

"Metaphorically speaking," said Marcus Bailey. "*Metaphorically* speaking, that's your husband's set of wheels."

It was foolish, stupid and foolish, but suddenly Noreen felt her stomach clench: she didn't like the look of that dark cloud with all its lightning. It must have showed on her face because Marcus shook his head. "Don't try to interpret for yourself, okay? You know what that card means? Lying where it does with them others, I'll tell you what it means. Famous man," he said. "You married yourself a famous man."

Noreen laughed. "Not yet," she said.

"That's correct," he said. "That's right, he's not famous *yet.* But someday." Then he glanced around behind him, and when he turned back to the table, his lips were compressed. His long fingers started to gather up the cards. Noreen looked, searching for his mother and her new husband, but nobody who fit that description was coming off the elevator: there were only a couple of Asian businessmen, several boys—obviously on their way down from the convention—and a slender peroxide blonde wearing red, wet-looking jeans and a white-and-black-striped gondolier's jersey. Marcus was on his feet. "Nice talking to you," he said, his friendliness suddenly gone, and he strode off. She watched, but he didn't go to greet anyone, he walked directly out of the hotel.

Soon after that, Roy and Nick showed up. Noreen kissed Roy and tugged gently on his arm till he sat down where Marcus had been. That left Nick standing, which was okay with Noreen. Roy started to show her what he'd gathered today, he had his hand plunged into his yellow shopping bag, when Noreen said—she blurted—"I just had my fortune told. Guess what? Guess what it said? I'm going to be married to a rich man! How about that, huh? I'm going to be married to a very rich man."

"Must be talking about your *second* husband," Roy said. Then he laughed and slid his goods onto the table. *Little Lulu and Tubby at Summer Camp, Uncle Scrooge* number 10, two or three *Sugar and Spike* comics, and—the "piece duh resistance"—a slightly damaged animation cel from Disney's *Pinocchio,* Pinocchio not a boy yet, still a puppet on a shelf, fifteen bucks, a freaking *steal.* Beautiful! Noreen slumped in her chair, feeling close—*this* close—to tears.

Then Nick bent down and picked something off the floor. It was one of the cards from Marcus Bailey's deck: the red wagon holding the giant white egg. Feeling a spike of embarrassment, Noreen snatched it from Nick's hand and stuck it in her bag.

"I really like your haircut," said Nick, and Noreen said, "Thank you." She looked up at him, and—oh, why not?—smiled.

OUR NOREEN
IN
"SHELF LIFE"
(PART 2)

Poor Nicky, thinks Noreen. God, he was an unhappy kid. Young man. God, was he ever. Nicky. Nick Loooooby. And it's crazy, it's probably cheap nostalgia, it's turning fifty, but she . . . she *what?* Feels regret? Yes . . . but no, that's not it, not exactly.

She misses him.

She misses Nick, *him,* not—

"Missus?"

"Heydar, do you mind?" Her son-in-law is behind her, peering over her shoulder at Marcus Bailey's fortune-telling card. Quickly, Noreen sticks it back in the white envelope and drops that back into the Tide box. "What is it?"

"Phone for you."

She takes the portable, covering the mouthpiece with her free hand. Whispering, "Who is it?"

"Your son."

"Thank you." She hasn't seen or talked to Walter in more than a month—even though he's living in New York (by himself, since he and Martine apparently have split for good) right on the other side of the Holland Tunnel, in Soho. At no salary, he's been operating the camera for a friend of his who's making a low-budget crime movie. Noreen understands he's busy, but it *has* been more than a month since he called. And you'd think he'd try to visit once in a while. It wouldn't take him more than half an hour to drive over here. But at least he's remembered her birthday. There's that, at least. "Walter?" she says. "How are you, sweetie?"

"Mom? Did you see the paper today?" There's a long pause. Then: "They found Roy. It's in the *New York Times*. He's down in Virginia— in a hospital. Mom? You there, you okay?"

"I'm fine." Seated on that old dinette chair in her attic, Noreen feels suddenly incapacitated. She feels a thousand pounds heavy, and light- headed. Her eyes fill, her throat closes, and her nose starts to run. Roy's *alive*? But here is what primarily occupies Noreen's mind at this precise moment: Walter *didn't* remember her birthday, that's not why he called, he called just to tell her about Roy. About what he saw in today's paper.

"Mom? You still there?"

Family, thinks Noreen. They'll always disappoint you. Always. But what's the use of kicking? There's *no* use. No fucking use at all.

THE END

TRAVELIN' NICK

IN

"BLOOD ON THE PANELS"

EARLY THAT MORNING . . . while there was still dew in the grass and a clammy dampness to the air, the two of us walked to Amity cabin. "I'm almost ready to be finished," said Roy. He held the waist of his dungarees bunched in one hand, and I thought, Holy Christ, how much does he weigh? A hundred pounds? Less? He looked like a kid, a skinny little bald kid. "How 'bout yourself, Clyde? Almost ready?"

"Whenever you are."

First thing, Roy fueled himself with a hash pipe, then with a hit of blotter acid. (Even though it gave him wicked hemorrhoids, he started each workday with a tab.) "I'm outta here," he told me, then winked and stuck it on his tongue. Then Roy untied the laces of his tennis sneakers, and we both sat down at our tables.

I took off my glasses, breathed on each lens, wiped them with my shirttail, and went to work, brush-inking panels, doggedly, one after the other. I laid ink on Eugene—dressed in chaps and riding a horse—lassoed from his saddle by a gang of masked dog-headed outlaws. Lettered "NOTHIN' DOIN'!" where my brother had indicated, and carefully scalloped the surrounding balloon. On my own, I added a cactus to the desert. A cactus and a cow skull. Roy was too damn skimpy with his props, too spare, and besides: what the fuck. I was feeling very what-the-fuck that morning. I drank a quart of Gatorade, pissed in a Skippy jar, smoked half a pack of cigarettes. Put on the radio and kept changing the stations. I turned it off for a while, then turned it back on. Every twenty minutes, I stood up and stretched, reaching toward the rafters. But I never once peeked at what Roy was drawing. And we didn't talk.

Nearly a month had passed since I'd arrived, and we'd hardly talked at all, except for the usual stock phrases ("How you doin', Clyde? You doin' okay?" "Fine, Roy, doin' just fine"). I'd say, "Once we're finished with this story, what next? Any ideas? I got some. Wanna hear?" Most times he just ignored me and kept right on drawing. At best, he grunted. And whenever I thought to relate some news from home, he pretended not to hear. Mom had pneumonia last winter. Candy had shingles. Walt likes to color, he likes to draw. Noreen has something called a bone spur in her left foot, she'll need an operation. No response. Nothing. So eventually I stopped talking. Roy penciled. And I inked.

That day, we both worked for almost three hours before his nosebleeds started again. Then came the Godzilla one, in a gush, and Roy suddenly was covered in blood. It was on his lips, his chin, his shirt, his hands, his dungarees. Eight on the Richter scale. I thought he was hemorrhaging. Scary shit. But it didn't seem to faze Roy. After it stopped, he calmly changed into a clean T-shirt—his third in two hours—and went out on the porch.

When I joined him a few minutes later, he was sitting with his eyes closed in the rocker he'd dragged over from the house. Alongside his chair was an upended milk crate, and on top of that was a can of Hawaiian Punch, several paperboard bathroom cups, and Roy's yellow wallet, smudged now with his bloody fingerprints.

"Hey, Roy? That page you were working on? I tried wiping it off, but it's ruined."

"Don't worry about it."

"I'm not worried, I'm just saying you're gonna have to redo it."

"Then I'll redo it."

And whenever he did, that would make it the twelfth time, at least, that he'd started the last page, page 65, from scratch. Through the first two and a half weeks of August, he'd penciled nine or ten new pages—ten, I guess—working quickly, manically, nonsequentially, but whenever he reached what he said was to be the last page, that's when things stalled and turned strange. Well, stranger than they'd been. He'd do all the faint panel layouts, but whenever he'd begin to draw the finale ("Why does it have to be sixty-five pages, Roy?" "It just does." "What happens at the end, Roy?" "You'll see."), he'd freeze up, or his nose would start to bleed, or he'd abruptly return to an earlier, finished page, add something minor, some dummy lines. When he turned his attention back to page 65 again, he no longer liked it, and he'd either tear it up or completely erase whatever he'd already penciled. Then he'd take out a clean sheet of bristol board, rule new panels, and start over.

But why didn't he finish? Why couldn't he? Every day I wanted to ask him, and every day I almost did, but then I'd bite my tongue.

I'd bite and swallow.

I sat down in an Adirondack chair and picked up the wallet from the milk crate. I had an impulse just to take it, to put it in my back pocket, stand up, and go away. *Run* away. It would serve my brother right, it would—

"Don 't touch that."

I shrugged and put it down. "Roy? Did I tell you that Uncle Neil's a Good Humor man now? He said he got too fat so they laid him off at the gas and electric. But I bet you he finally got caught stealing."

"Why do you always bring up stuff like that? I don't *care* what Uncle Neil is doing. I don't even know who the fuck you're *talking* about."

"Why're you acting like this?"

"Like what?"

"Telling me you don't know who I'm *talking* about! What is *that*? You don't remember Uncle Neil? What about Noreen? You remember her? How about Candy? You remember *me*—remember who *I* am?"

"Jesus, Clyde."

"And why do you always call me that?"

"I don't remember."

"Yeah, well, I hate it. I hate being your fucking Clyde!"

"You don't want to be Clyde? Then poof!" he said. "You're not Clyde. But now the question is: who do you *wanna* be?"

"Just Nick. Just your brother. I just want to be Roy Looby's brother."

He said, "Roy Looby? I don't know who the fuck you're talking about."

THAT AFTERNOON . . . I scrubbed the floor of Amity cabin, getting off, as best I could, the dried spatters and red footprints. You wouldn't believe all the blood. You'd think cows had been slaughtered there.

I was still down on my hands and knees when Cora Guirl opened the screen door and came in, rolling an inflated black inner tube ahead of her. "Wanna go for a swim?"

"No, thanks," I said, and sneaked a look at her hard-muscled tanned legs in purple cutoffs. Burn scars were clumped behind her left knee and ran in lumpy strings down her right calf. Her toenails were lavender. "What's Roy up to?"

"Sleeping in a kitchen chair." She leaned the tube against my stool. "Or at least he was the last time I looked."

"I hope he's keeping his head tipped back."

"Gee, Mom, I'm not sure about that." Whenever Cora laughed, her lips pulled away from her gums. I found that tic horrible, horselike, and very sexy. She watched me scrub for a minute, then began to follow the "Eugene Saga," as I'd dubbed it, in its tacked-up procession around the cabin's four walls. What she took in as she walked slowly backward (there wasn't much to read, God knows; this was something you just *took in*) were sixty-four identically sized bristol board pages, the single-image splash page (Eugene crouched, naked except for the bowler hat, in a corner of a room, despair cartooned on his face) and sixty-three interior pages that utilized a repeating grid, four tiers, three panels to a tier.

But if the grids were regular, predictable, the story was not. Nearly every adjoining panel was discontinuous, nonsequential, yet each was part of a pattern, too. I'd recognized that instantly the first day. But I hadn't been sure then, and still wasn't, whether the pattern was thematic or just schizophrenic, a work of genius or a freak-out in eight hundred tiny pictures.

I hated the goddamn story. It wasn't even a story, it was fifty, sixty, seventy stories! All chopped up. Everything just—flung. Candy Biggs would've hated it, too. The guy who yakked to us all the time about logical flow, about a story, even a *joke*, having a beginning, a middle, and an end? Candy would've loathed it.

You went from the Imp lying in his backyard hammock, to the Imp digging an underground tunnel with a wooden spoon, to the Imp pissing on a horse-and-general war memorial. Next panel: the Imp diving into an orgy, his hard-on prominent. And in the *next* panel, the Imp, surrounded by sharks, is treading water in the trough of an ocean wave. Next, he's trekking through a desert. There's a cactus, there's a cow skull. And now he's being chased by a gang of bloblike creatures across three panels in a row (a lawn, a roof, a kitchen). "NOTHIN' DOIN'!" says the Imp. Says the Imp. Says the Imp. "NOTHIN' DOIN'!" It was all so crazy.

But the last ten pages were the craziest. Eugene opening doors, passing through rooms (a poolroom, a barroom, a ballroom, a living room with snack trays and TV), then stepping outside into a blizzard. Now opening a vault, falling down a hole, bellying through an air shaft, riding a subway, kicking out a screen, dropping into quicksand, hobbling along the ditch beside a country road, using a tree branch as a walking stick. Arriving at a clearing in the woods. Approaching the door of a rustic cabin on stilts, climbing to the porch, crawling in through an open window . . .

Cora dropped into a wicker chair by Roy's table and helped herself to his Camels. "You having fun with all of this?"

"Hardly." I got off my knees, stood up, and stretched. "Christ, I can't make any sense of it. Can you?"

"Oh, I don't know. It's Eugene remembering. So everything's all mixed up. It's not *so* hard. See? Look, there's me as the chicken-girl. Giving great head. And that monument, there? Is pretty much like the one in Chicago. That Roy peed on. It's Eugene remembering. But it's Roy's life, kind of. That's pretty obvious. My problem is, it's just not funny."

"And it's depressing."

"Yeah, well, it's that, too," said Cora.

"People are gonna *hate* this."

"Maybe that's the whole idea. Look, you missed a place."

"What?"

"Over there." She pointed with her leg and foot. "You missed some blood." Then, after I'd grabbed my wet rag and knelt down again and started rubbing at it, Cora said, "Hey, Clyde? Clyde, whyn't you get back in that big dopey car of yours and just drive home?"

Before I could say anything, the screen door swished open, banged shut, the latch clicked, and Cora was gone.

LATE THAT NIGHT . . . I couldn't fall asleep, so I got up and sneaked across the upstairs hall and crouched outside the bedroom Roy shared with Cora. Old-fashioned doorknob, old-fashioned keyhole. I rolled forward, closed one eye, and squinted the other, but the only things I saw were the record player and, taped to the wall directly above it, that animation cel of Roy's, the Pinocchio cel he'd bought years ago at a comic-book convention. But then I saw Cora's legs and the scars on her legs as she passed in front of the door, and I heard her say, "Think you'd ever want to draw with me again? Roy? You think? Want to jam with me some day when you're not too busy?" But there was no answer, and then I was pretty sure they were fucking, and all I could hear was Tampa Red on the turntable doing "Nutty and Buggy Blues."

NEXT: CORA UNCOVERED!

PURPLE CORA

IN

"SEVEN DIFFERENT PEOPLE (AT LEAST)"

P.O. Box 301
Kelting, Idaho
May 22, 1972

Dear Clarky,

You are bothering the shit out of me! On top of that, you're making me break the rules. Around here we don't have any contact with men—haven't you heard? It's not allowed at "Goddess Farm." That's the first rule. It's the damn <u>cardinal</u> rule. If you're male, you're poison, you're verboten (sp?). And even though you always had much bigger tits than me, you still qualify. You're still a guy, you're poison. You'll get me in trouble. Yeah, but it's also kind of nice hearing from you again—hey, what's a little testosterone between old friends? And since I'm breaking the first rule, by writing to you like this, I might as well break another. I just lit a cigarette, in case you're wondering. It's <u>delicious</u>. (A Kent, smuggled home from the craft shop in town where they have me working 50 hours a week.) Of course, I'm not smoking indoors. I couldn't risk <u>that</u>. My wonder-women sisters would string me up. Here we don't use tobacco, alcohol, or dope of any persuasion. No, I'm outside in the deep buggy woods. Those little black specks all over the page are proof.

But enough chitchat. I'm thinking we could possibly make a deal. I could help you out, like you're asking me to, but only if you help <u>me</u> out.

I'm short of cash and I'd really like to get some to explore my options. This girl scout camp has pretty much turned into a cult and I'm sick of it.

So how's this for a plan? You're in Chicago (how come?) so I'll meet you there and talk to you about Roy, even though I think you're FUCK-ING CRAZY to be writing a book about him. I'll tell you what I know about him (what <u>little</u> I know), answer any questions, and in return you stake me $500. Take it or leave it. Reply A.S.A.P. And please note the above address. Make <u>sure</u> you use the post office box! I know mine wasn't the first pair of eyes to read your letter.

Fondly,
Cora Guirl

P.S. How did you <u>find</u> me? And I mean that "fondly."
P.P.S. I won't believe that J. Edgar fucking Hoover is really dead till some-body drives a stake through his heart. How about you?
P.P.P.S. Could you enclose maybe $50 in cash or an m.o.? Bus fare.

St. Mark's Place, New York City
November 3, 1975

Dear Clarky,

So you figured out that Claudia Cling is your old pal Cora Guirl! Did you recognize me, or did somebody tell you? Did somebody tell you, or do you actually go to the "adult cinema"? I blush to think of you seeing me in the flesh. I don't know why, but I do. (I'm a <u>horrible</u> actress, but that's kind of beside the point. Great new tits, though. And blonde for a change. I like it!) All right, down to business. I've read the transcript you sent along with your letter—shit, has it <u>really</u> been three years already since I talked to you in Chicago? Sorry I ditched you that day. Forgive me? I was in a rocky state of mind. Goddess Farm was no picnic.

Anyhow, this morning I put on "Born to Run," for the millionth time, fixed a cup of coffee, and went over the transcript, very carefully. Don't quote any of the stuff that I crossed out. <u>I fucking mean this</u>, Joel. And I don't want to be identified in your stupid book, either. You are NOT to mention that Cora Guirl is currently Claudia Cling, do you understand?

Under those conditions, it's okay to quote anything you like.

Sincerely,
C

Cassette Tape #14/August 11, 1972
CG: Cora Guirl
JC: Joel Clark

JC: Looking good, Cora.

CG: <u>You</u> go work on a goddamn farm for a year and a half, you'd look pretty good yourself. Lunch part of this package?

JC: Sure.

CG: Thank you. So what're you doing in Chicago?

JC: Oh, you know. Seeing if I can start up a new publishing thing, talking to some people. Seeing what I can borrow. <u>If</u> I can borrow.

CG: What happened to Final Reckoning?

JC: Don't ask! I lost my shirt putting out "The Last Eugene." Of five thousand copies printed? I must've sold eight hundred, tops.

CG: Hell, you should've asked me before you went and published that thing, Clarky, I would've told you don't waste your time, don't waste your money, nobody's gonna dig it. It's like I told Nicky Looby once, it's just not funny. And besides that, it's depressing. And besides <u>that</u>, it's all crazy and mixed up, so who could even follow it? And on top of all <u>that</u>, "they say it's cursed."

JC: Please. If I hear that "cursed" business one more time . . . I'd like to know one person who went crazy reading "The Last Eugene." Show me! Just one!

CG: Well, there's Roy. And Nicky. And I'm not exactly a poster girl for mental health. And what about yourself?

JC: Cut it out, Cora. I happen to believe "The Last Eugene" is a masterpiece and—

CG: You were willing to go broke proving it?

JC: Sure, why not? It's only money.

CG: Speaking of which, you got some for me, I hope?

JC: Some.

CG: Oh, fuck, don't you be doing what I think you're doing. You promised to stake me five hundred bucks.

JC: I already sent you fifty. And I can only manage another three hundred.

CG: All right. Whew. I thought you were gonna—all right. I can live with that. Thank you <u>so</u> much. I'll pay you back.

JC: I know you will. And we'll forget about the interest.

CG: So can I have it?

JC: After lunch.

CG: All right. But can I at least see it?

JC: Don't be insulting. I think we're ready, yes. I'll have the hamburger platter. And coffee. Cora?

CG: Same, I guess. No, wait, no! I learned <u>nothing</u> from my days on the dairy farm? I need to <u>ask</u> for what I want, <u>say</u> what I need. Speak up! All righty, then. Can I still get breakfast? Then I'll have the breakfast special. Scrambled eggs, no bacon. But you got sausage? Sausage. And a biscuit. Okay, Joel. Shoot. I can't believe you want to write a book about Roy. Anybody seen him lately?

JC: Not a soul.

CG: God, it's so fucking weird. Just to—where do you think he went? He's probably down in Mexico. With Jim Morrison.

JC: Do you think we could get started? I'm curious what Roy was like when you first knew him. In Milwaukee. Can we start there?

CG: Sure. He was much <u>nicer</u>, at the beginning. He was shy and very, very wary of anybody wanting to get too pally too fast. You know how in "The Imp Eugene," everybody is always trying to take a big bite out of him? I have to tell you, that's a pretty obvious metaphor. That's how Roy felt, I think. Like everybody was trying to take a bite. That's how he'd act. He'd show up at parties but keep his shades on, and he always watched what he said. Like, if you invited him to get stoned with you, he'd take a rain check. And he wouldn't shake hands with <u>anybody</u>.

I first heard about him from this girlfriend of mine. She worked at the elementary school where I taught, she was somebody's aide. Anyhow, she'd fucked Roy, and from what she told me about him I didn't come away with a very positive impression. She said he had genital warts. Gross, right? So that's how come I didn't sleep with him, not right away. Not for weeks. And the funny thing was, when it happened, he didn't have genital warts at all! She must've got him mixed up with some other guy.

JC: How'd you meet?

CG: ~~I was just coming out of shellshock mode~~, I was unemployed. ~~After that kid set me on fire, that fifth-grade devil, I put in a claim for med-~~

~~ical leave, I was so rattled. Who wouldn't be rattled? But when I got~~
~~turned down, I quit anyway.~~ [Clarky: Pls. Note Crossouts.]

I was kind of living with ~~this guy, but sometimes I'd go back and~~
~~live with my mom and her new husband. That sucked, though. They~~
~~had all these hobbies, they were always adding on a room or~~
~~antiquing furniture. So I'd go back to~~ this cute boy named Brian. He
played in a white blues band, and the rock guys used to hang out
sometimes with the Movement types and hippies that worked for the
underground weeklies, including cartoonists. I saw Roy for the first
time at Victor's place. Zits had one of those shotgun apartments, I forget where, and it was a big party. I met Roy in the kitchen. He was
drinking coffee at the table, that's all he ever drank when I first knew
him, he never even touched a <u>beer</u>. Boy, <u>that</u> sure changed, didn't it?
He had one leg crossed over the other, like this, and his sketchbook
propped up against his knee, and there he was, just drawing away.
The party was going full blast around him, but he just sat there, very
calm, very busy. I usually don't find bald guys attractive, and I <u>didn't</u>
find Roy attractive, but he wasn't <u>bad</u>-looking, and I really liked how
he drew. He sketched people talking by the stove or dry-humping
against the wall, and they were great little pencil studies. Very realis-
tic, except that Roy gave everybody an animal head. Very cartoony
animal heads. Rabbits, pigs, horses, dogs, all different kinds of dogs.
God, he was good with a pencil.

Clarky, <u>you</u> read. You know that writer Lawrence Durrell? He wrote
these novels set in Egypt. I think it was Egypt. I read one for my sophomore lit class, and I only mention this guy because of something the
professor said about him once. He said that Lawrence Durrell was a
"writer's writer," by which he meant somebody that other writers
admired, a guy who made them want to sit down and write a book
themselves. He said that Durrell's stuff was maybe not the greatest
stuff in the world, but it was inspiring. Well, that's how it was for me
with Roy Looby. He made me want to go out and buy some paper and
pencils and maybe some pens and a bottle of ink and draw something
myself! Which is just what I most needed to do right then. I needed
something new, to start over, and Roy kind of—I'd see his comics and
I'd want to do the same thing. And I did, or at least I tried, and it
changed me. I'd been in really bad shape for a long time, but now I
was better. ~~Roy was a prick later on, but he kind of saved my life. Not~~
~~that he ever put any effort into it, but he did. He really did. He saved~~

~~my stupid life.~~ [I don't care if this _is_ a great quote, use it and I'll track you down and cut off your weenie.]

When I first started to draw? I'm jumping ahead, sorry—but when I first starting drawing comics? Roy said I had talent. ~~Nobody else thought so, and~~ I realized that ~~part of it was that~~ he wanted to fuck me so of course he needed to be nice~~, but even so, I think he meant it, too. You've seen some of my early stuff. It's awful. It's really terrible. I admit that. But it got better, right? Roy could spot what I had. He was very encouraging, at first.~~

Hey, could I bum one of those? I haven't been smoking much lately, I've had to be very economical ~~since leaving the dyke farm~~. I dole out every penny. Thank you. But why do you smoke Merits? It's like not smoking at all. Don't they give you the hiccups?

JC: So you, what? Started living together?

CG: Never. I never knew where Roy officially lived in those days, but it sure wasn't with me. And it wasn't with anybody else, either. At least not with anybody I knew. Like I told you, he was cautious. He'd show up at my place, we'd make spaghetti. We'd have couscous. I was becoming more and more of a hippie chick. I wore granny dresses, granny glasses, no underwear, I walked around barefoot. You should've seen the soles of my feet. I stopped shaving my legs. And under my arms. I got into all that purple stuff, just to be cool.

I always had grass, we'd get wrecked, it was nice having sex that way. A little pot, that's all, that's it. He never <u>touched</u> acid till he got to San Francisco and hooked up with those fucking Galoots. Yeah, so we'd ball, and later on he'd get up, like in the middle of the night, and draw comics. Oh! I have to tell you this. One time I got up to go to the bathroom. It was maybe two in the morning and Roy was sitting at the table in the kitchen, and he'd dumped together something like half a dozen different jigsaw puzzles that I had, and he was fitting together pieces from all of them, and fuck if it wasn't turning into a picture! A <u>crazy</u> picture, but . . . well, somehow a red barn, and the Eiffel Tower, and polar bear cubs, and Mickey and Goofy, and the Grand Canyon, and a snowman, and the fifty states. Somehow he'd turned all of those mixed-together puzzles into a picture of, of—you know, I'm not sure <u>what</u> it was, but it was <u>something</u>. The borders were jagged, I remember, and somehow that was—maybe I'm imposing this in, like, retrospect, but the way it was so jagged, the four sides of the new puzzle, somehow it seemed very creepy. A nonsense picture drifting off into nothing. When he realized I'd come into the kitchen, he scattered the puzzle, he broke it all up before I could have a good look at it. That was the first cruel thing he ever did to me.

JC: Were all these puzzles by the same manufacturer? For instance, were they all Milton Bradley puzzles, or were they—?

CG: Oh wow. You're gonna try to explain away the magic, aren't you? Like those guys that say the Red Sea was parted by an earthquake or something.

JC: No. No, I'm just thinking that possibly each puzzle had been cut by the same jigsaw machine, so then all the pieces would be compatible. Theoretically. So theoretically you could put them all together.

CG: Can't help you out, Clarky. They might've been the same company. I bought them all at the same place, at a Woolworth's, ~~as part of my private therapy. I used to do puzzles so I didn't jump out of my skin. Or slit my wrists. Or cut up my own face again.~~

JC: God, if he'd only photographed it. Or mounted it!

CG: Joel? Can I have my money now? You finished eating?

JC: Can we continue our conversation?

CG: Here?

JC: I don't care. Here, someplace else, whatever.

CG: Yeah, all right. But the money first. I'll pay you back.

JC: I know you will.

CG: Hey, if we're gonna keep talking, I have to go pee.

JC: I'll be right here.

JC: For the record, Cora Guirl has apparently given me the slip. Our waitress just came over. I guess she felt sorry for me. Cora left five minutes ago, she said, by a side door. So I guess I'll go home now. That is all. Over and out.

> No return address
> (canceled stamp reads: Bangor, Me.)
> September 3, 1981

Dear Clarky,

Congratulations on "Nothin' Doin': The Imp Eugene and the Art of Roy Looby"! At the bookstore in town where I bought it, they had it shelved under "Humor." It was stuck in with the "Garfield" and "Doonesbury" reprints, the "Herman" treasuries, and Erma Bombeck. I never heard of the Big River Press, but that doesn't mean anything. (I didn't know they even had book publishers in Seattle!) Anyhow, it's a very nice-looking book, although when I got it home I discovered that one of its corners was all crumpled under the dust jacket. And the binding is not what you'd call excellent. I would've brought it back, but the store only had that one copy and I didn't want to wait to read it. Thank you for mentioning me, the old me, the Cora-me, in the Acknowledgments. And thank you for not mentioning Claudia Cling even though Claudia no longer exists.

I have a new name these days, and if my Redeemer wills it, I will carry that name to my final reward. (And no, I have no intention of telling you my new name, either; it's none of your business.) I am married now to a wonderful Christian man and we have two small beautiful children. They're angels. Angels on earth! I'm very happy, and I hope you're happy for me. You've been in my thoughts again ever since I spotted your "handsome coffee-table book," and now you're in my prayers. Clarky, I feel terrible that I never paid you back that $300. Well, $350. Please find it in your heart to forgive me. When I was Claudia Cling, I could've paid you back, but selfishly I did not. I spent every dime I had on rent and clothes and cocaine. Now I could no more part with $350 in a single lump than I could part with my liver. I have not forgotten, though, and as soon as I can I will repay my debt to you. In the meantime, accept my prayers.

It was very, very strange to open your book and see all those old comix of Roy's again. I think you've made a good selection, although you left out my absolute favorite story. I think it was called "Footloose Eugene." The one about the Imp, where he gets off the bus in a new city and hooks up right away with that beaky chicken-girl Carlene. She's a very sexy young girl except that she has a chicken's head. You remember the story? Wish you'd used it. (Roy drew that one in my kitchen. I'm pretty sure the chicken-girl is based on me. The walrus is Paul.)

That early stuff still holds up, I think, the stuff Roy did in Milwaukee and Chicago and Boston, before he moved out to California. Eugene is selfish and immoral, but he's still a <u>rascal</u> in those stories from '67 and '68, he's still curious, he's still funny. Like if Alfred E. Neuman had a penis. (Glad you chose "1001 Ejaculations," by the way; it's vulgar and very sexist, but it's a hoot. I may be a Christian, but I'm no prude.) That early stuff you reprinted—yeah, it still holds up.

But the stories from "Lazy Galoot"? Already, there's a very sharp decline. I know you wouldn't agree, since you were the publisher, but I

see a big decline in the quality of Roy's work after he moved to California. You can see the effect on him already of all those arty guys, Victor especially. Or at least I can. That interminable story where Eugene just
sits in a chair getting stoned and sucked off, what a load of crap. What a
load of idiotic, self-important, misanthropic crap! Definitely the work of
somebody who's taking way too much medicine to get through the day.
Who is just way too full of himself. And that bullshit monologue, all that
plagiarism from Kafka and Sartre. Sartre! Like Roy Looby ever knew from
existentialism. It was all so phony, and I think that he finally figured that
out for himself. I also think that was the _real_ reason he went up to that
stupid, horrible camp and then buried himself there—to get away from
flatterers like you and Zits and Ahearn.

I really hated those stories Roy did in California, and I told him so—
which is how come by the time he left San Francisco we weren't just not
lovers anymore, we practically weren't speaking. He may have known in
his heart that the stuff was a load of pretentious crap, but he couldn't
stand it when somebody told him so. Roy _hated_ being criticized. He
couldn't take it. After everybody told him he was so darn great, of course
he didn't want to hear any criticism from _me_.

But that wasn't the only reason we'd stopped talking. It was also
because he'd started to make fun of my comics. He DESPISED them.
Well, because they had unicorns in them, because they were _romantic_ as
well as sexy. He was such a bastard, Clarky, by then! Too much weed,
too much acid, too much praise. At least, that's how _I_ see it. Such a bastard. Still, if he's alive today, I wish him well. I hope he's happy. I've for-
given him. He's in my prayers.

It's weird, but when I looked at those pages you reprinted from "The
Last Eugene," I got a reaction that was totally not what I'd expected.
Because of my unhappy real-life connection to its creation and because
I'd never really thought much of Roy's alleged masterpiece, I imagined I'd
feel depressed seeing any part of "The Last Eugene" again. Not so. First,
I thought it was amazing, the drawings, an amazing piece of work, and
I'd never thought _that_ before. (Of course, if I tried to read all 64 pages,
rather than just the 6 or 7 that you've chosen, I might feel about it the
same way I felt the first time I saw it. It was so _jumpy_.) And, second—
how do I say this? Seeing those pages again brought back memories, but
not all of them were bitter. And even the bitter ones were almost bitter-
sweet. I'm three years away from turning 40, so maybe I'm just getting
old, but I couldn't work up the energy to be angry or too sad. (And even

though "they say it's cursed," I didn't feel the slightest inclination to climb on the roof or run naked through the streets.)

If I have one criticism of your book (so far—criticism of your book so far; I haven't read the whole thing yet), I'd have to say that you went a bit too easy on me. I hope that I'm a woman who takes responsibility for her own actions—I try to be—and I can see now that I bear some measure of responsibility for what happened. Your book presents me as a long-suffering girlfriend, poorly treated by the eccentric genius, and I guess I was that, but I wasn't stupid. I had my own agenda too, Clarky boy. Just like everybody else around Roy, I had my own little agenda. Roy had a great talent for simplification (of course he did, he was an excellent cartoonist), and he saw us all for what we wanted. We loved him, sure, but we were hungry, too. Starved.

I'm thinking of the day I drove up to the camp, it must've been around the second week of August, maybe 3 weeks or so before Roy disappeared for good. I hadn't seen him in over a month. I'd visited him there once, but he sent me away, like he sent away everybody else. So I was nervous going back, as you might imagine. It never crossed my mind, though, not to go back.

When I arrived, Roy was working in the studio with his brother. In that cabin he used. He stumbled outside soon as he heard my car, and you should've seen him blink in the sun, like some barfly hitting the pavement at 7 in the morning. I didn't know how he'd react to seeing me again. At first it was positive, though. At first it was swinish, actually. He followed me into the house—he didn't help me carry any of my things, of course, he just followed me into the house and then he whipped out his equipment and wanted me to put it in my mouth. Right there. Just do it. No preliminaries. And I gave him what he wanted. I can't say gladly, but I gave it to him. Then ten seconds after he was done, he zipped up and went in the kitchen and got a bowl of popcorn and sat out on the porch, in the rocker. I hated him so much, more than I loved him, much more, but I loved him too, and I couldn't leave. I couldn't. And whose fault was that? My own! And I take responsibility for it.

That was a very shitty month, that August. Your chapter about it in the book doesn't really capture the particular madness, as I recall it. Roy was in rough shape, always having nosebleeds and falling down, getting high or tripping and drawing for days at a stretch like composers composing in those crazy Ken Russell movies. He'd crawl into my bed at 3 in the morning wanting instant sex, a complete blowjob, chop-chop, but half the time he'd demand it and then pass out. He hardly ever came. And he kept losing weight, he just got skinnier and skinnier, and I'll tell you, Clarky, I think he was trying to kill himself. That's my opinion. I really think he was trying to kill himself. And Roy's poor brother! It was so pathetic. At first Nick tried acting like everything was okay, he just ignored all the warning signs and went on inking Roy's stuff and talking about what they might draw together next. Poor Nick. Are you still in touch with him? I saw his name, too, in the Acknowledgments. I wonder what kind of a man he turned out to be. Poor Nicky. Poor <u>Clyde</u>.

By that Labor Day weekend, even he was coming apart at the seams, even quiet, mopey, woebegone Nick Looby was slowly going nuts. He stopped eating, he smoked 3, 4 packs a day, and hardly slept at all. Strange days. They worked in that cabin almost around the clock, but they never showed me a thing they were doing.

I got into this daily routine. I'd get up whenever I woke up, then I'd do my yoga and have a cup of tea, then read for an hour (I was reading Tolstoy on civil disobedience, and Simone de Beauvoir—but I remember wishing I'd brought something by Agatha Christie). Then I'd walk down to the river with my tube. Float around for a while just mulling things over—like what in the name of God was I doing there? Later I'd make lunch for the Loobys and leave it at their screen door. Knock-knock. Lunch is served. (They hardly touched anything, but still I went on making them lunch and dinner.) Then I'd go read some more. At first, I did a little drawing, but finally I quit. Just stopped. I wasn't really into it by then. There was no market anymore for my kind of comix. All that goopy love and peace junk. And of course <u>you</u> never would publish my stuff, Clarky. Comics are such a boys' thing, aren't they? Such a boys' <u>club</u>. But I won't get started on that.

So I just wasted my days at Camp Galoot, reading and tubing and watching the door of that cabin where they worked, just waiting for them to take a break. Nick took a lot more breaks than Roy ever did. He'd come out and sit with me if I was at the house, we'd sit on the porch, and he'd be all bleary. I'd ask him, "So how's it going?" and he'd say, "Oh, fine." He wouldn't tell me a blessed thing. "How's it going?" "Oh, fine." It was a riot. They were drawing a *comic book*, for heaven's sake, and we all acted like it was the Beatles making *Sgt. Pepper's*. I was jealous.

Every night I made myself useful, or at least available, to Roy, and I don't think he ever spoke a single word to me. Except maybe "Suck it."

I'd ask him if we could maybe jam together some night, in the kitchen. He could draw a panel, I could draw a panel, could we? Like we'd done for a while in Milwaukee and Chicago? "You want to maybe do a jam some night, in the kitchen?" "Suck it." I was pretty sure that Clyde was right outside the door, listening. Oh, I was always pretty sure of that. Jealousy recognizes jealousy.

But I've rambled on for too long, and it's past time to start supper and I want to get this into the mail. Congratulations again on the book! I just hope, for your sake, that not everybody in the world has forgotten Roy, like he forgot us.

Cordially,
"Cora"

P.S. I hope the Big River Press forwards your mail.
P.P.S. It's too late to make it into your book, Clarky, and you'll probably say why didn't she tell me this when she had the chance, but that night when Roy finally finished drawing "The Last Eugene"? He seemed like a completely different man when he came back to the house from his studio. And I don't just mean that he was relieved to be done, that's not what I mean. It's hard to put into words. But he seemed like a different person. A much nicer person, for one thing. I remember—and this will sound like the goopy old Purple Cora who used to draw the unicorns, but so be it: I remember how he reached out and touched my hair, he just put his hand on my hair and stroked it for a few seconds. He'd never done <u>that</u> before, or if he had he'd never done it with such <u>tenderness</u>, and I was filled with just incredible joy! I thought maybe he'd finally come around to thinking that I was (oh blush!) the girl for him. And then he went back to the cabin where Nicky had started to ink the last page, and I stood at my bedroom window and watched him walk down there, but then once he was inside there was all that terrible yelling, Nicky was just screaming at Roy, and that was such a shock. Nick had never even raised his voice the whole time I'd known him, but that night he was just screaming his lungs out at Roy. Yeah, I know what he says in your book, that he was just "whooping" it up, that he was just celebrating the completion of the book. But that's bull, Clarky. Total b.s. He was angry and he was yelling, that was no "whooping," brother. I couldn't hear what he was saying, but he was mad. After it quieted down in the cabin, I went to bed and fell asleep and the next day, Labor Day, Roy was gone.

P.P.P.S. For a long time I thought Nicky might've <u>killed</u> Roy and buried him somewhere in the woods—that's another thing I never told you. But I did think that. Or at least I thought it was possible. Well, because of all that screaming and yelling and then the next day Roy was gone. But that was just my gothic imagination. Roy just split, for whatever reason or reasons. And I hope he's still alive. I pray for him. I still do, every night. And I'm still kind of touched (whenever I think about it, which is not every day, believe me) when I remember the way Roy Looby touched my hair and looked at me the last time we were together. And now I really do have to go—my children must be starving to death. God bless you, Clarky.

                                              Undated (probably 1995),
                                                no return address

Dear Clarky,

    Here's your throat back, thanks for the loan. Enclosed pls. find a postal money order in the amount of $350. We're finally square. I ran into Elmer Howdy not too long ago and he told me you were living in New York with your sister. I didn't even know you had a sister. I thought about looking you up since I knew I'd be in NYC for a few days this week, but I finally decided no, better not. We'd only reminisce (sp?). And fuck that. I'm just passing through, staying with friends before I move back out to the Coast. Back to California! (But <u>not</u> San Francisco!)

    You wouldn't believe the turns my life has taken over the past few years. The last time I wrote you I was married, right? To my "Christian" husband? Yeah, well, that's history. And I won't bore you with all the details of my fucked-up (but INTERESTING) life since then. Whenever I take the time for an overview—which is not very often, since I always seem just to be responding to one crisis after another—but whenever I do get reflective, I think, "Holy shit, how did I get from there to here, from her to me?" You know? It's like I've been seven different people, at <u>least</u> seven, and who I am now, whoever the <u>hell</u> I am now, it's like those seven different people are all still me, but they've been scrambled up like Roy's jigsaw puzzle collage. Everybody changes, it's just that some people change more than others. How about you, Clarky? Have you changed? I almost hope I wouldn't know you if I met you again.

Yours truly,
The Woman Formerly Known as Cora Guirl

P.S. I saw your book remaindered at Coliseum Books up near Columbus Circle. A buck! They're selling it for a buck! Didn't I tell you, Clarky? Nobody gives a <u>hoot</u> about Roy Looby. Who even <u>remembers</u> the Imp Eugene?

Venable & Gurlecki
Literary and Talent Representation
14106 Wilshire Boulevard
Beverly Hills, California 90212
April 24, 2000

Dear Joel,

Saw this in today's *L.A. Times* and just had to cut it out immediately. Can you fucking believe it? Roy? After all this time? And in Virginia, of all places! Strange old world. Will wonders never cease? Do clichés ever die?

(signed) Cordelia Gurlecki

P.S. *Who?* Guess.
P.P.S. How you doin', Clarky? You doin' okay?
CG/kk
Encls.

CLARKY

IN

"NEXT SLIDE, PLEASE!"

Our old friend Joel Clark has found himself an actual paying job. A teaching job! Granted, it doesn't pay much, just over two grand for the spring semester, fourteen night classes, but still he'd like to see Mandy call him a lazy bum now, he'd like to see her just try! He's an adjunct professor at the New School for Social Research. What a racket! Paid to stand up here and talk about comics. To use a laser wand (he had to buy his own) and point out dynamic compositional elements in Harvey Kurtzman panels from *Two-Fisted Tales* and in old newspaper strips by George Herriman, Billy De Beck, Elzie Segar. Roy Crane. Winsor McCay. The whole gang! All the boys. All the great dead boys. "American Comics: A Social and Aesthetic History." Three credits.

Clarky looks forward, perhaps too much, to his weekly lectures. Always wears a clean and ironed white dress shirt. An acetate necktie printed with Nancy and Sluggo heads. His one and only charcoal suit. And he makes certain there's a hard, brilliant shine on his black oxfords. Some of the students call him Professor Clark or Dr. Clark. He never corrects them. They assume he has a Ph.D., and he never finished college. God bless America!

For three hours a week he gets to stand up here at the front of the classroom behind a lectern—a blond-wood lectern!—and pretend that other people give a flying fuck about his lifelong obsession. Heaven, he's in heaven. Even so, he'll sometimes let his bitter feelings gush out. But he really should watch that. Clarky doesn't want to alienate the students, the paying customers, the potential converts. He wants them all to like him, to go and demand that Dr. Clark be given other, similar courses to teach. He has already proposed "Chester Gould and Harold Gray: Expressionism in the Funnies" and "The Melting Pot and the Ink Pot: Race and Ethnicity in American Comics." So far, he hasn't gotten approval for either course. The administration keeps telling him he's being too "specialized." Would there be sufficient student interest? Probably not, thinks Clarky, but he keeps proposing the courses anyway. What else is he going to do? He's the Johnny Appleseed of American funnies, a proselytizer, an "unaffiliated comics scholar." And that's all he is. He just *knows* stuff.

He knows, for example, that "Comics today suck the Big Dick." That was one of the first things he told the class, back in January. He deliberately used "shocking language" to get their attention. "Newspapers," he said, "are murdering the funnies, shrinking them down and killing them off. And don't get me started on comic books! How many superheroes does one country *need*? No vision, ladies and gentlemen, no originality, style, no subversion! Just coffee mugs! And greeting cards! And Dilbert on a mouse pad! What a disgrace! What a shame! What a crime! Any questions? Questions?"

None.

Tonight: a rainy Monday evening, the twenty-fourth of April 2000. The classroom smells of damp clothes and wet shoes, and Clarky has been lecturing nonstop for over an hour. "Comix in Flux: The Sixties Underground Revolution" is what it says on the syllabus, and he's covered a lot of that ground quickly, setting the stage with some glib social history, poking fun at the Eisenhower fifties with its baby boomers growing up under the draconian Comics Code (he's made it sound like a tyranny comparable to that of the Khmer Rouge), a code that stated that no disrespect for authority could ever be shown in the panels of an American comic book. Then he talked about the "incendiary impact" of *Mad* magazine, which thumbed its nose at everything in American culture from shampoo and cigarette ads to Hollywood movies, baseball, politics, popular songs, and the national faith in gadgets and medicine—a magazine that was, in Clarky's considered opinion, more responsible for the "sixties" than the Kennedy assassination, the Cuban missile crisis, the civil rights movement, rock and roll, and Vietnam. Well, okay, maybe that's extreme, but it played a major role. Most of the predominantly white, middle-class kids (guys, almost entirely guys) who became the vanguard underground cartoonists of the late sixties and early seventies had grown up reading *Mad* and very likely those EC horror comics, too. Questions? Any questions? Then let's move on, said Clarky. We can thank (or we can blame, ha ha) the counterculture/antiwar/radical press in New York and Chicago, Milwaukee, Austin, San Francisco, and dozens of other cities for the proliferation of underground comix—that's i-x, said Clarky, not i-c-s. Alternative newspapers like the *East Village Other* and the *Berkeley Barb,* the *Texas Ranger* and the *Chicago Mirror* gave generous space and total freedom to a group of drug-fueled hippie cartoonists like Vaughn Bode, Robert Crumb, Kim Deitch, Art Spiegelman, S. Clay Wilson, and Spain Rodriguez. Clarky then spoke for a while about the psychedelic poster stores of San Francisco that refitted themselves into publishing companies to produce black-and-white comic books like *Zap* and *Bijou* for sale—along with incense, bead curtains, *The Whole Earth Catalog,* and dope paraphernalia—in hundreds of small head shops across the country. Almost sheepishly, he mentioned the Final Reckoning Press, his own "modest comix publishing venture," and—whew!—now that he's zoomed through all that history in seventy minutes, he's finally ready to slow down, saying, "From here on in this evening we'll examine in depth one single underground comic strip and its creator. And considering the story that some of you, I hope, saw in today's paper, it seems particularly apt. So if there aren't any questions—any questions? no?—then let's get started. Joy, would you take care of the lights? Thank you. Glen? Whenever you're ready. First slide, please."

As always, Clarky is relieved when the room goes dark. Under those merciless fluorescents, he feels conspicuous. He knows that students speculate about his weight (325? 350?) and stare in awe at his tree-trunk thighs, wondering if he can still have sex. (He probably *could.*)

In the dark, Clarky can forget that he even has a body. "Glen? Anytime you're ready." Ka-chunk. First slide.

The projected image that appears on the screen, initially blurry, then growing sharp, is a line drawing of a small, evilly grinning figure in a tatty black sport coat. Competent but several degrees shy of professional quality, the drawing was done on a sheet of white bond paper with a soft pencil and then partly inked (the sport coat and the blank eyes). "This is the earliest existing picture of the notorious Imp Eugene and dates back to late 1966, early 1967. A sketch, really. Please note the striped jersey as well as the black coat, and if you look carefully, right around this area, here, you can see there was once a hat of some sort on the figure's bald head. But it's been erased. Keep that in mind, as we go to—Glen, next slide, please? As we go to *this*. The eternal optimist, Derby Dugan."

This image—of a trussed-up little boy in a derby and a striped shirt being lowered by hook and tackle into a vat of hot candle wax— clearly has been isolated from a daily newspaper strip and is probably the last panel of the sequence since it contains both the date— 4/11/34—and the artist's florid signature: Walter Geebus.

"Do you see the resemblance?" says Clarky. "Glen? Can we go back to the previous slide, please? This first-ever sketch of the Imp Eugene was made by Roy Looby when he was around eighteen years old. And can anyone deny that Eugene, here, bears an uncanny resemblance to poor hapless Derby Dugan in his Depression-era prime? They could be one and the same! Except, of course, for a significant difference in attitude—as we shall see."

Clarky loves to lecture, to hear himself talk. He believes he has a talent for teaching. His sister Mandy claims he has a talent for never growing up, for being twelve at fifty-seven, twelve at fifty-eight, twelve at fifty-nine, but she's wrong. Since when do twelve-year-olds lecture in a college classroom? Though Clarky would admit that he's maintained, clung to, some youthful enthusiasms, he won't cop to being immature. No way. He's a grown-up. With a grown-up's high cholesterol, shortness of breath, and need to pee four, five times during the night.

"Next slide, please, Glen. Thank you. And now we have Eugene again, circa 1970 this time, in his final comic-book appearance. Note here the character's bowler hat, in lieu of a high-crowned derby—but otherwise? Could that not be Derby Dugan? Ignoring the giant erect phallus, just forgetting *that* for a moment—is this not the spitting image of Derby Dugan? But how did it happen? How did America's once-beloved and always optimistic little orphan boy turn into this—into this *maniac*? Well—"

"Dr. Clark?" There's a hand vigorously waving back and forth, second aisle to Clarky's left, third seat: oh, him, the nicotine fiend, the guy who gets up and slinks out of the room for a smoke every ten, fifteen minutes. "Dr. Clark, it's ten to nine, and we usually take our break at eight-forty-five."

Clarky would like to throw that prick right out the window but instead he smiles amiably, thanks him for the reminder, and says, "Let's take a short break here and when we come back—Roy Looby and *The Last Eugene*. Five minutes, people. Joy, can you get the lights?" By the time the fluorescents come flickering back on, Clarky is holding up a paperback copy of *The Last Eugene* in his left hand and a hardcover edition of *Nothin' Doin': The Imp Eugene and the Art of Roy Looby* in his right. Behind him, on his desk, are stacks of each title. "People? Just a reminder. Anyone interested in purchasing either or both of these extremely fine books, see me now or after class. I'd prefer cash, but I'll take a check." When there are no customers, he heads for the classroom door.

Smiling at the students milling in the hall, Clarky takes the stairs to the third floor and heads for the men's room there. He never uses the one downstairs, it would just seem . . . awkward taking a whiz alongside one of his students. Although the men's room is empty and he can have his pick of urinals, he stands at the one farthest from the door, then zones out. While relieving himself he does a little Zen thing . . . like Clarky knows from Zen.

"Professor?"

Startled, Clarky turns his head as Glen Tiner steps up to the urinal next to his. (Or maybe it's not "Tiner." He'd have to check the class roster, but for sure it's "Glen," Glen the volunteer slide projectionist.) A skinny kid in his early twenties, short-haired, slightly walleyed, with a pasty I-live-indoors complexion. Wearing a white T-shirt with *The Scream* printed in black on the front and dark-brown jeans. He says,

"Did you get a chance to look at any of that stuff I gave you last week?" Glen is an aspiring cartoonist, and "that stuff" is a twelve-page Xeroxed minicomic, a little item called *Local News*. "Don't think I'm rushing you, Professor Clark, but—"

"No, no, that's all right. And I had a glance-through, yes, but I'd like to sit down and take a more careful look. If you don't mind." Clarky zips up and moves to the sink, runs the water.

"Oh, sure," says the Tiner boy, "that'd be great, thanks." In the mirror Clarky can see him shaking his dick and then zipping up. "But what do you think from, like, just your *glance-through?*"

"Very nice, Glen. You draw well." And Clarky's not lying, either. The kid has talent, and thank God he's not wasting it drawing X-Men rip-offs or his own version of Spawn. But his work is so confessional, so autobiographical, so in-your-face that it's unnerving. Glen's character is named Glen, a short-haired, *very* walleyed twenty-year-old who works part-time in a video store, hates both his parents, fornicates with his girlfriend, cheats on his girlfriend, gets drunk with his pals, smokes dope, masturbates, reads comic books, and—that's it. That's about it for *Local News*.

As Clarky cranks down, then tears off a sheet of paper toweling, Glen steps up to the sink. He doesn't wash his hands but instead finger combs his hair in the mirror. "Do you have any comments? Like at *all*? I mean, I'm really serious about this. I can take it, I want criticism."

"And I'll give it to you, Glen. Just let me have another look."

"Yeah, sure. But if you have any *first* impressions."

Clarky feels a bolt of annoyance—don't bug me, kid! But then: "All right," he says. "Okay. I'm wondering—what's your mother going to think when she reads it?"

Glen looks astounded. "She's not *gonna* read it!"

"You sure? What about your girlfriend?"

"We're not together anymore. But no, what I'm really asking you about—"

"Maybe you should disguise yourself."

"What?" He follows Clarky out into the hallway and toward the staircase. "What?"

"It's all about disguise, Glen. It's all about wearing a mask. It's all about showing your face while you're wearing a mask."

"I'm not sure I get you."

"I'm talking about art, Glen."

"Yeah, well, I'm talking about comics. You got any *constructive* criticism?"

Whoa. The kid turns on Clarky just like that! Just like Roy Looby could. Like Roy *would* if you made even the slightest criticism ("This panel feels a little busy") or asked him any questions about his intent. He was so touchy. And this kid, this Glen Tiner, actually reminds Clarky of Roy in the old days: that sneer on his mouth and that shine of panic in his eyes. Oh Christ, yeah, very similar. Although he hadn't consciously realized it until now, he must've subconsciously noted the resemblance. Hasn't he shown favor to the little twerp—didn't he agree to read his stupid comic book, and let him operate the slide projector? Halfway down the stairs, Clarky stops and puts a hand on the railing. "Constructive criticism?" he says to Glen. "Okay. You draw too many close-ups in a row. Try some variety."

"But that's my strategy, that's my style!"

"Well, then," says Clarky, "go for it. Do whatever the hell you like. Which you're going to do anyhow, aren't you? Aren't you? You'll do exactly what you want, so what the hell does it matter what *I* think?"

Glen Tiner's face turns blotchy red, and his jaw drops. "Jump down my throat, why don't you? Jeez!"

Clarky has a brief impulse to apologize—he *should* apologize, that was completely uncalled for, but to hell with it. He's the teacher, he's Professor Clark, he *knows* stuff, he's in *charge.* "I think we'd better get back to class," he says. "The Imp awaits."

YOUNG GLEN TINER

IN

"MISANTHROPY 101"

At the rear of the semidark room, standing beside a humming slide projector, Professor Clark is saying, "Escape, ladies and gentlemen, that finally is what this crazy thing is all about. Misanthropy, magic, cannibalism, memory, disguise, and escape. Not too shabby for a shitty little comic strip, eh?" That gets a laugh (polite, deferential, disingenuous) from everyone in the class except Glen Tiner. Escape? he thinks. Disguise? *Cannibalism?* Fairly certain it's a load of crap, he nonetheless writes it all down. Then he puts away his Bic, and using only thumb and first finger, he slowly removes a junky pink plastic hairbrush from a cloth shoulder bag hung on the back of the desk in front of him. His heart is going nuts, but you'd never know it. His face is mild and serene as a yogi's. The bag and brush belong to a chubby young woman with a drastic crew cut and artsy-fartsy wire earrings. A sweet perfume wafts off her neck, where there are several large black moles. Glen has a deep prejudice against people with moles, who knows why. He quietly unsnaps his own bag—he's been lugging around the same algae-green carryall with him since junior high—then lifts the flap and jams the brush inside, stashing it down among his sketchbooks, a spring-water bottle filled with Hawaiian Punch, a sleeve of

Chips Ahoy!, and several videos (*Barton Fink, Bugsy, Oral Love Girls, Fangs of the Vampire IV*) that he lifted earlier today from the Blockbuster where he clerks. Also stuffed in there are thirty getting-dog-eared copies of *Local News # 1*, his hand-stapled minicomic. (Tomorrow, he might just draw up this little theft, this *episode,* include it in the latest autobiographical strip that he's been working on; he'll give it two panels.)

Since he was twelve—the same age when he began drawing comics, drawing them at first because he needed something that could, every so often, catch the attention of his parents and flick it away from his big sister's ice skating prowess—since then, since he was a kid in western Connecticut balanced on the brink of puberty, Glen Tiner has been an occasional klep, swiping one or two Christmas cards on display in his Aunt Judy's living room, a miniature Phillips head screwdriver from a neighbor's garage, twelve-inch rulers, Mars bars, and confiscated yo-yos from Brother Damian's classroom desk at the parochial high school. Later, living on his own in New York City, he might pocket a card of sinus tablets from somebody's medicine cabinet during a party or a pack of razor blades from Gristede's. Always there was, and still is, the heart-racketing moment of taking, followed by a long, satisfying buzz of possession. It's practically the same claque of feelings, arriving in the same order, that he gets whenever he draws. He'll pick up his pencil and then all at once feel a body throb of self-contempt, of guilt and panic, and a prickly fear of ruin. But once he's started, once he's actually drawn something? Man, oh man, king of the world. So weird, truly weird, but stealing stuff and drawing comics? Give him an identical kick. They could almost be, at root, the same damn thing. But Glen won't delve into that, it's not in his nature. He's not a psychologist, dude.

Which is maybe why Glen Tiner has such a problem tonight with all this Roy Looby shit. Escape? Disguise? Memory? Cannibalism? And what the fuck is misanthropy? He could raise his hand and ask but suspects that everyone else already knows the definition. He fears they might all just look at him and smirk, and who needs that? All his life, practically, he's been getting those smirky looks, those rolling eyeballs. From neighbors. Rich kids at school (and not-so-rich ones, too). His mother. His father. His sister, Kendra. All right, so he's never been what you'd call a good student, he could never throw a ball or hit one, either, or put together model airplanes that didn't end up looking like they'd crashed, and no, he couldn't ice-skate, he couldn't *roller*-skate, and forget about tennis, even though for a while he'd tried his best. In this world, dude, in this *country,* you get those looks if you don't go along with the crowd. This is America, ain't it? Ain't this America? Glen heard a stand-up comic on Comedy Central say that once; actually, the guy kept saying it over and over, it was part of his act, his riff, his shtick, he'd punctuate his most cynical observations with it, and for a while Glen used the same phrase in his daily life, he sampled it, adopted it, made it his mantra whenever something shitty happened or something unjust or plain stupid. Like when he got suspended from high school for carrying Tylenol? He said to the principal, "If I got a headache, I got a right to get rid of it. This is America, ain't it? Ain't this America?" For wising off, Glen was bounced for an additional week. This world, man, this country, this *America.* Forget about it. Thank Christ he found comics. *They* were despised, *he* was despised: perfect match.

And now he wonders what brought all that on. "Misanthropy." Right. Misanthropy. No way is he going to raise a hand and ask what it means. Besides, he's ticked off at that fat-fuck professor. "Too many close-ups." What kind of bullshit constructive criticism was that? Plus, Glen is royally pissed at Professor Clark for taking over at the slide pro- jector. That was *his* job. He's been handling it every week of the semester, he volunteered the first night, said, "Me! I'll do it," but now suddenly the fat prick wants to show his own slides, what's that? Glen hates sitting in a desk, he just hates it. He taps his foot a mile a minute, he wants to stand up, jump up, he wants to punch that little button on the slide clicker. He's been *usurped* and that sucks. (Usurp. U-s-u-r-p. Usurp. A never-to-be-forgotten word; first place, all-city spelling bee, April 1991. A triumph, man. Glen didn't see any sneers *that* day. But then, neither did he see his parents in the auditorium; they were off at another rink, another fucking competition with Kendra, Kendra, stupid Kendra.)

Ticked off that he's been usurped at the slide projector, Glen thinks now that he might just leave. Hell with this class. This is all such bull- shit tonight anyway, all this Imp Eugene baloney. Just because there's something in today's paper about this Roy Looby dude (what it says, exactly, Glen has no idea and couldn't care less)—because this old fucker is mentioned in the stupid paper today, the class has to sit here in the dark and listen to Professor Clark gas about the Imp Eugene. Glen Tiner has never heard of the Imp Eugene, and even though he'd never heard of most of the dead comic strips that Professor Clark yammered about in previous classes ("Little Nemo in Slumberland," "Polly and Her Pals," "Krazy Kat," "Smokey Stover," "Derby Dugan," all that ancient history), for some reason he can't quite put his finger on, this particular one gives him a superqueasy feeling. Maybe because it's one of those hippie strips from the 1960s, maybe because Glen is sick and tired of hearing about the sixties. Who cares?

All his life until the great day when he packed a bag and motored, he had to listen to the old man tell him how great the Beatles were, the Rolling Stones, Aretha Franklin, the Byrds, the Doors, the Jefferson Airplane, all those *dinosaurs*; Glen had to sit there and listen to him talk about the antiwar movement, boasting how he'd helped "close down the university." Yeah? So what? You know? So fucking what? Age of Aquarius. Age of *Assholes*.

Clunk!

The sound of a new slide dropping snaps Glen alert; he looks up and toward the screen, filled now with a collage of different bald-headed cartoon boys. "In the upper left-hand corner," says Professor Clark, "is our friend the Yellow Kid, circa 1896. Richard Outcault's Yellow Kid. And proceeding clockwise from there, we have George Wreckage's Pinfold . . . Carl Anderson's Henry . . . and Little Lulu's pal Iggy. Next, there's Connie, from 'Terry and the Pirates,' and Casper the Ghost, and, of course, Charlie Brown, from the 'Peanuts' strip. Just a small sampling, ladies and gentlemen. Over the past hundred years, the bald-headed boy with the stick-out ears has been a staple, a pattern, a *presence* in American comics, appearing, flourishing, vanishing, then reappearing. He's always different yet always the same. Picked on and preyed on, the punch line, the punching bag. And the more he suffers, the more we like him. Sadists that we are."

Ha-ha goes the class while Glen tries to decide whether or not he finds this stuff at all interesting. Well, yeah, kind of. So he picks up his Bic and jots: "Bald. 100 years."

Clunk!

Another collaged slide: Derby Dugan again, side by side with the Imp Eugene.

"So if we look at the bald kid as possibly the oldest and certainly the most consistent archetype in American funnies, then the Imp Eugene seems less like a direct swipe from Derby Dugan and more like a part of the natural continuum, yes?"

If you say so, dude, thinks Glen Tiner.

"But at the same time," says Professor Clark, "Eugene with his shabby coat and his striped shirt and his bowler hat certainly resembles Derby Dugan a heckuva lot more closely than he resembles, say, Charlie Brown. Yet while the visual influence is direct and undeniable, Roy Looby's Eugene is the antithesis and a virtual repudiation of everything that Derby Dugan represented during that adventure strip's sixty-five-year run in newspapers. To put it simply, Derby was forever *heading* somewhere, hoping, even expecting, to find a nourishing meal to eat, preferably scrambled eggs. But Eugene, the Imp Eugene, was always running from wherever he'd been, hoping but never expecting that at the next place he paused to catch his breath he wouldn't be *eaten*. Derby lived in a nation of solid citizens where a few bad apples caused all the trouble, while Eugene lived in a country of greedy, grasping cannibals. And of course, Derby Dugan had his talking dog as a constant companion while the Imp Eugene traveled alone."

Glen jots "Alone," then his chin brushes against his chest, and . . .

Zzzzzzzzzzzzzzzzzzzzzzzzzzzzzzzzzzzzzzzzzzz

He flinches awake suddenly, figuring that, at most, he dozed for a minute or two, but—ah God, he hopes he didn't snore. His last two (no, three) girlfriends all told him he snored so loud they couldn't sleep. (Yeah? Well, screw them. Take me like I am or, like, just forget it.) Subtly, he glances to both his left and right, but nobody seems to be smirking. Instead, they're pensively staring straight ahead at the slide screen. At a black-and-white Imp Eugene comic-book panel. The Imp snoozing (hey, what a coincidence!) on a sofa, while three lumpish and practically identical figures (they remind Glen of the Pillsbury Dough Boy in triplicate) surround him with irritable expressions on their faces. And Professor Clark is droning, ". . . first few stories, which he drew shortly before leaving New Jersey and taking up residence for a while in Milwaukee, are fairly trivial things, interesting to us now only because they *are* the first ones. Even so, even then, all of the classic elements are fixed. So is the premise. And as in most great comics, the premise is simplicity itself."

Glen Tiner sits up straight. Simplicity? About freaking time!

"Eugene," says Professor Clark, "is some sort of magic boy, perhaps a visitor from the moon or perhaps just special or gifted, who knows? In these early stories, which are only two or three pages long, the Imp amuses himself by conjuring things—a sandwich, a Mustang convertible, a Duke Ellington record and an old Victrola to play it on.

"The Imp was magic, could *do* magic, and everyone else? Wasn't. And couldn't. This, as we'll see, introduced the central conflict of the series—jealousy. From the start, everyone around Eugene was intensely, insanely jealous of his magic powers, and their clumsy attempts to make him ply his magic for their own benefit provide the comedy—mostly slapstick—that fueled the earliest stories.

"Which brings us to Woozy, Floozy, and Claude, those three blobby-looking creatures you see before you now on the screen. Who, or what, these uglies actually were was never made clear. Originally, they lived in the same house as Eugene, but why they did and whether the Imp was their guest or their host, we never get a hint. They were simply there, always pestering the hell out of our hero. 'Show me how you do your magic, Eugene!' says Claude, the one that wears glasses. 'Heal me, Eugene—come on, be a pal!' says Woozy, the one with the bandaged head, the broken arm, the crutch. 'Hey, Eugene, babycakes, use your magic to build me a palace,' says Floozy, the one with breasts. Gimme, gimme, gimme. And Eugene, much to their disgruntlement, always says no. Or, in the phrase that's most often associated with the strip, 'Nothin' doin'!' Woozy, Floozy, and Claude drive him crazy with their endless demands, and he drives them crazy right back by refusing ever to meet them. These early stories, a veritable orgy of selfishness, are amusing enough and occasionally quite funny, but it's not until one of the last strips that Roy Looby drew in New Jersey that the premise takes on its most significant, and mature, elements."

Clunk!

Even Glen has to laugh now, along with most of the others in the class, as the slide that comes slowly into focus—presumably an image that is emblematic of Eugene's "most significant, and mature, elements"—turns out to be a nine-panel sex page. "All right, all right," says Professor Clark with a note of exasperation in his voice, "can we, can we, can we please see past our prurience? Thank you.

"Although not published till 1968," he continues, "this particular story, entitled 'Bite and Swallow,' was actually drawn in March of 1967. (Fortunately for us, Roy Looby had the habit of dating his work, usually noting the completion date in the last panel of a story.) Note here the vastly improved draftsmanship, the balanced compositions, the confidence in the figure work, but also note—and I gather you all have—that this is the first time Eugene clearly exists in the precincts of what would shortly come to be known as 'underground comics.' Previous to this, the Imp Eugene might well have appeared in a family newspaper or a children's comic book. From here on out, though, anything goes. Adults only.

"In panel one"—a thin red beam shoots across the room now from Professor Clark's pointer, tapping the upper left-hand quadrant of the pull-down screen—"we find Eugene lounging outdoors in a hammock, his magic right hand lifted idly above his smiling face. And skulking behind a tree in the foreground are his three nemeses. In panel two we see the Imp Eugene has conjured up a five-piece jazz band in his own backyard. (Incidentally, the musicians pictured here were copied from a 1924 photograph of King Oliver's Creole Jazz Band. That's Louis Armstrong, third from the left.) So, we have the band playing and Eugene smiling as he listens. In case you're wondering, those notes peppering the air, those clef notes and so on, are completely random and bogus; obviously Roy Looby didn't know his ass from his elbow when it came to musical notation. Anyhow, the band is playing, Eugene is smiling—and we see Floozy creeping toward the hammock.

"And in panel three, a little history, ladies and gentlemen, an historic first in the Looby canon: full frontal nudity. Floozy has shed all her clothes to reveal a rather, shall we say, Amazonian physique. And judging by the exclamation mark that's materialized above Eugene's head, the Imp is just as surprised as the reader by her brazen striptease."

Glen Tiner writes: "Panel three. Tits. First time."

"In panel four," says Professor Clark, "Roy Looby's surreal visual wit asserts itself as the Imp plucks down the exclamation point, sticks it between his legs, and—"

With a noisy exhale of disgust, the heavyset mole-girl seated in front of Glen Tiner abruptly stands up, grabs her bag, slings it on her shoulder, and galumphs toward the classroom door, momentarily cutting across the projector's white light and casting a huge, scary-monster shadow on the slide screen. The door slams behind her.

"Anybody else?" asks Professor Clark, and there's more laughter, but not much. "Then let me just pause here for a moment and point out to you all that while I, like that scandalized young lady, might—in fact, do—find much of the sexual content in the Imp Eugene mythos—"

Mythos? thinks Glen Tiner. What the—?

"—to be vulgar and obnoxious, even disturbing, it is never, in my opinion, gratuitous. Well, sometimes. But rarely ever. There's plenty of it, plenty of very graphic sex, throughout the stories that appeared in 1968, '69, and '70, but nearly all of it, in keeping with the prevailing theme of the work, is strictly transactional."

That does it. Glen is outta here, he's leaving, he's not going to put up with any more of this big-word bullshit; he didn't sign up for a class about *comic strips* only to feel stupid. If he wanted to feel stupid he could've stayed in high school. Comics aren't supposed to make him feel dumb, but that's how this fat bastard is making Glen feel. Dumb as a post, like what his grandmother used to call him. "Transactional?" Screw transactional. Glen is outta here, right now. In fact, he's rising from his desk when Professor Clark suddenly says, "And what do I *mean* by transactional? Simply that in Eugene's world, sex is always portrayed as a grudging negotiation, a kind of business exchange, each party wanting something from the other."

Oh. Well, why didn't he just say that in the first place? thinks Glen, slowly settling back into his desk.

"Here," says Professor Clark, "in this first-ever sex scene, which comprises panels four through nine, we can already see that transactional process at work. Eugene sticks the exclamation point between his open legs to create a giant phallus and Floozy leaps readily upon it. Et cetera. *But.* While the Imp—to use sixties parlance—just wants to get his rocks off, notice, please, all the images crowding the female's busy thought balloons. What do we see? We see a house, we see cars, we see cash, we see a barbecue grill crowded with sizzling hamburgers. And of course, what's most obvious here, we see the female's facial expression change to one of extreme avidity—"

Damn, thinks Glen.

"—and finally to shrewd calculation, till, in the last panel on the page, she opens her mouth wide, displaying a full set of needle-sharp teeth. Teeth which—"

Clunk!

"—on the first panel of the following page, she uses to bite a huge chunk of flesh out of Eugene's throat. Cannibalism, at last, enters the series. Cannibalism and *escape*. Eugene flies off that hammock and then—as the reader's eye moves rapidly from panel to panel to panel—he runs away spurting blood and swearing a blue streak of ampersands, asterisks, and exclamation points. In later stories, those typographical marks would be replaced by good old Anglo-Saxon four-letter words.

"From this point on, the Imp saga plays fluid variations on a rigid theme. Because Eugene won't give them what they want, Woozy, Floozy, and Claude—sometimes independently, other times working as a team—decide just to take it. If they can catch Eugene, they can eat him, and if they eat him, well, they can have his magic. So they think. Run and chase, run and chase . . . till suddenly the strip changes from a domestic one to a picaresque." (A picturesque *what*? thinks Glen.) "In a five-pager entitled 'Footloose Eugene,' the Imp runs completely away, to another city, and from then on out, in story after story, he just keeps going, keeps moving, and the three blobby irritants disappear from the cast. But everyone else that he meets on his travels—be it a chicken-headed girl in the big city or a gang of stagecoach-robbing dog-headed outlaws in the Wild West—everyone eventually sees the Imp as a nourishing meal. A free meal.

"In these stories—and all told, there are just twelve of them—published in a variety of underground comic books, including Roy Looby's own title, *Lazy Galoot,* Eugene employs, to quote a caption from one of the strips, 'disguise, deceit, and eventually his feet' to survive in a dangerous land of Imp-hungry cannibals. Questions? Then let's go on to the next slide, shall we? Here we now have the opening page from Roy Looby's final creation, *The Last Eugene,* the long, baffling collage-like story they say is 'cursed.' And what do we see? We see the Imp huddled naked in the corner of a—yes, Glen, you have a question?"

"Yeah, I, uh, do." I do? "Where does the, um . . ." Where does the, um, *what*? Glen has no idea what he wants to ask, he just knows that he wants to ask something. Needs to. But why did he raise his hand? He didn't mean to, it just . . . went up. His heart is racing, you'd think he'd just shoplifted—or sat down to draw. "Where does . . . the misanthropy come in? Where does *that* come in?"

"Good question," says Professor Clark. "But let me turn it around, okay, and ask *you* a question."

Oh fuck, thinks Glen.

"If people treated *you* like a piece of tasty meat, wouldn't you *hate* them?"

"Hate them?"

"Wouldn't *you* be misanthropic?"

"Oh!" says Glen. (Lightbulb on!) "Yeah, sure," he says. "Sure I would. Absolutely! Yeah. Right! I'd hate their guts." He snorts, laughs, nods his head. "Cool."

"Any further questions? Yes, Mrs. Hoffman?"

Oh God, *her*. The old bat with permed snow-white hair whom Glen Tiner dubbed "Snooty Grandma" the second or third night of class after she'd interrupted Professor Clark's lecture on "Women in the Funnies" to inquire how he could possibly suggest that Wonder Woman was a role model for teenage girls of the 1940s when all she ever seemed to do was tie men up in golden ropes or heavy chains (and Mrs. Hoffman did not appreciate the general chuckling that her comment provoked). "This may sound quaint and naive to anyone under sixty," she says now, "but why does Eugene refuse to give those lumpy whatevers at least a little bit of what he has? Misanthropic for what reason? Do you see what I'm saying? What's *he* got to be misanthropic about?"

"Good question, Mrs. Hoffman. And if we look closely at the stories, we can't really identify any specific—"

"Because from what I've seen here, this little stinker strikes me as nothing but a selfish egomaniac. No wonder the hippies took him to heart."

Feeling a spasm of unexpected anger, Glen says, "Hey, lady, they tried to eat him!"

"But only after he wouldn't lift a finger to help them."

"Yeah? But why should he?" says Glen. "Who says he has to?"

"And that is precisely my point," replies Snooty Grandma. "He doesn't *have* to do anything, just as you say. But you'd think he might *want* to from time to time."

"Good point," says Professor Clark, "very good point. This is clearly not a humanistic comic strip, is it?"

"No, it's not," says the old bat, "and I'd go further and add that it's very definitely pornographic."

"I have to disagree with you, Mrs. Hoffman."

"The proof is in the pudding, Dr. Clark. You've been showing us filthy pictures for the past ten minutes, and if I didn't find them all so offensive, I might think your highfalutin analysis was pretty darn funny. It's a dirty comic strip, Dr. Clark, as crude and dirty as those so-called Tijuana Bibles you were talking about a few weeks ago."

"Well, there again, I have to—"

"And what sort of *artist* names his most important female character Floozy?"

"Good question, Mrs. Hoffman, but often in satirical literature—"

"This is hardly literature, for heaven's sake."

"Whoa whoa whoa whoa, *whoa*," says Glen Tiner, and he is on his feet now, he's leaped up and is standing in the aisle beside his desk, chopping the air with an arm, staccato chopping while his temples throb. "Lady, you just don't get it!"

"Glen," says Professor Clark. "There's no need to take that tone. Let's all just discuss."

"That's what I'm doing, I'm discussing. 'It's not literature, for heaven's sake'? And *I'm* saying, What's literature, lady? Some books that nobody reads or, like, *wants* to read. You ever try to read *The Crucible*? Or *Jane Eyre*? What *is* that shit? But if you don't like it, man, if you can't get *through* it, what happens? They flunk you. That's not literature, man, that's terrorism! And they look at you like you're a jerk, like you're a fool, like you're dumb as a *post*. But who cares? Because that stuff is not literature, it's just *old*. Pilgrims, man. Some nutty wife in the attic! I know this stuff, I read it mostly, and it's, like, boring. But I'll tell you what *is* literature, man, it's anything that cuts straight through all the crap and gets right down to the—like right down to the *heart* of things." (What is happening here? What is he saying? Why is he doing this? Doing and saying all this stuff when all that's going to happen, for sure, is that he'll be sneered at in the end. God, fuck it.) "Filthy? Pornographic? Deal with it, lady, it's the truth! So it's got pictures, so what? So there's humpin', so what? So this guy Eugene won't give those pesty fuckers a piece of himself, what's wrong with that? He's smart, man."

"Glen, that's enough. Sit down."

"Eugene is smart. Very smart. And anybody with, like, native intelligence could tell you why. You want to know why?"

"Glen!"

"I'll tell you why! You offer yourself to somebody else? Anybody? Everybody? They're gonna laugh in your face! They don't want you. They don't want *it*. They don't! It can't be any good if you're just giving it away. If you want to give it away, it can't be worth dick. You know what I'm saying? This is the truth that *I* see here, lady, that I see right up there on that screen. They don't really want you to give them anything for free, or just for the damn hell of it, or just because you *want* to. No way. This is, um, this is, ah . . . this is what we learn from *true* literature. To say 'nothin' doin' ' and feel good about it."

"Glen?" says Professor Clark. "Maybe you want to step outside for a couple of minutes? Calm yourself down?"

"Don't *usurp* me, all right? *I'm* talking now! *I* got the floor! I paid tuition. And I—you say, you go, Here, here, take this, I want to give you this. Doesn't matter what, it's a model airplane, it's a cocksucking slide projector, it's twenty words you can spell in a row, it's some picture that you drew, it's your freaking *shoulder*. It's a gift, it's free. I'm *giving* it to you. But you know what? They'll say, Keep it, we don't want it, and you'll be left standing there like a jerk. Give nothing away! Nothing! And if that's 'misanthropic,' no prob. *That's* what Eugene can *teach* us, man. Screw everybody!"

Now his mouth is shut and his mind suddenly goes blank. Even in the ashy dark, Glen still can see what's happening, can see all the silhouettes, all the dumb fucks in silhouette, each head turned toward him. He wants to vanish, he wants to. He wants to. He wants to run.

OLLIE THE ROOMMATE
IN
"WHAT'S GOIN' ON?"

It's a long trudge up, and by the time Ollie Ruhl makes it to the fifth floor, he's out of breath, he's gasping. Black specks bounce and collide in front of his face. Damn, he's only twenty-two, he should be in way better shape, he has got to start working out. But when's he going to find time? This morning he left the apartment around quarter of four, and what's it now, ten, ten-thirty? But this is what he wanted, wasn't it? To work on a professional shoot. A feature film? To get experience, see how it's done? Yeah, sure, but driving a panel truck all over the five boroughs to pick up and drop off props (lamps, carpets, vases, machine guns) isn't exactly what he had in mind. No, but it's a start. Even though *Speak Low, Die Loud* is a dumb low-budget thriller that's probably headed straight to video, the job could lead to something better, right? So quit complaining and just breathe. Leaning back against the wall, which probably hasn't been painted since the nineteenth century, Ollie takes off his chunky black Elvis Costello glasses, unsmudges both lenses with his T-shirt. Then he gets out his door key and waits for Karla to drag her butt up. If he's out of shape, she's fifty times worse. She looks good, though. A little skinnier than he'd prefer, but she has that great red hair, genuine red, not dyed, and she knows how to—

"When. Are you going. To *move?*" Here she is now, half dead, practically crawling up the last few steps. "If I meet some cute first-floor guy, Ollie, you're gonna be shit outta luck."

"It's good for your heart."

"Yeah, right." She follows him down the short hall to his apartment—5B—and then stands behind him, leaning with her forehead pressed against his neck, while Ollie fits the key in the lock. "Any chance comic-book boy's not home?"

"Fingers crossed." Before pushing open the door, Ollie turns and plants a kiss on the top of Karla's head. Man, he does love a redhead. "Glen? Female on the floor!"

No Glen, but dumped on the kitchen table is Glen's filthy green knapsack, with the flap laid open. Most of its contents are spilled out in a jumble: water bottle filled with red juice, woman's hairbrush, empty Gillette razor bubble pack, several videos in blue rental boxes, and, of course, multiple copies of the dweeb's stupid "minicomic," the one he's been hawking on the street for the past two months because no comic-book shop in Manhattan would take it on consignment. The one that drove Ollie Ruhl up the freaking wall when he first saw it. "Draw what you want, man, but don't drag *me* into it." If Glen Tiner wasn't such a loser, Ollie might've put a fist through his stupid face. "Don't you know anything about privacy, man? You want to draw yourself whacking off, go ahead, but don't you ever dare fucking draw *me* again, you hear? Fucking voyeur." Jesus. Open a comic book and there's somebody named "Ollie the Roommate" acting rowdy at a topless bar, grabbing a dancer, being knocked flat on his ass by the giant bouncer. Ollie felt violated and very embarrassed. Yeah, and so what does dweeby Glen say? "It happened, man, didn't it? It's local news, man. Nobody owns the local news." What're you going to do with a guy like that? Yeah, so it happened, so what? That don't mean it's news, but what was the use of trying to explain anything to Glen Tiner? "Just don't do it again," Ollie told him. "And P.S., your drawings suck." (But that was just a low-blow coda—actually, they were pretty good. Glen definitely had talent. Jerks, Ollie supposed, sometimes did. I mean, look at the film industry.)

"Guess he's out," says Karla. "Good deal." As she passes Ollie on her way to the fridge, she gives him a playful squeeze on his ass. "What d'you got to drink?"

"There's beer."

"What else you got?" Karla snoops, then reaches in finally and takes out a can of Cherry Coke.

"I can't believe he's not here. Glen?" Ollie turns to go through the dinky living room, saying, "I bet you he's back there drawing," but Karla glides suddenly in front of him, blocking the way. She puts her arms around his neck and plants an open-mouthed kiss on his lips.

"We got the place to ourselves."

Ollie finds that hard to believe. "He's in his room, I'll bet. Fucking voyeur."

Karla knows about Ollie's cameo appearance in *Local News* #1. Two weeks ago, somebody on the crew, one of the sound guys, got hold of a copy and passed it around, and that whole day long Ollie had to smile at the jibes, the cracks, the kidding, even though, inside, he was royally pissed. Turned out all right, though, in the end. This whole good thing with Karla might never have started if it hadn't been for Glen's invasion of his privacy. She'd made some teasing remark about Ollie's penchant for titty bars, and he'd pled guilty but he swore—"to *God*, Karla!"—it was the first and only time he'd ever gone to one. And besides, he was drunk, which he additionally swore that he very rarely was. She leaned through the window of the quilted-aluminum catering van, handed him a cheese sandwich in Saran Wrap, and said, "You doing anything later tonight?" Which just goes to prove, right? That bad shit, even a shitty little comic book, can have unforeseen positive effects. Still, Glen Tiner is a first-class jerk, and if Ollie Ruhl could afford the rent by himself, he'd boot him the hell out.

Karla is tickling him now, her fingers running up and down his waist. Stepping away, out of his arms, she says, "Wanna get nekkid?"

Man, is this girl great, or what?

"Yeah, sure, but let me just check that he's really not here."

She rolls her eyes. "While you do that, I'm gonna go pee." Which means Karla has to walk back out and traipse halfway down the hall, because that's where the stupid toilet is. Some swank place. Toilet in the hall, tub in the kitchen.

After she's gone out, Ollie nudges—cautiously nudges—open Glen's bedroom door, steps inside, then stops dead. It's like that scene in ten million crime movies (there's even that scene in *Speak Low, Die Loud*), the one where the good guy comes home and discovers the place "ransacked." The cracked linoleum floor and the futon are strewn with sheets and ribbons of torn paper, and when it dawns on Ollie Ruhl that it's not just any paper but the good bristol board that Glen has been drawing on lately—when he realizes that what's been torn up is all the work that Glen has finished, or partly finished, for the second issue of *Local News*—when Ollie sees *that,* his stomach tightens and he mutters, "Oh shit." He glances around, half expecting to find his roommate's bloody corpse.

Instead, he sees, pinned up on the bedroom walls, several dozen pages torn from a black-and-white comic book. Appearing in panel after small panel is the same little character in a bowler hat, a hat that keeps shooting straight up from his bald head whenever somebody—a Michelin man (or maybe just a reasonable facsimile) with great big glasses, or a girl with a chicken's head, or a dog-headed cowboy dressed all in black, or a pig in a tunic—tries to grab him from behind.

Ollie's head is throbbing like it used to after he'd sniff model-airplane glue in a paper bag when he was an asshole thirteen-year-old in Queens. He suddenly pivots around and walks over to Glen's canted drawing table. Tacked down at all four corners is a large sheet of slightly textured drawing paper covered with quick sketches in grease crayon. Ollie recognizes both the artist—it's Glen's work all right—and the character. It's that little comic-book character in the bowler hat. The guy who's running like crazy in all of the pictures on all of the pages tacked to the walls.

At the top of Glen's table is a hardcover book—one of those coffee-table-size jobbies—with a red dust jacket: *Nothin' Doin': The Imp Eugene and the Art of Roy Looby.* By Joel Clark.

When Ollie picks it up, it flips open to where there's an uncapped highlighter lying slantwise across the page; he tosses that on the table and reads: Chapter X: The Last of Eugene . . . and Looby. "As much for its temporal and spatial disjunctions as for its fizzling finale, *The Last Eugene* found few champions among comics aficionados following its eventual publication in 1972." Blah blah blah.

"Hey, you. Forget about me or something?"

Ollie looks up at Karla the same moment her lusty big smile closes down. As she registers all the torn-up paper, the shambles, Ollie registers Karla's nakedness. Which strikes him as almost macabre, damn it.

She says, "What the fuck?" and Ollie says, "I think Glen must've done it himself."

"Yeah, well, we can ask him. He's in the bathroom and he won't come out."

"What?"

"I said he's down the hall."

"You talked to Glen?"

"How else would I know it's him? Yeah, I talked to him." Karla seems to remember suddenly that she's stripped off all her clothes, and gives a little shrug. "The best-laid plans," she says, "so to speak," and laughs. "I locked him out."

"Who? Glen?"

"I figured, well, *he's* busy, why not enjoy ourselves. And if he wants to come back in, he'll just have to wait till we're done. We're doing him a favor, you know? He could draw it in his comic book: the night you locked him out to fuck your girlfriend."

Ollie's smile comes a few seconds too late.

"Yeah, well," says Karla. "That was the *idea*. Although it doesn't look like ol' Glen is gonna be *do*ing his comic book anymore. Why'd he rip it up?"

"Shit if I know."

She walks to Ollie, leans in, and kisses him. "Maybe you wanna go talk to him?"

Ollie nods. First he'll talk to him. Then he'll *strangle* him.

He stalks through the apartment and out the door into the hall.

"Glen?"

No answer, so Ollie knocks on the toilet door. Still no answer, but the sink taps are running. Now they're off, and there's a quiet splash. "Glen, I know you're in there, man. You sick?"

"I'm fine."

"So open the door."

"Nothin' doin'."

"What happened to your room, man? You do that?"

"Leave me alone, Ollie. Stop pestering me. I'll come out when I come out."

"Why'd you tear up your stuff, man?"

"Because it was shit. I didn't know dick, but now I do."

"Now you know what?" Should he call the cops? Bellevue? "*What* do you know, Glen?"

"That it's all about fucking misanthropy." There's another splash, followed by a scraping sound. "And cannibalism."

"Glen?"

Silence. Splash. Scrape. Splash.

"Go away, Ollie."

"Hey, come on. If something's wrong, I'll help you, man. But you got to *tell* me."

"NOTHIN' DOIN'!"

"Then fuck you, asshole."

"Fuck *you,* cannibal!"

Ollie gives the toilet door a sudden kick, then bangs it once with his fist. When he goes back in the apartment, he finds Karla still in Glen's room. She's facing the far wall, peering closely at the last page in the row of tacked-up comic-book pages. Ollie's eyes jump quickly from panel to panel, from tier to tier: the guy in the bowler walking in a ditch beside a dirt road, coming to a clearing in the woods, walking up to a small cabin on stilts, climbing to the porch, crawling in through an open window . . .

Now there's movement, a sound, behind them, and when they both turn it's Glen Tiner—with a pair of scissors clutched in one fist and a safety razor in the other—standing in the doorway. His shirtfront is wet, and his skull, his *bald* skull, is bleeding freely from half a dozen places where he nicked it shaving.

"Glen . . . ?" says Ollie.

Glen just stares at the tall guy with the black-framed eyeglasses and the buck-naked girl with the large, heavy breasts—he stares at them till his eyes widen in horror. The moment Karla takes a tentative step toward him, Glen turns and runs like hell. Through the apartment and down the hall, down the stairs and out the front door and into the street.

And then? Then, just like that, Glen Tiner is gone.

TRAVELIN' NICK
IN
"THE LAST PAGE"

There was a river not far from the camp where Cora went swimming a lot, and that's where I found her on the Sunday afternoon before Labor Day. Flutter kicking every few seconds, she held on to a slimy rope that stretched from one bank to the other—we're not talking the Mississippi here, just some little nothing of a river that didn't have a name, so far as I knew, and was no wider across than a backyard pool. "Who's there?" Her eyes looked small without her big prescription sunglasses. They kept blinking in my direction. "That you, Clyde?"

"No," I said, "it's me." In swim trunks, flip-flops, and an Imp Eugene T-shirt. "It's Nick."

I moved from behind the brush down to the sopping grass, stepping carefully over mucky rocks, and waded in with my shirt still on. When I joined Cora in midriver and grabbed hold of that rope, my heart jumped. Jesus Christ, she was skinny-dipping! In general, my life sucked, so that was great. Roy *still* hadn't finished the last page and I'd inked everything there was to ink and there was nothing for me to do now except smoke a lot of cigarettes and reread old Walt Disney comic books. And I couldn't sleep. I'd been awake and feeling wired for three or four days. So being surprised by Cora's little tits underwater was totally great. Of course the trick was to make believe I hadn't noticed, to act blasé. I said, "You know how, like a hundred and twenty years ago, you told me I should go home? Remember?"

"Yeah . . . ?"

"Well, I'm thinking maybe you're right. But I'm thinking maybe I should take Roy with me."

"Fat chance."

"Cora, he's never gonna finish. He's stuck, he's—I could try, right? It couldn't hurt to try."

"Poor Clyde." Her left hand broke the water surface, to touch me on the cheek. Then she let go of the rope with her right hand, stretched out her left arm, and swam away. I watched her leave the water, hauling herself up by a tree root, then dashing for her towel. I caught a good glimpse, though, as she twirled it around her meaty torso. Jiggling buttocks and a burn-scarred back.

"I haven't figured out what I'll do if he won't come, though."

"You could always tie him up." Cora had been collecting her clothes. Now she ducked behind a bush to change.

"You serious?" I released the rope and swam. "You really serious?"

"I'm joking, Nicky."

"Yeah, okay, but I *could* tie him up. Except it's a long trip. Especially the way *I* drive."

"Did you say something? I missed that last thing."

"I said it's a long trip. Especially the way that I drive. I always get lost. I can't read a map."

"Oh, anybody can read a map. I'll show you."

"Nice of you to offer, but I'm beyond help." I'd just flopped down in the grass when Cora came out from behind the bush dressed in a long-sleeved grape-colored sweatshirt and lilac shorts, but still dripping. "What do you think?" I said. "You think it's a bad idea?"

"That's not what you're asking." She sat down beside me on a big rock. "You're really asking do I think Roy's crazy."

"Yeah? I guess I am. So is he?"

Cora let out a long, dramatic breath. I waited for her to say something, but she didn't.

"He's not who he used to be, Cora."

"Who is?"

"I am!"

"Yeah, well, maybe you shouldn't be."

"That's just a lot of hippie bullshit. Look at him! I can't let my own brother—"

"Yeah, you can. Clyde, he's a grown man. You'd be a kidnapper."

I thought about that for a minute, and about some other stuff too, then I told her, "I was thinking more in terms of being, like, a sheriff. Or a bounty hunter." But I smiled to let her know I was only kidding. Then I said: "But it wouldn't be the first time I brought him home. When we were kids, Roy must've run away a dozen times. And it was never like something happened, it wasn't like he got punished and got mad or got in trouble at school and couldn't face, you know, the consequences. He just . . . he'd walk away when nobody was looking, when your back was turned, and not come back. Not till Mom and I found him after we'd been driving around and around the whole city for, like, hours. She'd say, 'What gets *into* you?' and he'd just shrug."

Cora nodded, then went on nodding. She was a muller, that one. And while she mulled, I thought about how pissed, how murderously pissed I'd got every time he ran away, because he never, not ever, not once asked me to go with him.

"So what do you think," I said, "you think I should try and take him home?"

"This is a stupid conversation," said Cora, getting to her feet. "That's what I think."

We followed a path back from the river that ran behind the camp's single tennis court, where a crow was perched on one of the net poles and a doorless old refrigerator stood upright on the left service court. A pack of dogs barked at us from the baseball field. I picked up a stick, just in case. "You feel like doing something together?"

"Like what?" said Cora.

"Oh, I don't know—wanna draw with me? We could jam. I could ink your stuff, or we could take turns doing panels."

"I don't draw."

"But you did, right?"

"Unicorns and castles. And ladies in Victorian nightgowns. Yeah, I drew for a while."

"When'd you stop?"

"When I got tired of hearing how shitty it all was."

"Roy tell you that?"

"I don't want to talk about this."

"Could I see something you did? Because I'd like to."

"Cut it out, okay? I don't want to draw with you."

"Christ," I said, "you sound like Nancy Sinatra."

"What?" She couldn't help herself: she laughed. "I sound like Nancy *Sinatra*?"

"Not the daughter, the *wife*. The first wife, the one he left for Ava Gardner. She's always saying how could she marry anybody else, after being married to Frank Sinatra."

"And I'm like that how, exactly?"

"Never mind."

"No, this is fascinating. How exactly am I like Nancy Sinatra?"

"You won't draw with me—what, because how could *that* be any good, after you've drawn with Roy? After you've drawn with Roy Looby. After you've been with the best."

"That's not what I'm saying. I just don't want to draw—okay?"

"Fine."

"But you want to do a puzzle?"

"Yeah, all right," I said. "That's cool."

As we came abreast of Amity cabin, both of us turned our heads at the same time and looked and saw my brother, in silhouette, bent over his table, working. I split away from Cora and went up on the porch. "Roy?"

"Hey, Clyde, how you doin', you doin' okay?"

"Yeah, sure. How's it coming?" I pulled open the screen door. "Need me yet?"

"No, I don't need you, Nicky. But when I want you, I'll let you know."

"Great." I let the door slap closed. Then I caught up to Cora at the house, and as we were going inside, she asked me, "How the hell do you know what Nancy Sinatra says, anyhow?"

"I know lots of things," I said, "you'd be surprised."

Naturally, Cora selected one of those incredibly busy "adult" jigsaw puzzles, a million different-color gum balls inside a penny gum-ball machine. I was no help at all, and pretty soon, I grew stone-bored. I wasn't a puzzle guy, that's all. Some people are and some people aren't. Every time I looked again at the heap of pieces on the dining room table, I felt sick to my stomach. It was like vertigo.

Cora worked slowly, and slowly made progress. The puzzle started to coalesce: from the rubble, a coherent picture was emerging, and from time to time I felt an impulse to drive my hands through it, sending it back into complete disarray. But that always passed.

We opened a bottle of red fizzy wine and drank from jelly glasses. We ate Ding Dongs, salted peanuts, navel oranges. Cora smoked a joint. I passed but still must've gotten a contact high because when I stepped out on the porch for some fresh air, it was dark already with the moon up, and by my reckoning it should've been only three-thirty, four o'clock in the afternoon. I looked down the midway between the facing campers' cabins and saw lights on in Amity.

Back in the house, I walked up behind Cora and put my face close to the nape of her neck, where she had the tiniest brown mole. You couldn't see it till you were just inches away. I stayed there like that, breathing her. "El Condor Pasa," the Simon and Garfunkel song, came on the radio. I'd rather be a hammer than a nail. Cora turned her head just slightly, saw me, looked away. She took a swallow of wine and put her glass down. "You asked me if I thought he was crazy? Well, he's not," she said. Then she said, "I hate doing these stupid things. Time filler-uppers. Fuck it." She'd been holding, and jiggling, several puzzle pieces in the palm of one hand. Now she flung them like seeds across the table.

"Cora?"

"What? *What?*" When she turned around, I was still right there behind her, and I kissed her on the mouth. I almost apologized, the way I'd apologized to Noreen the first time I'd kissed *her*. But I didn't. Instead I kissed Cora again, and she opened her mouth and kissed me back, and then we both looked at each other for a long, long, super-long moment.

I guess she felt like an idiot, too.

Five, ten minutes later we still were standing there like that—but with our arms around each other by then, in a weary, sexless embrace—when there was a tiny squeak, and the front screen door opened. Roy came inside, stopping directly under the hall fixture. The top of his head gleamed, and in the harsh light his eyes were completely black. Two flat disks. His dungarees were bunched at his ankles and loose around his hips. His T-shirt, speckled with both wet and dried blood and damp with perspiration, hung on him like a barber's sheet. He glanced from me to Cora. From Cora to me. And I was almost convinced he didn't recognize either of us. But then, tipping an imaginary hat, he winked straight at me and said, "All yours."

"You're *finished*?"

Roy walked around us to the table, and when he leaned over it, I could see a corner of his yellow wallet sticking out from his back pocket. His right back pocket. He picked up a jigsaw piece and fitted it into the puzzle. Without even searching, he found the correct spot. As though the piece were magnetized and the hole magnetic. Then he grabbed another puzzle box from a stack on a chair, tossed the lid aside, dumped everything out. And mixed those pieces with the pieces already on the table. Then he emptied another box, and then another. As he began to fit pieces together, deftly, quickly, randomly, Cora watched and was fascinated.

That's when I left and walked up the midway to Amity cabin in a soft drizzle, the first rain we'd had since I arrived in California. As I went up on the porch, I could hear my transistor radio playing inside; it was tuned to a Dodgers game. That stopped me in my tracks. Roy had been listening to a ball game? Roy? Who hated sports of any kind?

I opened the door and, feeling exhausted, buzzy, and scared, I went into the cabin and looked at the last page.

WHAT HAPPENS NEXT?

BIGGS THE CARTOONIST
IN
"I GET ALONG WITHOUT YOU VERY WELL"

[1]

At least twice a month he wrecks the damn car again, in dreams. He'll be having a perfectly fine dream, an inconsequential dream, occasionally even a sex dream (at his age!), when the clear light surrounding him will suddenly darken, become dusklike. Then, after walking away from whatever he's been doing (following a hooker through an amusement park, painting grocery market display signs with his dad, or playing the sax—something that he couldn't and didn't ever want to do in real life—at an enlisted men's club during World War II), Biggs will climb a narrow flight of stairs or wend his way through a boisterous Italian restaurant or a sumptuous banquet affair, then step into the Gents, only it's not the Gents but someone's tiny bedroom, where he finds Ginnie, his ex- and only wife, seated in a ladderback chair. Next thing, he'll grudgingly collect her, often tossing her over a shoulder like a rolled-up area rug, as well as some pieces of valuable Derby Dugan memorabilia—a statuette, an electric fan, a bright yellow wallet—and then, just like that, Biggs will be in his car, jammed behind the wheel, driving fast. Somewhere, somehow, he's lost both Ginnie and the Dugan stuff. Alone now, he'll find himself speeding like a maniac in the pouring rain. And he'll think, Oh dear God, thank you, because he'll imagine, feel sure that he's being given a second chance, an opportunity to go back in time and not crash the stupid car. He'll be so happy he'll get careless and, without meaning to, he'll end up launching that Buick off the country road. A big wet tree fills the windshield.

"For going on forty years," he says, "that same dream." He's mentioning it now because he dreamed it yet again today, during a late-afternoon nap. "It's like the Twilight Zone."

"I've had a few recurring dreams myself," says Mary Laudermilch. "There's the witch-in-the-backyard dream I've had ever since I was a little girl—"

"This coming September, it'll be forty *years* since I wrecked my car. Half my lifetime ago."

"How old *are* you, Edward? I don't think you ever told me."

"I'll be eighty-one."

"Well, you certainly don't look it. What's your secret? You have absolutely no lines in your face. You must never worry."

Biggs laughs. Oh, for the love of Mike, "don't look it." He looks it, brother, and more! And never worry? If only. But still it's nice to hear Mary Laudermilch flatter him. If Biggs could find a way to finagle it, he'd have her to dinner every night, not just every other Monday.

This rainy April evening, he defrosted and broiled a couple of those steaks he gets airmailed from Omaha, Nebraska. A new delivery in the second week of the month, like clockwork. "I have to call them up and cancel," he says now, after Mary tells him how good her steak is, so tender it's like butter, you hardly need your knife. "I can't eat this much beef. Even with help."

"Plus, I'd think, they're very expensive."

"Not really. And it's good stuff. Only corn-fed beef."

"Oh, it's out of this world." Mary smiles, and Biggs is delighted. It was so smart—it was brilliant!—chatting her up three months ago when he had his late sister-in-law's rings and bracelets appraised. With her younger brother, Mary owns Laudermilch's Vintage Jewelry at Journal Square, where Biggs and she had a merry old conversation the day he was in, the day of their appointment. Later that same afternoon, he'd called her to ask if she'd let him take her out for a drink. God knows what had possessed him or given him the courage to pick up the phone. He was so nervous he doodled the whole while he was talking to Mary, filling the edges of his Word Find tablet with little pencil drawings of Derby Dugan's head. They came as naturally as his signature. After all this time! He hadn't realized, because for years he hadn't tried, that he could actually draw again, a little. Could doodle heads. Anyway, Mary said yes to drinks.

And drinks led to dinner at a safe American-cuisine restaurant (he picked her up in a cab), then to meals twice a month at his place. (Besides the frozen steaks, he also keeps boxes of frozen fantail shrimp and frozen Italian meatballs, all of them mail-ordered.) So far they're still just friends, Biggs and Mary Laudermilch. Friends with a business component: she had happily purchased all of Peg's jewelry. Not that there was a lot of it, but what Peg owned was quality stuff.

Although Biggs had never been especially fond of his sister-in-law (she was a big complainer), he continues to miss her. She's been dead a year now, and still he misses her; the daily phone calls, the inane chitchat, the occasional evenings spent together watching TV. Her late husband, Biggs's older brother, Gus, passed away, jeez, a long time ago. When was Reagan inaugurated? January of what? Eighty-one? Gus has been dead since then. Pancreatic cancer. He hadn't known that he had it when Reagan was elected but was dead of it two days before the Great Bullshitter was inaugurated. January 1981. Nineteen years. Poor Gus. Poor Peggy.

Biggs is alone now; who's left? Nick Looby stops by to visit three or four times a year and phones every few months. And once in a blue moon, Noreen Bozzo, who lives down in Bayonne now, drops by with slabs of ham and scalloped potatoes, or a mayonnaise jar of homemade soup, or a tray of lasagna. But she always seems anxious to leave two minutes after she's arrived, and Biggs can't quite figure out why she comes at all. They hardly speak. Well, they hardly spoke in the old days. It's good of Noreen to come, though. Even if it does end up leaving Biggs vaguely depressed. Thank God for Mary, for whatever it is that's going on between the two of them.

A vigorous beauty-parlor blonde and a compact (not exactly "sturdy," but getting there) woman of sixty-three or -four, Mary wears only solid-color, well-made dresses from Anne Klein. (This evening it's a dark-blue one.) She used to be married to a lawyer who later became a Democratic congressman from New Jersey and later still an inmate at a federal prison in Minnesota. Mary rarely talks about him, but why should she? They had no children and have been divorced since the late seventies. (A legal divorce, a church annulment.) She never remarried and has told Biggs that she rarely dates. He might've made some kind of pass by this time, but his entire skeleton felt like broken glass this winter and spring, so he wasn't, still isn't, feeling especially male. Besides, Mary is a devout Catholic. Biggs fears that if he tries anything, it could end the friendship. And companionable, everyday friends aren't easy to come by, especially at this late stage of the game.

Mary says now, "Can I help with that?" and Biggs says no, he's got it, and clears the table. Then, limping, he carries the dinner plates to the kitchen. He piles everything in the sink, runs the water, lets it all soak, then plugs in the percolator. When he comes back, he suggests they get comfortable in the living room. How about some music? Some music?

Biggs kneels down—slowly, arthritically—in front of the stereo cabinet and flips through his record collection, jammed alphabetically inside of it: Kingston Trio, Peggy Lee, Tom Lehrer, Thelonious Monk, Bob Newhart, Patti Page, the Platters, Johnny Ray, and finally what's he looking for: Sinatra. But wait a second, hold on, what's this one doing in with Ol' Blue Eyes? Dean Martin, *Everybody Loves Somebody,* a misfile. Well, at least he'd misfiled Dino with a pal. Looking at the photo on the album sleeve, Biggs marvels at what a handsome guy that Dean Martin was, back when. Such a head of hair! Always with a strong drink in his hand, but that had to be an act. A man simply couldn't perform night after night half in the bag. You'd *think* not, but, hey, we all drank too much back in those days. Look at me. All those parties in Westport. All those cocktail parties. The lost world. Biggs hasn't had an alcoholic drink since, well, since the tree. After taking a last glance at Dino's smiling face, he sticks the LP back where it belongs, in between *An Evening (Wasted) with Tom Lehrer* and *It's Monk's Time.* Then he returns to the Sinatra section, trying to decide which one he wants. Okay.

It's been so long since he played a record that Biggs is more than a little surprised when the stereo actually works, when the LP drops and the arm glides over, settles gently, and the needle, with some crack-ling, finds the lead-in groove. *In the Wee Small Hours.* What everybody used to call the suicide songs. Beautiful, though, just gorgeous. And that voice, ah Jesus. Biggs looks over to Mary, sitting in the easy chair that he usually takes, and she nods approval.

"Did you ever see him in concert, Edward?"

"Once. In the late fifties, I guess it was." He remembers taking Gin-nie, remembers squeezing her small hand while Frank sang "As Time Goes By." He remembers coming home after the concert and going straight into his studio to work—or maybe he doesn't remember doing that, maybe he just assumes that's what he did because that's what he did every night, night after night, in that crazy part of his life. "He was a wonderful performer, wasn't he?"

"The best," says Mary. "I saw him down Atlantic City, at the 500 Club in '53, and the place was packed, and I saw him again at the Riv-iera, in Fort Lee. But I saw him again just a few years before he died, up in Connecticut, and that was almost sad. He was a ruin by then, Edward, and his voice, it just wasn't the same. But still."

"Still, it was Sinatra."

"Yeah."

Biggs smiles, feeling happy, inexplicably happy. But no, it's not inexplicable at all. He's happy to acknowledge fondly a heroic decline. Sinatra kept going, didn't he? Even when he probably shouldn't have, he kept going. With his vocal cords all frayed and his breathing wrecked by half a billion cigarettes, the man kept singing, making records, *because that's what he did.* Maybe it was vanity, and maybe it was foolish, and maybe it even hurt his reputation and his legacy, but Frank Sinatra was a singer and so he went right on singing. He kept going. "They're talking about putting up a statue in Times Square. I hope they do it. The man was a legend, an icon. And that voice! Ah Jesus." Halfway through "I Get Along without You Very Well," Biggs, feeling sorry for himself now, says, "Poor Frank." Then he says, "Let me see if that coffee's done."

In the kitchen, while he's reaching for the cups and saucers, Mary suddenly comes up behind him. Touches him lightly on the shoulder. "Edward, I can't believe that I forgot, I feel like such a dope."

"Forgot what?"

"You said, 'icon,' and I remembered."

"Remembered what?"

"It was going to be the first thing I said when I arrived tonight but then I completely forgot. Did you see in the paper? About that fellow you're always talking about?"

Confused, Biggs says, "Buddy Lydecker?"

"No, no. No, the one from the neighborhood. That disappeared."

"Roy Looby?"

"That's it. Did you happen to see in the paper?"

"No. What about Roy?"

"And you're always telling me you figured he was dead. Well, he turned up in Virginia, he's in the hospital. And from what it sounds like, he was a homeless man."

"I don't believe it. Where'd you see this?"

"There was a little thing this morning in the *New York Times*. I thought for sure you'd heard. I'm sorry. I should have called right away."

"No, that's all right." Biggs stands motionless in the middle of the kitchen floor, having another one of those paralyzing lapses that he gets every now and then, confused about how to complete an action he's begun: flossing his teeth, finding his shoes, turning off the shower.

"Edward?" Mary moves in close beside him, trying to take the coffee cups from his grip.

He snaps out of it, gladly transferring the two cups to Mary, then excuses himself. Halfway down the hall, he remembers something and comes back. "Why don't you just slide that Mrs. Smith's pie in the oven and turn it on low. Just to warm it up." Then he goes back to the living room, clicks off the stereo, locates his address book, and dials a number. It rings three times.

"Hi! To leave a message for either Nicholas Looby or Signs by Clyde, please speak after the beep."

"Nick. Candy Biggs. What's this I hear about Roy? Are you there? Call me. It's Candy."

Mary takes the phone from his grip. How long has he been holding the earpiece pressed to his mouth like a big goof? Like some big senile goof? He can hear a computer-female voice saying, "If you would like to make a call, hang up and dial again. If you would like to make a call—"

Mary returns the handset to the cradle. "I'm sorry. I guess I thought you would've heard."

"Will he be all right?"

"It was vague," says Mary. "Whyn't you sit down? Sit down, Edward."

"I think I will."

"Can I pour the coffee? Or do you want a glass of water?"

"No. Coffee. Definitely coffee."

Mary returns to the kitchen, and Biggs has yet another lapse, this one leaving him with a semirigid jaw and his left arm useless and club-like with pins and needles. He flinches now in the upholstered chair. And now in his hospital bed . . .

[2]

He twists around slowly, it has to be slowly with his body a pathetic bag of badly mended bones, with drains here and there from his most recent surgery. Looking now through the open door and across the hall into the opposite room, seeing a small boy in a bed there with pillows bunched behind him. A small bald-headed boy turning a mustard-yellow wallet around and around in his hands.

And Candy thinks, Oh God, thank you, because he imagines that he's being given a second chance.

"Nurse?" He says, "Nurse, could you take this to the young man across the way?"

"Oh! Did you draw that yourself, Mr. Biggs?"

"Yes. Could you give it to him, please?"

"It's very good! As good as what you see in the paper." At that, he winces. It's a terrible sketch, the line ragged, shaky, but it's the best that Biggs can manage now, drawing lefty. "I guess you must love 'Peanuts.'"

"'Peanuts'? That's not Charlie Brown," says Biggs, "it's Derby Dugan."

"Is that a comic strip?"

"Would you just give this to him, please? Thank you," he says, then watches her cross the hall and speak to the boy, who bends forward, turns his head, and peers around her white bulk. When he sees Biggs waving, he frowns. Examining the sketch, he frowns more deeply. When he glances back up and toward Biggs once again, he looks suspicious, puzzled, on the brink of astonishment. Before sending it over, Biggs autographed the sketch, signing it the way he'd always signed the Dugan strip: *Ed ("Candy") Biggs,* his name surrounded by a scalloped border. He watches the boy study the sketch, then decides, against doctor's orders, to get out of bed and go talk to him. Throwing back the covers, Biggs manages to swing his legs around, sit up, then set his feet down on the cold linoleum floor.

But as soon as he's walking, things turn screwy. Even crippled, even recuperating from abdominal surgery, it shouldn't take him *this* long to cross the hall, and when he does finally step into the room, oh God, there's Ginnie in a chair, wearing a sweater and slacks and reading a thick paperback novel. Biggs plucks a souvenir yellow derby from the bedpost, thinking if he ever finds that bald kid again, if he ever finds his way back to the fucking hospital, he'll give it to him, something to match the wallet. "Come on, Gin," says Biggs, "time to go." But then *he's* gone, straight into the driver's seat of his Buick. It's pouring down rain. He has no intention of crashing into a tree. Why should he? Why ruin his life? He could always write and draw another comic strip. A different one. So to hell with crashing! But he's going so fast, and goddamn, he has one of those lapses again and can't remember how you slow a car down. How do you?

[3]

He flinches awake, and Mary says, "I hope it's not the company."

"It most definitely is not. This is just what happens when you have supper with a geezer. Oh, you've fixed my coffee. Thank you." He tests his arm, pinching the loose flesh just above his wrist, and it seems okay. No pins and needles. And his jaw works fine.

"I know you don't take milk," says Mary, "but I wasn't sure if you take sugar or not."

"Never any."

"Well, good for you, Edward. It's poison, they say. I wish I could give it up myself. I'm getting a little fat-girl potbelly."

Probably he should contradict her, tell her she looks wonderful, but he's suddenly in no mood to flirt. "I'm amazed the story was in the *New York Times*."

"Really? It said your friend was supposed to be a 'sixties icon.'" She laughs, obviously pleased, and surprised, that she remembered the headline. So why not say it again? "A 'sixties icon.'"

"You know, I haven't seen that guy since May of 1967." Biggs does a quick calculation. "Thirty-three years. God almighty."

"It must be a shock."

"Was there anything about what he's been doing all this time?"

"It was a tiny little article, Edward. I don't know what made me read it in the first place. But as soon as I get home I'll cut it out for you."

"Would you? I'd appreciate that."

Even though he tries to be good company, a genial host, Biggs remains distracted the rest of the evening. Mary does most of the talking, going on for a while about how gorgeous the altar at Sacred Heart cathedral looked yesterday for Easter services but mostly telling him about her decision to withdraw gradually from her jewelry business—she's not giving it up entirely, mind you, just planning to pull back some. It's that time of life, she says, when you should be enjoying yourself. She might take a few trips, and Biggs nods—yes, that sounds good. Uh-huh. Then it's nine o'clock and Mary looks at her watch and tells him she ought to be heading home, early day tomorrow. Usually when she comes to dinner, she doesn't leave till at least ten; often it's after eleven. Biggs feels a twinge of guilt. He's been monosyllabic for the past hour and a half and really should apologize, explain, but decides finally to say nothing.

Taking along his cane (he won't go down the porch steps without it, not since that time he fell), he walks Mary out. The rain has finally stopped and the air feels warm. Mary's car is parked directly in front of the house. She owns a white Honda Civic, this year's model, and Biggs is always anxious they'll come outside one time and discover it missing or vandalized—this isn't a terrific neighborhood, hasn't been for years. Every house, including the one that Biggs lives in, looks run-down, and a few, like those flanking his, are abandoned, dilapidated. Directly across the street, green outdoor carpeting covers the steps and porch floor of the house that once belonged to Biggs's closest boyhood friend (Billy Powell, killed at Normandy beach). Painted directly on the asphalt siding are several words in Arabic script. During the late eighties, early nineties, it was a mosque, but it closed several years back shortly after some of its members were arrested for bombing the World Trade Center. Now Biggs is fairly certain the house is full of squatters.

As he holds open the driver's door for Mary, he swings his head around, trying to see if they're being watched from a window, or a porch, or a stoop, or from any one of the old American cars, the Dodges and Plymouths, that line both sides of the street. Or even from behind a tree. He was mugged once, at Christmastime three years ago, and is terrified of its happening again. It doesn't take much for his bones to break, you know.

"Thank you so much for coming," says Biggs. "I'm afraid I was pretty lousy company tonight."

"No, you weren't," says Mary with a little smile, then she reaches through the driver's window and touches his wrist. "Listen to that!"

"To what?"

"Isn't that a train? Doesn't that sound like an old-fashioned train whistle?"

"You're right."

"You never hear trains anymore."

"No, you don't."

"I wonder where it's coming from."

"Hoboken? I don't know."

Mary shrugs off the conversation—enough!—then looks past him, back toward the house, and quirks up a corner of her mouth. Biggs knows exactly what she's going to say next, it's what she always says, last thing. "My lord, the electric company must love you." Because every downstairs light in his house is burning. And many upstairs lights, as well.

"Guess I'm just scared of the dark, Mary." He meant it to come out lightly, jokey, as it always has in the past, but tonight it comes out with a confessional sincerity he regrets at once. It *is* pretty silly, all those lights, and with the empty houses on either side, his place looks like the *Queen Mary* in the middle of the dark Atlantic. Like a passenger train stalled on the prairie at night. "I'll turn everything off before bed," he says. "Promise." Knowing it's a promise he won't keep. She pats his hand, covers it with hers.

He watches her pull away from the curb, then hobbles back up his steps. Thinking, Roy Looby? After thirty years. Thirty-*three*. Time goes by, all right. And by the same token, it doesn't. Biggs locks the front door, stands tentatively in the front hall, then walks into the parlor and takes down from the bookcase a tall bound volume stamped "1954" on the cover. He carries it to the sofa, settles himself, and reaches for his magnifying glass, the one he uses, must use, these days to read. (Contacts irritate him, and he can't wear eyeglasses, not with his ears misaligned!) He opens it to a still-pristine color proof of his first Sunday strip, the very first one.

Derby's on a train.

[4]

Not long after Candy Biggs took over "Derby Dugan," a librarian at King Features in New York shipped him by parcel post two dozen of those oversized volumes, each one containing a year's worth of Sunday-page proofs, 1930 through 1953. Biggs wasn't supposed to keep them, he was supposed to study them and familiarize himself with the strip's extended cast of characters—with their personalities, their speech patterns, the nature of their connection (friend or foe) to the hero and his talking dog—and to see how they had all been drawn by poor Buddy Lydecker and, before him, by Walter Geebus. Biggs had always meant to return them, but—well, these things happen—somehow he never got around to it. And nobody reminded him. When the syndicate discontinued the practice of having Sunday proofs bound annually, Biggs saved all his own proofs throughout his stewardship on "Derby Dugan" and had them professionally bound, again one calendar year per volume, at his own expense.

After Roy Looby, this kid he'd met in the hospital, had been coming to his house every day after school for a couple of months, Biggs brought up the complete set from his basement. And he didn't just show the books to Roy but let him paw through them as often as he pleased. Fascinated, the boy read every single one from beginning to end, but time after time he'd return to the Depression-era strips, to the Walter Geebus years, and those proofs he would pore over like a lawyer pores over a contract. Derby's in a breadline, he's in a boxcar. He's in a hurricane, a forest fire, he's bleeding in the alley. He's crawl-ing on his belly through the great American desert. There's a cactus. There's a cow skull. Roy just soaked that stuff up. He loved it. And why not? Biggs loved the Geebus version, too, as dark and as cheerless and even as clinically morbid (bullet through the neck, knife in the back) as those old-timey strips often could be. It was the picaresque stuff that Biggs himself had grown up reading on quiet Sunday mornings while his widowed father painted Bible scenes on plywood and his older brother did arithmetic problems on the window seat. No, Biggs was happy to see Roy Looby devour those classic strips; to read and reread them, and frequently—at Biggs's urging—to take out pencil and paper and copy different panels, entire pages. Derby's in a rowboat, it's night. Tongue poking from the side of his mouth, pencil held barely an inch above the point, Roy would copy it, perfectly. Nothing wrong with that. No, that was Biggs's intention, he wanted Roy to immerse himself in "Derby Dugan," it was just that . . . well, damn.

Sometimes Roy could be cruel, no other way to put it, and whether it was calculated or simply thoughtless, still he could hurt you. This one time, for instance. He'd been riffling through that set of bound proofs yet again when all of a sudden he lifted his head and called out to Candy Biggs, across the room watching TV: "Geebus could draw cir-cles around that Lydecker bum." And Biggs cocked his head, smiled indulgently, and said, "Well, yeah, but poor Buddy tried."

"And he could draw circles around you, too, Mr. Biggs."

Nick Looby was at the house that afternoon, practicing balloon ital-ics, filling page after page of a marble-covered copybook with the alphabet, and he was shocked pale by his brother's remark. "Roy! For God sakes! That's not funny."

"I got a right to my opinion."

"Yeah? Well, you don't got a right to—"

Biggs said, "Hey! Nicky? Forget it. Roy is absolutely correct, he *does* have a right to his opinion. And what's more, I happen to share that opinion. So don't think you have to defend me, thank you very much."

It was stupid and juvenile, but he didn't much care for Nick Looby; he resented him for always coming to the house, for tagging along after his older brother, and Biggs wished like hell that he wouldn't. What Biggs really wished? He wished Nick would just go away. Vanish. Hit the road, Jack—like in that Ray Charles song. Hit the road, Nick. And don't come back no more no more no more no more.

Nick Looby wasn't a boy in whom Candy Biggs had, or wanted to have, any sort of investment. And the awful thing was, he was a pretty nice kid. A little nervous, overly anxious to please, but nice. He mowed Biggs's lawn, for Christ's sake, had volunteered and wouldn't take a dime. He shoveled snow for Biggs. Took down the storm windows and put up the screens. He knew his way around a brush, too, and a crow-quill pen, give him that much. He was a bit too— what?—*literal,* the way he just followed the pencil lines, and was too careful and conscientious ever to be anything special, ever to be a comer, but at least he could do it, he never smudged, he never smeared, he had some talent, although Biggs felt that his real talent was for lettering.

In fact, several times he had suggested to Nick that he might consider a career in sign painting. Which Nick took as an insult until Biggs mentioned that he himself had once earned his living that way. "You, Mr. Biggs?" "Yeah, me—and my dad. It was a family business. It's a noble profession, people always need signs. Otherwise, they don't know what's standing right there in front of them." "I guess," said Nick, "yeah, I guess." A nice kid, all and all. But there was just something about him. Biggs couldn't figure out the antipathy that he felt toward the boy and that—occasionally, impulsively, unfairly—he displayed. He really couldn't figure it out, although it *had* struck him once or twice, but just once or twice, that Nick Looby reminded Candy Biggs of himself, a little. Of some facet. Some facet of himself. But which one?

So. Would you get a load of this? Roy acts like a royal shit, a real snot nose, and it ends up with Nick looking crushed and Biggs feeling ashamed of himself. What's wrong with this picture?

How it should've ended up? Biggs should've thanked poor Nick Looby for coming to his defense and then he should've reamed Roy out, put that seventeen-year-old fucker in his place. Taught him a lesson, some manners. Said, Listen, you little punk, I may not have been the greatest strip man that ever lived, but even with this dead fucking right hand I can still draw circles around you.

Which was total bullshit. Even with a *live* fucking right hand, even in his prime, even at his very best, Candy Biggs had never been as richly talented, as natural, as facile as Roy Looby. Never. And Biggs knew it, too. Had known it from the moment that hospital nurse delivered a sheet of paper back across the hall, a thank-you sketch (or, at any rate, a reply sketch) made for him by the small bald kid in the room opposite. Roy was special, that was clear enough. So Biggs restrained himself. When the kid insulted the only work that he'd ever been proud of? Candy Biggs bit the tip of his tongue and swallowed. He didn't want to chase him away, God knows he didn't.

[5]

When had he come into the kitchen? Jesus Christ, wasn't he just paging through that book of his old strips? He can't remember putting it down, or getting up from the chair, or walking out here. What the hell's the matter with him these days?

But since he's out here . . . Biggs squirts some Lux liquid into the sink water and swirls it around with a finger, starts doing the dishes. Scrubbing plates, rinsing glasses, he thinks about Mary Laudermilch, about the tiny, indulgent smile that her lips formed as she said, "Sixties icon." He thinks: 1967, but then shakes his head. Think about something else. In 1967, in 1967—in 1967, Mary Laudermilch would've been in her midthirties. And now Biggs is imagining what she might have looked like naked then. In *her* prime. In the prime of her life. He really doesn't want to imagine what she looks like naked at this point in her life, although for her age she's not half bad. And now, all at once, he thinks of Ginnie. The former Ginnie Kis. The Hungarian-born Ginnie Kis. Star-spangled Ginnie . . .

Biggs remembers exactly what she looked like naked in *her* prime. Dear God. She was, she was just, she was so amazing. As all the boys would corroborate. Paul Vessey. Jack Hayser. Don Haldeman. That traffic cop in Bridgeport whose name Biggs can't remember. Joe Haley.

Bill Skeeter.

Dan Sharkey.

They'd all tell you. If any of them were still alive, and some of them must be. They'd happily tell you. Fondly recall. Ginnie Biggs? Was a real knockout, they'd say.

She called her sugar Candy.

But never visited him at Norwalk Hospital, not once. Or at least he doesn't remember that she did. They kept him so doped up, though. So maybe she did.

She's Ginnie Krajewski now. Assuming, of course, that *she's* still alive. Ginnie Krajewski. Of Rye, New York. Married a guy who imported—from China? from Korea? from *one* of those cheap-labor countries—novelty items for banks and realtors and grand openings: ballpoint pens, combs, key rings with different-color plastic fobs, smiley-face buttons, American flag decals.

As Biggs is reaching to stick a saucer in the drain rack, a burning pain wriggles up his right leg, his shoulder throbs, and his vision becomes flocked.

He's thought about this. If he ever gets any real warning? If he's not suddenly felled? If he feels it coming on, he'll try to make it to bed, where he can shut his eyes and his mouth and just let it happen. That would be good, because then he won't look ridiculous or vulgar or pathetic when someone eventually finds him. And if he can't make it to bed, he'll try for an armchair.

He just doesn't want to end up on the floor.

Pulling a chair away from the kitchen table, Biggs sits down hard, a sopping dishrag still clutched in his hand. Dishrag? Why is he holding a dishrag? What's he supposed to do with the stupid thing? He can't remember. You don't eat off it, so why's it called a dishrag? It drips sudsy water on his pants, soaking his shirt cuff, his sleeve, but is that right? Is it supposed to do that? He stares at it. The phone rings. He doesn't answer.

[6]

"No, but he's right here," said Nick Looby, carrying the wall phone's receiver halfway across the kitchen, its kinked plastic cord pulled taut. "I'll get him." Then, with a worried expression, Nick silently mouthed, "Our mom," and handed Biggs the telephone. Seated at the table, Roy glanced up, frowned, then resumed drawing.

"Hello?"

"Mr. Biggs? Hi, this is Cathy Looby."

"Afternoon, Mrs. Looby." He poked Roy lightly in the shoulder, and when Roy looked, Biggs drew a circle in the air with his finger. Oval, *circle*. Oval, circle, circle, circle. "What can I do for you?"

"Well—actually I called to tell the boys to come on home for supper, but Nicky says you've already fed them. Now, I don't want them both thinking they can just impose on you all the time like this, Mr. Biggs."

"No imposition at all, Mrs. Looby, but I have to confess that *I* didn't feed them, although we ate like Polish kings. Thanks to our deli connection." Automatically, Biggs glanced to the grouping of take-out containers on the sink counter (there were open cold-cut wrappers beside them and a few seeded rolls), then he winked at Noreen Novick, seated beside Roy with her elbows planted on the table edge, her wrists crossed, and her bosom supported by her forearms. (God, was she ever top-heavy! Only fifteen, a sophomore in high school, and already she had a rack on her larger than Ginnie's!) "But I apologize if we've ruined your dinner plans, Mrs. Looby. I should've called you first."

"Well, no, it's not like we're having anything special. I just don't want the boys bothering you, Mr. Biggs." He had quit asking her to call him "Ed" or "Candy"; it was no use, she wouldn't.

"No bother, Mrs. Looby. None at all."

For a brief period he'd addressed the woman as "Cathy," but finally he'd gone back to calling her "Mrs. Looby." Although she'd stopped inviting him over to the house—the last time he'd been there was for Roy's seventeenth birthday, almost a year ago now—Biggs felt certain she didn't actively dislike him. But he was also convinced she didn't much care for him, either. She felt sorry for him, was how Biggs read things. Sorry that he was a cripple and sorry that he was forever going back into the hospital for more surgery and still more surgery, but she didn't much *like* him. Couldn't warm to him. There might have been a time, early on, when she'd had suspicions he might be a sex pervert, a boy-toucher, but those fears apparently had passed. While he'd never discussed it with either Roy or Nick—he would never have brought up such a thing, never, not in a hundred years!—he would have bet money she'd asked each of them, separately, whether Mr. Biggs ever said or did, or even suggested, anything that made them feel, well, funny inside.

For his part, Candy Biggs thought Mrs. Looby amiable enough but dull. Roy's mother, and she was dull as dirt! Watched her Cronkite, smoked her Kents, and probably slept in cotton pajamas.

And now she was saying, "Well, if you're sure you don't mind them hanging around, then I guess it's all right. But would you send them home by seven-thirty? They still have homework, you know."

"I'll chase them out at seven, how's that? Mrs. Looby? Could you excuse me for just one second?" Biggs removed the phone from his ear, cupped a hand to the mouthpiece, bent down to Roy. "That's too sharp an angle. No angles, it's a *kid,* draw him rounder. Here." But when he tried to guide Roy's pencil hand, Roy fiercely shook him off.

"I can do it myself, Candy, all right? *God.*"

Biggs glanced at Noreen, and her nostrils were flared. She was scowling at him deeply and territorially. Fat cow. Elsie the fat cow. And she wasn't at all pretty.

"Mrs. Looby?" said Biggs. "Thanks for waiting. I'll make sure the boys get started for home by—"

"She had to go turn off the oven."

"Neil? How you doing, Neil, you doing okay?"

"I'm doing well, Mr. Biggs, thank you," said Uncle Neil. "But she had to go turn off the oven. It's a meat loaf."

"Ah. Well, she's busy, so would you just tell her for me that I'll send the boys home at seven?"

"That'll be good, Mr. Biggs." Here was another one who refused to call him anything but "mister." "Mr. Biggs, Cathy would tell me to mind my own business if she heard me say this, but, well, I'm wondering. I know the boys like to draw, and it's nice of you to be giving them art lessons—"

"I'm not giving them lessons, Neil." Suddenly, Biggs was aware that both Roy and Nick were looking at him, Nick anxiously, Roy with a grin that locked finally into a sneer. Biggs turned his back to them. "But what's your point?"

"Now, I'm just a friend of the family, I'm not the boys *real* uncle—"

"I'm aware of that. Your point?"

"Well, I don't know, but I'm thinking they might be getting just a bit too old for that kind of thing. Funny books. And I know their mother worries about it, too."

"Well, then maybe *she* should talk to them about it, yes?"

"I don't mean to offend you, Mr. Biggs."

"And I'm not offended, Neil. I'm just curious why you feel you have to raise this . . . concern."

"Now, don't . . . I just have the boys' best interests at heart."

"And I haven't?"

"Of course, well, of course you do! It's only . . ."

"What are we talking about here?"

"I thought I'd just told you. The boys are in high school, so you'd think, oh, I don't know, they'd want to get more involved in *different* things. Dances. And whatnot. Clubs. Instead of always going to your house and drawing."

"I think you better go eat your meat loaf before it gets cold." As Biggs brusquely passed the receiver back to Nick Looby to hang up, everyone in the kitchen could hear Uncle Neil Cannon on the phone saying, "It just seems to me there's more to life than drawing funny books. Hello? Hello?"

"Maybe we should go home now," said Nick in a small voice. "Hey, Roy? You think? I mean, if Mom's gonna be all mad."

"Then go," said Roy. "Go home, Clyde, if that's what you want." Then he cocked his head and smiled, and the smile was for Biggs, and

Biggs alone. "What do you mean, 'angles'? What angles you talking about? I'm drawing the kid round—what, that's not round?"

"Yeah, sure, that's round, it's just not round enough," said Biggs, his words coming out breathy, choppy, as though he'd been running or climbing stairs. His heart speeding up. He felt a lump rise in his throat, and he laughed. "Just not round enough. Here, Roy, let me show you," he said, pulling up a chair.

Noreen stood and walked to the sink, where Nick joined her, and together they quietly wrapped the leftover lunch meat, bagged the rolls, and threw away the take-out cartons. Then they did the dishes. Nick washed, Noreen dried. "Tonight's Tuesday," she said. *"The Fugitive."*

"Oh yeah," said Nick. "Cool."

"This is round," said Biggs. "This, Roy, is how you make a line that says *round.*"

[7]

With a flinch (no tree in the windshield, just a little spasm in the heart), Candy Biggs sits up straight on the kitchen chair, his blank-out suddenly over. He stares wide-eyed and distastefully at the wet cloth still in his open hand, then throws it back in the sink. Getting up, he walks slowly around the table, keeping one hand, the fingertips, on it, just in case. Coffeemaker turned off? Turned off. According to the sunburst clock above the fridge, it is nearly eleven. Already? He leaves the kitchen thinking, Uncle Neil. The meter reader. The Good Humor man. A few years back, Biggs had seen the poor bastard's death notice—actually, it was a news story in the *Jersey Journal*. It wasn't funny, it was awful, but if anybody on this planet was going to be electrocuted reaching into the freezer of an ice-cream truck for a toasted coconut bar and touching a live wire instead, it was that guy. Mr. Luckless. Poor Uncle Neil.

In the living room, moving toward the dreaded flight of stairs (there's no chance in hell he will ever move his bed to the first floor; though it definitely would make his life easier, it would also make it more circumscribed, and it's narrow enough now, thank you very much), Biggs wonders if he should try calling Nick Looby again. No, he left a message, that should be enough. If Nicky doesn't call by, say, lunchtime tomorrow, or make it late afternoon, he'll leave another. Planting a hand on the newel post, then bracing himself, Biggs sets one foot down on the bottom step, looks up . . .

[8]

"And where the hell do you think *you're* going?"

"To the bathroom," said Nick. He was already near the top of the stairs, and though he'd been taking them two at a time, he'd been creeping. "I have to use the bathroom."

"Yeah? Well, there's one right off the kitchen. Use that."

"I'm already here, Candy."

"Down. Now."

Nick glared at Biggs for a long moment, his eyes half-lidded behind those clunky and perpetually smudged horn-rimmed glasses. Finally, with a blasted exhale, he clattered back down the stairs, deliberately being as noisy as he could. Christ, you'd think he was six, not seventeen going on eighteen, a peevish kid and not a senior in high school. To look at him as he stormed past Biggs that late afternoon, then flung himself on the sofa (guess he'd forgotten he had to pee!), you'd think he was a week away from starting kindergarten.

"Nicky, for Christ's sake."

"What?"

"Leave them alone, would you? They'll think you're a pervert."

"I'll tell you who's a pervert." Nick sat up, then whirled on Biggs. "*I'll* tell you who."

"That's enough."

"Why do you let them do it here? It's sick!"

"Nobody asked you to hang around waiting."

"Me and Roy, we're supposed to be drawing comics."

"Yeah, well. I'm sure you will. When he's done."

" 'When he's done.' You could get arrested for this, you know."

"You going to turn me in, Nick?"

"You *could*."

Biggs shook his head, then sat back down in his armchair to resume paging through Roy's latest sketchbook. It was mostly filled with dated (10/12/66, 10/15/66, 10/21/66) roughs that he'd done with a hard pencil (he'd also done a few with a Rapidograph pen, much to Nicky's vocal disapproval). These were the first drafts, the workups, for those idiotic girlie-magazine cartoons Roy had been churning out lately by the dozens. While Biggs understood that Roy needed to earn some money—after all, he was nineteen years old—it seemed just such a waste, all this crap. All these stale and stupid gags. All these desert-island castaways, adulterous husbands, hookers soliciting in fishnet stockings, all these nurses. (Biggs was an authority on nurses, and he was here to tell you that none of the ones that *he'd* ever met shed their caps and uniforms at a wink and a whistle.)

But at least the girlie stuff kept Roy from taking some dead-end job. From punching a clock. This stroke-book crud that he published in magazines like *Sir!* and *Mr.* and *Man to Man* didn't pay much, never more than twenty bucks a cartoon, but at least it kept Roy free. To improve his craft, develop his chops, to think about what he might really want to do. And Biggs, for some time now, had just the thing. The perfect move for Roy to make. He'd thought about it a lot, made a few inquiries, even dropped some hints—but not to Roy, not yet. He had dropped his hints in certain circles, ones that were not entirely closed to him, despite his current professional status as a nonperson. Biggs was biding his time, waiting for the ideal moment to speak with Roy. To broach the subject.

"It's going on five o'clock!" said Nick. "And they've been up there since three-thirty."

"It's *twenty* of five, and they've been up there since ten of *four*. But if you must be on your way, be on your way."

"Why don't you like me, Candy? You don't, do you?"

God, that came out of nowhere! Biggs looked over to Nick, sitting now on the edge of the sofa cushion, leaning forward, hands cupped to his knees. "Of course I like you. What a thing to say. If I didn't like you, would I let you come over here every day for the past two years? Lighten up, Nicky. They'll be down."

"Why don't you? Why don't you like me?" The kid just wasn't giving up. "You can tell me."

"Yeah? Well, for one thing, you ask stupid questions and threaten to turn me into the cops for letting your brother spend a little private time with his girlfriend."

"I'm serious."

"So am I." Biggs made an effort to wiggle his eyebrows like Groucho Marx. "I like you, Nicky. Honest. We're friends."

"Yeah, sure."

With a grimace and a stab, a physical stitch, of guilt—for not liking Nick? for making that so apparent? for allowing Roy and Noreen to slip away to the spare bedroom every afternoon? for all of the above?—Biggs turned another page in the sketchbook. "What the hell is this?"

"Is what?"

"This." Using both hands, Biggs held the book up, open to face Nick Looby halfway across the room. "He looks like a fucking maniac! Since when does Derby Dugan look like this?"

"Since never, I guess. Because that's not, um, Derby Dugan. It's this . . . other guy. Our new guy."

"What new guy?"

"Roy doesn't know what to call him yet, but I'm thinking—what do you think about Eugene?"

Biggs slammed the book closed. "What do I think about *plagiarism,* do you mean?"

"Oh come on, Candy."

"Your brother draws a kid in a striped shirt and a black coat and a derby on his head and you sit there telling me it's *your* guy, it's not Derby Dugan?"

And then Roy was standing there—since when?—standing there with Noreen crouched timidly behind him, Roy looking smug, grinning, on the verge, the brink, of a big laugh, and he said, "That's not a derby, old man, it's a bowler. It's a bowler."

[9]

Staying to the banister side and taking it slowly, Biggs has made it to the head of the stairs. Exhausted, breathless (and with every joint in his body screaming, Help! Murder! Police!), he drops onto the deacon's bench put here for just this purpose. His calves are twitching, his insteps ache.

Using the cane that he keeps hooked over an arm of the bench, Biggs gets up again and moves slowly down the hallway toward his bedroom. Midway, he pauses at a partly open door, the room that was his when he was a boy. He peers in. Nothing much to see: the bed, stripped to the mattress, a cheap dresser, its walnut veneer coming unglued in half a dozen places, old paper shades drawn to the sills at both street-facing windows.

Biggs had always taken it for granted that Roy's kid—Walter—was conceived right here, right there, in that bed, on that mattress. Stupid girl. Stupid *Roy*. Apparently, they'd used only condoms, can you believe it? (Biggs had once found a Trojans box in the wastebasket.) You'd think Noreen would have had sense enough to be on the Pill! Unless, of course . . . Which Biggs thought very possible, even likely. She knew what she wanted, that one, that cow, and didn't care what havoc she wreaked to get it. But it boomeranged, didn't it, girly? Didn't it? Served you right.

Pulling the door shut, Biggs realizes that the ceiling light is off; he flips up the wall toggle, then shuts the door.

In his bedroom, his dad's old room, Biggs sits on the padded cedar chest and takes off his shoes and socks. Then, standing, he unbuckles his belt, unzips, lets his trousers fall around his ankles. After giving the armpits of his shirt a good, objective sniff—he can wear it again—he hangs it on the bedpost. Deciding to leave his cane where it is and just shuffle, he goes into the bathroom, runs the hot and cold taps at the sink, washes his face. Of course, he gets the neck of his undershirt sopping wet (before turning in, he'll change into a fresh one), but he refuses, both when washing and when shaving, to stand bare-chested in front of the mirror. Too depressing. All that sagging . . . meat. All that stitchery. Not to mention the famous Lydecker scar. When he bathes, he actually closes his eyes while soaping himself. So it's neurotic. So what?

There's an old black-and-white portable TV on the dresser, but tonight Biggs decides to skip watching anything from bed. Since Carson retired, late-night television isn't worth the effort it takes to switch on the set; those two grinning morons they got now—Frick and Frack?—just further proof, if any was necessary, that American civilization has crashed and burned. After tuning in a classical station on the clock radio, he changes into pajama bottoms and a clean, dry undershirt, then climbs into bed.

Mary Laudermilch loaned him a book—it was his own damn fault for telling her it sounded interesting when it sounded anything but—and now he feels obliged to get through it. He's been reading a little every night for almost a month and he's only on page, what? Sixty-four. Biggs doesn't care about wizards, especially *boy* wizards. Not these days.

Sitting propped against two pillows, he removes his glasses, rubs his eyes, the bridge of his nose, and tosses Mary's book to the foot of the bed. Then he sits with hands lightly folded on his stomach: how he plans to position himself on his final day, in his final moments, if he ever gets any real warning, if he's not suddenly felled. And it is also how he used to sit, exactly how he used to sit there, during those bad weeks, sometimes months, in the early 1960s, following yet another round of surgery. Sitting propped up in his bed, day after day, just thinking about poor Buddy Lydecker. Ginnie. Dan Sharkey. Derby Dugan. Derby Dugan and his dog that talks. His cast of characters. The crazy years. Thinking about all of those wear-a-tie cocktail parties that somebody, some couple in his circle would host on Sunday afternoons. *Kill the kid, keep the dog.* Thinking about all that junk, that junk in his memory, in his attic. Obsessing. And later, when the Loobys would come by after school to keep him company, talking about it, too. All of it.

[10]

Day after day, during the bad weeks, the bad months. Propped up against pillows, recuperating. Telling Roy Looby, "First an oval, then a circle," and talking to him about the dead old times, the lost world, when everybody followed the funnies, when the funnies were a national glue, like politics and baseball and polio scares. Telling him, "After I took over the strip from poor Buddy Lydecker, I tried everything—anything!—I could think of to get it noticed again and save it from the cartoon boneyard." Remembering out loud all those stupid complaints, those letters and telegrams from parents and teachers, church groups, the cops, the FBI, even Art *Linkletter*—

The boys laughed.

Biggs said, "It wasn't funny, Roy. I was in trouble. Me and Derby Dugan."

Biggs said, "And then one day I got this call from King Features telling me to bring him home! Home? Derby Dugan didn't *have* a home, at least he'd never had one for more than a month, and always it was borrowed. That was the point! That was the premise."

Roy said, "So then what happened, Mr. B.? What happened next?"

"I'll tell you what happened next—but first lower that horizon line just a tad, okay? And try drawing moonlight on the water like the ragged outline of a Christmas tree. Try it. Nick? Would you get that? And if it's those goddamned Jehovah's Witnesses again, just say that we're heathens in this house, go to hell. Thanks. Make it a little more jagged, Roy. Good!"

It was 1964.

Biggs said, "We still lived together—"

And Roy said, "You weren't *married*?"

"Of course we were married! But over that summer she'd taken up with young Bill Skeeter, a third-rate illustrator living in Westport, and they weren't making any secret of it. I'll say they weren't!"

Nick Looby fidgeted, looked flustered, embarrassed. "Mr. Biggs," he said, "it's five to four. Don't forget your pills. You need a glass of water? Or do you want me to run downstairs and get you a Coke?"

Roy said, "She just took up with him? What happened next?"

And Biggs said, "Draw something for me first, then I'll tell you. Draw me Derby Dugan."

Biggs said, "And don't hold your pencil like you're squeezing a pimple, for Christ's sake. Lightly. Gently. Caress it."

Biggs said, "This guy. What're we gonna do about this guy? You don't keep an eye on him every second, what's he do, he does it backwards."

Then he said, "Yeah, Nicky, a Coke would be nice."

Biggs said, "He arrived in Westport the previous winter to take an instructor's job at the Famous Artists School."

Biggs said, "He rented a furnished apartment over a shoe store, a Thom McAn store."

Then Roy said, "You went to his house? When your wife was there?"

"Why not? I'd been through this same shit before. Pardon my French, Noreen."

Roy said, "This guy worked for the Famous Artists School?"

"Yeah, but he didn't last there long."

"Okay, but what happened after you got to the guy's apartment?"

"First, make me believe that our boy is in a *burning* barn. About to be cooked. Let me see you draw fire that says *hot*."

It was 1965.

Biggs said, "Nicky, make sure the druggist gives you four separate prescriptions. Last time he fucked up and there were only three. Pardon my French, Noreen."

Biggs said, "And do you know what Dan Sharkey told me? That I'd done in the kid myself. That it was my fault."

Roy said, "It really pissed me off when it just stopped in the middle of the story."

Biggs said, "And don't think I didn't tell Sharkey that! I said, 'It's the middle of a story—don't you even read it?'"

Biggs said, "Draw him again. Way I showed you. Now draw him again."

It was 1966.

Biggs said, "My left goddamn ear. And when they sewed it back on? At Norwalk Hospital? Well, as you can see for yourself, Roy, they sewed it on too fucking high. Pardon my French, Noreen."

And sixteen-year-old Noreen Novick pushed a smile, blushed a little. "I should go. Roy? Walk me?"

Roy drawing, Biggs watching, Nick saying after the quiet in the bedroom had stretched on for nearly a minute, "I should go myself. *I'll* walk you, Nor."

"No, that's all right, Nicky, you don't have to."

But he walked her home anyway.

Roy said, "Like this?"

"Better. But curve those flames, curve them."

Day after day, Biggs recuperating, recovering, and the best days were the rare ones when Roy, just Roy, Roy all by himself came and sat at his bedside with a lapboard and a pad of cheap newsprint. "Fore-shorten that arm, Roy . . . like so."

"Like this?"

"Like that, yes! Now *there's* Derby Dugan! Pass him over."

"I kind of thought I'd keep this one."

"Nope. Pass it over."

"Why do you want all these drawings, Candy? Jeez, what do you do with them all?"

"I collect 'em. So that when you're a hotshot cartoonist, a famous man, I can pull 'em all out and show the world how truly rotten you drew when you were eighteen. So hand it over."

And Roy did, tearing out a page, two pages, a dozen pages, what-ever Candy wanted. Day after day. Week after week. Month after month. Year after year.

[11]

Biggs is startled now when the classical station begins playing squeaky Bartók. He can't stand to hear violins and cellos being tortured into sounds like that, like something from the soundtrack of a horror movie. He reaches and turns off the radio, then—what a daredevil!—he continues leaning farther over, stretching halfway out of his bed and sliding open the deep lower drawer in the night table.

Inside is a handsome 12 x 18 book of good drawing paper bound in grosgrain leather that Biggs mail-ordered from a Sam Flax catalog more than thirty years ago. Removing it from the drawer, he leans back against his pillows and plops down the book in his lap. On the first and every subsequent page—and there are sixty-four, all told—is the unofficial, the very unofficial, Roy Looby version of the "Derby Dugan" comic strip, as assembled by Candy Biggs with a pair of scissors and a bottle of rubber cement. Biggs at the kitchen table cutting up Roy's sketchbook pages, trimming the cuts into equal-sized rectangles, fitting together some of them into strips of three or four "panels" apiece. The sample "dailies." Then fitting others—crowding them—into four tiers of three. The typical twelve-panel broadsheet "Sunday page." But sometimes fitting, at the top of each page, a preprinted Derby Dugan logo—he'd found a small batch of them in a carton that came down from Connecticut—then adding a small drawing directly to the right of it, for a thirteen-panel "full-tab."

Hundreds of Roy Looby's pencil drawings, the best ones, culled and furtively assembled by Candy Biggs. Derby poling a raft. Moonlight broken, jagged, on the water. Derby in a barn on fire. In a boxcar. In the desert. Crawling on his belly. There's a cactus. There's a cow skull. Derby on a broken-off chunk of river ice, freezing to death. Derby in pantomime, no dialogue, just empty balloons, ovals with tails that Biggs scissored from pristine Strathmore and then pasted down, strictly for position. Strictly to indicate that these were comic strips—or could be—and not just a series of pictures. True, the sequencing was jumpy, even jarring (in this panel here the kid is lost in a monkey jungle, and in the next panel, the very next one, look, he's staggering down an alley lined with garbage pails while blood drips from a coat sleeve), and it's also true that time, as well, seems woozy or spastic (snowdrift, parched field, trees in bud—panels one, two, three, in this daily here). True, all true, but none of this stuff was ever meant to be published, it was meant to be a collage, you see, a sampling.

A second chance. A crack at resurrection.

[12]

Same as in the Bible famines, it was seven years since Candy Biggs had last seen—and, in most cases, spoken to—any of his old cartoonist pals, and the anticipation was terrifying. When he arrived at the Waldorf-Astoria that evening in late May 1967, his breathing became so labored, the air so fatally thin, that he felt as though he'd been dropped by helicopter into the Andes. Crossing the lobby, he stopped and leaned on his crutches. Immediately, he felt Nick Looby's hand on his lower back. "You gonna be okay, Mr. B.? Want to sit down for a sec?"

"I'm fine," said Biggs with a spike of temper. When he'd invited Roy to come with him as his guest to this year's National Cartoonists Society banquet, he hadn't meant Nick, too. If he'd wanted the lesser Looby to come, he would've asked him. "Couldn't you do up your tie any better than that?" said Biggs now, and while Nick self-consciously touched his lumpy Windsor knot, he called ahead to Roy, "Hold that elevator!" But Roy let it go.

"Too crowded, old man. We'll catch the next one."

While they waited, Biggs reflexively glanced around, spotting a contingent of silver-haired Westport strip men and their wives coming at a stroll out of Peacock Alley. The wives were slender, pretty, modestly endowed blondes, and each could have been mistaken for Eva Marie Saint in *North by Northwest*. Taking a deep, fortifying breath, Biggs grew a smile on his face, fitting the crutch pads more securely under his arms, and then, automatically, glanced down at Nick Looby's left hand, making certain that it still held the briefcase. If Nick had to come along (which was Roy's condition for coming himself), at least he was making himself useful. Roy probably would have left it back in the car. Say this much for Nick, he never would have thought to ask Biggs what was inside. Roy would. Roy *did*. "None of your beeswax," Biggs had told him.

"Candy! Candy Biggs—how are ya?" said Clay Meeker ("Spy #9," a dismal and dying adventure strip launched by Clay's late father in 1938 and now running primarily in Swedish, Danish, and Central American newspapers). "Honey, you remember Candy Biggs?"

"Of course I do," said Meeker's wife, leaning in to give Biggs a kiss on the cheek but suddenly thinking better of it—what if she knocked him over?—and so backing off and showing her big white teeth instead. "It's a good to see you."

"Good to see you, too," said Biggs. He wished he could remember her name. Tina? Terry? Something with a T. Then he was being patted on the shoulder by Don Gargan ("Coin Op," a fairly new strip aimed— "targeted" was the syndicate's term—at young urban marrieds). "Candy man," said Gargan, "it's been too long." Chip Flexner ("The Lafftons," a long-running "suburban-domestic" captioned panel now drawn entirely with Magic Marker) just pointed his index finger and cocked his thumb. Flexner's and Gargan's wives (neither of whom were their wives during Biggs's Connecticut period; there had been different, older wives then) both smiled politely. Then Gargan's wife—the one who *most* resembled Eva Marie Saint, the hair, the eyes, the bone structure, the bustline—glanced at the Looby brothers and said to Biggs, "Are these your sons?" Ulp! Awkward moment.

"Afraid not," said Biggs. "This is Roy Looby, a friend from Jersey City and one hell of a promising cartoonist. And his brother, Nick." Then he introduced the Loobys to Gargan, Meeker, and Flexner in turn, in turn adding, ". . . and his lovely wife."

The elevator came. Riding it to the mezzanine, Clay Meeker asked Biggs what table he was sitting at, did he know the number? "Hope it's ours," he said, and Biggs almost laughed. Hope it's ours! Meeker was more likely praying, and praying hard, that Biggs would be seated at any table *but* his. There had been a brief Meeker/Ginnie affair, back in '58 or '59. They'd slipped away during a Halloween party, met once or twice at a Greenwich motel, and that was that. But Candy Biggs, of course, had known all about it. Because Ginnie had told him. "It'd be great getting caught up," said Clay Meeker.

"I'm sitting with Dick Macdonald," said Biggs.

"Darn. Well, let's get caught up sometime during the evening."

"You bet," said Biggs, letting the Connecticut six exit first from the elevator cab. They set off down the hall in a fast walk; long gowns didn't slow the women.

Roy said, "Are there gonna be any guys here that aren't a hundred years old?"

"Roy, please, don't embarrass me."

Dick Macdonald was already seated at the table when Biggs arrived in the banquet room with the Loobys trailing slightly behind. Although he had stayed in fairly close touch with Macdonald—phoning him on the last Sunday of every other month, marking his calendar ahead to make certain that he did—it was still a shock when Biggs saw how wasted his old friend now looked. Dick Macdonald had the red, blotchy complexion of a serious alcoholic, and a serious alcoholic's disconcertingly mobile smile, now apologetic, now bitter, now fey, now glazed. "Sit here right next to me, Candy," he said, not getting up from his chair and regarding with near horror Biggs's two sticks and the clumsy maneuvering it took for him to slide them both under the table at the same time as he plopped into his chair. "Dick Macdonald," he said then, reaching around and offering a hand up to Nick, then to Roy, who had taken the two seats next to Biggs. Biggs noted Macdonald's minutely lifted eyebrows and knew he was trying to decide whether Roy's baldness meant cancer, the military, or just bad genes.

Meanwhile, the six others at the table, three couples, sat there smiling in suspended animation, waiting for the signal to start in talking again. Amiably, Biggs nodded to them all, but he was thinking, What the hell is this? He didn't know any of these people. He risked a momentary frown, directed at Dick Macdonald; Dick got the message and shrugged. "Shall I make the introductions?"

"Yes," said Biggs, "why don't you?"

Their tablemates, it turned out, were a sports cartoonist from Toledo, an advertising illustrator who worked for Johnstone & Cushing (instead of a suit or a tux, this guy had come in his air force reserve uniform), and a freelance comic-book artist. Plus, of course, their lovely blond wives. The men were of Biggs's generation. The women were—midthirtyish. Nobody bothered with the fuss of shaking hands; grins sufficed. Biggs took over then and did the honors for the brothers Looby, introducing them exactly as he had earlier to Clay Meeker's party. Then he turned and whispered to Dick Macdonald: "I thought you said Joe D'Emilio would be at our table."

"Sorry, Candy, he was supposed to be, then he just—he's sitting over there, instead. Don't look. But he came with Dan Sharkey."

"Dick, you swore to me that prick wasn't coming."

"Lower your voice." Macdonald pressed a smile into his lips, beamed across the table at the Johnstone & Cushing guy, the *colonel,* who had just brought up "all that Muhammad Ali business."

"Did you tell Joe I'd be here?"

"Of course I did. I promised you I would, didn't I?"

"And what'd he say?"

"Candy, it's not polite, having a private conversation."

"What'd he say?"

"He said he was glad you felt well enough to get around."

"And?"

Dick Macdonald gave Biggs an irritable sidelong glance before turning back to the table at large. "I don't know how come that loudmouth thinks he can get any special treatment," said Dick.

"Conscientious objector!" said the reserve colonel. "If Cassius Clay—excuse me, *Muhammad Ali*—is a conscientious objector, then I'm a Ubangi."

Instead of dinner talk jumping breezily from the strip business to in-group anecdotes, as it always had done at previous banquets Biggs had attended, that evening it stayed lugubriously focused on politics, national news, and the generally unbelievable things going on every time you looked around or picked up the paper. In fact, the word *unbelievable* popped up with more frequency than the personal pronoun. It was unbelievable that the United States had just lost its five hundredth warplane in Vietnam. Five hundred planes! "How could we let that happen?" said the comic-book artist, a man named Capra, same as the movie director. *Bob* Capra, though. "How?"

"I'll tell you how," said Colonel John Mostly (mostly a pompous windbag, Biggs had already decided). "Because Johnson doesn't have the will to win. It's disgusting. It's just unbelievable."

And it was unbelievable, too, that men like Richard Speck were running around all over the place, killing nurses. But while Dolin, the sports cartoonist, agreed that it *was* unbelievable and said that you never used to hear about things like that, he was here to tell everybody that the *really* unbelievable "aspect" of the whole sordid business was that Richard Speck wasn't ever going to fry for his crimes. "Life in prison! What's that? Life with color television! Before we know it, we'll be reading about him getting married behind bars. To a pen pal. It just makes you sick."

By then, Roy Looby was on his third or fourth glass of red wine (he hadn't touched his chicken croquettes or spoken a word), and Candy Biggs was growing despondent. He hadn't expected everybody to flock his way, but you might think *some* people would drop by the table and pay their respects. He'd been out of circulation nearly seven years, and nobody had the courtesy to walk over and say hello? What were they afraid of? That he'd start in right away talking about poor Buddy Lydecker, the way that he used to? Jesus. He hadn't expected a round of applause, but nothing? And nobody?

While the dinner plates were being whisked away, he turned back to Dick Macdonald, again whispering: "You told Joe that I expressly looked forward to seeing him tonight?"

"Look, I did my best. You could've called him up yourself."

"I thought the indirect approach was better."

Macdonald—you could tell!—was two seconds away from shaking his head or even rolling his blood-veined eyes. But he checked himself. "What's this all about, Candy? You thinking of pitching him a new strip?" He skipped a glance to Biggs's right hand, where the fourth finger and pinky were misshapen and semiclenched. "You feel up to something like that?"

"Who said anything about pitching a new strip? I never—"

"Excuse me, Mr. B.," said Nick. "Is that Mell Lazarus? The 'Miss Peach' guy?" He pointed to a laughing man several tables away.

"No, it's Al Andriola."

"Wow, no kidding!" Nick's eyes went round, looked huge behind those chunky-framed glasses. "And that guy, that white-haired guy, is that—"

"Nick, you're interrupting me."

"I'm sorry." He blushed a little, then turned to Roy. "Hey, Roy? Candy just told me. That guy over there? That's Al Andriola. Who draws 'Kerry Drake.'"

Roy shrugged, wouldn't even look. What the hell was the matter with him tonight? Tonight and yesterday and last week and last month. It was time Roy snapped out of it, Biggs thought. High time. Snapped out of it, quit with the long face, made the best of his stupid marriage, and got on with the important things. Got on with his career. Abruptly, Candy Biggs leaned across in front of Nick, and said, "Roy. See that guy there? That's Hal Foster. 'Prince Valiant.'" Then he turned back to Dick Macdonald. "Do you think you might walk over to his table in a little while and remind Joe D'Emilio that I'm here?"

"Candy? Can I tell you something? If you want, I'll do it, but Joe and I aren't exactly on the friendliest of terms these last couple of months."

"You never said."

"Well. It's not like I want to broadcast it, but my strip is down to forty-seven clients and Joe's been acting a little bit cool toward me. My luck to be doing a strip about soldiers of fortune in freaking *Africa*.

Every Negro group on the map is calling for my head. Black is beautiful, and I'm dying, Candy."

"Forty-seven papers?"

Macdonald sat looking at his hands. "Why don't you get a mega-
phone?"

"Sorry," said Biggs. "But you never mentioned that things weren't . . .
you know."

"I guess I'm just not like this other guy I can remember who never
shut up whining about it."

"Guess you're not," said Candy Biggs. "Well, I'm really sorry to hear
this."

"What're you gonna do, right?"

"Kill the kid, keep the dog?"

Dick Macdonald sat back hard as though he'd been shoved in the
chest.

"I mean," said Biggs with a shrug, "if there *was* a kid in your strip.
Or a dog."

It was either Dick Macdonald would burst out laughing then or he'd
get really, really pissed. He got pissed.

"Fuck you, Candy," he said, too loud, and got up. "Call of nature,"
he announced to everyone at the table except Biggs, then he smiled
and staggered away.

"Who's that guy, Mr. Biggs?" said Nick Looby seconds later. "That
guy over there? Is that Stan Drake?"

"Oh, shut up, you."

While the waiters went around pouring coffee and delivering slices
of white cake with chocolate ice cream, from the head table came a
repeated tapping on the live mike and a call for silence. Bob Dunn
("They'll Do It Every Time") was emcee. Biggs couldn't recall a single
banquet when he hadn't been; some things, at least, didn't change.
Thank Christ.

Following five minutes of topical quips (none about Vietnam, but
there was one about the miniskirt ban in Greece), it was time, at last,
for the annual awards. Nick Looby polished his glasses with his necktie, then turned his chair around so he wouldn't have to look over his
shoulder. He seemed as excited as a boy at the circus and clapped
enthusiastically every time a name was announced—Bill Keane! Johnny

Hart! Orlando Busino! Will Eisner! But Roy not only didn't applaud, he paid no attention. He ate a little bit of his cake, drank another glass of wine. Then, just before the major award of the evening, the Reuben for Outstanding Cartoonist, was presented (and that year, the award, curiously enough, went to Rube Goldberg, the very guy it had been named after), Roy stood up. "Call of nature," he said, clearly soused and with a smiling glance at Dick Macdonald's still-empty chair.

"God," said Nick, "I can't believe I'm actually seeing Rube Goldberg!" He was grinning but quit when he saw Biggs suddenly press the heel of a hand against his forehead. "What's the matter, Mr. B.? You not feeling good?"

"What the hell's the matter with your brother? Can't he forget about Noreen for one night and just enjoy himself?"

"What's Noreen got to do with it? I think he's just uncomfortable." Nick lowered his voice, leaned in closer. "I don't think he likes these people."

Biggs snorted and gave a dismissive glance to the others seated around their table. "I can't say that I blame him."

"I don't mean just these people. I mean . . . *all* these people."

"What are you talking about? This is the cream of the crop! These are his fellow cartoonists. These are his colleagues!"

Nick's face turned red. Then he opened his mouth but shut it again.

"You don't know what you're talking about. He's drinking like a fish, is what's wrong with him. He's just not used to it."

"Yeah," said Nick. "I guess. So there's the answer to your question."

"What?"

"You asked me what was wrong with him. But you knew it all the time. He's drinking like a fish."

"Don't get snotty with me, Nick." But already Nick had turned away and was listening again to Rube Goldberg, "the dean of American cartooning," recollect his long, illustrious career. He looked frail standing at the microphone. He looked ancient. He looked a hundred years old. "Just don't you ever get snotty with me."

Fifteen minutes later, when couples (including Colonel Mostly and his missus) got up to dance, Biggs lifted the hem of the linen tablecloth, searching for his briefcase. "Get that for me, would you, Nick?" Now that the table was cleared of plates, he laid down the briefcase in front of him and drummed on it with his fingertips. He lit a cigarette. "Nicky, I need you to do me a favor. You see that man sitting way over there, by that pillar? Look where I'm pointing. The guy with the black hair. Next to that woman in the green dress."

"Yeah, I see. What?"

"His name is Joe D'Emilio and he's general manager at King Features, and what I want you to do is to go over there and—very quietly, as quietly as you can—I want you to tell him that Candy Biggs would very much like to say hello. You may tell him that I would've come over myself, but that I feel self-conscious on my crutches. You may not need to tell him that, but if he seems . . . hesitant, tell him. Got that?"

"Sure. The guy with the black hair. No problem."

"Nick! Nick, get back here, I'm not finished. You see that other guy? Sitting directly across the table from D'Emilio?"

"Yeah?"

"What I want you to do, I want you to turn your back to him while you're talking to D'Emilio. So he can't hear what you're saying. All right? You got that?"

"Yeah," said Nick hesitantly. "Okay. What's going on?"

"None of your beeswax. The message is strictly for Joe D'Emilio, that's all."

As Biggs tracked Nick's movement across the floor, his gaze happened to fall on a table of *New Yorker* cartoonists. Charlie Saxon was there, and Lee Lorenz, Whit Darrow and Otto Soglow, and—good God, so was Dick Macdonald! He'd pulled up a chair and squeezed in—crashed a *New Yorker* party!—and now, looking forlorn and very out of place in his cheap black suit, Macdonald sat there with his chin propped on his hand. Did this mean he wasn't coming back? Biggs felt both remorse and contempt push forward from the back of his mind. But by then, Nick Looby had reached D'Emilio's table, he was bending down, he was—

"Mr. Biggs. We've hardly had a chance to say two words." Bob Capra, the comic-book guy, had come around the table and slipped into Nick's vacated seat. A slender man in his late forties with a dry complexion, crow's-feet, and deep vertical grooves in both cheeks, Capra nevertheless had bright, pale-blue boyish eyes. The eyes of someone who would still love to play stickball, who found the Three

Stooges hilarious and probably continued to read Batman stories with keen pleasure even though he knew the sad men who drew them, knew about their stormy marriages, their prostate woes, their legal woes, and their tendency to welsh on debts. There were some comic-book guys who never grew up, and those were the only ones that Biggs could abide. They were pathetic, of course, but sweet. "Gosh," said Bob Capra, "wasn't it great to see Rube Goldberg? He's so amazing!"

Biggs smiled at Capra, then tried to look past his shoulder, across the room to Nick.

"I guess you're an old hand at these shindigs," said Capra, "but this is my first one. I didn't join till just this year. Well, for the longest time, you guys wouldn't let guys like us through the door, but I guess you finally figured what the hey, our money's green too. So! Enjoying yourself? I had the roast beef, what'd you have?"

"The roast beef."

"Good, wasn't it? Oh! I have to tell you, I really enjoyed my little chat with your friend."

"You talked to Roy?"

"Roy, is it? No—with the glasses."

"Oh. Nick." Would it be rude to ask this comic-book moron to please move out of his fucking sight line? Biggs couldn't see Joe D'Emilio, couldn't see—

"He tells me that he does a lot of inking. And lettering. I told him to give me a ring, I might be able to find him some work."

Biggs said, "What? I'm sorry, what are you saying?"

"I thought I might help your friend Nick get his foot in the door. I have some connections at Charlton and Top-Drawer. Archie Comics. Even at DC. And I think I could point Nick in the right direction. If his stuff is good enough, of course. Is it?"

"Is it what?"

"Ouch." Bob Capra laughed, already rising to his feet. "I better not leave the missus alone for too long, she might get scooped up by one of you suave syndicated types. Nice talking to you, Mr. Biggs. And tell your friend Nick that I'm serious, he should give me a call."

Now that Capra was gone, rejoining his wife, who had decamped to another table nearby, Biggs could see that Nick was strolling back but that Joe D'Emilio hadn't budged from his chair.

"What'd he say? Is he coming?"

"Did I just see you talking to Bob Capra?" Nick sat down. "Do you know that he draws Jughead?"

"Why am I not surprised? So what about it? Is D'Emilio coming over here or not?"

"He said he'd try."

"All right, we'll give him ten minutes." Biggs undid the snaps on his briefcase, opened it, and took out the leather-bound drawing book. "But if he doesn't come in ten minutes, you just go back over there and tell him I have to leave soon. Tell him my legs are starting to bother me."

"Are they? You feeling okay?"

"Nicky. Please."

"You think I should go and find Roy?"

"That's not a bad idea. But Nick, whoa. Hold your horses. I want you back here in ten minutes."

Biggs smoked another cigarette, and he must have slipped into a kind of trance because it wasn't until he was rubbing it out in the ashtray that he noticed he was now alone at the table. His coffee was cold, but he sipped it anyway. At other tables, more couples got up to dance as the four-piece combo segued from "Night and Day" to "Strangers in the Night."

"Candy. Hello." It was Joe D'Emilio, standing a few feet away. He showed no inclination to come any closer.

"Joe! Good to see you. Sit down. Please."

"Well, just for a minute. I promised the wife we'd cut our early. She's flying up to Boston in the morning to visit her sister."

"Oh sure. Sure."

Biggs noticed that Joe D'Emilio had spilled something, probably coffee, on his foulard, and there were a few speckles down his shirt-front, as well. Which was probably the real reason he wanted to leave so early. (Assuming, of course, that he really did.) He was one of those impeccable dressers, the kind of man who seemed always fresh, who could look clean-shaven at five-fifteen in the afternoon. Not that Biggs ever seriously wondered about it, but it might have been interesting to find out how many times a day the man actually shaved. Was there a bathroom attached to his office? Good chance. D'Emilio had jet-black hair (had to be dyed), an olive complexion, an unlined face, and teeth like you saw only in the movies.

"How're the kids?"

"We only have the one."

"Girl, as I remember?"

"Boy. Finishing up his third year at Princeton." D'Emilio's eyes took on a suspicious look. "How've you been keeping yourself, Candy?"

"Busy." As D'Emilio grudgingly parked himself in Dick Macdonald's chair, Biggs lifted the drawing book and placed it between them on the table. "I've been keeping myself very busy, Joe. Actually, I've been working with this young man, and I think he's someone you're going to be interested in. I think he's going to knock your socks off. He's terrific."

"Candy?" D'Emilio put out a hand and laid it flat on the closed book, for emphasis. "This is not the time or the place, okay? You can't really expect me to look at samples. Come on, we're at a banquet."

"You mean to tell me you haven't talked a word of business all night. *You* come on." Watch it, Biggs told himself.

D'Emilio sighed. "What's this young man's name?" He removed his hand from the drawing book.

"Looby. Roy Looby. As a matter of fact, he's here with me tonight—"

"Of course he is."

"—but I don't know where he's off to at the moment. No, I'm telling you, this young guy is amazing, and the really amazing thing is what he's been up to." Biggs opened the book, then angled it so that D'Emilio could see the first page dead-on. "Anyone here you recognize?"

"Ah shit." Leaning back, D'Emilio closed his eyes. Then he lifted his shoulders and dropped them. "Candy, what're you trying to do to me?"

"What am I trying to do? Is show you it's time you dug up the kid and brought him back."

"And why should I want to do that? Derby Dugan is finished, Candy. That strip had its day, and that day is passed. It's gone. You remember all the trouble we got into when you were on it? And that was already ten years ago."

"The trouble, Joe, the real trouble was you guys made me bring him home. Remember that? Like I told you then, the kid doesn't *have* a home, that's what made him so great. So American. Let Roy take him back out on the road and then just watch this strip hit the heights all over again."

D'Emilio was shaking his head. "Candy, you got it upside down. You got it backwards. Where have you been? Home is the only thing that anyone does give two shits about. Especially now. Especially these days. That's how come we keep looking for new family strips."

"Families! Excuse me, Joe, but I'm sick and tired of hearing about families."

"Yeah, well, maybe if you'd ever had one of your own—oh Christ, I'm sorry. I'm really . . . I'm sorry, Candy, but see what you've done? See what you made me do?" He looked behind him with irritation, then stood up. "I really have to run."

"No, no, no, wait! I deserved that. You don't have to apologize. Look. I'm just thinking—family strips are great, they're terrific, but there's still a place for Derby Dugan, I know there is."

"It was good seeing you, Candy."

"Would you just look at what I'm showing you here?" Frantically, Biggs turned another page, then another. "Look! Derby's in a blizzard, he's on a raft, he's in the desert, he's in the fucking jungle. Look!"

"Candy, that world is dead. Okay? As a doornail. Nobody, except maybe you, thinks drifters are cute anymore. Drifters kill student nurses, that's what *drifters* do. They're not cute. Now, if you'll pardon me, I have to run."

"Grow him up a little, then."

"What?"

"He's been gone—the kid's been gone for a few years and he grew up a little. He's what now? Maybe eighteen, nineteen? We bring him back and he's no longer a kid-kid, he's—Joe, I read the papers. I know what's going on. There's plenty of kids eighteen, nineteen, twenty years old wandering around on their own these days. Right? So we make a new Dugan, a Derby Dugan for them. A hero for them. What do you say?"

D'Emilio tightened his jaw. "We? I thought you were trying to sell me on some guy named Roy Loogy."

"Looby. Roy Looby. And that's exactly what I'm doing." Biggs tapped the drawing book again, turned another page. Derby floating down the river on a chunk of ice, freezing to death. In an alley, bleeding down his coat sleeve. Back in the desert. Another cactus, another cow skull. "I can't draw anymore, but this young guy, this kid, he's perfect. I'd help out. But just in a kind of advisory way, and I wouldn't expect any compensation. I'd just . . . do it."

"Why?"

"Why?"

"Yeah, why the hell do you still care about it? For God's sake, Candy, it was only a job, it was just a damn comic strip. And you didn't even create it."

Biggs held his eyes down. "No. You're right. You're absolutely right. I didn't. But I was put in charge of it, see, and look what happened. It's like, it's like . . . somebody drops their kid off at my house—will you watch him? Sure I will. And what happens? I'm watching, I'm doing the best I can, but somehow I turn my back for two seconds and the kid falls out the window! How do you think that makes me feel?"

Joe D'Emilio had reared back. "Jesus, Candy, you're screwier than—"

"Don't say it," said a voice from behind him. "Don't you fucking say another word to this man."

"Who the hell are you?"

"Loogy, Roy Loogy." Roy smiled and winked, but not at D'Emilio, at Candy Biggs, who'd turned pale and sat rigidly now with his fingers splayed on the open drawing book. Roy sat down, reached over, and pulled it out from under his hands. "Christ," he said, giving the pages a quick flip. "Clyde, you seen this?" Nick stood frozen behind him, arms hanging straight down at his sides. He shook his head no.

"Candy, I'm sorry," said Joe D'Emilio. "But this—it just wasn't the time or the place." He turned an expression of dark hostility on Roy, then walked away.

"How long were you standing there?" asked Biggs, never raising his eyes.

"Long enough. What the fuck were you thinking?"

"What were you? I almost had him interested!"

"Bullshit. He was trying to get away from your sorry ass."

"I could see it, the wheels were turning. When I said we could grow the kid up a little, make him eighteen, nineteen—I could see his mind start to consider."

"Bull. Shit."

"And you had to go piss him off!" Biggs ran a hand through his thinning gray hair. "Roy. Help me with these." He grabbed one of his crutches by the upright and slid it partway out from under the table.

"What do you think you're doing?"

"Just give me a hand."

"Nothin' doin'," said Roy, flipping quickly through the book, moving his lips as he counted pages, shaking his head in shocked amazement.

"Nick! Come around here and give a hand. Now!"

Looking torn, Nick rubbed his mouth. "You want to leave? We're leaving?"

"Just help me with these!"

Using the back of his chair, Biggs rose unsteadily, and Nick passed him a crutch. He snugged it under his arm. Second crutch.

"Mr. B.? We going home now?"

"We'll go when I say we go." Biggs half turned, looked across the room, past the dancers, past the *New Yorker* table, and took a deep breath. "If I can bring him back over here, you'll apologize. You hear me? Roy? I'm talking to you."

Roy flipped the book closed.

"I don't know if I *can* get him back, but if I do, you'll apologize. Otherwise, we'll just write him. You were sticking up for me. D'Emilio will respect that, when he has a chance to think. It's a virtue. You were defending a poor cripple. But even so, you need to apologize. You don't understand business negotiations, Roy. I could see the wheels turning. I had him intrigued."

"You had him ready to call Bellevue, is what you had him, old man."

"Roy!" said Nick. "Cut it out."

"And how fucking dare you?" Roy lifted the drawing book and tossed it across the table. It bounced when it hit, and the cover jumped open, fell closed. "You are so out of it, old man, it's not even—"

"Roy, I'm warning you, shut up!" Nick put a hand on Roy's arm, then instantly withdrew it.

By then Candy Biggs had set off, crutching his way across the parquet floor, heading toward D'Emilio's table, ignoring all the open stares, saying "Excuse me" over and over as he avoided dancing couples and small groups of three or four men huddled in conversation. "Excuse me," he said, "excuse me."

Dan Sharkey stepped in front of him.

"Excuse me," said Biggs, and tried to go around. But Sharkey took one step to his left, and blocked him again.

"Hello, Candy."

"I asked you to excuse me," said Biggs. "I need to have a last word with Joe."

"Joe is trying to get out of here. And since I just, thirty seconds ago, heard him call you a maniac, I doubt he wants to hear any last word from you. What are you trying to pull?"

"Get out of my way, Danny boy, or I'll knock you down."

And what happened next—Biggs was never certain in his own mind exactly what really did happen next, who said what, who said what first, who pushed, who pushed back, but suddenly, oh good Christ, Dan Sharkey—who looked about fifty but was probably closer to sixty-five—suddenly his foot was braced against a crutch tip and he was shoving . . . or maybe it was just that Biggs *saw* the foot there, Sharkey's foot, and in a split second decided he wanted to go down, imagine the sympathy, imagine . . .

Who knows?

There was shouting, and Ginnie's name was mentioned, Ginnie's name went flying around with all the *fuck you*s and the *you bastard*s, Ginnie's name and poor Buddy's name, and then both crutches flew out—seemed to *squirt* out—in opposite directions from his armpits, and Biggs crashed, landing hard on his coccyx. The pain was excruciating. He lay on the floor helpless, agonized, ecstatic, and mortified. There was a long moment of electric silence, followed suddenly by a roar of voices, all of them pitched at accident-scene level. Did you see that? What happened? He shoved. He fell. Who? Oh God, him? Biggs closed his eyes because they stung with tears, and when he opened them again, there was Nick Looby, squatted down trying to slide his arms under Candy's lower back, Nick saying, "You okay? You all right?" Candy Biggs looked past him, searching for Joe D'Emilio, who would just have to be ashamed of himself now. Who would surely fire Sharkey on the spot and call Biggs first thing in the morning, wanting to talk. But while he looked avidly for D'Emilio's face, he didn't find it. No D'Emilio, and no Roy, either.

No Roy.

Just Nick.

"Scooch up a little, can you, Mr. B.? And let me help you."

Later, during the car ride home, Biggs from the backseat told Roy in the front, "I wanted to give you the strip. To pass it on. Don't you get it?"

"Jesus Christ, don't *you* get it? There is no strip! You heard the man, it's dead. And so is Derby Dugan."

"But this is America, ain't it? Nothing stays dead. We can bring him back, give him a second chance."

" 'We'! What 'we' is this? When did I ever become part of a 'we'? When did I ever join anything?"

"Roy, cut it out," said Nick, who was driving, steering the car through the Lincoln Tunnel. "Just cut it out!"

Biggs said, "Our boy was gypped, Roy, he was fucked—they killed him in the middle of a goddamned baseball game!"

Biggs said, "Let's bring him back. Dig him up and bring him back."

Biggs said, "It's your turn now."

"Nothin' doin'!" said Roy Looby, twisting around to glare behind him at Candy Biggs. "Nothing. Fucking. Doing."

Then Biggs all of a sudden lurched forward. "If you won't do it for yourself, at least—at least do it for me, son." Biggs moved to touch Roy on the wrist or maybe to clasp it, but Roy drew back—"Keep your hands off me, Candy, I'm not your fucking son!"—and looked out the passenger-side window.

They didn't speak after that, or ever again: less than a week later, Roy Looby packed a bag and moved to Milwaukee. And Joe D'Emilio never called Biggs, and Dan Sharkey wasn't fired, and the scene, the set-to, at the Reuben Awards banquet passed quickly into cartooning folklore, like the story about the house, the goddamn house, that fell on Ted Dorgan's drawing hand, and the one about the fatal Al Capp/Ham Fisher feud, and the one about young Frank Sweeney poisoning Walter Geebus with arsenic back in the Great Depression. But Candy Biggs was *twice* a legend. Once for the Buddy Lydecker mess—which had always included his wife's punishing affairs and the suspicious automobile accident—and then again for the banquet fiasco.

Biggs had always considered himself a damn good story man, and now his whole life had boiled down to a couple of damn good stories.

[13]

A few minutes before midnight on this April Monday in the year 2000, he wonders if cartoonists still tell stories the way they used to. Or if that's all changed, too. Like everything else. Every other goddamn thing. His generation of newspaper cartoonists, the one that came up right after the war, is passing, is nearly finished, its few surviving members living either in Sedona or in poverty. If he thinks back to the guys he saw at that banquet in '67, four out of five are dead, most of them for a long time already. Dick Macdonald, jeez, he never even made it to the 1970s. So many guys. So many guys. And so many strips. Whenever Biggs happens to glance at a comics section these days, which is rarely, there aren't many that he recognizes, and the ones he does are being drawn, pathetically, by other hands. He saw "Dick Tracy" in the paper last year and almost wept, it was so stupid and homely. Same with "The Phantom." All the good old story strips, like their creators, are dead and buried, they're six feet under, they're under ground or will be soon. And the gag strips aren't funny, they're desperate, and it all seems . . . over. But what can you do? Everything changes. Every fucking last thing in the world that you know and you like, or look forward to, or even love, for Christ's sake, it just goes and changes on you. Turn your back, it's different. Turn around, it's gone. Well, sure, this is America, ain't it?

The phone rings.

Biggs doesn't answer (he looks at it, though) and it finally stops.

He sits up in his bed braced against the pillows, the drawing book still in his lap, but with the cover closed. Oval, he thinks. "Oval," he says.

The phone rings again.

Should he answer? It could be Mary Laudermilch, calling to tell him she'd found that little article in the paper, did Biggs want her to read it to him? Or it might be Nick Looby calling back to say yes, it's true, Roy has resurfaced. Even so, Biggs doesn't pick up the receiver because he doesn't want to, he doesn't need to, because it makes no difference now. Too late, Roy.

For all of Biggs's melancholy, he feels physically wonderful at this moment, tip-top, almost . . . athletic. Which is very odd since at night his aches and pains almost always are at their worst. Nevertheless, he's positive that if he climbed out of bed now, jumped out of bed, he could sprint up the hall, and leap down the stairs, and charge through the rooms, and—

He's fallen asleep, he realizes, and this is just a dream. It's *that* dream, starting again. And if he got up, he might sprint for a second, but soon he'd be opening a door, some door, and walking into a room, some room, to find Ginnie in a red sweater and pleated white slacks, reading a book. And then? Then, as he'd done a thousand times in forty wasted years, he'd be driving his car like a maniac through sheets of rain. To the same end. The same wet black tree.

How come everything changes but that?

Oval, he thinks. "Oval," he says, and balks at entering any further into the dream. He refuses. Flatly fucking refuses.

For a period of several years Biggs had believed there could be such a thing as a real second chance, a faith awakened the day he turned in his hospital bed and discovered, in the room across the hall, a bald-headed small boy clutching a yellow wallet sized for a much younger child. He'd believed, honestly believed. But no.

Nothin' doin'.

The failed suicide is still a suicide. You never can be alive again, not really, not like before.

Oval, he thinks. "Oval," he says.

Circle, circle, circle.

The phone rings again, and rings for a couple of minutes before it stops.

TRAVELIN' NICK
IN
"AIN'T GOT NO HOME"

By the time I got back to Jersey it was late October. Three or four days before Halloween 1970. I'd spent two months, just about, crossing the country. I'd gone to—gone *past* Las Vegas. Slept in the backseat of my car out in the desert. So now I could say that I did it. And what else? In Arizona I broke my nose walking into a plate glass door I thought was open. That was at a Howard Johnson's restaurant in Tucson, and my nose hurt and bled so incredibly much that I stumbled around in circles moaning for ten minutes. Nobody asked me if I was okay, nobody came over. Well, I'd grown a beard, I probably looked like a drifter. Dangerous, even. Another Manson. Or maybe not.

Also in Arizona—in Tempe—I went with a black prostitute in a blond wig. Velma. *Verna.* But after that twenty-minute adventure (she gave me what she called "half and half") I was so strapped for cash (okay, yeah: she robbed me, too) that I stuck around town for a week, manning the drive-through window at Dairy Queen. Then in Arkansas I had a small accident—sideswiped a parked car—and two state cops searched my Bonneville, looking for drugs. Of course I didn't have any, but I had a few bad moments worrying those redneck troopers might, you know, plant something. I had that beard, and by then it was

full, it was bushy. And besides, I had on an Imp Eugene T-shirt. Why
had I taken the "southern route"? Served me right for buying a road
map! What was I thinking—I'd seen *Easy Rider*! Starring Peter Fonda,
who, it seemed, had never hung out with Roy. Cora told me that. My
brother never even met Peter Fonda, she said, no matter what it said in
Rolling Stone. And I believed her. I also believed her when she'd told
me that Roy never propositioned a Playboy bunny for a hand job. It
was the other way around—she'd offered *him* one and he told her to
get the fuck out of his space. But he'd said it too loud and was nasty,
I guess, and that's how come he ended up being ejected from Hugh
Hefner's Chicago mansion.

After leaving California, I drove for twelve, fourteen hours every
day, but I never listened to the radio or played any tapes. During my
first weeks on the road, I'd make up stories while I drove, little
vignettes starring the Imp Eugene: he could . . . he could join a rock
and roll band, or . . . he could meet God, or the Abominable Snowman, or . . . *girls.* He could meet girls, lots of girls, and bang some
chesty waitress (named Velma) from a sandwich shop, or he could . . .

From time to time, I'd pull over, leave the engine running with the
parking brake on, grab a drawing book and a pencil, sketch out a few
panels, make some thumbnails. But later on, whenever I looked over
what I'd done, it all seemed pointless and tired and stupid.

And besides, I really sucked with a pencil.

So finally I quit making up stories and just drove.

I phoned Joel Clark a lot, but he never had any news for me about
Roy. After he'd disappeared from Camp Galoot early on Labor Day
morning, he never showed up again either in San Francisco or in
Berkeley. No one had seen him. And Clarky wasn't sure what to do
about *The Last Eugene.* The damn thing, he said, was such an awkward
length—sixty-four pages!—that he was thinking he might publish it as
a book, a large-size paperback book, and not as part of the long-
delayed *Lazy Galoot #3.* But considering the frantic, disjointed nature
of the "work," that seemed a risky venture, and Clarky couldn't afford
to lose any more money.

Meanwhile, the Galoots were pissed. They'd taken one look at *The
Last Eugene* and hated it. It was just a bunch of pictures, it wasn't
comics, there was no story, everything just happened and nothing hap-

pened next, and it wasn't funny, and how many times could you read the same two words? And it didn't end, it just stopped. Fizzled out. It was just a big piece of crap. Either Roy had lost the magic or else he was thumbing his nose at them. Well, fuck you, baldy! They weren't sure whether they'd publish a comic book without Roy's stuff in it, but this much they were sure of: if they ever saw that bastard again in person . . .

By unanimous vote of Zits, Breitstein, Ahearn, and Howdy, my brother was duly cashiered out of the Lazy Galoots Comix Collective.

"Jesus, Clarky, you really haven't heard from him? Nothing?"

"Not a thing."

"What about Cora?"

"Somebody told me she moved to Oregon or Idaho, but I'm not sure."

"If you hear from Roy, you'll let me know?"

"Yeah, sure, but how do I get in touch with you?"

How infuckingdeed? The answer was, he couldn't. I was living on the road, driving east (most of the time), but taking it slow. In theory, I could've done that forever, gone anywhere I pleased, taken this road or that road, stopped here or not stopped, stayed there or stayed *there,* for as long as I liked. In theory. But I knew that eventually I'd end up back in New Jersey. "How about if I just keep checking in with you, Clarky?"

But then sometime in the last week of September when I tried calling him again at Final Reckoning Press, an operator said the number had been disconnected, and so even before I reached the Garden State Parkway, I'd lost touch with Joel Clark. And I wouldn't hear from him again for a couple of years—not till he started to line up people to interview for *Nothin' Doin': The Imp Eugene and the Art of Roy Looby.*

I arrived back in Jersey City on a Saturday morning. Uncle Neil was out sweeping leaves on my mom's front walk, but I didn't stop. I drove past Candy's house but didn't stop there, either. Finally I drove to Noreen's. The porch was decorated for Halloween with a plastic skull, a jack-o'-lantern, cotton cobwebs, rubber spiders, and a headless body in a rocking chair. (Upon closer inspection, the body turned out to be an old flannel shirt of mine and a pair of my dungarees stuffed with newspaper.) In the side yard, a chained English setter was stretched out asleep on the dead grass. It heard me coming, though, and looked at me, but seemed wholly disinterested and put its muzzle back on its paws. Noreen had a dog now?

She answered my knock still in her bathrobe. God, her boobs were great.

I said, "New haircut? I like it." And that was true, I did: shingled in the back, crimped on top. Very cute.

"Jesus Christ." I'd expected anger, maybe sarcasm, or a little or a lot of both. But not that shrug of resignation. And she looked a little guilty. What did *Noreen* have to look guilty about? "Well, come on in, I guess."

In the parlor the electric broom lying across the radiator tubes was just where it had been—if memory served—when we'd had our last big argument. I remembered because for a moment I'd considered grabbing it up and conking her on the head with it. July. August. September. October. Four months and nothing about the place seemed any different. It looked the same as it had the night I'd stormed out. *That* was comforting. But then I started to notice little things. Some ashtrays I'd never seen before. A Princess phone. And a stack of textbooks on the coffee table. *Principles of Accounting. Introduction to Economics. Conversational French.*

Textbooks? *College* textbooks? Noreen hadn't finished *high school.*

"You're looking good, Nor."

"You look skinny. And the beard."

"Well. It doesn't mean anything. I just didn't shave." Golden Books were everywhere, and bristle blocks, a Peanuts sneaker, and a bowl of dry Cheerios. A loud Sylvester and Tweety Bird cartoon was on TV. "Where's Walt?"

"Out."

"Who with?"

"He's just out, Nick." She turned off the television and the silence was spooky.

"When'd you get the dog?"

"It's not mine."

"So whose is it?"

"You have breakfast? I still have some pancake batter."

"Yeah? That'd be good. Thanks."

We went out to the kitchen and I sat down at the table. On the wall calendar practically every day of the month had some reminder jotted in the square—the panel—with a Flair pen. I couldn't read the handwriting. It wasn't Noreen's.

"So how's Walt doin'? He doin' okay?"

Noreen stood with her back to me pouring batter from a huge glass measuring cup. "He's good."

Then I said, "Noreen—" just as the wall phone rang. She answered it, then pulled the cord to the far side of the kitchen, twisting away as she spoke in a low voice.

I got up and finished cooking the pancakes, flipping them, waiting half a minute, then sliding them onto my plate. I helped myself to coffee. Noreen was looking at me as she listened on the phone. I smiled. She stared back.

"I'm sorry," I said. "I'm sorry, Noreen. I'm really sorry." She turned her back to me and continued speaking on the phone. I heard her ask, "Is he enjoying himself? Does he like the animals? No, you don't have to put him on." I sat down at the table, listened to the weekend weather on the all-news radio station, and doodled on the Formica tabletop with my fingertip. Oval, circle, circle, circle. I heard Noreen say, "When do you think you'll be home?" Heard her say, "No, it's no problem, I can handle it." What I actually heard her say was, "I can handle it, *Larry*." Then I took my cup of coffee with me down to the cellar.

My drawing table was gone, and so were all the cork squares I'd glued to the wall for tacking up roughs and clippings. Now there was a second TV, an overstuffed chair, a table with two filled ashtrays on it. And a thick paperback book. James Joyce, for Christ's sake. *Ulysses*. On the flyleaf, printed in blue ink, it said, "Lawrence Bozzo/Eng 224 Modern Brit Lit."

Two minutes later Noreen came down.

"We're gonna put the couch and TV there," she said. "Make it like a family room."

"Larry *Bozzo?*"

"Don't say a word, don't you dare."

"From Stegman Parkway? Junior Chamber of *Commerce* Larry Bozzo?"

"Nick, I'm warning you . . ."

"Sorry, sorry."

She walked over to the easy chair, absently picked at a clot of dried chocolate on the upholstery. "You saw Roy?"

"Yeah."

"And?"

"He ditched me, Noreen. And nobody's seen him since."

She walked over to where I was standing by the coal furnace and stared at me. Right into my face. I got a funny little feeling in my belly. That look, the way she never blinked? Was telling me something. It was telling me she'd take me back, give me a second chance—that all I had to do was ask. I'd known her nearly all my life, and certain signals, certain signs, you just recognized.

She said, "Nick?"

I said, "Yeah?"

She said, "Your nose is bleeding."

CLARKY AND CLYDE
IN
"THAT TAKES THE CAKE!"

Where Clarky lives with his sister is a buff-brick apartment building on the corner of West End Avenue and Ninety-fourth Street. In the lobby he nods to the night desk man, then rides one of the two boxy elevators tucked away in an alcove. Mandy's apartment is 9C. Clarky never thinks of the place as hers and *his,* even though he's been living with her now for God knows how many years—seven? Almost eight. For most of those years, he contributed next to nothing to the rent, and while he's been able to give her some regular money this spring, he's still not paying his fair share. But home is where they have to take you in, right? "They" may not like it—and Mandy, bless her heart, has been a saint, despite her not being thrilled about Clarky's presence—but they take you in anyway. He's lucky to *have* a home. It's not so hard for Clarky to imagine himself as one of those pathetic gray-faced guys you see in the street dragging around their belongings—most of it inessential, even absurd—in a shopping cart. A homeless guy. Like Roy Looby.

When he comes through the door, Mandy is in the living room with her friend Betty Scocco from the fourth floor. The Lionel train clicks around an elaborate double-gauge track set up on top of a trestle table.

Locomotive, coal car, tank cars, boxcars, and a caboose speed past a
siding, through a nostalgic miniature small town and the forested outskirts, then through the tunnel in a brown-and-green papier-mâché
mountain. Mandy manipulates the transformer while Betty stands nearby
eating a slice of white cake from a paper dessert plate. Both are dressed
up, made up, their gray hair permed and identically cut.

"How'd it go?" says Clarky. "Enjoy yourselves?" His sister and Betty
went to see a Broadway musical tonight, *Miss Saigon*.

"Oh, I just loved it," says Betty. "It was so much fun. And that helicopter! It was fantastic!"

Mandy brings the train to a stop, the refrigerator car lined up perfectly at the dairy loader. "It was enjoyable," she says with a shrug.
"But the music was so-so."

Betty dismisses Mandy with a languid wave of her hand. "Oh, you
and your imported dramas! She's a snob, isn't she, Joel? What's wrong
with musicals?"

"Nothing," says Mandy defensively. "I just happen to prefer drama."
She looks irritated, but for only a second. "How was class, Joel?"

"Don't ask," he says, dipping a shoulder and letting his carryall drop
onto a chair. He unzips it, spreads open the fabric. "One of my students went postal. And not only that—after class? I think he stole some
of my books!" And why does he think that? Because he knows for a
fact that he'd brought four copies of *Nothin' Doin'* and fifteen copies of
The Last Eugene—just in case anyone in the class wanted to buy either
or both—and now there are just three of the one and thirteen of the
other. That little son of a bitch! Clarky dumps out the books on the coffee table, then begins slotting some of them into the built-in bookcase,
where there are dozens more of each.

"Went postal how?" says Betty Scocco.

"He got into a ridiculous argument with another member of the
class and—you know, I'm still not sure what all really happened. He's
just a bizarre kid."

"Well, put it behind you," says Mandy. "There's some cake on the
kitchen table. Have a piece. And relax."

"I think I will. Betty," he says with a nod, "good seeing you."

"Good seeing you too, Joel."

Even before he's in the kitchen, they've lowered their voices and are whispering. About him, of course. People have been whispering about Clarky practically all his life—about his weight, about his effeminacy, or at least about that high-pitched voice of his, about his lingering juvenile enthusiasm for the funny papers, about his complete lack of ambition. Over the last twenty, thirty years, he's done legal proofreading as a freelancer and worked the glove or watch counters, during Christmas season, at different department stores in Manhattan, but that's about it. Even Mandy, as close as she is to her younger brother—she's sixty, he'll turn fifty-nine in the summer—is at a loss to explain what happened to him. She'll say, "Joel used to have his own publishing company in San Francisco. But after that went bust, he never really got his act together again." She never mentions his work on the Roy Looby "companion." In deference, he believes, to his huge disappointment when the book failed to sell more than five hundred copies.

In the kitchen are several iced cakes on the long sink counter, on top of the refrigerator, and on the butcher-block table. There are *always* fresh-baked cakes around. Mandy the mad baker. (And people think *Clarky* is eccentric!) He may take a year and a half to write goofy essays like "Providence and the Platonist Ideal in 'Dick Tracy,'" which he publishes (if he's lucky) in no-paying university-based popular culture journals, but she bakes a damn *cake* every day. And some days more than one. She's a CPA with an excellent head for numbers, but beyond that? Kind of a screwball.

After cutting a slice of marble cake, Clarky takes a carton of milk from the fridge and pours himself a glass. Then he leans against the counter, staring into space. Damn. That little maniac stole my books! What got into Glen tonight? Clarky finishes his cake and cuts another slice—trying the chocolate strudel this time. Mandy comes in and sits down across the table.

"Betty gone?"

"Yes. I think she wanted to watch something on the tube. You know Betty and her 'programs.'"

"So you really didn't like the play?"

"It was all right, Joel. But I find it hard to feel nostalgic about Vietnam. Or to even give a shit about it." She watches him eat, then points to another cake on the counter. "You should try some of that. It's orange."

He grunts with his mouth full.

"I'm sorry your class didn't go well. I know how much you look forward to it every week." She doesn't say it, of course, but it's implied: I know it's the *only* thing you look forward to. And that's the sad truth.

"I'd expected tonight's class to be pretty special, too. After that story about Roy in the paper today, I thought everybody'd be eager to hear about his work. But not really. I don't think more than two or three of them even saw the piece."

"Well, it was easy to miss."

"Damn right it was! 'National News Briefs,' Jesus Christ. If Jimmy Hoffa suddenly showed up again, you can bet they'd do better than page A14."

"Poor Joel," says his sister and heads back into the living room.

"What's that supposed to mean?" He starts to follow her, realizes that he's still holding his cake plate, and puts it down on the table. "Mandy? What's that supposed to mean?"

She's back futzing with the trains. The set belonged to her former husband, who taught drafting at a trade school on Staten Island. He was considerably younger than Mandy, had a stammer, and was a war-games enthusiast as well as a model-railroader. When they divorced, well over ten years ago, Mandy let him take away all of his armies and terrain, but she demanded the trains, for spite. In time, she developed a real passion for the hobby, and now there's scarcely an evening when she doesn't play with the set.

Clarky and Mandy watch the train go round and round.

"What'd you mean by 'poor Joel'?"

"Nothing."

"No, what?"

"You just looked so—disappointed, that's all. That it wasn't on page one."

"Well, God, I think it's pretty incredible, don't you?"

"I suppose. Are you going to go see him?"

"To Richmond? I'd like to, but I'm not sure I can—"

"If you want to rent a car, I'd loan you the money, Joel."

"No, no, that's okay. I'll just wait till I hear something more from Nicky. But I appreciate the offer." He sits down and watches his sister watching the trains. "Remember that junky little train set Dad used to have?"

"That he put around the Christmas tree every year. Oh sure."

"I miss him like crazy."

"You just liked Dad because he read every comic strip in the paper."

Clarky laughs. "He did, though, didn't he? He'd say to me, 'Joel, if you look hard enough, you can fall right into the pictures. Right into the panels—into another world. That's the magic of those things.' And it's true, you can, you can fall right in." He kicks off his shoes and lifts his legs onto the ottoman. "Hey, Mandy? What was the name of that song—it was famous because people supposedly committed suicide after they heard it. You know which song I'm talking about? Billie Holiday made a recording of it, I think."

"'Gloomy Sunday.'"

"Right! You figure that was true? About people killing themselves when they heard it?"

"Joel, are you okay?" Suddenly she looks alarmed.

"What? Oh no, no, no, if that's what's you're thinking, no. I was just reminded of that song, I guess, because of what happened tonight."

Mandy switches off the transformer and the train immediately stops. Giving Clarky a quizzical look, she sits down opposite him on the sofa. "What about tonight?"

"Oh. You know. I've mentioned it to you before. That silly business about *The Last Eugene*. 'They say it's cursed.' All *that* business. How it's supposed to drive you crazy if you read it."

"Is that what happened to you, Joel?" She smiles, reaching over and touching his knee.

"I'm afraid I was crazy long before *The Last Eugene* came along. No, I was just thinking about the kid who went a little berserk in class. He lost it while I was showing slides from Roy's book."

"For heaven's sake, you don't seriously believe that silly comic book is cursed."

"Of course not. But it is a miserable thing, and nobody that was ever connected to it . . . well. It's a work of genius, but it's a miserable thing, too."

"I know you were crazy about your Roy Looby, but I can't say I ever saw anything in this stuff."

"That's because you're a prude." But he winks.

"No, the sex didn't bother me, or the dope smoking, or the nose snubbing at anything and everything. No, it just struck me as so—angry and unhappy and confused."

"So were the times, Mandy. Let's not forget."

"I still prefer 'Beetle Bailey.' If you'd published 'Beetle Bailey,' Joel, you might not be sponging off your poor sister today."

They both laugh, then Mandy looks at her watch. "I'm getting ready for bed. Sorry your class was spoiled."

"I'll live. And there's always next week."

"There always is, Joel. Until there isn't."

When he's alone, Clarky switches off the floor lamp and shuts his eyes.

Two or three minutes later, the phone rings.

"It's Nick, Clarky. Nick Looby. Feel like going out for a drink?"

"A drink? Where they hell are you?"

"Downstairs. I'm calling from the lobby."

"What're you doing here? I thought you'd be with Roy."

"I'll tell you all about it. Want to go out for that drink?"

"Whyn't you just come on up here?"

"You sure?"

"Sure I'm sure. Come on up, Clyde."

Clarky tiptoes back to Mandy's bedroom to let her know what's happening, but she's already asleep, so he pulls the door closed. He waits in the foyer till he hears the elevator open. Then he steps into the hall, and here's Nick, in an outfit that's so typically Clyde: brown sport coat, blue shirt, tan cuffed slacks. Loafers. Clarky hasn't seen the guy in five, six years. Last time they met, it was by accident, and it was on the street. Christmas season. Nick was heading into Macy's and Clarky was coming out through a revolving door. He let Nick assume he'd been shopping, not working there at the leather-goods counter. They'd promised to get together for a proper reunion, but neither ever called.

Till last Wednesday, when Nick had phoned him from Richmond. With the news.

Nick's hair has turned completely gray, the former waves and curls changed to Brillo. There are deep lines across his forehead, dramatic vertical grooves in both cheeks, and he's still wearing those square black eyeglass frames, the brainy kind with temples on them as broad as tongue depressors. But otherwise he doesn't look too bad; in fact,

he looks pretty good. That last time Clarky had seen him, his complexion was spooky—well, it hadn't been all that long after Nick had
that heart attack.

"Can I get you something to drink? Mandy has everything except
white wine."

"No, I'm good. Unless maybe you got a Coke. With ice?"

"I can manage that. Sit. I'll be right back."

When Clarky returns from the kitchen—carrying the cola, a nonal-
coholic beer for himself, and four slices of cake, each one different—
he finds Nick at the train table, bent forward and examining the small
buildings in Tiny Town. The bank, the church, the filling station.
"Yours?"

"My sister's," says Clarky, handing Nick his glass. "Go ahead and run
the train if you want."

Nick declines, and they clink a toast.

"To the miracle," says Clarky. "So tell me—how's he doing?" Then
he scowls and says, "You're not mad at me for calling the *New York
Times,* are you?"

"I was. But not anymore, what the hell."

"I was pissed they didn't give it more play. Nice headline, though:
'Sixties Icon,' that was nice. But I'm really disappointed they didn't
make a bigger deal of it."

"You would be, Clarky. But that's just because you were his biggest
fan."

"Still am! Except I had to laugh, calling some of his strips 'antiwar.'
Did Roy even know there was a war *on?*"

Nick twiddles with the train transformer; the locomotive lurches forward, stops, lurches again, stops again. Behind it, all the cars click.
There's a buzz, Nick rights the Exxon car, then leans over the table and
picks up a small metal figure, the filling-station attendant. "The detail
is incredible." He sets it back down.

"Yeah. But come on now, tell me everything. What do the doctors
say? Any change in Roy's condition?"

Nick smiles. He picks up a miniature telephone pole, puts it down.
"He's gone, Clarky."

There's a long, long silence. "What?"

"Roy's gone."

"You mean he's—?"

"No, I mean he's *gone*. He did it again—he disappeared. Flew da coop."

"No way! I thought he was in a fucking coma!"

"He was."

"Come on, Clyde, you're teasing me."

"I wish. Or maybe I don't. After the newspaper guys showed up— thank you very much—it got so crazy for a while that I figured I'd stay with him around the clock. This was—what day is it today, Clarky? I'm losing track."

"Monday."

"Still? So it was late last night or early this morning. God, it seems longer ago than that. They set me up with an air mattress and I went to sleep around ten-thirty, eleven, and everything was the same as it was all week. But when I woke up later in the dark, I had this funny feeling. And when I put on a light—no Roy. His bed was empty. At first I thought—well, you know. Empty bed, you think the worst. But that didn't make any sense, they would've woke me up if he'd . . . so I . . ." Nick jiggles the ice in his glass. "Nobody knows how he got out of there. But he did."

"Jesus Christ." Clarky looks pale. "Then what happened? They call the cops?"

"No—I specifically asked them not to. I didn't want this to be a fucking details-at-eleven thing."

"Why not?"

Nick has been staring at the train table; now his eyes widen, he smiles and points. "What the hell is that?"

"Exactly what it looks like," says Clarky, getting up from his chair and coming over. "A hobo jungle." The two of them look at the group of tiny tramps positioned near an exquisitely small and carefully enameled campfire, the grouping surrounded by a stand of two-inch-high metal trees outside the railroad yard at the edge of town. "Did you look for him?"

"Sure I did. Even went over to the men's shelter where he'd been staying."

"And?"

"Nobody'd seen him. But I found some old guy who'd known Roy when he stayed there. Some poor old guy named Bob. 'Sure,' he says, 'that bald fella with the funny yellow wallet.'"

"Roy still had that wallet?"

Nick smiles and nods, then he takes off his glasses and holds them up to the light. "Know what else Bob said? That Roy was a 'nice fella.'" Deciding the lenses aren't too smudged, after all, he puts his glasses back on. "A real nice fella."

"What else did old Bob tell you?"

"That Roy seemed happy."

"What the hell did he have to be happy about?"

"I'm just telling you what the man said."

"He threw away his fucking life! Turned his back on his talent. On us. How the hell could he be happy?"

"I don't have an answer for you, Clarky. Except that maybe his real talent was something that none of us ever knew about."

"Bullshit. He's got a real talent for being a *homeless* guy? Come on, Nicky—somehow he just . . . snapped. Finally we have to admit that."

"Yeah?"

"Yeah," said Clarky. "We finally have to—wait a minute! This all happened last night and you're back already?"

"Why stick around there?"

"Yeah, but he could still *be* there, someplace."

"And what if he is? Which I kind of doubt, but what if he is? So what? This was all a big fluke, Clarky, just a fluke. It wasn't supposed to happen. But somehow it did. Look. I spent six days in that hospital room, just talking to Roy, talking *at* him, talking to myself, trying to make sense of what happened to us. And I never did.

"I'd talk to him for hours, then I'd go back to the hotel and sit in my room and feel . . . wrung out. Then I'd go back to the hospital and talk at him some more. This went on all week. Till I took a good look at myself and couldn't stand what I saw, this bitter middle-aged sign painter who's been blaming his brother for his own fucked-up life. So when I went to the hospital yesterday morning, I didn't have anything left to say, I was done. *I* was done. Then I went to sleep on his floor last night and when I woke up, it was like he'd never been there. But of course he had. I don't know why he came back—"

"He got hit by a truck!"

"I don't know why he came back, but he did, and now it's all done, and I feel like a two-ton feather's been lifted off my shoulders. I loved him, you know. I loved him so much he couldn't stand it."

Clarky is shaking his head, shaking his head. "You're not the only one who loved him. I was his—I just wanted everybody to know how fucking great he was, that's all. And even after he went and dumped me, even then I didn't give up on Roy—I spent and lost every last cent I had publishing *The Last Eugene,* and for all the impact it had, I should've saved myself the trouble. If only he'd done the kind of work I knew he could do. But he had to go draw that miserable sixty-four-page . . . whatever it is."

"Sixty-*five*-page." When Clarky frowns, Nick shrugs and picks up one of the copies of *The Last Eugene* still on the coffee table. Flips through it.

"As you can see there, Nicky, it's sixty-four."

"You only *published* sixty-four. You only *got* sixty-four, but there was another page, Clarky. The sixty-fifth. Believe me, I should know—I tore up the fucking thing."

"You what?"

"Tore it up, tore it all to pieces. The last page of *The Last Eugene.* When I went to Roy's studio that night? After he said he was done? I looked at what he'd left for me on his table and I—wouldn't do it. Couldn't." Nick looks directly into Clarky's face. "It was the final appearance of the Imp Eugene and I refused to ink it."

"Why?"

"Oh come on, Clarky, guess what happened."

"I don't know, you tell me."

"On page sixty-four, Eugene is just walking, remember? Out into the countryside, down a dirt road, and he comes to a clearing, and there's a cabin. And the cabin looks exactly like Amity cabin, remember? And he climbs through the window in the last panel . . . and that's how the book ends. And everybody hated it. What the fuck, that's no ending. And they were right, Clarky, it wasn't. Because there was another page, the real last page, page sixty-five, that takes place inside the cabin. Where the famous Imp Eugene climbs on a drawing table, ties a rope on a hook, puts a noose around his neck, steps off into space, and hangs himself. Roy drew him dangling there for seven panels in a row. And left the last two panels on the page empty."

"All those times I interviewed you—why didn't you say anything? Fuck you, Nick. Why didn't you tell me?"

"Because it was none of your business."

"The hell it wasn't!"

"Well, that's how I saw it. The Imp was my guy as much as Roy's— I helped create him and Roy thought he could just kill him off? I'd junked my life with Noreen to go after him, gone across the goddamn country to find him, spent a month working beside him, and he never told me what he was planning? I could've killed him. Instead, I tore up the page. And when Roy came in later, I started screaming at him like a fucking maniac."

"What'd he say?"

"Nothing. But when he saw all the ripped-up pieces on the cabin floor he laughed his ass off."

"Then what?"

"I told him—I said if he tried to redraw that page the same way, I'd just rip it up again. Because there was no way I was going to let him kill off our magic boy, there was no fucking way I'd help him bury Eugene. But the madder I got, the fucking happier he looked. Like he was glad I'd done it. And so I said okay, great, now that *that's* settled . . . now that we agree that Eugene stays alive, maybe we could talk about what he *really* does on page sixty-five."

"And?"

"Roy said yeah, sure—tomorrow. So I went to bed and fell asleep for, like, the first time in days, and when I got up—when Cora came in my room the next morning and *woke* me up—Roy was gone. He just took off in the night."

"Nicky, how could you have destroyed that page?" For a moment, Clarky feels an impulse to strangle the guy, he even glances at his hands—as if. But then he just shakes his head and sits down on the sofa. "You son of a bitch."

"Yeah, sure. But you know what? I thought I ripped it up because I wouldn't kill off something that me and Roy created together, but you know what I only just figured out this week? The Imp *wasn't* mine, it was all Roy's. It was Roy. *He* was Roy. By drawing that page, my brother wasn't just killing off the Imp—you know?" Walking back over to the train table, Nick reaches down into the miniature hobo jungle and picks up a tramp with his traveling sack on a shoulder. He glances at the bottom—MADE IN CHINA—then sets it down among other, similar figures. "Couple days ago, when I realized he still had that stupid wallet, know what I did? I took it. I took it and then later? At the hotel? I tried to stick all of my credit cards in it, and my Blue Cross card and my AAA card and my Social Security card, and everything else. Well, it was just too small. No way that stuff would fit. Nothing fit. Except a few bucks. What the hell did I think I was doing? It was so funny I had to laugh. Just another thing that wasn't mine, and I didn't want it. Fuck, I couldn't use it. So yesterday I took it back to the hospital and put it on the table next to Roy. It was his. He could have it back. You can have it, Roy. It's yours." Nick smiles. "Hey. I should get going."

Clarky doesn't move. He refuses to walk Nick to the door, won't even look at him when Nick opens it to let himself out. Instead, Clarky picks up a slice of lemon pound cake from the plate he brought in from the kitchen earlier. Takes a bite.

"Clarky?"

"I don't want to hear anything else from you," he says with his mouth full of cake.

"That guy Bob that I talked to? At the shelter? That told me Roy was such a nice fella? He wasn't the only one who said that. The people running the place said the same thing. Roy didn't just flop there, he helped out. Fixed the beds, swept up. That kind of thing. Made scrambled eggs for everybody in the morning."

Clarky turns his head finally and meets Nick's gaze. Nick's smile.

"And oh, by the way? Roy took his wallet when he left. So long, Clarky."

And so long, *Nick.* And so long, Roy, wherever you are. So long, Candy. So long, Ginnie. So long, Buddy Lydecker. So long, Dick Macdonald, and Joe D'Emilio, and even you, Dan Sharkey, you lousy prick. So long, Bob Capra and Marcus Bailey! So long, Bill Skeeter! So long, Noreen Novick-Looby-Bozzo, and Walter—so long and good luck with that movie career! And so long to Clarky's sister, Mandy, the cake was delicious, thank you, and so long, Betty Scocco. So long to

Breitstein and Ahearn, to Howdy and Zits! So long, Cora, whoever you are! So long, Glen, you crazy nut. So long, Nurse Carol—why don't you give Nick Looby a call sometime, he'd like it a lot. So long, Karla, so long Ollie. So long, Heydar and Laurie! So long, Cathy Looby. So long, Uncle Neil, and God bless! So long, Eugene! So long, Derby! So long, Derby Dugan—so long, kid, see you around . . .

"Let's Talk It Over!"

We'd love to hear from you! Send your letters to The Editor, *Dugan Under Ground*, P.O. Box 301, Jersey City, New Jersey 07331. Remember to tell us your full name and street address, and let us know if it's okay to publish it. We'll print whatever interesting letters space will permit.

Dear Editor: Enjoyed *Dugan Under Ground,* but wish to register my disappointment that Uncle Neil (Neil Cannon, my favorite character) didn't get a fuller treatment. Might I suggest—are you ready?—that Uncle Neil be given his own series. At least think about it.

Allen Middleman
Ventura, Calif.

Allen, thank you for the very thoughtful letter! Your idea about a new series starring Uncle Neil is an intriguing one, but we'll have to pass. What more can be said about him? He was a nebbishy neighborhood character, he was unlucky in love, and he was electrocuted on July Fourth weekend, 1996. He's dead. He was a nice guy, but he's dead. And life belongs to the living, Al. So—what do you think about a Cora Guirl series? (She is a MAJOR Hollywood agent, with clients that include Bette Midler, Susan Sarandon, and Celine Dion. Her story is a potential blockbuster.) Is there any fan interest in Cora Guirl? Or how about a Noreen and Heydar series? Interested? Older woman, younger man . . . but it's not what you think. They go into business together, importing stuffed animals from Japan. Another All-American success story! Any interest? Write and let us know!—ed.

To the Editor: I think you should be willing to give any reader his money back if he feels your so-called novel is below par, which I do! We hardly see Roy Looby at all and I thought this was supposed to be a book about him. This, to me, demonstrates poor planning.

Mark Scaduto
Mount Kisco, N.Y.

Dear Mark, poor planning? We don't think so!!! Know what your problem is, pal? You have a completely misguided idea about what Dugan Under Ground *is all about. And frankly? We don't need readers like you—so we'll be glad to send you a full refund as soon as you remember to send us your FULL ADDRESS!!! Moron.—ed.*

Dear Gang, After reading all about Joel Clark's book on Roy Looby, I find that I'm dying to get hold of a copy for my "collection." (I've amassed quite a good collection of "comicana.") Could you please forward this letter to Mr. Clark, in case he might have a copy that he would be willing to sell me. Thank you.

Josh Elliott Freiberg
Bowling Green, Oh.

Dear Josh, no sooner said than done! We sent your letter to Clarky this afternoon, and we're sure he'll be in touch with you shortly. "In case he might have a copy"? MIGHT have? Hoo-ha, Josh. Clarky must have 2,000 copies in his bedroom.—ed.

Dear Editor: Why do so many novels these days make fun of religion? I'm fed up. I don't happen to be a Moslem, but if I were, I might take offense at the portrayal of Heydar and his family. It smacks of racism. Watch you don't find yourself on the receiving end of a fatwah!

Lee Thomas
New York, N.Y.

Lee, is that a threat? There was no disrespect intended for any of the great religions of the world in our modest little novel. Dugan Under Ground has nothing but admiration for Islam as well as for Catholicism, et cetera. In fact, if you paid a little more attention to the story and less to finding offense with every little blessed thing, you might be surprised to discover that this very novel you call "irreligious" (you do call it that, don't you?) is in fact deeply concerned with spiritual issues and themes. And no, we are not going to

point them out for you. That's not our job.—ed.

Dear Editor: I don't know whether you people were being coy or just couldn't make yourselves come right out and *say* it, but I feel you owe it to your readers to tell them unequivocally that Edward (Candy) Biggs, my friend, passed away in his sleep on Monday, April 24, 2000, at the age of 81.

Mary Laudermilch
Jersey City, N.J.

Mary, Mary, quite contrary, we cop to being coy. That ringing telephone was supposed to cue the alert reader that poor old Candy was gone. Sorry if it didn't do the job for you, but let me just say in our defense that we were afraid we'd be accused of cheap irony if we'd been any more overt at that point in our narrative. Guess we can't please everybody! Thanks for writing—and we hope you're enjoying your semiretirement.—ed.

Dear Editor: Could you please give me a list of titles of all the Claudia Cling XXX movies? Are they available on video, do you know?

(Name Withheld)
Pottstown, Pa.

Isn't there always one? Isn't there? Look, buddy, those movies were made a long time ago, and if you have any respect for Cora Guirl at all, you won't go looking for them. If you simply have to have them, however, here's a partial list: Oral Love Girls, Oral Love Girls II, Oral Love Nurses, *and* A Toiler in the Sex Film Industry Finds Jesus—Her Moving Story of a Life Shattered and a Soul Redeemed.

There's no nudity in the last one, but it's our favorite.—ed.

Dear Editor: I admit I've been scratching my noggin! I can't figure out whether I'm supposed to like Nick Looby or think he's a real jerk. Any hints?

Kelly Dillon
Richmond, Va.

P.S. I hope your readers don't take Nick's word for it about Richmond. There's lots more to do here than look at Civil War monuments. And even though there are still racial tensions, we've come a long way!

Dear Kelly, can't you both like Nick and think he's a jerk? Does it have to be one or the other? We wanted to throttle him ourselves when he was so whiney, but at other times—for instance, when he was solicitous of poor Candy Biggs at the cartoonists' banquet—it was hard not to like the big dope. Or are we wrong here? Let's have a contest! In fifty words or less, tell us whether we should like Nick Looby or think he's a real jerk. Or both. First-place winner gets a copy of Nothin' Doin': The Imp Eugene and the Art of Roy Looby, *second- and third-place winners get paperback copies of* The Last Eugene, *with a foreword by Allen Ginsberg and an introduction by Joel Clark. Contestants are warned, however, that exposure to* The Last Eugene *can be hazardous to your mental health. So, come on, Readers, let's hear from you!—ed.*

Dear Editor: As not only his agent but, I hope, his friend, I was annoyed that you didn't mention the title of Walter Looby's award-winning

documentary short about sweatshops in Rhode Island, *Who Will Hear Our Cry?* Walter is a major talent in the film industry today, and I'm very excited to be with him as his career takes off for the heights. After helming the second unit on last year's smash action hit from New Era Films, *Speak Softly, Die Loud,* Walter is about to start preparations for a surprising new film which is sure to catapult him into the first rank of American filmmakers.

J. L. ("Harry") Pierson
The Granzinger Agency
New York, N.Y.

P.S. Just curious. Are first editions in good condition of *Lazy Galoot* comics very valuable? If so, could you give me a ballpark figure? Thank you. By the way, I very much enjoyed reading DUG. Parts of it made me long for my long-gone stoner days.

Harry, Re: your question. Prices fluctuate all the time, but the current high price for a copy of Lazy Galoot *# 1 in mint condition is $75. But that doesn't mean you'll get $75. The underground comix of the late sixties and early seventies are only a fair-to-middling investment possibility. Re: Walter Looby. See his letter below. You really ought to keep a tighter rein on that boy, Harry.—ed.*

Dear Editor: Being a filmmaker, I rarely read anything besides trade magazines and scripts, but recently I had to make an exception for *Dugan Under Ground.* Not only does your publication deal intimately with members of my immediate family but I, myself, actually make a cameo appearance, albeit as a toddler.

Though I wish I could tell you I remember speaking on the telephone long distance with Nick Looby during the summer of 1970, I really can't. And while I have no cause to doubt the conversation actually occurred, still, that dialogue about a leaking roof and a spaghetti pot struck me as too convenient and *far* too cute. Perhaps in *your* medium (and I cast no aspersions, I respect print) such a scene might convey pathos, but I can tell you with confidence that in *mine* it simply wouldn't work. On screen, it would look both corny and contrived.

But now let me get to the real reason for writing. Early in the summer of 2000 (before I even became aware that a book such as yours was in the making), I was approached by an independent film producer (who must, for the time being, remain anonymous, though you surely would recognize his—or her—name if I told it to you). During the course of our meeting, which took place in New York City, my current base of operations, and which lasted for over an hour (I need hardly point out that the meeting's length was highly significant), I was asked if I had any interest in making a documentary film about my father. (This was scarcely two months after he had disappeared from his hospital bed in Richmond, Virginia, and only a week after *People* magazine published a three-page feature about the "mystery" of Roy Looby.) I said that I had an interest in making a *film* about my father but wasn't convinced it should be a documentary. (As you probably know, I have a solid reputation as a maker of hard-hitting

documentaries—the most recent being *The Nerd King: Bill Gates and the Siege of Microsoft*—which have won major awards and been shown in prestigious film festivals around the globe.) As I now have a strong interest in branching out into narrative film, I proposed the idea for a *bio-pic* about Roy Looby, instead, and suggested some fine young actors (Haley Joel Osment is my first choice to play "young" Roy). Long story short: my idea was seized upon wth great enthusiasm, and happily I am now preparing a feature-length script based on the life and career of Roy Looby tentatively titled "Mr. Counterculture," although we expect that will change.

But now let me *really* get to my reason for writing.

Although I honestly can't see all that much material I might adapt directly from your publication (I plan to minimize and possibly eliminate the roles played by Ed Biggs and Nick Looby, which for some unfathomable reason you felt the need to stress), I thought it wise, as a precaution against any possible legal unpleasantness in the future, to option *Dugan Under Ground*. You will find the terms reasonable and compatible with the terms Joel Clark has accepted (snapped up, greedily) for a similar option I've taken out on *Nothin' Doin': The Imp Eugene and the Art of Roy Looby*. (There, again, I doubt that much of his material will find its way into my screenplay, although Mr. Clark's admittedly florid and fannish descriptions of my father's life and work in San Francisco might prove *somewhat* helpful.) I can assure you that, when completed, my film will stand as a fascinating and dramatic portrait of a great and mysterious American artist, as well as a powerful evocation of a most exciting time in our nation's history. I can also guarantee you (and I don't mean this to be as critical as it may sound) that my film will present Roy Looby with much more clarity and focus than your book managed to do. Reading *Dugan Under Ground* (awful title, by the way; it's misleading), I felt that I was constantly looking at my father through the wrong—and smeared— end of a telescope. And I can't imagine why you allowed a singularly unpleasant and untalented hack like Nick Looby (a sign man, for God's sake!) to play such a prominent role in your telling of the story. You took a wrong turn there, editor. Also, the organization of your material seemed haphazard and unnecessarily difficult. There is much to be said for beginning, middle, and end—in that order.

Please get in touch with my agent—Mr. Harry Pierson at the Granzinger Agency—as soon as possible.

Walter Looby
New York, N.Y.

Walt, sorry, but we don't like your tone, and your prose (way too full of parentheses) is tortuous. So because of that, and becaue we're not too crazy about film as a "medium," we're not going to sell you any option. Nope. And be careful, son, the editorial board at Dugan Under Ground *is a mighty litigious group. Use any of our copyrighted material, and you'll find yourself in court before you can even say "albeit a toddler." Are you sure you're Roy Looby's son? And while we've said it before (see above), we might as well say it again: Where'd you get the idea that* Dugan Under Ground *was even about your dad? So long, kid, see you around.—ed.*

Hey, editor, how you doing, you doing okay? Just a quick note to say that all is well—don't worry about me. Sun's out, sky's blue, and the highway goes on forever. Like me. Whoops, gotta run, gotta run—here's my ride.

No Name
Dayton, Oh. (postmark)

P.S. Don't get me wrong—sometimes freedom sucks. Sometimes it rains.

????????????—ed.

Dear Editor: Who's stronger, Nick Looby or the Incredible Hulk?

Brian McIntyre
Tulsa, Okla.

Nick Looby! Next time ask us a hard one, Brian.—ed.

That's all we have room for now, folks. But keep 'em coming! We read every single letter, and don't just give us the bouquets, let us have the brickbats, too. We're tough, we can take it. This is America, ain't it? Ain't this America?—ed.

ACKNOWLEDGMENTS

When I started to work on *Funny Papers,* the first novel in this "cartoonists' trilogy" about Derby Dugan and his multiple creators, it was 1980, I was thirty-one, and my daughter Jessie was an infant just several months old. Now the third book is finished, it's 2001, I'm fifty-two (but so youthful), and Jessie is about to graduate from college. It wasn't supposed to take me this long! But even though I'm bewildered and embarrassed that the "project" ate up more than two decades of my life, still I'm very, very happy that it's done. A large number of people—family members, friends, fellow writers, colleagues, agents, editors, and an awful lot of cartoonists and comic-strip scholars—contributed significantly to the making of these novels, and I'd like to thank just some of them before I give a final tip of the yellow derby and bid a fond farewell to the Dugan gang. So: to Kate, Jessie, and Santa De Haven; to Margaret Hussey (my mom), Julia Markus, and Michael Rockland; to Francis Greenburger, Chuck Verrill, Gary Panter, Art Spiegelman, Michael Naumann, Sara Bershtel, and Elizabeth Kaplan; to Bill Burnett and Peggy Black, Walter Gallup, Kim Deitch, Mandy and Harry Matetsky, Richard and Margaret Cammarieri, Chris Rowley, and Anitra Brown; to Denis Kitchen, Chris Couch, Richard Marschall, R. C. Harvey, and the editors and interviewers at *The Comics Journal*; to Andy Helfer, Joel Rose, Faye Prichard, Clare Lowell, Laura Browder, Richard Fine, and Frank Miller of Richmond Comix; to the graduate fiction students who were members of my Novel Workshop at Virginia Commonwealth University, and to the many syndicated-strip cartoonists and comic-book artists, both mainstream and underground, who generously welcomed me into the world of their art, their passion, and their profession . . . to each of you, my sincere gratitude.

ABOUT THE AUTHOR

Tom De Haven is the author of several novels, including *Derby Dugan's Depression Funnies* (winner of the 1997 American Book Award) and *Funny Papers*. A frequent contributor to *Entertainment Weekly* and *The New York Times,* he also teaches at Virginia Commonwealth University. He lives in Midlothian, Virginia.